ALL I NEED IS YOU

Also by Julia London

Historicals

The Devil's Love
Wicked Angel

The Rogues of Regent Street

The Dangerous Gentleman
The Ruthless Charmer
The Beautiful Stranger
The Secret Lover

Highland Lockhart Family

Highlander Unbound
Highlander in Disguise
Highlander in Love

The Desperate Debutantes

The Hazards of Hunting a Duke
The Perils of Pursuing a Prince
The Dangers of Deceiving a Viscount
The School for Heiresses, Anthology. "The Merchant's Gift," Sabrina Jeffries, Liz Carlyle, Julia London, Renee Bernard

The Scandalous Series

The Book of Scandal
Highland Scandal
A Courtesan's Scandal
Snowy Night With a Stranger, Anthology. "Snowy Night with a Highlander," Jane Feather, Sabrina Jeffries, Julia London

The Secrets of Hadley Green

The Year of Living Scandalously
The Christmas Secret, novella

The Revenge of Lord Eberlin
The Seduction of Lady X
The Last Debutante

Contemporary Romance and Women's Fiction

The Fancy Lives of the Lear Sisters

Material Girl
Beauty Queen
Miss Fortune

Over the Edge (previously available as Thrillseekers Anonymous)

All I Need Is You (previously available as *Wedding Survivor*)
One More Night (previously available as *Extreme Bachelor*)
Fall into Me (previously available as *American Diva*)

Cedar Springs

Summer of Two Wishes
One Season of Sunshine
A Light at Winter's End

Special Projects

Guiding Light: Jonathan's Story, tie-in to *Guiding Light*

Anthologies

Talk of The Ton, "The Vicar's Daughter," Eloisa James, Julia London, Rebecca Hagan Lee, Jacqueline Navin
Hot Ticket, then: "Lucky Charm," Julia London, Dierdre Martin, Annette Blair, Geri Buckley
The School for Heiresses, "The Merchant's Gift," Sabrina Jeffries, Liz Carlyle, Julia London, Renee Bernard
Snowy Night with a Stranger, "Snowy Night with a Highlander," Jane Feather, Sabrina Jeffries, Julia London

ALL I NEED IS YOU

AN OVER THE EDGE NOVEL

Previously available as *Wedding Survivor*
(Thrillseekers Anonymous)

Julia London

Montlake
Romance

Text copyright © 2005 Dinah Dinwiddie
Previously published as *Wedding Survivor* in 2005, 2011
Montlake Romance Edition published in 2013

Published by Montlake Romance
PO Box 400818
Las Vegas, NV 89140

ISBN-13: 9781477805817
ISBN-10: 1477805818

Dear Reader:

I am thrilled that my earlier series Thrillseekers Anonymous is available to you once more. Now titled Over the Edge, these books are about a few men who love a good thrill. They have become fearless and brazen, and will try any extreme sport for the adrenaline rush. But there is no sport more extreme than falling in love.

They have dodged danger many times. But when they get the idea to form Thrillseekers Anonymous, creating extreme sport vacations for the very wealthy, they run into the sort of trouble where their brawn does not help them. Eli, the thinker of the group, runs across the wedding planner, Marnie, whose bubbly personality is more than he can bear. Marnie's only goal is to put on the wedding of the century for an A-list celebrity couple...until she finds out how much she needs Eli to make that happen. Michael is the newcomer, arriving with plenty of baggage. When he runs into Leah again, he is reminded that she was The One—only Leah doesn't quite see it that way after the way he dumped her. Finally, Jack is saddled with providing security to the latest, hottest pop star, Audrey. He doesn't like her high-handed ways and Audrey doesn't like mouthy bodyguards. But circumstances keep forcing them together, and the sparks begin to fly.

This series idea came to me after a family member enthusiastically described a helicopter ski trip. It made me wonder about men who have no fear of jumping out of helicopters in remote terrain, then skiing down mountain faces where there are no trails. I could picture them, bruised and battered, but very proud of themselves. And then I pictured what sort of woman could bring a man like that to his knees. It was delicious fun! I hope you find some thrills of your own in this resurrected series. Happy reading!

CHAPTER ONE

There she was, their next victim...only she didn't really look like the other wedding planners.

That was not necessarily a bad thing.

On the edge of Beverly Hills, at the corner of Third and Fairfax, Marnie Banks, their next victim (as Eli McCain liked to think of them, for reasons that would soon be apparent to Ms. Banks), walked into the Original Farmer's Market wearing a red baseball hat.

At least she followed instructions.

From the backseat of the Lincoln Town Car, Eli watched her stroll deeper into the market. She had a bag over one shoulder and wore a pair of snowy-white sneakers. He didn't know a lot about women's fashions, but he didn't think the shoes jibed with the rest of her outfit. She was supposed to be dressed in simple, banging-around clothes, not like she was headed for a schoolteacher convention. Her pants reminded him of something his mom would wear, and her blouse was buttoned almost to her hairline.

Whatever—she'd done what they'd asked, worn the red hat and sneakers, and was presumably on her way to buy a piece of fruit so she could be distinguished from all the other schoolmarms that might be lurking in the market.

She turned right and *whoa*—that was a thick tail of coppery red hair falling out the back of her baseball hat. At least now Eli understood what the hell she was talking about when he'd called her to set up this interview.

He and his partners were, inexplicably, interviewing wedding planners to coordinate a very high-profile wedding. Yes, Thrillseekers Anonymous, the premier LA boys' club, was going to add a *wedding planner* to its ranks.

It was a convoluted story and one Eli didn't like to think about, but the long and short of it was, when he'd called Marnie Banks to give her the rundown of how the interview for this gig would occur—including the red hat, piece of fruit, sneakers, and casual clothing—she hadn't questioned any of it. Unlike the other three candidates, who seemed a little freaked out by the prerequisites, this one instantly began to chatter like a flock of magpies about how mystery and stealth were absolutely necessary to pull off the wedding of two megastars.

Eli appreciated the fact that she seemed to take their unusual request in stride, and ticked off the prerequisites for the interview. At the end of the list, she'd asked, "Could I make just one teeny-tiny suggestion?"

"A suggestion?"

"Just a little one. I mean, fruit, shoes—I get that. But what would you say to a black hat instead of a red one?"

Her question had stumped him—he could not imagine what the color of the hat had to do with anything. "Why?" he'd asked after a moment. "What's wrong with a red hat?"

"My *hair* is red."

She said it very matter-of-factly, as if it were perfectly obvious what the color of her hair meant to anyone. Eli was so baffled that he could not respond. As he was trying to work through what she could possibly mean, she'd clarified, "A red hat would really clash with my hair."

He told her to hang on a minute, then covered the phone with his hand and stared blankly at the wall.

"*What?*" Cooper, one of his partners, asked, peering at him suspiciously. "Is she a whack job?"

"Yes. No. I don't know. But she thinks a red hat would clash with her red hair."

"What do you mean, *clash?*" Cooper demanded hotly, looking as confused as Eli felt.

"I think she means that they don't go together. Like green and…hell, I don't know, whatever green doesn't go with."

Cooper blinked. "Get out."

Eli frowned, uncovered the phone. "No," he said sternly to Marnie. "Red hat."

"Okay. Just thought I'd ask. It never hurts to just ask, right? I've never been shy about asking, because I fig—"

"Marnie? Is that you?"

The older woman's voice on the line startled Eli, and apparently Marnie, too, for it was the first time she'd shut up since he'd called.

"*Mom!* I'm on the phone!"

"Are you? I thought I heard the phone ring. Well, sorry for the intrusion, honey. Bye now." The phone clicked off.

"I am so *so* sorry about that," Marnie had gushed. "How embarrassing." She laughed a little too hard. "You know how mothers are."

She lives with her *mom?* "Right," he said, mentally adding a check in the con column. "So, are we straight? You know what, when, and where?"

"Yes, absolutely."

"Great. See you then," he said, and hung up.

He turned around and folded his arms across his chest and frowned thoughtfully at Cooper. "She's chatty. Not good."

Cooper winced. "But they've all been kind of chatty, haven't they?"

Good point. But this one…Eli didn't know why, but he had the feeling that this one was different from the others.

I was right, he thought now, as he settled in to wait for her to reemerge with her fruit. She was certainly different from the others in physical appearance, and in the best way possible. She had an athletic build. A *nice* athletic build. Long legs. Strong back. A nice ass and that excellent dark-copper hair. Hopefully, she could survive the interview.

About fifteen minutes later, she reappeared holding an enormous casaba melon that looked like it weighed thirty pounds.

He had told her, very explicitly, to purchase a piece of fruit that could be seen by the casual observer—he'd meant like a bright orange. Apparently she thought he meant they were blind.

She stopped next to a trash can, balanced the melon on top of it, swung the bag off her shoulder, and bent over to rummage around inside.

Eli glanced at his clock. It was a minute to two, the appointed time. She was punctual—another point in her favor. He told the driver to pull up to the curb, and as she continued to rummage, Eli got out, leaned up against the back fender of the car, hands in pockets, waiting. She finally stood, slung the bag over her shoulder, and heaved the melon to her chest again. That's when she noticed Eli standing there and did a strange little hop-in-place.

"Marnie Banks?"

"Ah…yeah," she said, smiling a little. "That's me."

"Great. You can get in," he said, and opened the door of the Lincoln.

Still smiling, she dipped a little to see inside the car, her maple brown–colored eyes squinting.

"Why don't you just dump the melon?" he suggested.

She jerked her gaze from the car to the melon she was holding, then to him. "*Dump* the melon?"

"Dump it."

"But I paid seven bucks for it."

Why? "Okay, so keep the melon," Eli said. "You wanna get in?"

"Okay." She straightened and looked at the Lincoln. For a very long moment.

Expressionless, he watched her. She was having the same reaction that the others had, and in hindsight, he thought that maybe this wasn't the best approach to hiring a wedding planner.

"Ah…" Marnie took a tentative step forward and bent at the waist, trying to see inside the Lincoln again. "You're the Thrillseeker guy, right?"

"Right. You mind getting in before we call attention to ourselves?"

"Do you have a name?"

"Yes. Eli," he said, looking behind her. You could never be too safe—if she'd told anyone about this and the rag press got wind of what they were up to, they'd be all over the girl. And him.

Marnie took another step forward. "You *are* the dude with the same Thrillseekers outfit that is arranging the wedding of Vin—"

"*Yo*—" he said, cutting her off before she could utter the names of the two biggest superstars in America. "No names, remember?"

"Oh. Right." She peered inside again, then at him with those big maple eyes. "And it's perfectly understandable, given that you're dealing with a supersecret wedding— well, technically, a *second* attempt at a supersecret wedding—"

"Ah...I think that would fall under the category of *no names,*" he reminded her. "Just get in, will you?"

She stepped closer, directly next to him. Eli detected a very pleasant scent as she peered inside. "The windows are black on the inside."

"That's right. We have clients who don't like anyone to know they're inside."

"Oh," she said, as if a light had just popped on inside her head. "Right, right." She dipped under his arm and carefully put one long leg in the Lincoln, bent to have another look, then reluctantly slid the rest of her body inside. Eli shut the door, walked around to the other side, got in beside her, and locked the doors.

"Are you locking the *doors*?" she cried with alarm.

"You can unlock them from your seat," he said, nodding at her seat controls.

"Right, okay," she said, squinting at all the buttons on her door.

Eli waited until she had found the unlock button and tried it once or twice. When she settled back, apparently satisfied that she could flee if necessary, he asked, "Okay?"

"Okay," she said firmly. "I'm good."

"Yo," he said to the driver, and pushed a button to roll up the window between the front and back seats. The driver pulled away from the curb, and Eli settled back.

Out of the corner of his eye he watched Marnie Banks remove her red hat and perch it atop the casaba melon between them, fuss with her hair a minute, then try to see out the thick, smoky glass. But she bored of that and settled back again, turning slightly in her seat to face him. "So," she said brightly, all her reservations apparently gone. "Your name is Eli, is that right?"

"Right."

"*Riiight.* Do I detect a bit of a drawl? Where are you from, Eli?"

"Texas."

"Ah! I *love* Texas. My uncle used to live in Austin. Great place. I love the music scene, do you? And the lakes. I had the best time at that huge lake down there, what's the name? Tavish? No, Travis. Travis, that's it. So what part of Texas are you from?"

Oh God, she *was* chatty. "West. We'll arrive at our destination in half an hour."

"Okay," Marnie said, and picked up her bag, looking inside. "Would you like an orange?" she asked, and pulled one out, sticking it under his nose to show him. "I picked some up at the market. I figured as long as I was there, I might as well pick up a few things," she said cheerfully.

Eli glanced down. The orange was enormous, almost the size of the melon. "No, thanks."

The orange disappeared. She put the bag down and straightened her blouse. She was really pretty, he thought. Not gorgeous or reed-thin like the Hollywood types he was used to working with, but a lot prettier than a schoolmarm and definitely a lot curvier.

She glanced up, but did not seem to notice Eli checking her out. "I'm from LA," she said. "Born and raised."

Eli shifted his gaze forward.

"I used to be in high tech," she said, casually propping her arm on the melon and crossing her legs. "I was doing pretty well until my company went bankrupt."

Eli said nothing.

"That's why I'm a wedding planner." She laughed. "Yep, I finally got the opportunity to jump into the wedding business with both feet when I got laid off. But I'd wanted to do it for a long time, you know. I figured the high-tech thing really wasn't for me," she said with a sniff. "I'm really better suited to planning weddings than designing Web pages. Honestly? Getting laid off was the kick I needed to jump right in there and start doing it. And then I heard about *this* wedding!" She suddenly twisted toward him again. "So how do you know them? Vincent Vittorio and Olivia Dagwood, I mean. I knew this would happen, by the way. I read in *People* that they started seeing each other again on the set of *The Dane*."

That much was true. Eli had worked that movie, and it was the second affair they'd had. The first one had ruined their marriages. And then they'd broken up over a makeup girl. When Vince dumped the makeup girl, their second affair had been pretty much in the open, and Olivia's quickie divorce from the dancer she'd married while Vince was doing the makeup girl pretty much sealed the deal.

"I guess it goes without saying that this would be a fabulous boost to my portfolio," Marnie waxed dreamily, and faded back into her seat.

"So how is your portfolio?" Eli asked idly as the driver slowed for a red light.

"What do you mean?"

What did she mean, what did he mean? How should he know what he meant? "I guess I mean how many weddings have you done?"

"Oh. How *many?*"

What else would be in a portfolio?

"Well, none, technically," she said firmly. "I mean, this potentially could be my first solo wedding, but that doesn't mean I haven't been involved. Oh no—I've done *puh-lenty* of apprenticeships," she said, sweeping her arm out to show just how puh-lenty, "so I feel perfectly capable of handling *this* wedding. I interned with Simon Dupree. I bet you've heard of him. He is *the* most famous event coordinator in all of—"

"Relax," Eli said easily. "You can give the rundown of your experience when we reach our final destination."

"But what do you think? Do you think that sounds okay?"

"Does what sound okay?"

"My pitch."

"Yeah, I guess," he said with a shrug. What he knew about wedding planning was absolutely zilch. Jack was their resident expert, because his sister had used one to plan her wedding. *They order the flowers and help with the dress and shit like that,* he'd told them. Frankly, the less Eli talked about weddings, the better, and he was only doing this one under official protest.

"What is our final destination, anyway?" Marnie asked, trying to see out the window again.

"Where the audition will be."

"Audition." She laughed at that.

Eli glanced at her again. "What's funny?"

"That just sounds funny. Like I'm going to have to try out or something," she said, and laughed again.

She had no idea. Eli suppressed a smile.

"So what's the deal with the Thrillseekers?" she asked. "Anything you can tell me about them? What they're like?"

"Well…they don't like to talk a lot," he said, and looked at her meaningfully.

"Really?" Marnie asked with a charming smile, missing his point completely. "That's too bad. I like to talk to people. Don't you? I like meeting new people and hearing about them and what they do. I guess that's why I'm such a good wedding planner. I really *listen* to the bride and groom and try and make their vision of their perfect day come true," she said, and blithely launched into all the ways she did that.

With a small sigh, Eli folded his arms and stared forward.

CHAPTER TWO

Marnie was fully aware of the bad habit she had of talk-ing to fill the space around her, especially when she was nervous. But she really didn't know how to stop, espe-cially not when she was this nervous. She was beginning to think that maybe she'd jumped a little too hastily into what was really a whack job.

That wasn't so far-fetched, seeing as how she'd found out about the job to begin with by eavesdropping on a hushed conversation at a wedding trade show. While Marnie was not in the habit of eavesdropping on other people's con-versations (well...unless it was something *really* juicy), she'd been a little desperate. She needed this job in a bad way—if she had to live with Mom and Dad another month, she'd hurl herself into the ocean and let herself be washed out to sea. And besides, a certified wedding planner without an actual solo wedding under her belt couldn't afford to be too choosy.

Oh, who was she kidding?

The very thought of doing Vincent Vittorio and Olivia Dagwood's wedding sent chills up her spine. They were the two biggest stars in the universe and Marnie couldn't *wait* to meet them—she could imagine her and Olivia becoming best friends as they planned everything, and then, when Marnie had pulled off the wedding of the century without a hitch, Olivia would hook her up with some of her A-list stud friends and refer tons of fabulous clients to her so that Marnie could become *the* wedding planner to the stars.

Hey, a girl could dream, couldn't she? And that dream alone prompted her to put on the red hat and purchase the fruit, per the bizarre instructions of Thrillseekers Anonymous.

Then the Lincoln had appeared.

When she'd seen Eli leaning against the Lincoln in a black Astros hat, with dark glasses resting on a straight nose and a sexy shadow of a beard dusting a strong chin and some killer lips, not to mention the long, lean look of him in general, Marnie had been pleasantly surprised. Bonus! The job had a really good-looking guy involved.

Unfortunately, good-looking did not mean particularly friendly. He reminded her of a cowboy in one of the old westerns, the strong silent type. A Clint Eastwood with steely eyes—well, she presumed there were steely eyes behind those shades.

And what was all that about an audition?

The Lincoln turned, and Marnie caught a glimpse of towering iron fences through the front window that could only be surrounding huge monolithic houses, and she felt a tingle of excitement. *Wedding planner to the stars,* here she was!

Actually, telling Clint Eastwood that she'd wanted to pursue a career in wedding planning was a big fat lie. When the dot-com she'd been working for went belly up, she'd tried to get another job in the tech industry, along with everyone else and all their mothers—it felt like hundreds were competing for the same few openings.

Weeks went by without a nibble, and her unemployment status at last led to her greatest humiliation yet—having to move home with Mom and Dad. But she hadn't had a choice—she couldn't pay her rent and she couldn't pay her credit card bills, which were, she was embarrassed to note, pretty damn high. Honestly, she'd not realized how large she'd been living on her humongous dot-com salary before the company tanked.

So after about three weeks with Mom and Dad, when Marnie was contemplating living under a bridge on the Santa Monica Freeway, she'd seen the ad for the wedding planner certification class.

Wedding planner. The term had sort of circled around and tickled her thoughts for a while. It actually sounded fun. Who didn't like a wedding?

So she'd taken the class. At the very least, it got her out of the house and away from the TV, and Mom and Dad, and Mom's book club. And though she'd never really envisioned herself a wedding planner, once she got into it, she was sucked in by all the beautiful white dresses and lovely cakes and flowers and fancy china—not to mention all the fabulous high-heeled shoes.

And she suppressed a shudder of delight just thinking about the sparkly wedding shoes Olivia Dagwood would wear on her third walk down the aisle. Or was it her fourth? She'd have to check E! Online.

The Lincoln turned again, and she had the sensation they were traveling up and around. Then the car slowed and made a sharp left. Eli lowered his window. They were at a security box. He punched in a code, then raised the window as the driver eased the car forward, through the gate, coasting down a hill and stopping in a small parking lot.

Eli lowered the back windows; the driver stopped the Lincoln and got out. "Wait here," he said to Marnie as the driver opened his door. "I'll be back for you in a minute or two."

"Where are we?" Marnie asked.

He got out, stuck his head back inside, and said with a sexy, lopsided grin, "We're here," and shut the door.

"Thanks for the info, Chuckles," Marnie muttered as he walked in front of the Lincoln in a pair of faded Levi's—which looked damn good on his butt—and disappeared into what looked like a garden path or something.

Marnie sighed, looked down at her hat, her melon, and the straw bag full of giant oranges, then leaned her head back, closed her eyes, and mentally reviewed her best selling points.

While Marnie was mentally preparing herself, Eli walked around the six-car garage of the Vittorio Bel Air estate, past the service entrance to the house, and down the garden path to a little pavilion where the guys were waiting for him.

"You get one this time?" Jack asked with a chuckle. He'd thought it was hysterical that the last candidate had refused to get in the Lincoln with Eli.

"Yeah, I got her all right," Eli said, and perched against the railing of the pavilion. "I was right—this one's a talker. I already know half her life story."

"Good," Cooper said as he pushed away from the post he was holding up. "Maybe that will save us some time. So come on, let's get this over with. I've got a meeting with DreamWorks later. What do we have on girl number four? And please tell me it's not one of those giant photo books of weddings like the other two brought."

Michael pulled out a phone, punched a couple of buttons, and squinted at the screen. "Marnie Banks, thirty-four years old. Recently laid off from a six-figure job at a dot-com that developed security portals for other dot-coms."

The guys looked questioningly at one another; when it appeared no one knew what the hell that meant, Michael shrugged and continued. "Up to her eyeballs in debt, living with Mom and Dad, and driving a BMW."

"Figures," Jack muttered with a roll of his eyes.

"Interesting—no actual wedding gigs, according to her résumé," Michael added, looking at the guys. "But she checks out. No arrests, no mysterious trips to the Middle East. No marital strife on record, no gigs in strip joints. Looks like good, squeaky-clean fun—except that she has no concept of money."

"No wedding gigs?" Jack asked, frowning. "That can't be good. How's she going to pull off a wedding like this if she's never done one?"

"No *solo* wedding gigs," Eli said. "She worked with some big-shot event coordinator."

"We'll check it out," Michael assured them. He was their security guy, because he had more contacts than God. "But let's not forget she's the only one we have left. And we agreed—we *want* an unknown, to keep the press off our trail. If this one doesn't work out, we've got nothing."

15

"Whose fault is that?" Cooper interjected. "You scared that last one half to death with your scorpion deal."

"What, we're not supposed to mention bugs?" Michael protested. "Dude, have you ever seen a woman with a bug? There can be one bug in the same county as a woman, and the minute she knows it, she is screaming her head off—"

"Okay, but couldn't you have just said there might be some bugs instead of, 'What would you do if you woke up with a scorpion in your sleeping bag?' Come on, dude, that was just gross. Even I was thinking of bailing when you said that."

"Guys," Eli said, holding up his hands. "I think we have proven in spades that we have a deplorable lack of interviewing skills and the finesse of a bunch of snails when it comes to talking to wedding planners. So let's be smart about how we're going to do this."

"Do the physical stuff first," Jack said. "We've wasted too much time talking about weddings only to find out they won't do the physical stuff. Tell me what you think of this," he said, and proceeded to lay out the physical course as he saw it, which was met with immediate argument from Michael, who felt particularly bad for the girl who'd worn a dress.

But Jack countered with the widely held view—at least in this group—that the successful wedding planner had to be able to climb a rope.

At the *very* least, she had to do that.

They were firmly entrenched in their respective and loud opinions on that subject.

The Lincoln quickly turned into an oven; Marnie could feel perspiration on her forehead. "Ridiculous," she muttered, and flung open the door and stepped out. "I'm not waiting in some oven," she announced to the driver, who was having a smoke under the trees, and bent over, scooped up her hat, her melon, and her bag, then kicked the door shut with her foot. "What am I, a dog?"

He shrugged. She marched to the front of the vehicle, put on her hat, anchored the melon under her arm, flung her bag over her shoulder, and proceeded to march in the direction she'd seen Eli go.

She walked down the garden path to the large garage, and paused for a moment to count the doors. Six in all. Wow. Only someone huge in the movie industry would have a six-car garage.

A smile curved the corner of her lips, and Marnie marched on.

She rounded the garage, saw the walkway up to the main house, and proceeded—but she didn't make it as far as the keypad on the gate when a man the size of a mountain appeared from nowhere and stepped in front of her. He folded his arms across his chest and frowned down at her. "May I help you?"

"I hope so," she said smartly. "I was about to boil to death in the Lincoln. I'm looking for Eli."

"Who?"

"*Eli*," she said again. "The guy who drove me here."

"Right. And I suppose he's staying here, huh? A close, personal friend of Vince's?"

"Who?" she asked, but the moment the question was out of her mouth, she knew exactly who Vince was and gasped with delight. "*Vincent Vittorio* lives here?" she squealed. "Am I going to meet him?"

The guy laughed and grabbed her elbow none too gently. "*No*," he said, and pushed her back. "Take a hike," he said, escorting her roughly down the path.

"Hey!" Marnie protested. "I'm here with Eli!"

"I don't know any Eli—"

"The Thrillseeker guy!"

The man stopped pushing her. "Oh. You're here for the auditions."

"What is the deal with the *auditions*?" she cried, and wrenched her elbow free of his grasp.

"Got me," he said, and pointed in the opposite direction to a path that led into the garden. "That's their deal, not ours. They're down there. Up here is off limits. You understand me? *Off limits*," he said again, making a slashing motion across his neck.

"All right, already," Marnie said, pouting.

The guy turned around and started to walk away.

"But wait!" she called after him. "Is Vincent *here*?"

"*Off limits!*" he barked and stalked off.

Whatever. Maybe Eli would introduce her before he took her back to the Farmer's Market. If she could find Eli, that was.

She wandered down another path and did indeed find him, as well as some other men, as she rounded a bend in the path through a large garden. They were standing inside a beautiful white pavilion with hanging ferns and cushioned seats and boxes of flowers along the rail. By the sound of it, they were arguing. Well, wasn't that just great—she was roasting on a spit and they were having some sort of argument.

"Helloooooo!" she shouted as she made her way to the pavilion with her melon and oranges. "Hel-*loooooo!*"

All four of them stopped and jerked toward the sound of her voice. As she strode toward the pavilion, Eli stepped out of the group and moved quickly out from the cover of the structure and down the steps, as if he were somehow surprised to see her here. Another guy, almost as good-looking as Eli, stepped out with him and peered at her as if she were some sort of space alien who had just landed in the garden.

The other two men—okay, make that four gorgeous guys—walked to the edge of the pavilion to stare at her. Marnie halted directly before them and paused for a moment to lose the melon, which was beginning to feel like it weighed two tons.

She straightened up, eyed them curiously, and smiled as brightly as she could, given the circumstance. "Hi! I'm Marnie Banks."

No one said anything.

Oh come *on!* "Surely *you* remember me, Mr. Eli," she said with a forced bit of laughter. "You brought me here, remember?"

"Oh, I remember," he said and smiled a little. "Ah...this is Cooper," he said, gesturing to the man next to him, who extended his hand to her in greeting.

Marnie grabbed it and shook it vigorously. "It is a pleasure to make your acquaintance, Mr. Cooper."

"Ah, it's Cooper Jessup," he said, withdrawing his hand from her grasp with a bit of a wince. "And these are our partners," he said, motioning to the others around him. "Eli McCain, you know," he said, indicating Eli. "And Jack Price and Michael Raney."

The two guys each moved forward to shake Marnie's hand. She smiled at the lot of them, straightened the only sensible blouse she had that was nice enough for an interview but might also be considered a "banging-around" blouse, and clasped her hands together. The four men stood there, towering over her, as if they expected her to say something.

What she wanted to ask was if any of them were single— she hadn't been in the company of so many good-looking, buff men in…well, never. But okay, she was here for a job, not to ogle the team. "Well!" she said, smiling. "Thanks so much for interviewing me. I am really excited about this opportunity."

"Right," Eli said, glancing at the others. "So Marnie, there are a couple things we'd like to ask you."

"Great. Fire away. I have some résumés here in case you forgot to bring the ones I sent you," she said, digging in the bag of oranges and pulling out a manila folder. "I didn't bring my entire portfolio, but of course I can make that available to you," she added, handing them each a double-sided, colorful résumé. "Nevertheless, I think there's enough information here to demonstrate that my background is perfectly suited for this wedding," she added confidently. "So please, ask me anything you want."

"Great," Eli said, without looking at her résumé. He seemed reluctant to ask whatever it was.

Marnie smiled brightly. "I'm ready if you are."

He glanced at something over her shoulder and said, "Okay, well…first of all…can you can climb that rope over there?"

Marnie laughed politely at his lame joke.

No one else laughed. Eli nodded solemnly to a point over her shoulder. Still smiling, Marnie turned to look. It was a rope, all right, hanging from a sycamore tree.

"Climb a rope?" she asked, and jerked around, expecting to catch them snickering over some weird joke. Only they weren't snickering at all, and Eli nodded again, as if it were perfectly reasonable to ask a wedding planner to climb a rope.

Her eyes narrowed with suspicion.

"Just...you know, give it a quick run up and down," Eli suggested. "Nothing fancy."

He was serious. They were *all* serious. They were peering at her, actually, glancing anxiously at the rope then at her again.

"You want *me* to climb *that* rope."

"Yeah, it must sound really strange," Eli agreed. But then he patted her on the shoulder, leaned over so that his head was directly next to hers, and said softly, "But we really need you to climb that rope."

CHAPTER THREE

E li caught her arm before she could grab her melon and
run, and at least got her to agree to hear what they were
trying to accomplish with the audition.

Thrillseekers Anonymous, he said, was an ultrasecret,
ultraexclusive, members-only sports club catering to the
extremely wealthy.

The "extremely wealthy" point instantly caught her
attention, and she had stopped wrestling Eli for the melon
and demanded suspiciously, "Like who?"

"Like...we can't tell you unless you get the job," Cooper
said.

That clearly disappointed her, but she did agree to come
into the pavilion and sit down to listen to their spiel—a spiel
they'd given so many times that they all knew it by heart.

It went something like this: Eli, Cooper, and Jack had
grown up best friends on the West Texas plains. Their love
for anything sporting had started then—football, baseball,
basketball, rodeo—whatever sport they could play with the
goal of outdoing the other two. They were still pups when
it became clear that regular sports were not enough to sat-
isfy them. They began to create elaborate, double-dog-dare
tricks using rooftops, trampolines, and swimming pools.

And they created a dirt-bike trail through the canyons that rivaled the professional circuit. They made a game out of breaking horses without using a bit and built motorized conveyances that they would race across fallow fields.

As they grew older, their competitive spirit grew more extreme, and they became experts in white-water rafting, rock climbing, canyon jumping, kayaking, surfing, and skiing—name a sport, any sport, and they had tried it.

After college, Jack went into the Air Force so he could fly higher and learn how to do stunts in airplanes. Cooper and Eli weren't as interested in flying as they were in jumping off buildings and blowing things up, so they headed out to Hollywood to hire on as stuntmen.

With Jack in the Air Force, Eli and Cooper got their start working on some of the biggest action films in Hollywood. Their ability to do any stunt and their willingness to go the extra mile eventually led them to choreographing huge action sequences. Through a series of big blockbuster films, they earned a solid reputation for being fearless, unconquerable, and astoundingly safe, given what they did.

And still, with all the action in their day jobs, Eli and Cooper routinely trekked out on weekends to ocean kayak, or kite surf, or helicopter ski—whatever caught their imagination.

But it wasn't until they got the bright idea to take along a couple of pals who just happened to be movie stars that their outings began to be the talk around movie sets. Their reputation as tough guys grew exponentially—the more Hollywood bigs they took along on their adventures, the bigger their adventures became.

Perhaps more important, and amazingly without a lot of forethought, what Eli and Cooper proved adept at doing was keeping these jaunts out of the press. In fact, they became masters at it.

It was Cooper who came up with the idea of making a business out of their love of adventure—after all, extreme sports didn't come cheap. And an increasing number of Hollywood moguls wanted the exclusive and exotic outings they offered, particularly if the adventure came with the guarantee of total privacy.

When Jack started making noises about getting out of the Air Force—he'd learned to fly anything with wings, and was ready to move on—they persuaded their old pal to come and join them in California. They figured if they could provide their own transportation and fly their clients to their adventure destinations themselves, they'd be that much more mobile and private.

Jack was more than willing to do it—he missed his old pals, missed the extreme sports with them. But he had one condition—he wanted to bring a friend.

During his years of service, Jack had become friends with Michael, a fellow extreme-sports enthusiast. It so happened that Michael was also considering moving on from his job—he was a CIA operative who was growing weary of being out in the cold.

As Jack had explained it to Eli and Cooper, what Michael brought to the table was invaluable—the guy had a contact for just about anything anyone could imagine. He'd known arms dealers, jewel thieves, opium traders. He'd dined with Saudi kings, had lived with a Parisian diplomat, and had at least two Swiss bank accounts that Jack knew of. He was a gold mine of information and resources.

Eli and Cooper said they didn't care about that, but could the dude ski? Repel down cliff faces? Sky surf or kite surf? Jack said he could, so a few months later, during a Lakers game one night, Thrillseekers Anonymous, or TA, as they called it, was officially born. The four of them agreed that night that no fantasy adventure was too fantastic for them. They agreed they would not fulfill fantasies that were illegal or included illicit sex or drugs, but anything else they considered on the table. Their motto became *Name your fantasy and we'll make it happen.*

In the last two years, TA had grown to the point that they were scheduling adventures monthly, if not more often. Word of their business had spread beyond Hollywood, and high-tech billionaires, European royalty, and New York real estate aristocracy, among other wealthy and famous people, sought their services.

The adventures were top notch. They had surfed thirty-foot waves off the coast of Washington, had canyon jumped through the alpine mountains of Europe. They had forged new helicopter skiing in Canada, going where no skier had gone before. They had careened down some of the meanest Class V white waters in the world, had raced motorcycles across the roughest terrain in South America, had climbed the frigid mountains of Russia. Whatever the fantasy sport, they had done it.

But then something peculiar happened.

Their clients were men of power and extraordinary means. But behind every one of those men stood a woman, and over the course of a year, some of their best clients had begun to call up inquiring about the same sort of gig, usually beginning with a heartfelt apology for even asking.

The wives and girlfriends of these men were just as attracted to the privacy TA offered as were their mates. But they didn't want extreme adventures—they wanted extreme social events. They wanted someone to organize an Antarctic cruise for fifty of their closest friends, or arrange an anniversary party on a remote island and give it a Gilligan's Island theme. They wanted someone to organize a girls' week out, which would include someplace very cool—floating down the Amazon River in luxury, for example. But most of all, they wanted the privacy.

At first, the guys balked. They rarely attended social events, and usually only when one of them happened to have a girlfriend, which was a hit-and-miss sort of thing, given the nature of their business. They certainly didn't do social events, and the first time they received a call requesting one, they had been collectively insulted. They specialized in dangerous, breathtaking, thrilling trips into the wilds of the world—not tea parties.

But the requests kept popping up, and they began to realize if they didn't go with the flow on this, they might start losing some valuable clients.

And then *this* happened—this being the wedding of the century, of course.

What made *this* different from the previous requests was that the two stars involved—Vincent Vittorio and Olivia Dagwood—wanted their wedding to occur at the end of an extreme sports trip. Sort of a hybrid, Vince explained to them.

Specifically, they wanted to return to the remote mountains on the border of Colorado and New Mexico, where they had filmed the epic movie *The Dane*. Vince had done some extensive training for that film, and his idea was that he and Olivia and a couple of TA guys would all go canyoning, which involved riding waterfalls and rappelling down rock faces or jumping in alpine pools so that they could slide down a water chute to the next foaming pool, only to climb out and up the next rock and do it again.

At the end of their jaunt, Vince proposed that they would hike up to a pristine and beautiful little dale at the top of the San Juan Mountain range. The dale was only a quarter of a mile up from the Piedra Lodge, the luxury summer resort where they had resided during the filming of *The Dane*. In that tiny dale was an old miner's cabin that had been converted into a plush honeymoon cabin. It was, Vince said sheepishly, the setting Olivia wanted—between towering mountains covered with summer alpine wildflowers and spruce trees.

And he was willing to pay them a shitload of dough for what Olivia wanted.

The request had been an agonizing development for TA. They didn't want to lose out on the chance to go canyoning—the four of them had bemoaned the fact they didn't have the time to do it before *The Dane* wrapped. They did not, however, want anything to do with a wedding. Even one tacked on to canyoning.

But Vincent Vittorio was one of their best clients. He was a short guy, had a bit of a Napoleon complex, and was constantly trying to prove his mettle through extreme sports.

In his zeal, he had brought TA some of their most lucrative contracts. Worse, not one of them could deny the lure of the money Vince was willing to pay them. They had quickly determined they could book an entire year's worth of expenses against what they would make off this one event.

At first, the guys had tried to find a way out by searching for some hole in the logistics of doing a wedding there, but really the logistics weren't that difficult—the spot was remote, and the nearest airport, a two-hour drive, was only a regional one. A single two-lane road led up to the old mining sites, and even that was closed for most of the year. As a result, no one was up there save cattle, elk, and the occasional bear. It would be a cinch to keep the event private. Moreover, the lodge and honeymoon cabin were available at the time they wanted it.

No matter how they looked at it, they couldn't find a really good reason to say no. It was just that none of them wanted to be involved in a wedding, because none of them knew *how* to be involved in a wedding.

They needed, Jack said then, a wedding planner. He convinced them that with a wedding planner, the rest of them had to merely show up.

But *hire* a wedding planner? Let a *female* into their inner sanctum? It seemed impossible, inconceivable, and a really bad idea. Much argument and discussion and—after a trip to the store for a case of beer and some ribs—even more argument had ensued, until the four men resolved the issue by taking a vote.

It was three to one, Eli voting against.

He had his reasons.

They all knew his reasons. It had been only a year since he'd been jilted at the altar in another big to-do. Yep, Eli

McCain had been left standing holding the proverbial bag while the rest of the world read about it in the tabloids. The last thing he wanted or needed was a wedding in his life.

Nevertheless he was voted down—they would hire a wedding planner. But they agreed they would hire an unknown planner who didn't have a public relations office so the press wouldn't get wind of it. And as the wedding itself would require some hiking and lifting and various other physical activities (the dale was beautiful, but it was awfully remote at eleven thousand feet), they would need a wedding planner who could at least climb trees and rocks. Thus, the idea for the audition was born.

At that point, the guys had tackled the even harder issue of who among them would lead this expedition into virgin territory. No one stepped up. All of them said, "Not me, pal." Several bawdy and impolite things were said about weddings and marriage in general. They had at last decided which of them would lead—from the canyoning all the way to through the wedding—in their usual customary fashion.

In a cruel and ironic twist of fate, Eli lost his round of rock, paper, scissors.

Personally, he didn't think there could possibly be a worse choice than him. As Cooper explained everything, just watching Marnie's eyes light up at the very mention of wedding plans and exotic locales made his stomach churn. What was it with women and fancy weddings? If Eli ever contemplated marriage again, which he'd never do, he'd run off to Vegas or something.

"So what do you think, Marnie?" Cooper asked after the spiel.

It was clear what Marnie thought—she beamed like a ray of pure sunshine, the light coming right out of her maple eyes. "Are you kidding? A wedding in the mountains? I can't think of a more romantic setting!"

"I guess it's romantic," Cooper said with a shrug, "but it's not easy. It involves a lot of physical stuff. And we can't afford to have a team member who isn't in shape and can't pull her own weight, you know what I mean?"

"Absolutely."

"That's why we need you to climb that rope."

Marnie's beaming smile faded a little. "Well...okay. Sure." She didn't sound very sure, but she put aside her bag, her melon, and her red hat nonetheless. "I'm not exactly dressed for it," she said, looking down at her black slacks.

"That's why I said to dress in banging-around clothes," Eli explained.

She gave him a brief, withering look. "I didn't realize 'banging around' meant rope climbing." She walked past him to the edge of the pavilion and stared at the rope. "Just up and down once, right?"

"Right," Coop said.

With a small sigh, she headed for the rope. The guys followed her. She stopped at the rope, rubbed her hands on her black slacks, then rubbed them together as she eyed the thing. Eli stepped up to spot her. "It's easy," he said. "Watch me." He jumped up on the rope, quickly scaled to the top, then just as quickly lowered himself to the ground.

Marnie frowned.

"Marnie...have you ever climbed a rope?" he asked carefully.

"Of *course* I have climbed a rope," she said. "Granted, it's been a few years, like maybe twenty-five, but hey, I've climbed one. I can do this."

Okay, then, it was clear they weren't going to find a wedding planner who could climb a rope. And honestly, Eli felt a little sorry for her. She seemed so...so *spunky* and so desperate to get this job. She definitely got extra points for being the only one of the four women they had talked to who'd made it to the rope.

"Listen," he said, "if you can't get all the way up, don't worry about it. We're not going to cut you for failing the rope climb. It's just so we can get a feel for your strength."

"You might want to stand back," she said, ignoring him, and with a grunt, she launched herself at the rope, jumping up and grabbing on about halfway up.

And there she hung, clinging desperately to it, her legs wrapped tightly around it, her hands white-knuckled in their grip as the rope swung lazily.

Eli winced when she didn't move for a long moment. "Just use your legs and inch your way up," he suggested.

"Right," she said brightly. But she didn't move.

"It's okay, let go," Eli said, putting his hand on the rope.

"No! I can do it," she gasped, trying to shake his hand off with a wiggle of her hips. "I just have to pull..." She made a very strange sound and managed to get one hand above the other.

For a moment, he thought she was going to make it. But then she began to whimper.

"Let go, let go," Eli urged her, grabbing her rope and peeling her fingers from it, began to peel her fingers from it, one by one. When she was in danger of falling, she let go and landed off balance, knocking into him. Eli grabbed her shoulders and straightened her up.

A frown creased her brow as she pushed some loose hair behind her ears. "You made me lose my grip!"

"Actually," he said with a hint of a smile, "you were gripping the hemp out of that sucker."

"I was?"

He nodded.

Marnie sighed. "That bad, huh?"

Worse. It was horrible. No upper-body strength at all. Marnie groaned, but Eli said, "Hey, it wasn't too bad," and patted her kindly on the shoulder. "I thought it was great. A for effort."

Marnie smiled gratefully, and Eli noticed with some surprise just how warm that smile of hers was.

"Well," Coop said, shaking his head as he sauntered up to them, "I guess we can try running."

They escorted Marnie through the garden and around a stand of trees to a small, half-mile track Vincent kept to stay in shape. She exclaimed her surprise when she saw it, and exclaimed even louder when Michael told her they wanted to get a feel for her endurance. "If you could just run around the track a couple times," he said, making a circular motion with his hand. "Maybe four. That's all we need."

Marnie looked down at her white silk blouse. "I wish I'd known to wear something a little sportier."

"I said 'banging around'," Eli objected again.

She flashed him a look that said she thought he was clearly a moron and walked to the starting line. She paused, fixed her hat and her hair, and pulled her shirttails out of her pants. "Do I have to be fast?" she asked.

"Nah," Michael said easily. "Just run." And the four of them lined up behind her, watched as she started to jog… well, bounce, really…around the track.

"Gotta say, this one is a definite improvement over the last one," Coop said with a grin.

"Not bad, not bad," Michael added, smiling appreciatively, too, as they watched a very nice ass bounce as she ran by. "But she runs like a girl."

"This is the dumbest idea we've ever come up with," Eli snorted. Not that he wasn't appreciating the package bouncing around the track along with the guys. "We're making a wedding planner run around a track. Do you know how stupid that is?"

"Shut up," Jack said. "I'm enjoying the show."

Marnie made it around one and a half times before she had to stop and put her hands on her knees to get some air. When the guys joined her, she apologized between gulps of air, and admitted to being very amazed that her trips to the gym hadn't yielded a better performance.

While they all hastened to assure her that it was quite all right—they admired her willingness to try—there wasn't a man among them who didn't wonder if she could pull her own weight at eleven thousand feet. They were used to enduring extreme conditions with strong men. Not women who ran like girls.

Fortunately, Marnie fared much better on the next phase. The idea, as they had developed it, was to make sure their wedding planner could handle the press. In the pavilion, Michael began to fire a set of nonsensical questions at her, asking and reasking the same thing, trying to shake her up.

Marnie did a great job—none of the questions about affairs or babies or drugs rattled her in the least. She had a great laugh and a charming smile, and laughed appropriately at the ridiculous questions but still answered them with aplomb. Better yet, she gave up just enough of her made-up version of the wedding for the press to have a story, but not enough where they could actually learn when or where it was.

The last phase of the audition was Jack's creation. He thought it necessary to give the candidates some what-if scenarios to see how they'd react. "The bride hasn't decided what to wear for the wedding," he said, harking back to an Oscar moment that Olivia had told them about. "She has three or four dresses. When she gets up to the site, she decides to wear a Vera Wayne, but you don't have a Vera Wayne," he said, making it sound like a matter of life and death. "What do you do?"

"Wang," Marnie said.

"Huh?"

"Vera Wang. This is a tough one," she said thoughtfully. She tapped a manicured forefinger against her lips, then said, "Okay, here's what—I'd try and talk sensibly to her and point out all the good things about the gowns she's got."

No one had anything to say to that.

"Okay, that's dumb," she said hastily. "This *is* Olivia Dagwood we're talking about. How about...I'd try and pass off one of the gowns there as a Vera Wang?" she asked. When no one spoke again, she said, "No? Okay, I give. What is the right answer?"

"Hell if we know," Jack said.

In the end, having exhausted everything they could think of, and being in turn exhausted by Marnie's knowledge of weddings, the guys sent Marnie back to the Lincoln to wait, and they caucused in the pavilion.

It was clear they had their wedding planner. Jack lamented that she didn't have the physical stamina they were hoping for, but they all agreed that she likely wouldn't look as hot as she did if she had the physical stamina of a discus thrower, which was, if they boiled it down, what they were hoping for.

"So what do you think?" Cooper asked them all. "Do we take her on?"

"Have we got another choice?" Jack asked. "She'll do, assuming she comes up clean on a thorough background check."

"I like her," Michael said. "She's cheerful. I like cheerful in a wedding planner."

"I like legs on a wedding planner, and she's definitely got those," Coop snorted. "I say we do it."

The three of them looked at Eli. He sighed wearily. "I still say it's the dumbest thing we've ever done."

"Great," Cooper said, and with a grin, shoved Marnie's forgotten melon at Eli. "Then you can call her with the good news when we finish the background on her."

CHAPTER FOUR

M arnie was waiting on the front bumper of the Lincoln when Eli strolled up the path, and she couldn't help noticing that the man looked as good coming as he did going in those old Levi's.

He smiled in a very soft, very sexy way that made her belly do a weird little flip as he reached the parking lot. "You forgot something," he said, indicating the now- bruised but still enormous casaba melon she hadn't even noticed until now.

"Thanks." She quickly took the melon from him and waited for him to say more. Like, *You're hired.*

But he lifted his hand to signal the driver and said, "You can get in."

That was hugely disappointing. She'd thought she'd done pretty well at her audition. She was really hoping that he'd come up and tell her, while she was standing on Vincent Vittorio's property, that she had the job. And she thought he ought to be a whole lot more cheerful than this, because she deserved at least cheerful after what they'd just put her through. And really, why couldn't he have told her to wear some *workout* clothes instead of some *banging-around* clothes?

It was the rope, she thought as he opened the door to the Lincoln for her and she carelessly tossed the melon inside. It was that damn rope! It had been her bane from the moment she'd first met it at age six, and it was still kicking her ass.

She climbed in; the driver shut the door as Eli got in beside her. A moment later, they were backing out of the little lot.

Her arms crossed, Marnie let the casaba melon roll listlessly on the seat between them. Okay, maybe she didn't have the experience they needed for this sort of wedding, as in *no* experience, but if that was the case, couldn't they have just said so instead of making her run around a track in pants? The nerve, the absolute, unmitigated gall!

Eli said nothing as they drove through the electronic gate and turned onto a street. The farther away from Vince Vittorio's property they drove, the more irritated Marnie became. Her failure was partially his fault, she thought, stealing a glimpse of Eli from the corner of her eye. He should have told her to wear something a little more appropriate. She stewed until she caught him regarding her with a curious expression. "It was the rope, wasn't it?" she blurted.

"Pardon?"

"The rope. You guys cut me because of the rope. For your information, I couldn't climb the rope because of my pants—they're a *linen and silk blend*. If I'd been wearing something different, I could have done it."

"That's why I told you to dress in banging-around clothes."

God, if he said that one more time, she could not be responsible for her actions. "But..." She sat up and twisted in her seat to face him fully. "But you didn't say *casual*, you said *banging-around*, and really neither of them mean the same thing as gym shorts, do they?"

"Apparently not."

She fell back in her seat. "And who calls workout clothes 'banging-around clothes'?" she asked irritably.

Eli shrugged. "Sorry. I didn't know there was a difference."

Were men just born fashion-challenged? "There is," she said with much superiority, "*clearly* a difference."

"I consider myself enlightened," he said with that easy smile.

A moment later the Lincoln turned and stopped. The driver got out and opened Marnie's door. Eli got out, too. Marnie stoically collected her fruit and her bag and awkwardly stepped out, juggling the stupid melon. Eli stood, his weight on one hip, patiently waiting.

"Thank you for the interview," Marnie said pertly, and tried to stick her hand out.

Eli put his hand under the melon, and took her partially extended hand into his big callused palm. Something tingled beneath her skin where her hand touched his, danced up her arm, and slipped right into her chest. Marnie looked up—somewhere along the way Eli had removed his shades and had the most amazing blue eyes she'd ever seen, a gorgeous mix of blue and gold. And there were little feathery lines on tanned skin fanning out at the corners. *Damn.* No job, no bonus gorgeous guy.

"I appreciate the opportunity," she said dejectedly.

He smiled lopsidedly. "Yeah, you really sound like you do. So listen, we're going to run a background check," he said smoothly, "and if you check out, I'll give you a call in a couple days and we'll talk about ground rules. If you're cool with the ground rules, I'll take you to meet Olivia…that is, if you want the job."

Wait a minute…was she hearing him right? Marnie stood frozen, her mouth open, the melon in her hand. But then she gasped and lurched all at once, and Eli caught her melon. "You mean…you mean, I got the job?"

"If you check out."

"Oh, I'll check out," she said, nodding her head. "There's an alarming lack of anything in my background."

"We'll need to go over a few things—"

"Right, right—I'll bring my portfolio to your office at a time that is convenient for you and show you—"

"No, I mean about how we work. And there's a contract you need to sign that basically says if you die or something, it's not our fault."

"Okay," she said, nodding and pumping his hand vigorously. "Oh, thank you, Eli! You won't regret it, I promise. So when can I expect your call?"

Eli smiled fully then—a stunning display of even white teeth and deep dimples. "Take a breath, girl. We'll call in a couple days," he said, and handed her the melon. He lifted his cap and pushed his fingers through a head of thick, dark gold, sun-streaked hair. "Take care." With a touch of his hat, he moved to the open door of the Lincoln and stepped in.

Grinning so widely her cheeks hurt, Marnie watched the Lincoln disappear into traffic, and then whirled around and marched for the parking lot and her car, the melon on her shoulder now. *Marnie Banks. Wedding Planner to the Stars!*

They did not call her the next day. Or the day after. By Friday, Marnie had lapsed into despair and had gone for a run to clear her head. And okay, to see if she could run the high school track at least twice.

When she got home, feeling better about herself after making two circuits without passing out, Mom was sitting in the kitchen in her new embroidered capris and red Keds, talking on the phone.

Marnie walked straight to the fridge, opened it, and took out a bottle of water.

"Well, you can put them in a fruit salad, too," Mom was saying. "You just section them, get a nice sweet dressing, and mix it all up. It's a really good summer meal."

Marnie started to leave the kitchen, but Mom gestured frantically at the phone. "Would you like to talk to Marnie? She just came in." Mom paused, and laughed, looking at Marnie. "Yes, she *does*—a little anyway. Nice talking to you, Eli," she said, and pulled the phone from her ear and thrust it at Marnie, who almost dropped her bottle of water, mortified that her mother had been talking to Eli about a fruit salad.

She suppressed a squeal and snatched the phone from Mom's hand. "Hello?"

"Hello...ah, Marnie. Good news. You can't climb a rope, and you can't run very far, but you check out. So... you wanna do this wedding?"

"Yes!" she cried, and whirled around to her mother, who was, unfortunately, bent over, her head deep in the fridge. "Thank you. I'm thrilled, and I promise I'll do a great job for you. I have a lot of ideas—I was thinking that maybe we could attend a trade—"

ALL I NEED IS YOU

"Ah, Marnie," he said, quietly interrupting her. "I'd save it for Olivia if I were you. It's all lost on me. So listen, let's get together tomorrow and go over some ground rules. Then I'll take you to meet Olivia."

Oh sweet Jesus, she was going to meet Olivia Dagwood. "Great!" she chirped. Eli told her when and where to meet him and the very generous amount they thought to pay her; she silently danced around the kitchen, twirling around her mom, twirling right into the wall.

"So remember," Eli said, wrapping it up, "this is all hush-hush. No talking to your girlfriends about it, okay? I'll meet you tomorrow at the Blue Bamboo. You know where that is?"

"Yes, it's very close to my house, so I'll see you tomorrow around one," she said, and clicked off the phone before tossing it onto the counter and turning to her mother, her arms wide open. "I got the job!" she shrieked.

"I knew you would," Mom sang confidently as she opened a can of tuna. "I knew the minute they saw you they'd want to hire you."

"Mom, *I* am going to coordinate the wedding of Vincent Vittorio and Olivia Dagwood!"

"I know! And I'm so excited for you. I told Linda you'd get the job."

Marnie's smile faded. "You told Linda Farrino?"

Mom clucked her tongue. "Of course I told Linda. She's my best friend."

"But Mom, no one is supposed to know. It's a huge secret."

"Yes, Marnie, I *know*," Mom said with a hint of exasperation. "I'm not some doddering old woman who doesn't remember what you tell me. I told Linda, but don't worry—she won't tell a soul."

Marnie wasn't so sure of that, but it was too late to worry. Besides, she had a bigger problem. What would she *wear?*

Really, what exactly did one wear to meet a huge international superstar? Olivia Dagwood would be dressed in something really fabulous, and Marnie...Well, one thing was certain; she was not wearing the skirt she'd gotten on sale at Dillard's. Maybe Mom would lend her some money to buy something new. And where would she meet Olivia? In her house? She could just see her and Olivia going through fashion books to decide what sort of gown—no, wait! Even better, they'd go to Vera Wang's studio and Vera would show them gowns she could make just for Olivia.

If Vera Wang had a studio in LA Wow. She really had some research to do.

"Marnie?"

She jerked her head up.

Mom nodded at her hand.

Marnie looked down; water was leaking out of the top of the bottle she was holding at an odd angle. "Oh geez," she said, and moved to get a paper towel to mop up what she'd spilled.

CHAPTER FIVE

At least Eli now knew that Marnie came by the gift of gab honestly. When he'd asked if Marnie made it home with all the fruit, her mother had launched into a tale of oranges and fruit salad that had gone on and on and on.

And here came the daughter of the fruit queen now, walking down the sidewalk toward him with a very large portfolio in hand. More notably, Eli was pleasantly surprised to see that she was wearing something besides schoolmarm clothes. She wore a pair of white hip huggers that did their part by hugging her like a glove, and a dark-blue shirt that sort of wrapped around her middle and left no curve undefined, and even gave him a peek of her belly.

The woman had some great curves. *Outstanding* curves. Curves like he hadn't really noticed—okay, wanted to notice—in a long while.

She said hello with a very winsome smile, juggled her stuff, and finally managed to sit across the table from him. Her dark-copper hair was loose today; it hung just below her shoulders and she had long bangs that sort of draped to one side.

Okay, all right. It wasn't news that she was damn attractive. Of course he'd noticed it during the auditions.

Christ, he was still a man, even if he had been effectively neutered by Trish.

But he honestly hadn't appreciated how naturally pretty Marnie was the other day. Maybe because she'd been sweating so profusely. But now she had a look about her, like she'd walked off a Wisconsin cheese calendar. He could just imagine her with a pitchfork—or whatever implement they used to make cheese—a pair of cutoff overalls with nothing underneath, one side unhooked, the flap just covering the nipple of a perfect breast...

Damn. That wasn't where he wanted to go. He squinted and tried to concentrate on what she was saying—not surprisingly, she'd been chattering since the moment she'd shown up. Something about venues as she shoved a pink book at him. An organizer, she said, and hauled the portfolio up onto the very small café table and opened it to the first page.

"This is a wedding I assisted. A beach wedding," she said, proudly smoothing the page. "I wanted to show you because it was outdoors, and this one will be outdoors. By the way, do you guys have an office? Because I will probably need the address. But anyway, you can see how we set it all up with the white chairs and the altar and the red carpet, so the bride wouldn't ruin her gown, although," she said with a mischievous little smile, "there was an incident with the gown, but it was at the very tail of her train, and to this day, I don't know if she knows." She laughed at that. "And the reception was just next door," she continued, turning the page, "with the same view, but we put down a dance floor and hired a little six-piece combo, and in the end, everyone kicked off their shoes and they were dancing on the beach to great music. We had these really cute lights, too."

She glanced up at Eli, obviously waiting for him to say something. Only he didn't say anything, because he had no idea what he was supposed to say about cute lights. Where can I get some?

A tiny little frown creased her brow, but she looked down at her portfolio again. "Here's another outdoor venue. This one was in Lake Tahoe. Have you ever been to Lake Tahoe? Gorgeous. So anyway, this one was on a private estate, and we did this great theme of skiing, even though it was in the summer. You know, trucked in some handmade snow, set up these little hills—"

"Question," Eli said, leaning back and stretching his legs long beneath the table.

"Shoot."

"Do you always…talk so much?"

"Yes," she said, without missing a beat. "Do you ever talk?"

Eli grinned. "When I can get a word in edgewise, sometimes I'll open up."

A smile curved the corner of her lips. "I have another one," she said, turning the page.

Eli stopped her again by putting a hand on her open portfolio. "Why don't you save it for Olivia? She'll be thrilled to have pictures to look at."

Her bright eyes narrowed a teeny bit. "Okay," she chirped and shut the portfolio firmly on his hand. "When do I get to meet her?"

He smiled and gingerly withdrew his hand from the portfolio. Marnie pushed her hair out of her eyes, leaned back, crossed her legs, folded her arms like him, and watched him, too. But with a glint in her eyes. If he wasn't mistaken, it was a smarty-pants glint.

He made a mental note of that as he withdrew a small notebook from his pocket and flipped it open. "After we go over some ground rules."

"Great," she said, and began to swing one foot. But she made no move to get a paper or pen.

"You might want to write some stuff down."

She sighed, leaned over, and fished around her bag for a neon-orange pen and lime-green spiral notebook, straightened up, flipped it open, pressed her neon-orange pen tip to the paper, and gave him a derisive little smile.

"Rule number one—and this one is the most important rule you'll hear," he said with a slow smile. "It's so important that if you don't follow it, I will can you so fast that you will never even feel my boot in your butt. And here it is: *No one knows.* No one. Not your best friends, not your mother, not your priest. *No one.* TA is successful because we guarantee privacy for our clients and that means never mentioning their names, or where you are going, or even that you are working on a wedding. You cannot even begin to imagine how resourceful and sly the press and paparazzi are in this town. You have to keep this under wraps until it's all said and done. Any questions?"

"Nope," she said, and instantly dropped her gaze, wrote something down.

He leaned over, saw the word *bossy.* Oh great—he instantly suspected that her mouth had already opened and gums had flapped. He tapped her on the hand with his pen. She just inched her hand away from his pen. Eli frowned. "What's the matter, Marnie? Do we have a problem? Have you *told* someone?"

She looked off to one side and muttered, "Mom."

"Oh God—"

"But she won't tell a soul," she insisted with big maple doe eyes. "I swore her to secrecy, and I swear, my mom won't tell a *soul.*"

"Who else?" he demanded.

"No one, I swear it!"

"No one? You're sure about that? You haven't been sitting around with your pals doing each other's nails and gabbing about your great new job? About meeting a couple major Hollywood movie stars?"

Her expression instantly went from pleading to miffed. "Sitting around doing my *nails?*" she echoed. "Are you serious? Is that what you think I do? You think just because I am a wedding planner that I don't have anything better to do with my free time than my *nails?*"

"Have you been talking, Marnie? Because in case you haven't noticed, you seem excited about this gig and you have a tendency to talk."

"At least I *do* talk," she shot back. "At least I don't sit there glaring at the world around me like I'm mad all the time like *some* people. And you're right. I am very excited about this job. But I am a professional. And for your information, Mr. Personality, I have a very full and busy life. I do not sit around and do my *nails* and gossip with my *pals.*"

"Okay, Chatty Cathy," he said, holding up a hand. "That's all I'm asking."

She petulantly flipped her hair over her shoulder.

"So I'm sorry about the nail thing. I didn't mean to be offensive," he grudgingly added. "I just want to make sure you haven't been gabbing with your friends about this."

"I don't *gab* with friends. If you must know, I had to move home with my parents because of some...*issues*...and my friends are four hours away. Unfortunately, I don't sit around with anyone but Mom and Dad."

"Issues," he snorted, and looked down at his list.

"Yes, *issues*. Issues you know nothing about."

"Oh, really? Would it be issues like maybe too many shopping sprees? What is it with women and shopping, anyway? Why would anyone spend every dime they ever made and then some on shoes and clothes and spray-on tans?"

Marnie gasped. "How did you know that?"

"We run a very thorough background check. We can't afford to have some flake infiltrate our operation."

"Is there a reason you act like we're working on some top military secret?"

"That's a great description, because this is exactly the way we treat our business. The sooner you start thinking that way, the better off we'll both be."

With a huff, she slid down in her seat like a chastised child. "Is there anything else, General?"

"Yeah, Private," he responded with a grin, and explained how they would work, how she would bill for expenses, how she was to report in to him on a daily basis. How he and Olivia and Vince would leave for the mountains a week ahead of her for the canyoning, and how *no*, Marnie could not go, because she had work to do.

"There's one last thing," he said. "You need to manage the couple's expectations."

"Meaning?"

"Meaning, we are going to be high in the San Juan Mountains and very remote. It's not exactly Santa Monica where you can truck in a bunch of cute lights or whatever, or have limousines drive the wedding party around. Trust me on this—I know Olivia. She's going to want the sun and the moon. It's your job to give her that, but on a scale that matches up with a wedding in a remote mountain location. Just keep thinking about logistics."

Marnie nodded pertly. "Manage expectations," she said, jotting it down. "Got it."

She didn't have it. He knew she didn't have it because she knew nothing about the way these people lived. Eli did know, and that's why he and Marnie would be talking on a daily basis. He'd worked beside a number of Hollywood stars, befriended them, dined with them and knew them to be self-centered egomaniacs who thought the world revolved around them. Hell, he'd almost married one of them.

That prompted a dull thump in his chest and he abruptly flipped his notebook shut. "You ready to meet the bride?"

Marnie's face instantly lit with an enchanting smile. "I can't wait," she said, and quickly began gathering her things.

Marnie met Olivia Dagwood in her trailer on the set of *WonderGirl*.

Her trailer was really cool, decked out in great, really cool Scandinavian-looking furniture, a big mirror and makeup lights, a separate room with a bed, a Jacuzzi, and a plasma TV on one wall. There were a couple of people inside—one man Marnie thought was a makeup artist, because he was holding a palette of what looked like eye shadows. And there was a woman with a iPad and the earbud of a cell phone in her ear.

Marnie didn't even see Olivia Dagwood until she stood up. She was wearing a very sleek and very modern superhero WonderGirl outfit. "Eli!" she purred, and went up on her perfect little tiptoes to air-kiss him before bending her head back to greet Marnie with a lovely smile. "So you're my wedding planner!"

Olivia, Marnie was extremely disappointed to see, was no bigger than a child. She was maybe two or three inches over five feet and might have weighed one hundred pounds. Marnie herself was five feet, eight inches, and a perfectly acceptable size ten. But next to Olivia, she felt like the Incredible Hulk.

Frankly, she was stunned by Olivia's tininess, because she looked so much bigger than this on the silver screen. And that outfit had to be a kid's outfit she was wearing. And her *head*—of course Marnie would never say this to another living soul—but Olivia's head seemed about two sizes too big for her tiny body. And if Olivia Dagwood was *this* tiny, and she and Vince Vittorio always seemed to be about the same height in the movies, that meant—

"It's Marnie, right?" Olivia asked, extending her tiny little hand.

"Marnie, yes," she said, recovering, and quickly shook Olivia's hand and dropped it before she broke it. "It's so great to meet you, Miss Dagwood. I've seen most of your films and I think you're great. I loved *A Late Summer's Tale.*"

"Oh, thank you. I was nominated for an Academy Award for that performance." She smiled appreciatively. "Please call me Olivia. We're going to be working very closely together, so we should be friends."

Okay. She had officially died and gone to heaven. She was beaming and could practically feel her face splitting in two with a ridiculously huge smile.

"Why don't you have a seat? Peter was just touching me up for the next scene."

Peter, the makeup guy, gave Marnie a cool once-over before he turned his attention to Olivia again.

"And this is my assistant, Lucy. You'll be seeing quite a lot of her."

"Hi," Marnie said.

Lucy nodded her head and dipped her gaze to her iPad, as if something in there was too fascinating to break away from and say hello.

"Have a seat, Marnie. Would you like something to drink?"

Marnie eased down onto a lounge chair. "Ah...a diet soda if you have one."

"*Soda!*" Olivia exclaimed delicately. "Well, no—I should have said bottled or mineral water," she said apologetically.

"Oh. Bottled water is fine."

Without words or eye contact, Lucy got up and walked across the trailer to a small fridge, opened it up, then slammed it shut again. "We're out of water."

Olivia, who had reseated herself in front of a lighted mirror, sighed wearily. "That's the third time in two weeks. Do these people read their contracts? Can you *please* do something about it, Lucy?"

Lucy stepped out of the trailer. Marnie looked at Eli. Eli winked at her.

"Okay, Olivia, you remember what we talked about, right?" he asked, shoving his hands into his pockets. "Nothing too elaborate."

"I know, I know," she said, and looking at Marnie in the reflection of her mirror, she playfully rolled her pale-blue eyes. "Men. They have no appreciation for weddings, do they? Especially Eli. But honestly, I'm not a wedding person. I'm really doing this for Vince."

What did she mean, 'especially Eli'? Why Eli? And why was Eli coloring a little? He didn't seem the type to color. Ever. At anything.

He looked at Marnie. "I'll be back in a half hour."

"That's okay, Eli," Olivia said. "I'll send her home in a car."

"You sure?"

"Of course! We've got so much to talk about, and I am sure you don't want to wait around. Is that all right with you, Marnie?"

Was she kidding? "Ah—sure."

Eli didn't look so keen on the idea, but he shrugged. "Okay. So I'll call you tomorrow, Marnie," he said, and with one last look at Olivia, he stepped forward, bent his head, and whispered in Marnie's ear, "Remember what we talked about." And then he gave her a very pointed look, stepped out of the trailer, almost colliding with Lucy and a guy in a green service shirt, who carried a flat of bottled Perrier.

"Is it cold?" Olivia asked him. "I don't want it if it's not cold."

The man silently hoisted the flat onto his shoulder and went out again.

"Morons. Who wants warm water? I'm so sorry, Marnie. Hopefully the morons will get us some cold water before my next scene. In the meantime, tell me a little about yourself," she said.

"Oh, Well, I suppose I should tell you that this is my first solo wedding, but I have apprenticed extensively under Simon Dupree—"

"Dupree. Yes, I've heard of him. He did a strike party for a Miramax film I did, I think."

Marnie didn't think so but continued on with her experience. And as she talked more and more about herself, she had the very distinct impression that not only was Olivia listening, she was *interested.*

Oh yeah, this was going to be the job of a *lifetime.*

Much later that afternoon, after a long chat about chefs, Olivia sent Marnie home. Literally.

Dad was puttering around the garage and Mom's book club was standing at the front window when Olivia Dagwood's car pulled into the drive. Marnie climbed out, thanked the driver, and with her portfolio in hand, practically floated up to the door.

"Who was that?" her dad called to her as she floated by.

"A friend," she said dreamily.

"You have a friend that drives a car like *that?*" Dad asked, his voice full of incredulity.

"Yep."

"Where's your car?"

"On La Cienega. Mom can drop me later," she said, and floated inside. She was instantly met by five women, all menopausal, and all on at least their second cocktail. They stared at her curiously as she entered the dining room, where they typically held court.

"Who was *that?*" Mom asked.

"No one you know."

"Was it Olivia Dagwood?"

That earned a collective gasp from the book club group. "Olivia *Dagwood*? The movie star?" Mrs. Randolph demanded, crowding in closer than anyone. "How would *you* know Olivia Dagwood?"

Mrs. Randolph was not a big fan of Marnie's, not for twenty years since Marnie broke up with her son Tim in middle school. "Olivia Dagwood? No!" Marnie cried and followed it up with a high-pitched, desperate bark of laughter. "Don't be silly. That wasn't Olivia Dagwood, that was *Lucy*."

"Lucy?" Mom asked, looking very skeptical.

"Lucy! Lucy, Lucy, Lucy. From my old job, remember? She and I used to take Pilates together. She's in town for a couple days."

"Oh…" Mom said, her skepticism turning into confusion. "Yes. I think I remember a Lucy. Of course. *Lucy*."

Crisis averted. At least until later when a canny Mom would want to know what happened to this so-called Lucy. "Okay, gotta jet," Marnie said with a smile and cheerful wave, then darted down the hall to her bedroom before her mom could utter the name Olivia Dagwood again.

Her bedroom, all yellow-and-white gingham, had remained unchanged since 1985, and usually Marnie hated it, but today, she tossed her portfolio on the bed and sank onto the bench in front of her vanity, grinning like a fool into a mirror that still had a picture of Sylvester Stallone as Rambo tucked into the mirror frame.

But Marnie didn't see Rambo. All she could see was a vision of her new future. Tomorrow, the car was going to pick her up and take her to Olivia's *house*. She was going to Olivia Dagwood's house in Brentwood to talk about dresses and cakes and...and something about an arch that Marnie didn't really understand, but would figure out later.

Could this be happening? After suffering the layoff and having to move home and not being able to find a job and generally feeling pretty crummy about herself, could it be possible that she was about to climb out of a hole and start a new exciting career?

Not dressed liked a frump she wasn't.

Marnie jumped up and headed for her meager closet. She was really going to have to find something that made her look a lot less incredibly hulkish if she was going to be the wedding planner to the stars.

CHAPTER SIX

At the DreamWorks studio, Jack and Eli met with the executive producer of the live-action period movie *Graham's Crossing*, which was set to start filming in October in Ireland. TA had been tapped to choreograph and coordinate the film's stunt work, and they were currently negotiating the terms of the agreement.

At the conclusion of the meeting, Jack asked Eli to wait—he had something he needed to do with the director, who happened to be in the building.

Eli was hanging out in the executive lobby, flipping through *Variety*, when he felt a familiar presence. He slowly looked up and idly wondered if he'd go his whole life feeling like he'd been kicked in the stomach every time he saw her. "Hello, Trish," he said, his voice gone depressingly soft.

"Hi, Eli," she said, smiling prettily, as if they were old acquaintances. As if they'd never been more than that.

She didn't look any different—still pretty and small and blond. Her clothing looked top dollar, but Eli would have been surprised if it hadn't—she was with Tom Malone now, a successful actor on his way to the big time and one of a horde of multimillionaires in this town.

"What are you doing here?" she asked casually.

"*Graham's Crossing.*"

"Oh," she said, flipping voluminous blond hair over her shoulder. "That's a Spielberg film, isn't it?" When Eli didn't answer, she smoothly moved on. "Guess what? Tom is backing a film for me to star in. We're shopping it around to the studios," she said very matter-of-factly, as if he could possibly care. As if it were typical for a star on his way up to give a vehicle to a B-list actress. But that's what Trish had expected, Eli supposed, when she started sleeping with Tom Malone.

Eli had worked a dozen of Tom's films, had even been on a couple of extreme-sport outings with him, and had always thought he was a good guy. But he'd never thought, never once suspected that Tom Malone was sleeping with his fiancée, Trish.

Trish, damn her. He tried not to think of her. Ever. It was easier now, because it had been almost a year since she'd given him the good news that she was "seeing" someone else a week before the massive wedding that *she* had insisted on. He hadn't wanted a huge production, but Trish had, and he had jumped into it with both feet because he adored her.

"That's great, Trish," he said, and tossed the rag aside and leaned back, folding his arms over his chest. "Glad to hear things are working out for you."

"*Eli,*" she purred, with a sympathetic smile. "Don't be that way. It's water under the bridge, and besides, we might end up working together someday."

He couldn't help himself; he laughed at that and stood up, towering over her at six feet two. "Don't think so," he said pleasantly. "I'll leave this town before I work with you again."

"Eli!" she exclaimed, smiling coyly at him with big blue eyes.

"Have a good life," he said, and walked away, leaving her gaping at him as if she couldn't believe he'd just walked away.

How could she expect anything less? She'd destroyed him a year ago, and that he could walk away now instead of crawling was a small victory for Eli. He'd never been in love with anyone before Trish—he'd been the kind of guy to flit from one girl to the next, moving on about the time they started getting serious. But with Trish, he'd fallen hard, like King Kong off the Empire State Building.

And with a year under his belt to obsess about it, Eli wondered several times how he could have missed her cheating, why he hadn't seen any signs, hadn't felt a little nudge deep inside him telling him the whole thing with Trish was off kilter. Maybe he had. Maybe he'd had the nudge and ignored it, and that was what made him such a putz. He'd been totally blindsided by Trish's announcement that night they were lying in bed together. Oh yeah, he'd been lying there thinking about how happy he was and wondering how many kids they'd have, and if they'd take after their mom or their dad.

Putz.

Sometimes, late at night when he was sitting on his deck in the Hollywood Hills and staring out over the valley, he would think back to the eighteen months he spent with that woman, remembering how incredible it felt to be in love, to feel so strongly about another person that you'd do anything for them. He wondered if he would ever be able to do that again.

He was fearful of it, truth be known. He was afraid of being King Putz again. He was afraid of that deep, soul-wrenching ache that went with it.

But it wasn't really a problem, Eli thought as he walked out into bright California sunshine, because he didn't meet a lot of women unless he was on a set, and after his experience with Trish, he treated starlets like lepers and just stayed the hell away. In fact, he couldn't think of a woman he'd met in the last several months.

Well. There was Marnie. But she didn't count.

So what if she had that sunny smile that could make a guy's balls tighten a little? It didn't mean anything. He'd just noticed, that was all, which meant he wasn't completely dead.

At the moment, it only served to remind him that he needed to call her and make sure Olivia hadn't gone off the deep end. While he waited for Jack, he tapped her number into his cell phone.

"Hello!"

He recognized the singing voice as Marnie's mother, with whom he was becoming very well acquainted. "Hi, Mrs. Banks. Eli McCain."

"Oh, hello, Eli! How are you today?" she trilled.

"Great. Is Marnie around?"

"Oh no, she's gone shopping. And you'll never guess with who!"

Oh *Christ.* "Who?" he asked obligingly, knowing very well who.

"*Olivia Dagwood!*" her mom shrieked in a whisper. "She drove here *herself* and picked Marnie up!"

Great. Fabulous. He'd told Marnie that Olivia was not to drive. The paparazzi would be all over her, and if they found out who Marnie was, the whole thing would be blown. And he could just imagine what was going on with the so-called shopping trip, too. He didn't trust Olivia Dagwood as far as he could throw her, and given that she might weigh ninety-five pounds, that was pretty damn far.

"Does Marnie have a cell phone, Mrs. Banks?" he asked.

"No, she doesn't," her mother sighed. "I'm upset with her about that because *I* think she needs one, you know, because women can't be too careful these days. But what did she do? She cancelled her cell phone because she couldn't afford it. Now her father and I offered to pay for it, but she said oh no, she has her pride and—"

"Well, if you hear from her, would you ask her to give me a call?" he politely interrupted. "She has my number."

"Oh sure, sure, I'll do that. Bye now!" she sang, and clicked off.

Eli frowned, punched the phone book on his cell, and retrieved Vince's number. Maybe Vince would have Olivia's cell phone number on him.

They were supposed to be brainstorming ideas for Olivia's wedding organizer. Marnie had sectioned it into budget, task timelines, vendors, themes, food, flowers, decorations, and photography. But Olivia was adamant about starting their talks with the wedding cake. Her idea for a wedding cake was pretty spectacular, too—six tiers and covered in edible flowers. Pretty fancy for a woman who really wasn't into weddings.

"Remember," Marnie said gently, "that we'll have to have it flown in."

"How much could it cost? And besides, have you ever been to a wedding that didn't have a cake?" Olivia had asked forlornly on the phone. "I can't even *think* about a wedding if I can't have cake."

That sounded very Marie Antoinette-ish, but Marnie figured Olivia had to be a little goofy to be such a great actress. Didn't all artists have their quirks? "Okay," she said slowly, her mind already racing ahead to how they'd have a wedding cake from some famous chef flown in.

"Listen, why don't we meet for coffee and make a list of potential chefs I would even consider," Olivia suggested brightly. Marnie was all over that idea and suggested a couple of low-profile places they could meet up. She was certain Eli would be proud of her for thinking low-profile.

But Olivia blew that by saying, "Oh, I'll just pick you up!"

Warning bells sounded in Marnie's brain—Eli had said Olivia was not to drive and risk putting the paparazzi on their trail.

"Ah...why don't I come to you—"

"Nonsense! Anyway, I just got a brand new Lamborghini SUV and I am dying to take it out," Olivia said brightly. "Don't you want to ride in it?"

Well, of course she did. Who *wouldn't* want to ride in a Lamborghini anything? Okay, maybe there was one stick-in-the mud who sprang to mind—she could see Eli in her mind's eye, and he didn't like it.

But she didn't say no.

When Olivia arrived, she did not slip into the neighborhood unnoticed. All the men on the street who were out tending their lawns stopped whatever they were doing to watch her SUV slide by, and even worse, Mom's book club—who Marnie was beginning to believe lived in the basement—were all in the living room.

She knew her ride had arrived when she heard the collective squeal down the hall as they all rushed out to meet Olivia Dagwood.

The megastar was extremely gracious, and even signed autographs for the ladies. Marnie actually had to push her way through them to get to the vehicle, and practically had to pull Linda Farrino out of the passenger seat.

Mrs. Farrino did not take kindly to being pulled out of the Lamborghini. She pushed Marnie back from the car a little and went toe-to-toe with her, her hands on her hips. "You better watch it, little miss," she said hotly. "Do you remember how I used to spank you?"

"Are you...are you threatening to *spank* me?" Marnie asked, aghast.

"Marnie, mind your manners!" Mom added hotly.

"Sorry, Mrs. Farrino," Marnie muttered, but quickly stepped around her and dove into the car and pulled the door shut before the woman could stick her overprocessed head inside once more.

Olivia smiled and waved, but hit the gas and tore away from the neighborhood crowd that was growing. "Why does anyone want an autograph?" she demanded of Marnie. "What good is it? I don't understand why people won't just leave me alone. Am I not allowed to drive on a street? Must I be accosted everywhere I go?"

Okay, that was asking a little much, Marnie thought, seeing as how Olivia was a huge movie star and was driving a Lamborghini, of all things, on a street right smack dab in the middle-class neighborhood of Hancock Park. These people crowded around the mailman, for heaven's sake!

Fortunately, Olivia seemed to get over it, and as they drove into Beverly Hills, she looked around at every stoplight wondering aloud when the paparazzi were going to jump out and start snapping photos.

"I can't believe they haven't picked me up yet," she muttered. "They really haven't picked me up yet," she repeated, frowning slightly as she drummed her fingers nervously against her wheel. "Oh well. It's only a matter of time."

Honestly, Marnie couldn't tell if Olivia was miffed that it was taking them so long to jump out or that they would eventually invade her privacy.

Olivia turned off Venice Boulevard and made a couple of more turns, then finally turned into a residential neighborhood and into the drive of a typical California bungalow. "I hope you don't mind," she said breezily to Marnie's puzzled look, "but I need to see my spiritual advisor something awful. Are you into Kabbalah?"

"Ah…not really," Marnie said. "I'm not really sure what it is."

"No!" Olivia exclaimed, wide-eyed. "*Everyone* is into Kabbalah. Come in and meet Ari. He's wonderful," she said with a dreamy smile.

"Ari?"

"My spiritual advisor," she said, and hopped out of the car. "He practices a new kind of Kabbalah."

Marnie followed Olivia, and as she stepped inside, she stifled a gasp of surprise.

Inside looked like a fancy spa. There was a fountain in the middle of the front room, a cherub standing on one foot and spouting water. The floors were teak, the walls were painted a deep red, and the smell of incense wafted through the air. Light was provided by a set of very low-hung Chinese lanterns. There wasn't any furniture to speak of, just two teak stools in a minimalist decor.

A tall man with a close-cropped beard and a ponytail stepped through some beads hanging across a doorway. He was wearing a Hawaiian camp shirt, linen pants, and leather sandals, and when he saw Olivia, he smiled and held his arms wide. "Ah, my little raindrop," he said kindly, and Olivia dropped her bag on one stool and rushed across the room into his arms.

He engulfed her tiny body in a bear hug and held her tightly to him for a moment. Then he loosened his grip and glanced up at Marnie. "Where is your Lucy?"

"She has the day off," Olivia said. "This is my friend, Marnie."

"Ah," he said, putting a big hand on top of Olivia's shoulders. "Is Marnie a believer?"

"Not yet," Olivia chirped.

Ari chuckled and let go of Olivia. He very languidly glided forward to stand before Marnie, then placed both hands on her shoulders and smiled. "Marnie. If you are not to yourself, then who is?"

She blinked. "Pardon?"

He laughed gently. "Little sunburst, that is what I shall call you, for you have the sun in your mien."

Marnie had no idea what that meant, much less what to say, so she gave him a very weak smile. He laughed again and turned around, walked to where Olivia was standing, and put his hand on her back. "Come, little raindrop, and let us see what life has in store for you today."

"Watch my stuff, will you, Marnie?" Olivia asked, but she was gazing up at her advisor like a puppy.

Marnie watched them disappear through the beads, then glanced around the room. She took the empty stool, picked up Olivia's bag, and balanced it in her lap, wondering why everything in this town had to make her feel so huge.

The ringing of Olivia's cell phone startled her out of her wits—it sounded ferocious in the bare room.

She gaped down at Olivia's bag—who was calling her? *Who?* Her director? Her agent? Her mom? That's who called Marnie all the time when she had a cell phone, which was why she didn't have a cell phone—wait. What if it was Vincent Vittorio?

The thought that she had completely lost her mind flitted across her brain somewhere, but it was too late—Marnie had already reached into Olivia's bag and snatched the phone and tapped to answer.

"Hello?" she whispered breathlessly.

There was no response for a long moment. Then Eli drawled, "Well, I guess you two have hit it off real well if you're answering her phone."

"She's not here right now," Marnie whispered.

"Why are you whispering?"

"Because she's inside with her spiritual advisor."

"Ah, for the love of—what are you doing, Marnie?" he demanded in that bossy way he had going on.

"*Sssh,*" she cautioned him, forgetting for a moment that no one could hear him but her. "I'm not doing anything. We were going to grab a latte and make a list of chefs for her wedding cake, but she needed to see her spiritual advisor."

"A cake." He said it like he'd never heard of wedding cake before.

"A wedding cake," she clarified in a whisper.

"You need a chef for that?"

"Yes, you need a *cake* chef for that."

"And how are you going to get this chef's cake to Colorado?" he demanded a little testily.

But it was, she had to admit, an excellent question. "I haven't thought through everything yet. But I'll think of a way."

"Maybe you better think again, because we didn't budget for a chef to make a cake."

Okay, now the dude was really beginning to annoy her. Her fruit was too big, she wasn't supposed to drive around with Olivia, they didn't have money for a cake chef..."Well, maybe the budget needs to be rearranged," she said pertly.

There was dead silence on the other end of the line, and then a low, throaty chuckle that swirled up her spine. "I think you and I ought to get together and go over what damage you and Olivia have managed to rack up so far," he said. "Maybe rearrange that budget, as you suggest. I'm going to be out of town for a couple days. Are you free for dinner later or are you having some lettuce leaves with your new best friend Olivia?"

"I'm sorry, but I don't recall seeing a clause in the contract you made me sign that said I couldn't be friends with Olivia."

"Olivia doesn't have friends. She has keepers—don't confuse the two."

Now she was just pissed. He probably thought she wasn't up to snuff for Olivia. Single. Living at home. Frumpy clothes. Well, maybe she wasn't up to snuff, but she would be by the time this was over. "Thanks for your advice, Eli, but I'm a big girl. I think I can handle it."

"All right, so handle it. Get rid of the cake. Are you free for dinner?"

"I'll have to check my schedule," Marnie lied. "I'll call you later."

He laughed again. "I think Mom and Dad will let you out. I'll swing by and pick you up around eight...all right?"

"Whatever," she muttered.

"See you," he said and hung up. She made a face at the cell phone and tossed it back inside Olivia's bag. She was thinking that he was awfully good-looking to be so bossy when a moan from the back of the room startled her; she jerked her head up and stared at the beads in the doorway, still swinging slightly from Olivia and Ari's push through.

She heard another moan and felt a tingle in her groin. Slowly, she stood up...could that sound be what she thought it was? *Nah.* No way. Ari was her spiritual advisor.

But when Olivia emerged a half hour later, she was smiling that dreamy smile, and her hair was mussed and her little miniskirt was twisted around.

"You should really check out this new Kabbalah," she said sweetly as she picked up her bag. "Come on, I could really use a smoke."

Marnie looked back at the beads swinging in the doorway again, then dumbly followed Olivia out, her jaw practically dragging on the floor.

CHAPTER SEVEN

Marnie's folks lived in a standard-issue California bungalow that looked like it had been built circa 1930. It
had a tile roof, a back alley and garage, and lots of windows.
In the drive were a Buick Regal, a Dodge Spirit van, and the
smallest BMW they made.

As Eli climbed out of his Z-250 pickup truck, he absently
wondered how many times a teenaged Marnie had climbed
out a crankcase window in the middle of the night to terror-
ize the neighborhood, because he could certainly envision
it. If her audition was any indication, it was a fortunate thing
her house wasn't a split-level, or she probably would have
hurt herself trying to climb down a tree.

He actually smiled at that visual image as he walked up
the drive.

A man with silver-gray hair and a little taller than Marnie
appeared from the detached garage and stood just below
the roof eaves, eyeing Eli curiously. He was holding a rag
and polishing something in his hand. "Hello there," he said.
"Friend of Marnie's?"

"Yeah…Eli McCain," Eli said, striding forward to shake
the man's hand.

"Bob Banks," he said, wiping his hand before taking
Eli's. "She's inside with her mother and the book club. Just

knock on the door there, and if they don't hear you, go on inside. I'll warn you, it's a gaggle of geese—they can't hear one another speak because they all talk at once."

He said it with a grimace that Eli understood very well. "Thanks for the warning," he said with a grin, and walked on to the front door.

He hadn't even reached the porch before two women appeared behind the glass storm door to peer out at him. They were wearing tight tank tops and short skirts. Both of them were holding tumblers with a suspicious-looking, tea-colored liquid.

One of them said something to the other, and they both lit up like twin Christmas trees.

The woman with dark red hair flung open the glass storm door. A huge, lumbering mutt came bounding out and launched himself and his nose at Eli's crotch. "Well, come in, stranger," the woman insisted, while the other woman laughed unabashedly at the dog's sniffing of him. "Bingo, stop that!"

That laughter, as it turned out, was the call of the wild, for three more women suddenly appeared behind them, all dressed in short pants or tight skirts, and all holding identical tumblers with a drink that was most definitely not tea.

"Don't be afraid," the woman with yellow hair called out. "It's not like we're going to eat you."

That prompted another howl of laughter from all the women. Eli stopped midstride. The woman with the dark red hair instantly stepped outside and smiled at him—Marnie's smile.

"Mrs. Banks?"

"How could you tell? Come on in, Eli, and don't mind us. We're just having a little fun. It's not often we get such a handsome man at the door, you know. Girls, this is Eli. Now Eli, don't call me Mrs. Banks. That makes me sound so old. I'm Carol, just call me Carol. And this is Linda, she lives next door and has for thirty years, and that's Alicia who lives in the cute blue house right over there, and Bev who lives behind me—you can't see her house, but if you come in, we'll show you her pool, and last but not least, that's Diane, who moved into the brown ranch house four years ago. We weren't looking to expand our group, but we let her in the day she showed up with a margarita machine."

The five of them howled again.

Eli really wished he'd had the presence of mind to have Marnie meet him somewhere. "Ah...pleasure to meet you, ladies," he said uncertainly. "Is Marnie in there anywhere?" he asked, gesturing to the house. "Or did you eat her?"

The women looked at one another for a moment of surprise, then laughed uproariously again. "Bring him in here, Carol," one of them demanded. "Let us play with him a little before Marnie gets him." And before Eli could react, he was being ushered inside to a front room with a full view of the street as the dog pranced excitedly along with them.

In the room was a round card table littered with full ashtrays, coasters, a couple of overstuffed handbags, and a couple of paperbacks. The women all took a seat around the table—Eli had the impression they took the same seats each time they were together. Mrs. Banks insisted he take her seat while she went to fetch Marnie. The dog, Bingo, collapsed next to Eli's boot with a grunt.

Sitting there with four middle-aged women giggling at him made Eli more uncomfortable than a visit to a doctor. He tried not to squirm in his seat, but they just kept watching him. And giggling. And two of them had assumed provocative poses, so that their cleavage was clearly displayed to him.

"Bev, is there anymore Wahoo left?" one of them asked sweetly. "Maybe our guest would like a Wahoo."

"I don't know, sugar, but I'll look," Bev said, and hopped up, grabbed the empty pitcher from the table, and swished out of the dining room in her denim miniskirt.

"So!" the one named Alicia said. "Are you and Marnie dating?"

"Ah, no," he quickly corrected her. "No, we're not. Just a business arrangement."

"Oh!" she said brightly. "Then are you available?"

"Alicia!" the one named Linda said, slapping Alicia's shoulder. "You know if there are any leftovers, I get them."

Eli could feel the heat building under his collar.

"Oh, don't worry, hon. We're not going to do anything that you wouldn't beg us to do," she said slyly. "So what sort of business are you in?"

He forced a smile. "It's boring."

"Guess who Marnie's friends with," Alicia said, leaning across the table so that her cleavage was even more clearly displayed. "Olivia Dagwood, the actress."

"Is she?"

"Have you seen her movies?" the third one, Diane, asked. "I loved *The Dane,* but I thought she was so lame in *The Goodnight Girl.*"

"Diane, please!" Alicia cried to the ceiling. "She was brilliant in *The Goodnight Girl*. She got a friggin' Golden Globe for it, hello!"

"Who cares about a Golden Globe? It's the Oscar that counts, and she didn't get the nomination there, did she?" Diane said. "So what does that tell you? Her acting sucked."

"I liked it!" Bev shouted from the kitchen. "I'll tell you who sucked in that movie, and that was that English guy, Damian Reese. He's so girly he makes my skin crawl."

Diane and Linda gasped and leaned to one side to see Bev in the kitchen. "You think Damian Reese is girly?" they both shouted at her, almost in unison.

"Ah...excuse me, Mrs. Farrino? Can I get Eli and then you can argue about Damian Reese?"

The women all jerked around at the sound of Marnie's voice. Eli thought it was possibly the sweetest sound he'd ever heard in his life.

"Do you know Damian Reese, Marnie?" Linda asked.

"No," she said with a smile and a sly wink for Eli. "So, are we ready?"

Eli was instantly on his feet, as was Bingo, watching him closely as he backed out of the dining room.

"Oh, that's not fair," Bev cried as she came running into the room with a glass pitcher of what Eli surmised was more of the Yahoo, Wahoo—whatever—drink. "We were just getting to know your friend. I haven't gotten a good look at him yet."

"He's not really my friend, Mrs. Campbell. And we've got a meeting to get to, so please excuse us," she said, and slung a very tiny purse over her shoulder and headed for the front door.

Eli and Bingo did not need a second invitation. "Nice to meet you, Mrs. Banks," he said, striding forward to catch Marnie's arm for safety. "And the rest of you ladies."

"Bye!" they laughingly called to him as Bev refilled everyone's glass.

"Now Eli, don't be a stranger," Mrs. Banks was saying as she followed closely on their heels, hopping around Bingo. "Marnie doesn't have a lot of friends down here."

"*Mom!*"

"We're always home, so you can stop in any time you want."

"Mom, stop," Marnie hissed in a low voice.

"What?" her mother innocently protested. "What's wrong with making your friend feel welcome? Marnie, remember Dad and I are going to the club tonight," Mrs. Banks added as she crowded Marnie and Eli at the door, then pushed it open. Bingo was out in a flash. "We're going to be late because there is a dinner dance and we never get out, and besides, Dad's friends are going to be there, so I think he'll want to stay a little while, so if we're not here when you get in, that's where we'll be."

"Okay, Mom," Marnie said impatiently as Mrs. Banks leaned out and looked around.

"Where'd that silly dog go? Marnie, don't forget to let Bingo out when you get home!" her mom called after them as Marnie marched down the walk.

"I won't," she called over her shoulder, then paused at the open garage. "Bye, Dad."

"Oh…bye, kiddo," came the response from deep within the cave somewhere.

"Marnie—where are you going?" Eli asked as she walked around to the driver's side of her car.

She stopped her march and turned around. He noticed for the first time that she was wearing a wispy dress that hung by tiny little straps off her shoulders and floated like clouds around her knees when she turned. And he likewise noticed that sliding out from that pretty dress were some of the best-looking legs he'd ever had the privilege to see. Long and lean and shapely. Hell, Marnie looked...well, fantastic.

The schoolmarm, it seemed, was dead and buried.

"To my car," she responded, sounding slightly confused.

"There's no need to take two cars."

"Oh." She glanced uneasily at his truck. "I just thought that maybe this way, either one of us could take off, you know...when we wanted."

Eli smiled. "I don't think I'm *that* bad, darlin'," he drawled as he walked toward her. "And besides, haven't you heard about global warming? The cost of gasoline? Smog? Think of your great-grandkids and ride with me," he said, and put his hand lightly on her elbow. "I promise to get you back in time to let Bingo out."

Marnie looked at his truck suspiciously. "Okay," she said, and let him lead her down the drive to his truck. "By the way, I'd just like to go on record as saying my parents are impossible."

"I have to admit, that was an interesting group of women," he said as he opened the door of his truck for her.

"Oh my God, you cannot *begin* to imagine," Marnie said very dramatically and stepped into his truck, giving him another nice view of her fabulous legs. He shut the door behind and walked around the truck to the driver's side.

As he pulled away from her house, Marnie checked her lipstick in her compact, shut that, put it back in her tiny little purse, then folded her hands in her lap. "Where are we going?"

"If it's all right with you, there's a restaurant down in Santa Monica I'm sort of partial to. It's a seafood place that makes a mean margarita."

She laughed lightly. "You've got a great Texas drawl, you know that? Even when you're being bossy, you have a very cool accent."

"Hey, watch it," he said with a grin. "I don't have an accent."

Marnie laughed, that pleasant, genuine laugh again. He really liked the sound of it—it made him feel happy. "Does that sound okay to you? Seafood?"

"Anything," she said, and Eli thought that was probably true. He had the impression that Marnie Banks was an agreeable, cheerful woman. Not high-maintenance, not like Trish had been.

At the restaurant on Ocean Avenue, they managed to snag a decent table with a view of the ocean, and after a lively discussion about wine—because Marnie was quite the connoisseur, and Eli was most decidedly not—she chose a Chianti. The only thing Eli knew about Chianti is that it went well with fava beans. So Marnie gave him an enthusiastic and basic education about red wines in one long breath.

"You know a lot about wine," he remarked once they'd ordered.

"Yeah," she said with a sad smile. "I learned it in my last job. Our company did a lot of entertaining when they were trying to drum up new clients. And we all know how well that went."

He smiled. "You were the entertainment coordinator?"

"God, no," Marnie said with a laugh. "I was a computer geek. But the guy who owned it needed someone to help out, and it was either me, or Daichi Ichiro, who never left his cubicle that I could tell. I'm worried that he's still there. And get this—his entire cubicle was filled with *Star Trek* memorabilia. Little captains and Mr. Spocks and pictures of Daichi at *Star Trek* conventions and beam-me-up thingies."

Eli laughed and settled back as Marnie launched into a very colorful and amusing tale of her old job, where they all lived in cubicles and worked long hours. Nonetheless, she was very upbeat about it, and professed to miss the high-tech world where every day in cyberspace was a new adventure. He liked that about her, too—the pervading enthusiasm she seemed to have about life.

By the time they had drunk a glass of wine and poured a second and were eating oysters on the half-shell (his suggestion), Marnie had told him her entire life story. High school at Los Angeles High, college at SoCal. Tons of friends around the States, but none in her neighborhood. She did not, he noticed, mention a significant other of any type. Not that he cared, because he didn't—he couldn't have cared less. Really.

When the main course was served, Marnie artfully turned the conversation to him. "So Midland, huh?" she said with a grin after she'd gotten him to admit where in Texas he'd grown up. "A redneck?"

Eli chuckled, took another bite of his steak. "You could say that."

"So what did you guys do in Midland?"

"What did we not do?" he asked with a snort, and told her about growing up in the middle of dirt. His parents were ranchers—they had cattle and some oil. Cooper's folks, too. Jack's dad owned a body shop, which came in handy when the three of them started to drive.

"How'd you get started in the thrill-seeking business?" she asked.

"Blowing up stuff," he said.

She blinked. "Blowing up stuff?"

Eli laughed low, remembering the three of them and their homemade explosives. "Coop has an older brother, the orneriest cuss you'd ever meet. In fact, he's probably doing time somewhere now. Anyway, we were maybe eight or nine when he taught us how to make cherry bombs and throw them in the toilet. The thing was, after we'd dumped cherry bombs into all our toilets, we weren't satisfied. So we thought we'd blow up Coop's fort."

"Cardboard boxes?" Marnie asked, leaning back in her chair, one arm slung over the armrest, her fingers dancing on the stem of her wineglass, her eyes glimmering so deep that Eli could feel them tug at him a little.

"No, a *real* fort," he said, frowning playfully at the suggestion they'd have anything less than the best. "Made out of actual wood, built up on the fork of an old oak tree. We built the biggest cherry bomb ever seen—worked on that sucker for days, it seems like. And on the day of the big blast, we put it up in the fort, set it off, and ran like hell to get away from it."

"And?" she asked, beaming.

"And it worked, all right. Wood was flying in every which direction. Only we forgot one thing," he said, smiling broadly now. "Coop's mom had an old tomcat. And that tom liked to take his morning nap on top of that fort."

"Oh no!" Marnie exclaimed.

"Oh yes. Now don't look at me like that. We didn't kill him—just singed him a little."

"What happened?"

"Well, I can only speak for myself. Coop's mom called mine and Jack's mom in tears. I'll never forget the sight of my mom's pickup hauling ass down that old caliche road to Coop's house. I was shaking in my short pants, and I had good reason. When my mom got out of the pickup, she was as angry as I'd ever seen her. She latched on to my ear and didn't let go all the way home. And that's when she turned me over to Dad. I don't think I sat for two weeks."

Marnie laughed roundly. "I had a similar experience with a Barbie doll. A virginal sacrifice gone awry, thanks to my next-door neighbor," she said, and told him of how her older brother Mark had been the one to rat her out.

It was, Eli thought as they ordered dessert, one of the most pleasant evenings he'd spent in a good long while. He was enjoying her company, loving the way she laughed so openly and fully. She had a great sense of humor, was engaging when she talked, and the best part about it, she was very easy on the eyes. Extremely. No shit—he could look at her all night...although he'd prefer it if she were naked.

As their talk turned to the wedding, and she very confidently began to rattle off facts about linens and silver, something like that, something miraculous happened. For the first time in months, Eli was beginning to feel alive. Not the dull, dead lump of flesh he'd been feeling like for so long. It seemed impossible, but he was having a good time and really didn't want the evening to end.

But then she had to go and mention the arch.

CHAPTER EIGHT

After shopping in a trendy boutique on Rodeo Drive (because Olivia said Marnie could really update her look there, and by the way, had she considered Botox?), Marnie was now sitting in a happening restaurant, wearing a wispy new dress, dining with a very fine man who sported a very sexy five o'clock shadow.

Did it get any better than this?

She was on top of the world, and hey, Eli was really turning out to be not quite as bossy as she'd originally thought. He was a little more talkative tonight—he actually told her something about himself. Even though it was something violent and involved a helpless animal, it still made her laugh. He was really a great guy, she was deciding.

And when Eli smiled, ho Jesus...he had these beautiful blue eyes, and they crinkled in the corners. His lips were full and so damn sexy, especially for a man, just like the models in *Vanity Fair* she thought were lip-enhanced. Eli's lips spread across even white teeth and ended in those fabulous dimples in each hollowed cheek. Marnie imagined he used that smile on women all the time. She could picture the cowboy sauntering into some saloon, and with one smile, the dance girls would come running.

She might, if she weren't working for the guy.

Oh yeah, she was really beginning to think she had lucked into the job of a lifetime and settled back in her chair, one arm propped on the polished armrest, her legs crossed and a foot, encased in a new Rodeo Drive shoe, swinging carefree. She laughed at Eli's stories of three daredevil boys in Texas dirt while she surreptitiously admired her dress (Olivia was right—it *did* drape beautifully), and somewhere in the back of her mind, she was telling herself that she had arrived, that it was only up from here, that she was meant to be hanging around the rich and the famous, and obviously, that was why the dot-com thing hadn't worked out. It wouldn't surprise her at all if people were seeing her right now, checking her out, wondering, who is that girl?

And then Eli asked her about her meeting with Olivia. And she said—which, in hindsight, perhaps wasn't the brightest thing she might have said— "I bought this dress!" And she sat up, so he could see how cool it was.

Eli looked. His gaze was sort of hidden beneath really long lashes and heavy lids, but he looked a good long minute, long enough for her to feel her blood start to heat. He looked from the top of her dress, which draped low on breasts encased in a new lacy push-up bra, to the hem, which was on her knee. And on down to her toes, and her very cool, very strappy beaded sandals.

Then he lifted his gaze and looked her in the eye. "You didn't go shopping, did you, Marnie? I thought maybe you'd sworn that off with the debt you're in."

Oh hell, *that* again.

"And weren't you supposed to make a little progress with our client?" he added.

"I did," she protested. What did he think, she was a complete novice? Well, okay, he might have reason to think that, but she had done more than shopped. All right, not a *whole* lot more, since they had shopped most of the afternoon, and he was right, dammit, that she had sworn off shopping. But hey, she was due to get a big payment here soon!

Anyway, she hadn't left Olivia without getting *something* about the wedding accomplished. In fact, the insinuation that she had "just shopped" was insulting the more she thought about it, and she snorted, "*Honestly*, Eli, I know what I'm doing." And she rolled her eyes.

"I'm sure you do. But I'm thinking you probably can't do a whole lot of wedding planning in the middle of some pricey dress shop."

He had a point, but Marnie tossed her head nevertheless. "For your information, we talked about the chef and how many guests she'd like to invite, and stationery, which Olivia is not big on, and linens, which she is very big on and *must* be BBJ linens, and the music, and then how we might incorporate an arch into the ceremony."

His heart-stopping blue eyes immediately narrowed at that, and he shot forward like a striking snake. "What did you say? You talked about *what*?"

"A chef—"

"Not that," he said, gesturing for her to move forward.

"The guests?"

"No," he said, frowning. "The last thing you said."

"Oh! A little arch she wants to incorporate into the ceremony. You know, get married under it."

Eli closed his eyes and sighed for a moment. Then he opened them and pinned her with a look that made her shiver a little. "Marnie," he said evenly, and put his giant hand on her wrist, let his long, thick fingers wrap around it. "Do you know what arch she's talking about?"

"Yes. It's an arch that they used in the filming of *The Dane*." Right, like she didn't know what arch. It held great sentimental value for Olivia, and she said it was made of plastic, so it wasn't a big deal as far as Marnie could see, and Olivia said she'd pay for the shipping. Bottom line, she'd *saved* TA money today.

But Eli's fingers tightened on her wrist. "Just out of curiosity—have you seen *The Dane*?"

"Not yet. I was going to rent it this weekend."

"Well, when you do, try and envision Olivia and Vincent's wedding under the Arc de Triomphe."

Marnie blinked. Then laughed. "Oh, Eli! Not that arch. She was talking about another one."

"How do you know?"

"Because she described it to me," she said and yanked her hand from his grip so she could sketch an invisible arch with her hands. "Not so big, and it's plastic, and she offered to ship it, so what's the big deal?"

"The big deal," he said calmly, "is that it's not that size." He mimicked her invisible outline. "It's actually about the size of Kansas. And Olivia is right. It's made of plastic—about three hundred pounds of it."

Marnie's earlier feeling of being a player was rapidly disintegrating. "Huh," she said, biting her lower lip thoughtfully. "Three hundred pounds, you say?"

Eli nodded.

"Mmm…that is a little different, isn't it?"

"Uh-huh."

She winced. "But I think it's a deal breaker."

"Excuse me?"

"'Fraid so," Marnie said, nodding sympathetically. "If Olivia can't get married under that arch, then she's not getting married."

Eli surprised her by laughing. "Promise? Because that wouldn't hurt my feelings one bit," he said, and intercepted the waiter who was about to lay the check on the table as he simultaneously reached into his back pocket, took out a wallet, and pulled out a platinum card of some sort and handed it to the waiter without even looking at the bill.

"What's that supposed to mean?" Marnie demanded.

"I mean, if Olivia wants to pull the plug on this stupid idea of getting married up there—or at *all*—I'd be the happiest man on the planet."

"You're not serious. You would ruin her wedding over a stupid arch?"

He shrugged. "I wouldn't lose any sleep. It sure ain't the gal's first rodeo and I'll bet big bucks it won't be her last."

"That's horrible!"

"Maybe, but it's true."

Frankly, he looked so smug about the whole thing that Marnie bristled. "What is the matter with you?" she demanded. "Everyone deserves a nice, pretty wedding—"

"You ready?" he asked coldly, suddenly sitting up and planting an elbow on the table. "Where's that waiter?" he asked, looking around the room.

The man was a horse's ass, and Lord help the poor woman who eventually hooked up with him, because Marnie was certain that *his* wedding would be an event in front of the justice of the peace, over and done within five minutes and topped off with a trip to Taco Bell before everyone got back to work. What a goon.

"Gee," she muttered, reaching for her purse. "Throw in one little arch and look what happens."

"That's right, just look what happens," he said, snatching the bill from the waiter when he appeared and dashing off his name on the receipt. He slammed the bill holder shut and looked up at her with glittering blue eyes. "I thought I told you to manage her expectations."

"What, she's not allowed to have an arch? Is that such an unreasonable expectation? *Lots* of weddings have arches, but I wouldn't expect you to know that, because I doubt you've ever been close to a wedding, and with your views on the subject, I doubt you ever will be."

His face colored slightly, and he pressed his lips together for a moment. "She can't have a fucking three-hundred-pound *arch*," he snapped, and stood, caught Marnie by the elbow and pulled her to her feet. And he kept his hand tightly on her elbow as he steered her through the maze of restaurant tables and out the door.

"Jesus, Marnie," he continued as they walked, "did you ever think how we'd ever get it up there? I showed you the map. You know what we're up against."

"Yes, you showed me the map, atlas man," she shot back. "But I didn't realize it was so high in the mountains that it might as well be on Jupiter. *We're* getting up there somehow. Can't an arch get up there, too?"

The maitre d' pushed open the door for them, and Eli and Marnie marched through it, side by side, halting together in front of the valet stand. Eli flipped his claim ticket at the kid, then turned to face Marnie. He was so close she could smell his cologne, the faint scent of wine.

She tried very hard not to look at his lips.

"This isn't a made-for-TV movie. You need to keep a lid on things. She may have more money than God, but that doesn't mean she has to spend it all."

She hated it when people—okay, men—talked to her as if she were a turnip. She folded her arms, lifted her chin, and glared right back at him. "Here's an idea. Why don't you just let me do the job you hired me to do?"

He blinked. And a grin slowly spread his lips. A very dark and dangerous grin. "All right. And why don't you just do the job we hired you to do and stop playing Hollywood Barbie?"

"Hollywood *Barbie*? You're going to call me names because the bride wants some stupid plastic arch?" she exclaimed indignantly.

His pickup screeched to a halt in front of them before he could answer. The valet jumped out of the driver's side and rushed around to the passenger side to open the door for Marnie. She glared at Eli and marched forward.

But he was right on her heels, and in a confused moment where the valet tried to get out of the way at the same time Marnie tried to get in the truck, she hastily stepped out of the valet's way and backed right into Eli. Or rather, the brick wall that was Eli. Brick chest, concrete posts for legs. Solid and thick, the man was as hard as his head, and it felt like she'd just been zapped—the sort of zap that stings and makes you shiver all over at the same time.

She quickly jumped forward before he could zap her with any other hard body part, and practically dove head-first into his truck.

Eli stepped up to close the door, and for a brief moment, a *very* brief moment, his eyes swept over her again, lingering for a split second on her breasts before he slammed the door shut and strode around to his side of the truck.

He got in, put the truck in gear, and pulled away from the curb. "So where were we?"

"Let's see…Oh, I remember. You were impugning my professionalism by implying that I am not taking my job seriously."

"Oh right, right, you had decided to take a three-hundred-pound arch to the remote mountains of Colorado. An arch I bet she told you about *after* you'd spent a fortune shopping. Which is exactly my point, Marnie—don't get caught up in the glamour."

"Glamour. Ha!" she cried derisively. "That is the most ludicrous thing you've said yet. Caught up in the glamour." She snorted.

"Oh yeah? Well, just look at you," he said as he headed for Santa Monica Boulevard.

She gasped indignantly. "Whaddaya mean, *look* at me?"

"Your *dress*," he said, as if that explained it all.

"What about my dress?" she cried, getting very irritated now, and looked down at her most excellent dress. "For your information, this is just about the coolest dress on the planet, thankyouverymuch, and please don't be offended when I say that I'm not about to take any fashion advice from Howdy Doody who thinks workout clothes are the same as banging-around clothes."

That made Eli laugh. "I may be Howdy Doody to you, but I ain't blind, sweetheart. It's because that dress is so fine that I'm saying this to you, all right? You wouldn't *have* a dress that fine if you weren't out shopping and getting carried away with Olivia Dagwood and her little sphere of stardom. But I promise you, the moment you become inconvenient or irrelevant to Olivia, she will cut you off and act like she never heard your name. I'm just saying things will go a lot easier if you just do your job and don't buy into the pals bit."

Marnie flew right past the tone of his voice and the telling her what to do to *that dress is so fine.* She tried to keep the smile from her face but was horribly unsuccessful. Actually, she was beaming. She glanced at him from the corner of her eye. "You really like it?"

He groaned. But he was smiling a little, too. "Try and absorb what I'm saying, will you, coppertop? No arches. No fancy cakes, no china, no silver, no sit-down dinners."

"Aha!" she said brightly. "So you *do* know a little something about weddings."

"Maybe a little," he said, and looked out the driver's window for a moment. "Just listen to me, Marnie."

She laughed. "How can I avoid listening to you? When you actually talk, you're usually complaining about something."

"I wouldn't be doing my job if I didn't try and mentor you a little bit here."

"Are you serious? Are you actually serious?" she exclaimed in disbelief. "You don't mentor. You spout opinions."

"Come on. No I don't."

"Yes, you do. You have a tone. I don't have a tone, but you *so* have a tone."

They argued about the perceived tone of his voice and her inability to listen, as well as how he came off like a frozen stiff who spoke only to bark orders until they reached her neighborhood.

As he turned onto her street, Eli said, "Okay, woman, all kidding and bitching aside—we're leaving in less than two months to go canyoning. We have to have the details of this so-called wedding nailed down by then. Do you understand? You can't sit around talking about cakes all day. You have to get her *nailed down.*"

"Roger, *el capitan.* We'll show up in Colorado in our combat gear and have the kind of wedding *you'd* like to have."

Eli glanced at her from the corner of his eye. "You assume too much, you know that? You assume you know where I'm coming from, and you really don't."

Whatever. He was a wet blanket and she sort of figured it really didn't matter where he was coming from. Nothing was going to change. "All right, all right—I don't know you, I don't get you, but that's okay. I don't really *need* to get you to plan their wedding, right?"

"Well...right," he said, sounding unconvinced. "Just please do what we need."

"Fine," she snapped. Miffed by the change in his demeanor after such a great dinner, she turned away in a huff and looked out her window. And saw a shape lying against the curb. As Eli drove past, she shrieked.

Eli jerked the wheel with a start. "What the hell?"

"Stop the car, stop the car!" she cried, pounding the dash.

Eli slammed on the brakes. "Jesus, what is it?"

She didn't want to say, didn't want to believe it. And besides, she was already out of the truck, running back to the shape.

Bingo was lying almost motionless, but at the sound of Marnie's heels on the pavement, he lifted his head and looked back over his shoulder at her, his big brown eyes full of fear and pain.

CHAPTER NINE

They wrapped Bingo in Eli's jacket and took him to the twenty-four-hour pet emergency room. Marnie went running inside, demanding help, as Eli lifted the dog in his arms and carried him in.

The vet told Marnie it was a good thing she'd spotted the poor dog, or else he might have died of hypothermia and shock. Eli wasn't sure how badly he'd been hit, but he suggested to the vet that the fact the dog was alert and whimpering was a good sign. The vet agreed and asked them to wait while he took Bingo back for X-rays and an assessment.

They watched the vet carry him back, then Marnie slipped into a seat and buried her face in her hands.

She looked so forlorn, so distressed, that Eli sat next to her and put a comforting arm around her shoulders. For such a spunky woman, she sure felt fragile beneath his arm.

Marnie slowly slid into him, so that she was pressed against him, with her face still in her hands. "*Mam-mu,*" she muttered tearfully.

He tried to decipher that for a moment before bending his head down to hers. "What?"

"*Mam-mu,*" she muttered again, only an octave higher.

He squeezed her fragile shoulders. "I'm sorry, Marnie. I can't understand you."

She drew a big gulp of air and lifted her head; her eyes glistened with tears. "Thank you," she said, dragging a hand under her nose. She grabbed his knee with both hands. "Thank you for saving Bingo, Eli. I don't know what I would have done if you hadn't been with me. I know you probably think I'm silly, but I love that old dog."

Eli's gaze fell to her hands on his knees. "I don't think you're silly at all," he said. "I love dogs, too."

Marnie blinked, and more tears spilled down her cheeks. "It's just the way that you took control, and you knew exactly what to do, and you didn't freak out, and you didn't hurt him, and you were so calm and assured..." She paused, gulped more air.

Eli sat staring at her slender hands clenching his knee, feeling a little self-conscious. "I did what anyone would do."

"No, you didn't," she said sternly. "You saved my dog." She sighed, let go of his knee, and collapsed against the chair, folding her arms across her. "I may not know where you're coming from, but I know one thing—you're a lot softer than you let on."

"No," he said with a snort, "I am not soft."

"Yes, you are."

"No. I'm really not."

She glanced at him from the corner of her eye and sniffed. "You're sure?" she asked with a tiny lopsided smile. "Not even a little?"

"Not even a little," he said, and stretched his long legs, shoving his hands into his pockets.

"Yes, you are," she murmured.

"Marnie—"

"You *are*," she insisted, laughing now.

Eli sighed. But he was smiling big on the inside.

They waited for what seemed hours. Marnie dozed off while he read a magazine, and before long, she had teetered to the right, propped up against him, dead weight on his shoulder. Her legs were sprawled before her, one cocked at the knee, the other leaning against the first.

She was cute. He grinned appreciatively at how far up her thigh her dress had ridden. Nice thigh. Nice, shapely thigh. He could imagine sinking his head between a pair of thighs like that. Could imagine it so vividly that his pulse began to pick up a little.

Thank God the vet reappeared when he did. "Bingo is going to be fine," he said after Eli nudged Marnie awake. "He's got a fracture, but there doesn't seem to be any internal bleeding. I'd like to keep him overnight for observation. I'd suggest you folks go home and get some sleep. You can pick him up tomorrow afternoon."

"Thanks, doc," Eli said, extending his hand. "Thanks for taking care of Bingo."

"It's my pleasure and my job," he said, taking Eli's hand.

He said good night to them, and Eli and Marnie walked outside into cool night air. "Are you cold?" Eli asked as Marnie wrapped her arms around herself.

"A little."

Eli glanced back at the emergency vet. "Bingo's got my jacket."

"I'll be all right." But she was clearly shivering.

Eli put his arm around her and pulled her into his side. "You've never been right is what I'm thinking," he said.

91

"Me?" she protested, nudging him with her elbow as they began to walk to his truck. "This from a man who was obviously impaled on a stick because he's so stiff and unbending all the time."

Eli opened the truck door for her and watched her long legs bend to get in the cab. He shook his head once to clear it as he walked around the back of the truck to the driver's side. But her legs were still there in his head, and he knew, as he turned the ignition, that he was going to have a hard time getting them out of his head. And that smile. Not to mention the hair.

"I can't stand to think of him lying there," Marnie said as they drove out of the parking lot. "He must have been so scared."

Eli couldn't stand to think of it, either—it brought to mind the dozen dogs he'd had in his life, ending with Hank, his golden retriever who had died of cancer a couple of years ago. God, he'd loved that dog, and felt the lump at the back of his throat even now. So he changed the subject. "He's going to be all right. So listen, I'm out of town for a couple days. Let's review: No arches, no spectacular waterworks, and no sky-diving routines for this wedding, right?"

Marnie groaned and dropped her head back against the headrest. "You are impossible. What is it with men and weddings? Why can't you just admit that the day is as special for men as it is for women? It doesn't make you any less macho to get married under an arch," she said, and proceeded to tell him how special arches made the world in general until they reached her house.

He pulled in behind her car and got out, walked around to her side as she opened the door, and offered his hand as she slid out of the car.

Marnie took it. And didn't let go. She just kept holding his hand with a shy smile and a look of tenderness in her big brown eyes. "Thanks, Eli. I mean it. From the bottom of my heart," she said, and squeezed his hand.

"Don't mention it."

"I have to mention it." She smiled, stepped closer, so that she was brushing against him in that skimpy dress, and looking at him with eyes that could swallow a man whole if he let them. A warning went off in Eli's brain, clanging like a railroad crossing, but he felt paralyzed, unable to get out of the way of the freight train that was headed right for him.

Marnie rose up on her toes, touched her lips to the corner of his, and just sort of lingered there for a moment...her very soft, very warm lips on his. Then she slowly slipped down.

"Thanks," she said, and slid her hand from his before stepping back. Only now she was flashing a sexy, devilish smile at him. "I'm going to go look at some china settings with Olivia tomorrow. I suppose when you get back you'll want to get together so you can tell me she can't have china settings, either?"

Eli blinked, made himself step back into the here and now, and laughed. "I'm not waiting until I get back, coppertop. I'll be calling you every day. Which reminds me," he said, and he stepped around her, reached into the glove box of his truck, and handed her a cell phone. "Keep it on you. I want to be able to deep-six china settings at a moment's notice."

Marnie smiled broadly as she took the phone. "Nice one. I'll see if I can get it to work." And she winked back at him, touched her hand to his once more, and stepped around him. "Thanks again, Eli. For dinner. For Bingo..."

"Yeah," he said, and shoved a hand through his hair, feeling awkward, as if he were on a date or something. But this was not a date. Not even close. This was not even in the same universe as a date.

Marnie seemed to sense his awkwardness and laughed lightly before starting up the walk to her house.

"Remember what we talked about," he called after her.

"Manage expectations," she responded over her shoulder and continued on, swinging that lovely ass as she walked.

Eli watched her walk all the way to the door. It was the polite thing to do, he told himself, although he knew damn well it had nothing to do with polite. She put a key in the lock, and pushed it open a little, then turned and waved to him before disappearing inside.

Only then could Eli make his legs move, and he got in his truck, started it up, and wondered what the hell just happened to him. Whatever it was, it felt alarmingly good.

CHAPTER TEN

Marnie awoke the next day feeling on top of the world. Even Bingo's accident couldn't bring her down. When she went to pick him up from the emergency vet, he bounded out of the back room like a puppy in a cast. Bingo, it seemed, was going to be fine.

Marnie returned the dog home to Mom, who was busy making enchiladas for the book club party that night, which, she cheerfully informed Marnie, was going to include the husbands.

"What's the occasion?" Marnie asked as Mom got down on her knees to greet Bingo properly.

"*Ah buh buh buh*," she said to Bingo as she mashed her forehead to his. "Nothing really. We just want them to feel included. *Ah buh buh buh.* Look at his cast. My poor puppy needs a treat," she said, and motioned for Marnie to help her up. "They're in the pantry, honey. Get him a pig ear, will you?"

"So okay," Marnie said as she gave Bingo a pig ear, "I'm outta here."

"Are you going off with that nice man?" Mom asked coyly as she rolled another enchilada.

"No, Mom," Marnie responded, trying her best to sound disgusted. But it wasn't working—she sounded downright giddy. Nevertheless, she continued. "That nice man is my boss, and besides, he's out of town."

"Oh, that's too bad," Mom said, then suddenly gasped and jerked around to Marnie, her eyes as big as saucers. "Are you going to be with Olivia Dagwood again? Is that where you're going? With Olivia Dagwood?"

"Mom!" Marnie cried, and slid across the saltillo tile floor to grab her mom by the shoulders. "You have *got* to stop saying her name! I told you, it's a huge secret. Quit talking about Olivia to the book club, and quit running to the front window every time you hear a sports car."

"Where are you two going today?" her bright-eyed mom asked. "Shopping? Are you going shopping with Olivia Dagwood? I wonder where she shops. Probably Montrose, right?"

"You're too hip for me, Mom," Marnie said, and grabbed her bag with the new cell phone in it, the very same cell phone she would never tell her mother about, and said, "I'll see you later" as she raced out of the kitchen.

Once outside, she put a hand over her eyes and peered down the drive into the garage. "Bye, Dad!" she called.

"Bye, honey! Drive carefully now," came a reply from within the cave.

As Marnie backed out of the drive and headed down the street, she caught a glimpse of her mother in the front window, the cordless phone on her shoulder. "Oh gawd," she muttered, and hit the gas.

Her destination was Brentwood.

When she arrived at Olivia's house, she punched in the pass code Olivia had given her, and a gate swung open. As she pulled through in her BMW, four men suddenly appeared in her rearview mirror and scared the crap out of her. They were all holding cameras with the long lens thingies on them. Marnie sped up and around the corner as the gate swung shut behind her. She grabbed her purse and briefcase, opened the door, and crouched low, then sort of ran and crab-walked around the front of her car to the front door.

Before she reached the door, however, Olivia opened it. And she was laughing, her hands on her bare belly, doubled over. "You look so funny!"

"Are they always like that?" Marnie asked as she slipped inside. "They just appeared out of nowhere and started firing."

"They're always like that. But you get used to it," Olivia said. "Come on, we're all in here."

Marnie wondered who "all" was. She followed Olivia, who was wearing velour sweatpants extremely low on her hips and a tight camisole that barely concealed her breasts. She led Marnie down a marble corridor, then turned right into a large sunken room. Opposite the door was a wall of plate glass windows that overlooked the pool and tennis court.

The room itself was completely white. The carpet was white. So were the furniture and the walls. It gave Marnie the sensation of being snow-blind.

"Hey, everyone, this is Marnie," Olivia said, and Marnie gathered her wits about her and smiled. She recognized Lucy, the assistant, and the man she thought was Olivia's stylist. An older woman in clothes very similar to Olivia's was lying on her side on the couch. Sprawled in a white bean bag was *the* biggest star in all of Hollywood, Vincent Vittorio.

Vincent Freakin' Vittorio!

Marnie almost dropped her briefcase. She tried to come off as cool, but she could not keep the damn grin from her face.

"Marnie, this is my mom, Della," Olivia was saying.

"Oh! Pleasure to meet you, Mrs...ah, Della," Marnie said, juggling her briefcase to shake her hand.

"Hi, Marnie."

She turned to Lucy. "Ah...hi, Lucy. We met once before, on the set," Marnie reminded her, stepping over a white cat to shake her hand.

Lucy looked at her like she was nuts. "We did?" Clearly confused, she shook Marnie's hand as she squinted up at her through matchbox glasses. "Which set?"

"It was just a few days ago. *WonderGirl.*"

"Huh," Lucy said, as if she found that to be particularly curious.

"And this," Olivia said with a sigh, "is my alleged fiancé, Vince." And with that, she fell onto a beanbag beside him.

"Ah...it's really great to meet you, Vince," Marnie said.

He lifted two fingers and turned his attention back to a magazine he was reading (*Star*, she was fairly certain). Marnie glanced around the room for a place to sit.

"Sit anywhere," Olivia said, flicking her wrist at the room. Marnie chose a white butterfly chair, as it seemed to be the only thing in the room sturdy enough to hold her, save the two occupied beanbags.

"So," she said, balancing her briefcase on her knees. "We've got ideas for a chef, ideas about linens and the size and scope of the reception. Shall I review the details for the groom?"

"Please don't," Vince muttered.

"Oh," Marnie said, taken aback. "Okay…where would you like to begin?"

"Where do you suggest?" Olivia asked with a yawn. A woman appeared from a door at the far end of the room, carrying a tray with two Perriers, a beer, and something that looked like oatmeal in a glass.

"I suggest we go over some basic questions and make sure we're all on the same page," she said, pulling out the pink wedding organizer. "Then we can see what needs work and more research."

"Great," Olivia said, and sat up to take the oatmeal. "Would you like something to drink, Marnie? Water or maybe a sea grass?"

"A sea grass?"

"Oh, it's great for cleaning you out," Olivia said as the maid delivered the waters to the women and the beer to Vince, who smiled up at the maid and winked his thanks. *Damn.* He looked as good in person as he did on the big screen.

"Bring her a sea grass, Maria," Olivia said before Marnie could answer, and smiled at Marnie. "You'll love it."

"No, she won't. She'll barf," Vince said.

"Vince"—Olivia sighed—"could you please try and help us out here? It's *our* wedding, remember. Not just mine."

He tossed aside the magazine, took a huge swig of beer, and settled deep into his beanbag. "All right, so let's go. What are the basics?" he asked Marnie.

"Well, the venue is decided, of course. Let me ask this— have you given any thought to a theme?"

"*Theme?*" Vince echoed, as if the very notion of a theme pissed him off.

"Yes, I have," Olivia said instantly. "Starlight. I think it's perfect. I mean think about it. We met under the stars. We're getting married under the stars. We *are* stars. So I think starlight should be our theme...okay, Vince?"

He looked at Olivia as if he couldn't believe she was serious. She returned his look with one that said she was dead serious. "Sure. I guess. Whatever," he lazily gave in.

Olivia frowned darkly.

"Hey, no one told me weddings had to have a theme."

"Really? You didn't have a theme in any of your other weddings?" Della asked Vince in all seriousness.

"Ah...if you want to make starlight your theme," Marnie jumped in, "then you might want to choose colors around that idea. Maybe a pearl white and midnight blue?"

"Oh, that sounds gorgeous," Della said. "Are you getting this down, Lucy? Starlight. Pearl white and midnight blue."

Lucy wrote it on her iPad.

"I don't get this theme business," Vince said, looking very perplexed.

"Come on, Vince, it's not rocket science," Olivia said testily.

"If your theme is starlight," Marnie said, "you could do something like have a lot of tiny tea candles around to represent stars. And in the pavilion, you could have a midnight-blue cover and suspend white roses to represent stars in the night sky."

"I don't want a pavilion," Olivia said instantly. "I want it all to be under the *real* stars!"

"Well...you might want to have something set up in case of rain," Marnie suggested. "Eli said it will be monsoon season, and there are not a lot of places to take shelter from what I understand."

"I don't care if it rains. I think that would be beautiful," Olivia said, and smiled sweetly at Vince.

He shrugged. "I don't care."

Marnie made a quick note to speak to Eli about that. She felt very strongly there needed to be some sort of shelter. She wasn't a mountain woman or anything, but she had an idea that if it rained at ten to eleven thousand feet, it would be a very cold rain. "What do you think of the candle idea?" Marnie asked.

Olivia looked at Vince, who looked at his bare feet. "I guess that's okay," she said with a shrug. "But I sort of wanted flowers."

"Oh, you'll have flowers, too," Marnie assured her.

"No, I mean like...*flowers*. Thousands of them. Flown in from somewhere. That's it! I want white tulips or roses flown in from Holland. We can decorate the arch with it."

"The arch?" Vince repeated, and looked at Olivia. "What arch?"

"You know what arch, Vince! The one from *The Dane*."

Vince blinked and looked at Marnie. "But...how are you going to get that arch up to the top of the mountain where there is nothing but four-wheel access? Am I right, Marnie? There's only four-wheeler access, right? Remember, Livi? They couldn't even get that fat-as-shit producer up there."

"Transportation is something we haven't quite figured out," Marnie said with a bright smile. "I'm working on that."

Vince snorted. "Sounds like a huge problem to me. Forget the arch."

"But I don't want to forget the arch!" Olivia cried. "That was the most romantic thing we ever did, Vince. You remember that night on the soundstage after we wrapped and we made love beneath that arch?"

"Jesus, Olivia!" Vince cried. "Your mother is sitting on the couch right there."

"Oh, I've heard it all before, believe me," Della said cheerfully.

"Vince, I want that arch," Olivia insisted.

"No. There is no way we can get that arch up there again, and I am not paying TA a ton of money to get it up there. This gig is already costing a million five, remember?"

Marnie choked on a small shriek.

Olivia and Vincent looked at her. "Are you all right, Marnie?" Olivia asked as the maid came into the room carrying oatmeal in a glass.

"Fine, fine," she said hoarsely. Her eyes were watering. She was literally choking on "*a million five*." Her poor brain could not compute. She could not, even in her fantasy, spend a million and a half dollars on a wedding. The maid handed her the oatmeal, and Marnie took a big swig of it.

It was nothing short of a miracle that she managed to keep from spewing that slop all over that insanely white room.

"Don't you like it?" Olivia asked, and seemed genuinely disappointed that Marnie's eyes were bulging out of their sockets.

"Love it," she croaked.

"No arch, Livi," Vince said again. "I'm not going there."

Olivia gave him a look as Marnie discreetly put the sea grass aside. "We'll talk about it later, Vince." And she turned a smile to Marnie. "What about the flowers? Can I have the flowers?"

"Sure, sure," Marnie said, her mind still reeling from the cost of this wedding.

"I would like...thirty thousand white roses," Olivia said. "Flown in from Holland."

No one else said a word. Everyone in that room—save Marnie—seemed to think that was perfectly reasonable. "That's...that's doable," Marnie said brightly. "But, ah... you'll have to have them flown in from Holland the day before, you know."

"Yes."

"And then transported to Colorado."

"Right," Olivia agreed.

Marnie cleared her throat, pasted a bright smile on her face. "The thing is, that's a logistical nightmare to have flowers flown in from Holland, clear customs, then moved to another plane and flown to some place in Colorado or New Mexico, and then, you know, driving thirty thousand roses up the mountain..."

Olivia blinked.

"I think she's saying shoot for a more reasonable number," Vince suggested to Olivia. "Like maybe, ten thousand."

"That won't be enough," Olivia said, lifting her chin. "I want roses at the wedding site and at the reception. I want them everywhere."

Marnie opened her mouth to reply, but Olivia cut her off. "We'll figure out something," she said brusquely.

She couldn't imagine what Olivia thought they'd "figure out," but whatever. This little planning session was going nowhere fast. "So," she said, smiling so hard her cheeks hurt. "We've got flowers and theme...What did you have in mind for the dinner?"

"Filet mignon," Vince said at the very same moment Olivia said "Lobster. And sushi appetizers."

Vince scoffed. "You think they can get lobster up there?"

"You think they can get beef?"

"Yes, I think they can get beef. There's a million cows walking around those mountains, remember? Those hombres can probably slaughter a cow and cook it right there."

"Ooh, yeah, *that's* appealing!" Olivia snapped. "I'm not having food made from animals at my wedding."

"Well, honey, what do you think a lobster is?"

"A crustacean. It's not the same thing."

"Then I guess you haven't heard the lobsters scream when they put them in the pot to boil them alive."

Marnie kept the smile pasted to her face as the conversation deteriorated into what constituted an animal, and wrote on her little notepad:

Help!!

At some point in the argument, Olivia and Vince determined they'd think more clearly about what they wanted with some wine and french fries, which they agreed was a food group that hurt no one, and they all loaded up in a limousine and headed for Zax. Olivia and Vince decided to smoke a joint on the way over, and even Della had a couple of hits. Only Marnie declined, sitting across from them next to the hairdresser or whoever he was, with her wedding organizer on her lap, trying in vain to wave the smell of pot away from her clothes.

For the record, it was at Zax that the paparazzi got the shots of Olivia slapping Vince that showed up on *Access Hol-*

lywood and *E!* that night, along with the speculation that the love affair between the two hottest stars was over.

It also happened to be the place Marnie was sitting when her cell phone began to ring a cheerful little tune.

"Hello?" she asked anxiously as Olivia and Vince were in a heated discussion about the use of professional guests, who would be hired to keep the dancing alive at the reception and make sure everyone was having a good time.

"Hey, it's Eli. How's it going?"

"Great. Just *great*. In fact, we're sitting here at Zax talking about the reception."

"Who's there?"

"Olivia. And Vince. And Olivia's mother and her assistant, Lucy, and—"

"I get the picture," he said, and then he asked, so quietly she almost didn't hear him, "Are you doing all right?"

Marnie was uncertain if he was asking her how she was after their little adventure last night, or if he was asking if she was doing her job well. In the moment she was trying to figure it out, Olivia slapped Vince.

The place suddenly erupted into a hail of flashbulbs. It seemed to Marnie as if they appeared from thin air to surround them.

"Hey!" Vince shouted, oblivious to the cameras as he caught Olivia's hand before she did it again. "Stop that shit!"

"I'm sick of this, Vince. Every time I turn around you are checking out someone's ass."

"I'm not checking out anyone's ass."

"What about that waitress? She's practically drooling all over herself and so are you."

"Marnie?" Eli asked. "What's happening?"

"Ah…there seems to be a little argument," she said, and tried to laugh it off, but Olivia looked like she was on the verge of tears. She suddenly stood up, knocking the table and tipping over stemmed water glasses when she did. "That's *it*, Vittorio! You want that piece of ass? Go get it, because you're damn sure not getting any from me!"

Vince tried to grab Olivia's arm, but Olivia jerked it out of his reach and accidentally hit her mother, who was trying to stop Olivia from making a scene.

"Holy shit. Come on," the stylist said, grabbing Marnie's arm. "Let's get the hell out of here."

"What's going on?" Eli demanded.

"Ah…I'm gonna have to call you back," she said shakily, and clicked off, grabbed her purse and briefcase, and headed out with the stylist in the opposite direction of Olivia, her mother, and Lucy. At least she thought it was the opposite direction—she'd been blinded by the light of camera flashbulbs. But she thought only Vince remained, and he was looking like a sad little puppy for the benefit of the cute waitress.

Marnie and the stylist dude ducked out through the kitchen and ended up in the alley. "What do we do now?" she asked, still blinking.

He shrugged, pulled out a joint, and lit up. "I'm gonna walk down the street and get a cab."

"But my car is at Olivia's," Marnie said.

He exhaled loudly. "Sounds like a personal problem."

Marnie frowned. He winked and started walking toward the street, pausing once to look back over his shoulder at Marnie. "You coming?"

She sighed, slung her briefcase over her shoulder, and went with the stylist guy to catch a cab.

When she made her way back to Olivia's, she walked up to the gate and punched in the pass code Olivia had given her.

"Hey, sweetie, get Olivia outside for us, will you?" one of the permanent paparazzi called out to her from the hood of his car.

Marnie snorted, walked through the gate swinging open, and made sure it closed behind her before walking up the long drive to her car. But as she reached the car, the door of the house flew open and Olivia came running out, tears streaming down her face.

How did Olivia know the moment Marnie was at the door?

"It's over, Marnie," she said, and caught a sob in her throat, wiping the tears from beneath her eyes.

"Oh no, Olivia, are you sure?" Marnie asked.

"Yes. I never want to see him again," she said, and choked on another sob. "I can't marry a man who's always looking for a piece of ass, and can get it whenever and wherever he wants. Do you know that slut waitress gave him her number while I was sitting right there? And he *took it!*" Olivia Dagwood let out a wail like Marnie had never heard. "How I am supposed to have children with that man?"

Excellent question. Marnie dropped her briefcase and purse on the hood of her car and ran around to Olivia, putting her arm around her tiny shoulders. Olivia turned her face into Marnie's shoulder and cried. "Olivia, I don't know what to say," Marnie said. "If you can't trust him, you can't marry him."

"So…you don't think I should marry him?" Olivia squeaked.

Was she serious? "Well…" Marnie said in a play for time, "I'm not telling you what to do—"

The sound of a vehicle startled them both; they turned around to see a cab coming up the drive. It pulled up behind Marnie's car, and Vince got out the back, pulled some bills from his front pocket, and tossed them in the window at the cab driver, then slapped his hand on top of the cab, telling the driver to go on.

"What are you doing here?" Olivia shrieked.

"Livi," Vince said, walking toward her, his arms wide open, an inch or two shorter than Marnie, the giant. "Come on, Livi, don't be this way."

"Marnie thinks I shouldn't marry you," she said, squaring off.

Marnie winced, raised a hand. "Hey, don't listen to me. I'm just the wedding planner—"

"Yeah, well, maybe you ought to plan someone else's wedding if you're going to go around making asinine suggestions," Vince snapped.

"She's right. I shouldn't marry you if I can't trust you, Vince. You let your dick lead your life, and where does that leave me?"

Vince frowned at Marnie. "Do you mind, wedding planner? I'd like to talk to Olivia."

No, she didn't mind in the least, and in fact, was grateful for the out.

"Don't go, Marnie," Olivia whimpered. "Don't leave me alone with him."

"Okay, well…the thing is, I've got to pick my mom up from the hospital," Marnie lied, backing around the front of her car. But neither megastar heard her. They were too busy staring daggers at each other, and Olivia was still wiping tears from her face.

Marnie made a break for it, grabbing her purse and briefcase and throwing them into the car. "Talk to you later!" she cried, and got in before either of them could respond if they were so inclined, and tore away from the whacked-out Brentwood scene as fast as she could.

When she finally turned onto Sunset Boulevard and headed for home, she realized she could hear the cell phone beeping. She dug around her purse for it, finally retrieved it, and looked at the display as she pulled up to a red light.

She'd missed ten calls. And she had six messages. She wondered how Eli would take the news that Vince would want her fired. Probably okay, considering the wedding was now off. Maybe Eli would thank her. Maybe he'd buy her a big expensive gift for ending his nightmare so quickly.

She didn't call him back and didn't answer the cell when she heard the cheerful tune on her way home.

When she walked into the house, the book club was sitting around the table. A stack of paperbacks, untouched from the last meeting, was still in the middle.

"Well, well, look who is home," Mrs. Donaldson said, and sipped daintily from her tumbler.

"Oh honey," Mom cried, and jumped up from her chair and hurried to intercept Marnie before she headed to her room. "Eli McCain has been calling you. He *really* needs to talk to you…" She glanced over her shoulder at the four pairs of eyes fixed on the two of them, then leaned forward and whispered loudly, "about you know what."

"Thanks, Mom."

"Marnie? Did you go shopping today with anyone we'd want to hear about?" Mrs. Farrino asked.

"*Mo-om*," Marnie protested.

"Oh now, I didn't tell them a thing. They're just very clever and they guessed," Mom said, and bustled Marnie along. "Be sure and look in on Bingo," she called, just as Marnie's cell began to ring. "What is that noise?"

"Nothing," Marnie called over her shoulder and ran down the hall into her room and shut the door. "Hello?" she asked timidly.

"Where in the hell have you been?" Eli asked loudly. "I've called you a hundred times. I gave you a cell phone so I could speak to you when I needed to."

"I know. I'm sorry. I was in the middle of a crisis," Marnie said dejectedly, and let her bags drop to the floor, then with her back pressed against the door of her room, she slid down to her haunches. "It's been a really long day."

"I gathered as much. You wanna tell me about it?" he asked, his voice gone quiet and sure again.

Strangely enough, Marnie did want to tell him. She told him about the wedding plans, and the pavilion, and the flowers, and the arch. Eli said nothing. So Marnie told him how Vince and Olivia got into an argument about the reception, and that the group moved to Zax, at which point Eli groaned a little. She told him how Vince was making moon eyes at the waitress who slipped him her number, and how Olivia had slapped him and stormed out in a hail of paparazzi fire. And she told him how the stylist rescued her—

He interrupted her with a chortle. "He's not a hairdresser, Marnie. He's their connection."

"Their *connection?*"

"Weed."

"Oooh," she said. "No wonder that guy wanted out of there so fast."

"Yeah," Eli said with a chuckle. "So then what?"

"Then," Marnie sighed, "I opened my mouth and inserted my entire size eight foot." And she told him how Olivia had come crying to her, and what she'd said, and how Vince had not been too happy, and that Olivia said it was over. And when she finished, her head in her hand, her new sandals flung across the room, Eli laughed.

He *laughed.* Not big and hearty, but a low and long laugh, as if he didn't believe her.

"I'm serious, Eli."

"I know you're serious, girl," he drawled. "I'm laughing because they aren't through. They've only just begun."

"What do you mean?"

"I mean that tomorrow, there will be a flurry of pictures and sound bites and speculation that the on-again, off-again affair is over, and Olivia and Vince will be incensed that their private lives have come under such a public microscope, and then they will laugh about it and conveniently forget it ever happened."

"I don't know, Eli," Marnie said morosely. "I think this time it's for real."

"Wanna bet?" he asked.

"Yeah, I do," she said. "Remember—I was there."

JULIA LONDON

"All right. When I get back, we'll pay a little visit to the lovebirds. If they aren't together, you win, and you get to name your prize. If they are together, I win, and I get to name my prize."

Marnie smiled. "What's your prize?"

Eli laughed so low that Marnie's skin tingled. "If I told you my prize now, that would ruin the fun, wouldn't it?"

Was he *flirting* with her? Hey, she didn't mind a little phone flirting with a hunk like Eli, and smiled broadly, stretched out, so that she was lying on her stomach on the floor of her room. "I don't mind telling my prize up front. You want to hear it?" she asked in a voice as husky as she could make it.

There was silence on the other end. "I'd rather you surprise me."

Actually, that was an excellent idea, as Marnie didn't have the slightest idea what her prize was. "Oh, I'll surprise you, all right," she said in her sexy voice.

"I just bet you will." He chuckled. "In the meantime, why don't you surprise me by not letting Olivia get too carried away with the flower thing?"

Wow. Talk about taking the zing right out of the conversation. "Hello? Did you hear anything I said?"

"Yeah, I heard every word. I just want you to try and talk some sense into her tomorrow. You know, maybe something like a thousand flowers instead of ten thousand. Or maybe an enchilada bar instead of lobster and sushi."

"You sound like you don't think I tried, Eli. You sound like I'm just jumping right in and encouraging her."

"Well, it's like we say in Texas, Marnie—you took to her like a bear to a honey tree."

112

All I Need Is You

"That's not a Texas saying. That's a saying everywhere."

"You get my point."

"Oh yeah, I get your point, I'm never at a loss about your point. Did it occur to you that maybe, just maybe, it's hard to talk Olivia Dagwood out of *anything*?"

"Oh hell, I know it is," he said cheerfully.

"Then cut me a little slack, will you?"

"I'd like to. The only problem is we don't have a lot of time. We need to have the wedding of the century wrapped up pretty quick."

"I'm not sure there is going to be a wedding of the century, and even if there is, I probably won't be involved once you talk to Vince."

"Vince won't remember anything about it. Trust me. I'll be back in a day or two. When I get in, we'll go patch it up. Okay?"

"Whatever," she muttered.

"Hey, coppertop," Eli said kindly, "don't worry. You gotta believe me on this one—it's all gonna come out in the wash."

She smiled at his attempt to reassure her, but she wasn't so easily swayed.

"More important, how's Bingo?" Eli asked.

"Bingo is great," Marnie said, grinning now. "He wants to give you a dog bone for saving him."

"Well, I'm glad to hear it. I'm sort of partial to big ol' gangly mutts. Okay, I'll talk to you later. And listen—next time your new cell phone rings, pick it up, will you?"

"Okay," she said, and a little voice in the back of her mind shouted at Marnie to ask him to call tomorrow, but she said, "Talk to you soon," and hung up.

113

She was really beginning to like this guy. He had a crusty exterior that could really piss her off at times, but underneath that crust, the man had a big heart.

For some reason, the image of Eli the cowboy flashed into her head. Wildflowers in hand, he was standing on a wooden porch, at the door of a woman.

CHAPTER ELEVEN

A TV was blaring in the convenience store where Eli stopped the next morning for a cup of coffee. He was standing at the donut case when a word caught his attention, and that word was *breakup*.

He spied the TV behind the clerk and walked over, putting his coffee and donut on the counter. It was a local morning talk show by the look of it—two talking heads with giant coffee cups were smiling and talking about the spectacular breakup of Olivia Dagwood and Vince Vittorio. Apparently, one of the more enterprising paparazzi had been carrying a handheld minicam and caught Olivia's dramatic exit from Zax. And there, sitting in the booth across from Vince, was one wide-eyed, slack-jawed Marnie Banks.

Damn.

Eli paid for his coffee and his donut and walked outside, looked up at the blue California sky, and sighed.

He went on to his first appointment in a tony office building outside San Diego, in Coronado. He was shown to a richly appointed conference room paneled in oak and with a view of the ocean, where six Japanese businessmen in dark suits were waiting to meet with a representative of Thrillseekers Anonymous.

JULIA LONDON

Through an interpreter, Eli learned the gentlemen wanted to take a trip down the Amazon River. They were very excited about the Amazon River, and every time he said the word *Amazon*, they would all chatter at once and nod energetically. He couldn't help but be reminded of a flock of turkey buzzards.

He was trying to figure out how they wanted to take this trip down the Amazon when his phone rang.

There was an immediate chattering of Japanese, and the men started bobbing their heads at him. Eli looked at the interpreter.

"They like you answer," she said.

"That's okay," he said, waving a hand at them. "It can wait."

She translated that, and they bobbed their heads again. A few moments later, the phone rang again, and the chattering started all over again.

"They like you answer," the woman insisted.

"Okay," Eli said, smiled sheepishly, and answered the phone.

"You know your girl is in trouble up here," Cooper said, dispensing with any greeting.

"I heard."

"Thought you might want to get back here. The press is all over the place trying to get a scoop."

"Yeah, I know," he said, and tried to imagine Marnie, in spunky good humor, holding a bunch of piranha-like reporters at bay. "I'll get back as soon as I can," he said. "I'm still working through this other deal." At that moment, two of the businessmen sitting next to him started to converse excitedly.

"Anyone speak English?" Cooper asked.

"Not a one."

"Damn," Coop said.

Eli told him he'd be in touch later, then ended the call and asked the interpreter how, exactly, the men wanted to tackle the Amazon.

"Tackle, please?" she asked.

"How do they want to go," he said, making a swimming motion. Why he made that motion, he had no idea.

The woman looked at his hands and said something to the men. There was some lively discussion between them, and then they looked at the interpreter. She turned stoically back to Eli and said, "They please no swim. They please sticks one."

Eli blinked. "Come again?"

"Sticks one." She made a gesture that escaped him.

It was going to be a long meeting.

When Eli finally left that day, he understood that the Japanese men wanted to take a rafting trip to the Amazon the week after the wedding. TA normally didn't like to book trips so close together, but the Japanese men had some sort of national holiday or something like it and really wanted that week or no dice.

Eli tried to explain through their interpreter that unless they were well versed on the wildlife and people of the Amazon, a raft might not be a good idea. He tried to explain piranhas and snakes and natives, but every time he thought he'd made a little headway, they would do the buzzard thing again and grin at him.

He did, however, have pictures to show them. He and Jack had done the Amazon once, and it was not exactly his favorite spot. But they didn't seem to care about anaconda snakes or giant beetles—they remained enthusias-tic about it.

That meeting took a lot longer than he'd anticipated. He wouldn't make it back to LA until late, not with the last stop he had to make.

Eli drove to Escondido. In a neighborhood of small cot-tage bungalows, he pulled up at the curb of a yellow house that had green shutters and pots of bougainvillea hanging off the porch. As he got out of his truck, the front door flew open and a girl came bounding off the porch, dodging the bike and the discarded toys in her haste to reach him. "Eli!" she cried, and threw her arms around his waist.

Eli grinned and hugged her back. "How you doing, Isabella? You behaving yourself?"

"Yes," she said, turning her gap-toothed smile up to him. "Did you bring me something?"

"Maybe," he said, and with her standing on his feet, him holding her hands, he monster-walked around to the pas-senger side of the truck, opened the door, and took out a stuffed panda. Isabella shrieked and let go of Eli for the bear, burying her face in the fur. "Thank you, Eli! I love it! I'm going to name it Marco."

Eli ran his head over the top of her curly black hair. "Is your mom home?"

"She's in the kitchen," Isabella said, and went racing ahead of him to show her mom her new stuffed bear.

Eli followed her in and sat with Isabella's mom, Leonore, for a while, and even stayed for dinner. Before he left, he gave Leonore an envelope full of cash. It was a little unorthodox, he knew, and illegal as hell—but he didn't want Leonore to have to declare the five grand as income on her tax return. She had it hard enough, working in a local grocery.

Eli'd been coming to Escondido every three or four months for about five years now, ever since Armando had died in the course of working a stunt Eli had designed for a movie they were filming. His death had been a crushing blow, because Eli had really loved that cheerful Mexican.

The whole thing had been a freak accident. Armando was one of his best guys, and he never had trouble on a stunt before the one that killed him. Armando was skiing down a fake mountain slope on fake snow and was to jump over an old Jeep made up to look like a war vehicle. But something went horribly wrong—the Jeep was in the wrong place and Armando crashed into it. The crash propelled him off the slope and he landed head first, the equivalent of two stories down, on concrete. He died a couple of days later, and Eli had never been able to rid himself of the guilt...especially because of Isabella.

Armando had been crazy about his little girl. He always talked about how he was going to make sure she had the best of everything, had every opportunity to be whatever she wanted to be. Seeing the girl and her distraught mother at Armando's funeral had almost been Eli's undoing. He swore to himself he'd make sure Armando's dream came true.

Shortly after Armando died, Leonore moved to Escondido to be close to her family. Eli started bringing food and toys, and when it came time, he persuaded Leonore to put Isabella in a good private school, for which he was quietly paying.

But Isabella was growing up. She was almost thirteen, and she wanted things Leonore could not give her. So far,

Eli had been able to come through. Xbox, Game Boys…that was stuff he could handle. Tonight, however, Leonore told him Isabella needed clothes for school. That confused Eli—he'd given Leonore more than enough to clothe Isabella. But as she talked, he realized that Isabella wanted the sort of clothes Leonore did not purchase, or know how to purchase. "Designer," she said.

"Designer," Eli echoed dumbly. What the hell did he know about designer clothing for kids? "I'll see what I can do," he'd said, feeling very sure he'd not get a clue anytime soon. But nevertheless, he gave Isabella a kiss good-bye and drove back to Los Angeles, wondering where in the hell he was going to get designer clothes for a twelve-year-old.

Eli got home too late to call Marnie. So he kicked back with a beer in front of the boob tube. He watched part of a Lakers game but that was quickly boring, so he started surfing. When he surfed past *Entertainment Tonight*, Marnie caught his eye.

Eli sat up so fast that he knocked over his beer.

Yep, it was Marnie, all right. She was standing out front of what looked like a taco stand near the beach somewhere. A breeze kept blowing her hair all over the shot, but he considered it a good sign that she was smiling and not crying. The *ET* guy was talking over whatever she was saying, but when they cut to Marnie's sound bite, she said, "At this point, any speculation about a relationship between Vince Vittorio and Olivia Dagwood is pure fantasy," she said. "At the moment, I'm not coordinating a wedding for anyone, much less those two." This, she said with a bit of an incredulous laugh that had the reporter grinning. "I should say I *wish* I were coordinating their wedding, but I'm not."

The studio *ET* guy smiled, too, and said to his companion, "That's what they always say, don't they, Mary?"

"That's right. Coming up…"

Eli clicked off, picked up the beer bottle, and went to the kitchen for a rag. He came back with a fresh beer and a kitchen towel, which he used to clean up the beer on his coffee table. Then he walked outside and stood on his terrace that looked out over the valley, sipping his beer.

He was thinking about Marnie. And he couldn't help but smile to himself. That was, he had to admit, a pretty damn good answer. She'd nailed it—at this brief moment in time, it was fantasy. And she wasn't working for them. Tomorrow, it would be a different story, she'd be working for them again. Just not at the moment. Yeah, the girl had done good.

He was sort of looking forward to telling her so.

He was at her doorstep at ten sharp. Mr. Banks's car was missing from the drive, and in the front windows, he could see Mrs. Banks doing some sort of tae kwon yoga thing. She grinned Marnie's grin when she saw him and waved at him to come in.

"Hi, Eli!" she said as she stretched one arm long in front and bent both knees. "This is the lotus," she said, and moved, very slowly, into another bent-knee, arm-weird position. "This is the lion. Do you do tai chi or yoga?"

"Ah, no," he said, and stayed against the rail that lined the three steps into the sunken living room where she was doing whatever she was doing.

"You should. It's very relaxing."

"I'll give it some thought," he said, smiling as she turned away and crouched again.

"You're up and at 'em early this morning," Mrs. Banks said cheerfully as she stretched one arm out and bent the other.

"I figured I needed to talk with Marnie after what happened yesterday," he said.

Mrs. Banks turned slowly, still crouching. She reminded him of a raptor. "She's still asleep," she said. "You can go on back and wake her if you want."

"Wake her?" he asked skeptically.

"Don't worry, hon. She's decent. Go on—last door on your left," she said, and took a crouching step across the floor.

Eli leaned back, glanced down the hall warily. He wasn't too keen on waking Marnie up, but it was pretty obvious Mrs. Banks wasn't going to interrupt her exercise to do it, and really, who slept until ten? Half the morning was gone.

"Thanks, Mrs. B.," he said, and pushed away from the rail and walked down the corridor, hoping like hell that his boots clopping along the tile floor might wake her up before he had to.

No such luck, apparently. He tapped on the door and stood patiently, waiting for someone to answer. No one answered. In fact, he couldn't hear anyone inside at all.

"Don't be shy. Just go on in, Eli," Mrs. Banks called to him. "You'll never wake her mewling like a kitten."

Eli glanced to his left, down the hall. Mrs. Banks's dark red head was floating above the railing she was leaning over. "Go *on*," she urged him with a smile.

He knocked again, turned the knob, and pushed the door open a little. The room was dark—even the blinds had been closed. He pushed the door open a little wider and stuck his head inside. The floor was strewn with clothes and shoes and handbags and lacy things he didn't want to look at too closely. A fan turned lazily above the bed...at least Eli thought that was the bed. And he thought he could make out the shape of a body beneath the comforter.

Cautiously, he stepped inside. "Marnie?"

No answer.

Eli tiptoed through the debris to the bed and reluctantly put his hand on the lump near the head of the bed. It felt strange, he thought, because it almost felt like a leg. He leaned over, picked up the edge of the comforter...and almost had a heart attack when a red-toenailed foot kicked out and Marnie shrieked.

Eli came up like a shot and Marnie rolled over onto her stomach in her comforter cocoon and stuck her head out. She was sleeping upside down with her head at the foot of the bed. Her hair was sticking out in every direction, and her eyes were the size of baseballs.

"What are you *doing* here?" she cried, pushing up to all fours and scrambling out of her cocoon to stand in front of him in a skimpy little silk number with spaghetti straps— and one strap, he couldn't help noticing, had slid down her arm. Damn, but the thing skimmed over her perfect boobs and perky nipples and flared out at her hips. It didn't even pretend to cover her long legs. Somewhere in the recesses of guy central, that nightgown got a standing ovation.

Marnie seemed to realize what he was seeing in the same moment he was seeing it and dove for something on the floor. She came back up with a little silk robe, which she quickly shrugged into. Only the robe wasn't much of an improvement—it barely covered her, either.

"What are you doing?" she cried.

"I'm sorry!" he said, throwing up his hands. "Your mom—"

"*Augh!*" she shrieked and shook her fists to the ceiling. "I *seriously* have *got* to get my own place." She lowered her hands to her head. "Shit!"

"I'll just go out," Eli said, pointing to her open door, "and ah...wait?"

"Yes, wait, wait," she said, now covering her mouth with her hand. "I'll be out in a minute." She didn't wait for him to move; she turned and disappeared into what was obviously a connecting bath.

Eli quickly backed out of the room and shut the door. He stood there a minute, staring at the door, trying to erase the image of her in that slinky nightgown from his mind's eye.

"Did you find her?"

He all but jumped out of his skin and jerked toward Mrs. Banks. "I sure did," he said simply. "She's, ah...I think she's putting something on."

"Then come on into the kitchen with me, Eli. I just made a pot of coffee and have some cheesecake left over from our book club meeting last night."

Eli took one last look at Marnie's door and followed Mrs. Banks.

She led him into a big white-on-white kitchen with an island and a pattern of ducks on the tile backsplash. It reminded him of his mom's kitchen—cheery and bright and full of familiar smells.

One of the smells was dog, and he heard the unmistakable thumping of a big tail. Sure enough, Bingo was on a pillow in the corner, his leg in a cast and one eye banged up. Other than that, he looked a whole lot better than he had the night Eli last saw him. He squatted down; the dog rolled onto his back and held up one paw so that Eli could scratch his belly. "How you doing, Bingo?" he asked, and reached into his pocket, withdrew a couple of gourmet dog biscuits, and gave them to the dog.

"Oh, how nice!" Mrs. Banks crowed. "He's doing great. Bob actually took him on a little walk yesterday," Mrs. Banks said at the other end of the kitchen. "Bob is my husband. Have you met Bob?"

"Yes. In the garage."

"Well, of course, in the garage. He's so antisocial, Bob. Every time the girls come over, out he goes to that damn garage. The Lord only knows what he does there. Cream?"

"No thanks. Just black," Eli said, and straightened up, looking around the kitchen. The door to the dining room was open, and as he moved to take the cup of coffee Mrs. Banks offered him, he noticed something from the corner of his eye. He turned fully toward the dining room.

The table had what looked like two dozen or more little moons stuck on a stick, and around the moons were tiny little stars. They stood about a foot tall, and the stars spanned about a foot around each moon.

"I think they're cute," Mrs. Banks said, standing beside him as he looked at the moons.

"What are they?" he asked.

"Decorations. Little galaxies."

"Oh," Eli said, and sipped his coffee. "Are you having a party?"

Mrs. Banks laughed at that. "Not *me*, silly. They're for you-know-who."

Frankly, it took Eli a minute to figure out you-know-who. And about the time he did, Marnie appeared with her hair in a ponytail and wearing some gym shorts that said *SoCal* across a pleasantly plump ass, and on top, a tiny little tank top thingie.

"Good morning," Mrs. Banks trilled.

"Mom," Marnie said, frowning. "I would appreciate it if you would not send strangers back to my room in the morning."

"Don't be ridiculous. Eli is not a stranger."

"You know what I mean," she said gruffly and stomped toward the coffeepot.

Mrs. Banks winked at Eli as Marnie went sailing past and whispered, "Marnie is not a morning person."

"I can hear you!" Marnie exclaimed to the kitchen sink. Mrs. Banks tittered gleefully and drank her coffee.

Marnie poured some coffee and turned around, clutching what looked like a soup bowl in both hands, and tried to smile at Eli. "I'm sorry," she said. "Just let me get some coffee in me, and then I'll be all right." And with that, she slid down on a stool at the kitchen island and slurped coffee.

Eli walked to the island and sat across from her. "I caught you on *E!* last night."

Marnie instantly perked up. "You did?"

"You *did?*" Mrs. Banks cried happily. "Did you tape it? Oh God, I hope you taped it."

"Ah, no," he said uncertainly. "I didn't even think to."

"How'd I look?" Marnie asked anxiously. "Was I a geek?"

"No, not at all," he said genuinely. "You did great, Marnie. I was very impressed with the way you handled it. You're a natural with the press."

Marnie suddenly beamed at him and almost knocked him off his bar stool with the intensity of it. "Thanks," she said through her enormous smile. "I was a little worried— I thought it was one reporter, but it turned out to be like, eight or nine, and I sort of panicked."

"No, really," he insisted. "It was great."

Marnie and her mom exchanged twin beaming smiles.

"So, ah...if you don't mind me asking...what's with the galaxies in there?"

"Oh, those," Marnie said, flicking a wrist in the direction of the dining room. "They're just decorations for the reception. I was down at the Third Street Promenade, and I saw them in this funky little boutique, and as it turned out, they had about twenty of them. The stars light up, isn't that cool? I thought if I wasn't fired, I should snatch them up. So I did."

"Okay...but why the galaxies?" Eli asked again.

"Oh, because that is Olivia's theme," Marnie said patiently. "Stars. And I've got a jump on some cool table decorations, too."

"Great, great," Eli said. "And how are we going to get them up there, again?"

"Ah, don't worry. I have an idea," Marnie said, and tapped her head with her forefinger as she winked at him. Then she lifted the giant cup of coffee and sipped from it.

"All right. I'll bite...how?"

Marnie smiled again. "Nope, I'm not telling you. I talked to Cooper yesterday, and he thought my idea was peachy.

He's gotta check out a couple things, but he's going to let me know."

"He is, huh?" Eli asked skeptically, and made a note to self—call Coop and ask him kindly not to interfere with Eli's friggin' gig.

"So, think we've got two questions that have to be answered," Marnie said. "One, is there going to be a wedding—"

"I hope for your sake there is, because I don't know what you're going to do with twenty of those," Eli said.

"Oh, we'll find a use for them," Mrs. Banks assured him.

"And two, am I still the wedding planner?"

Eli's gaze narrowed slightly. "I say it's about time we found out. You wanna go pay a visit to the happy couple?"

Marnie's brows dipped into a V over her eyes and her smile. "As a matter of fact, I do."

"Ooh, where are you going?" Mrs. Banks asked. "Bel Air?"

At Marnie's long-suffering sigh, Eli chuckled. "Give me fifteen minutes," Marnie said, and stood up. "Mom, promise me you will not badger Eli while I'm getting dressed."

"Don't be silly."

"*Mom*," Marnie said in a voice full of warning.

Mrs. Banks gave her daughter a wide-eyed look of innocence.

With a groan, Marnie left Eli with Mrs. Banks, who trotted over to the fridge and returned with a half-eaten cheesecake that looked, Eli had to admit, out of this world. "So Eli," she said slyly, as she sliced off a piece and put it on a plate. "My friend Diane says she heard from a hairdresser friend of hers who has a friend that is a massage therapist that Jude Law and Nicole Kidman are getting together." She pushed the plate halfway across to him. "Is that true?"

"I don't know, Mrs. Banks," he said, and reached for the plate, but Mrs. Banks suddenly snatched it back, out of his reach.

"You don't *know?*" she asked with a devilish smile. "Or you won't *say?*"

Jesus. How long was Marnie going to be?

CHAPTER TWELVE

It was a half hour later, not a quarter, before Marnie returned to the kitchen, because she had a small crisis in her closet. Now that she was fully awake, having seen Eli again had her thinking…what did one wear when one definitely wasn't trying to seduce her boss, but wouldn't mind too much if he seduced her?

In the end, she decided there really wasn't a perfect dress for that scenario, and settled on the slightly casual but good enough for Bel Air halter dress, matched with a pair of cute kitten-heeled gold sandals that had little flowers on the straps.

She left her hair in a ponytail because of a major case of bedhead and no time to correct it after her closet crisis.

She thought she must have done okay, because Eli sort of did a double take when she returned to the kitchen. He had his head between his hands and there was an empty plate with cheesecake crumbs in front of him. Mom was sitting across from him with a big man-eating smile on her lips.

"Eli knows Tom Cruise," she chirped.

"Oh man," Marnie said with a wince. "I'm so sorry, Eli."

"For knowing Tom Cruise?"

"No. For knowing my mother."

"I resemble that remark," Mom said brightly and hopped off her stool. "I don't have any more time to chat, kiddos. I'm meeting Bev in an hour and we are going to get spray-on tans. So if you will excuse me," she said, putting away the cheesecake, "I'll see you guys later. Oh, Marnie, don't give Bingo any treats. After the two fat gourmet biscuits Eli brought him, that silly dog will just get enormous lying there. Okay. Bye, Eli!" she said cheerfully, and went out of the kitchen whistling, pausing to pet Bingo.

When her mom had disappeared out the back door, Marnie looked at Eli. "You brought Bingo biscuits?" she asked. Eli shrugged sheepishly. "That was so sweet, Eli," she said, and gave him a smile that emanated from somewhere near the bottom of her heart.

"It was nothing. Just a couple dog biscuits." He stood up, checked her out with one brow cocked above the other, his blue eyes shining appreciatively. "Nice dress," he said. "You ready?"

"Yes. Can we take the BMW this time?"

"Why?"

She didn't want to tell him that she didn't think she could get in the cab of that truck with this dress, so she said, "Because your truck is too bouncy."

"Bouncy?"

"Yes, bouncy," she reiterated as she stood up. "Every little bump in the road makes me bounce."

"Well, yeah," Eli said, looking a tiny bit perplexed. "It has a very stiff suspension for all the obvious reasons."

There was nothing *obvious* about Eli McCain or his truck, and besides, she didn't really know what a stiff suspension was and was too embarrassed to ask. "Yes, obviously," she said, as if she knew what she was talking about. "But is it okay if I drive this once?"

He sighed, pushed his fingers through his dark-gold hair, and Marnie could imagine him standing at some split-rail fence in Texas, one foot on the railing, taking off a cowboy hat to shove that hand through that hair, then putting it back on again, real slow. And maybe a long blade of prairie grass between his teeth—

"Are we waiting for something?" he asked, interrupting her cowboy fantasy.

"No! No, let's go," she said, and stooped to say good-bye to Bingo. So did Eli.

Eli started griping about her driving the minute she pulled out of the drive. Granted, she had not seen Mr. Simon walking his dog behind her, but she had stopped in plenty of time for him to get out of the way. They motored up Rimpau Boulevard, past LA High School. "That's where I went to high school," Marnie said as they drove past. "Right over there," she said, pointing to a street behind the high school, "is where I had my first kiss. Brett Lipshitz."

Eli laughed. "With a name like that, you might think he wasn't very good at it."

"He wasn't," Marnie said. "He made out like a fish. I was very disappointed and swore to all my friends I'd never kiss a guy again."

"And?"

"And?"

"Did you ever kiss a guy again?"

She smiled coyly and punched the brakes for a red light. "Maybe a couple," she admitted with a grin. *But none as good-looking as you, Cowboy.* She stole a glimpse of his lips. She imagined him standing beneath a big Texas moon, those blue eyes gazing down on her, those fabulous lips of his pursed…"What about you? Kiss many girls?"

"Maybe a couple. And the light is green," he said.

Marnie jerked her gaze to traffic that was already moving and hit the gas, making Eli buck in his seat. His hand snaked up and caught the handle above the passenger window.

Marnie laughed as she swung a wide left onto the boulevard. "Are you scared?"

"No. I'm terrified," he said, and winced as Marnie darted around a bus and sped past it.

"Not to worry," she said reassuringly. "I've been driving in LA traffic for almost twenty years and I haven't had an accident yet."

"What about tickets?"

"Oh yeah," she snorted. "Tons." She changed lanes again.

"That's not making me feel any better," Eli said as Marnie turned onto La Brea to shoot up to Wilshire Boulevard.

"So do you really know Tom Cruise?" she asked, looking at him while she shifted lanes again, and noticing that he was now gripping the console between the seats, too.

"I worked a couple films with him, that's all."

"You're very closemouthed about the movie business," Marnie opined, hoping a little reverse psychology might result in some good dirt on Mr. Cruise.

Now Eli glanced at her from the corner of his eye, but only briefly before he quickly turned his attention to the road again. "I'm not closemouthed. You wanna watch where you're going?"

"I am watching where I'm going."

"Well, when you get to Bel Air—and it appears we will reach it in record time—you're gonna want to turn onto Stone Canyon Drive."

"So you're not going to talk about it?" Marnie asked as she sped up Sunset.

"Talk about what?"

"Who you know. Who you don't know. What you do."

"Why are you so interested?"

She braked for a red light and gripped the wheel. "I don't know. I guess I'm warming up to you," she said with a sly wink. "I'm starting to wonder if there is more to Eli than a general revulsion to weddings."

He frowned at that instead of laughing, as she expected. "I don't have a revulsion."

"I think you do," she said, and playfully poked him in the side.

"Look," he said sharply, "can we just keep the conversation to the job at hand?"

His reaction stung her, and Marnie quickly withdrew her hand and shifted her gaze to the road in front of her. "Sorry," she said. "I didn't realize I was bothering you."

Eli sighed, relaxed his grip of the console, and looked at Marnie. "You're not bothering me," he said quietly. "I'm sorry I was so…"

"Mean?"

"Mean," he admitted. "It's just that I think we ought to keep our personal lives separate from this gig, that's all."

"Why? Why keep our personal lives separate? You know an awful lot about mine, I'd like to point out. Anyway, it's not like I'm going to *do* anything with the information, it's just a way to know you better, so you know…we *work* together better, and—"

"Not a good idea," he said, quickly cutting her off.

What was with this guy? One minute he was giving her warm fuzzies, and in the next minute he was cold as ice, making her believe she was an enormous pain in his ass. It made her so crazy that she abruptly demanded, "What is the matter with you, Eli? Don't you have any friends?"

"Of course I have friends, but if you let the personal stuff mix with work, you run a risk…"

"A risk of what? Being human?"

"Of allowing people to get under your skin. To poke you. To make you uncomfortable when you're trying to work."

"That's ridiculous," she said, but suddenly remembered that Daichi, the *Star Trek* guy in her office, had once told her she was on his last nerve when she was just trying to be friendly. Maybe she was really bugging Eli. Maybe her thoughts of being seduced by her boss were too out there, she thought with much disappointment.

They didn't talk about anything but traffic until they reached Bel Air—Eli made a lot of comments about her driving, and Marnie just drove faster. In Bel Air, she followed his instructions until they arrived outside a very simple stone gate that she recognized. Eli jumped out of the car and went round, punched in a code, then got back into the car. Marnie slipped the Beemer through, and Eli told her to wait until the gate had closed behind her. When he was certain it was closed, Marnie drove on.

This time, they drove to the front of Vincent Vittorio's mansion, a big Mediterranean-style house that had to be ten thousand square feet at a minimum. "Wow," she said, as she parked the car on the circular drive. "He lives here by himself?"

"Hell if I know," Eli said, and got out of the car and came round to the driver's side like a gentleman to help Marnie out. She paused to straighten her dress, and then the two of them went to the front door.

They were greeted at the door by a small Asian man. "Hallo, Mr. Mac," the man said with a quick nod.

"Hello, Steve. Vince said he'd be around. Do you know where he is?"

"Yes, Mr. Mac. He's by the pool."

"Thanks. We'll just go on out if that's okay with you."

"Yes, yes, okay," he said, nodding enthusiastically and opening the door wider.

They walked through a tiled entry and into a living area with twenty-foot cathedral ceilings. At one end of the room was a massive fireplace in front of which were two leather couches, four overstuffed armchairs, and a large coffee table that looked as if it had been carved from a tree. Big, thick rugs covered the tile floors. The back wall of the room was windows and doors—six floor-to-ceiling windows and three sets of French doors in all—overlooking a sparkling pool and pristine lawn.

Eli walked across the room, opened a pair of French doors and looked back at Marnie, who was taking her sweet time moving across Vince Vittorio's living room, trying to absorb as much of it as she could.

"Sprain your ankle, slowpoke?" Eli asked, and stepped outside.

Marnie really wanted to check out the framed pictures that graced the built-in bookcases but reluctantly followed Eli. As she stepped outside onto the tiled porch, she saw that the pool was the popular lagoon style—made to look as if it were some wild pond. At one end, the pool disappeared over the edge—she wasn't quite sure how that happened, but it literally looked as if it spilled over the edge. On the other end was an airy loggia—a roofed gallery, open on the sides and enclosed with sheer silk drapes that lifted on a breeze. Inside the loggia was a chaise longue—double wide, she noted—as well as a bar and a smattering of padded deck chairs. It was like walking onto an American Classic Movie set.

The only thing missing was the leading man and woman. "They're not here," Marnie said, looking around.

"They're here," Eli said, and when she looked, he nodded to the end of the pool that seemed to disappear. There, in the corner, she saw two bobbing heads, face-to-face. "I'm gonna venture a wild guess here and say they made up," he said, and winked at Marnie before he called out, "Vince!"

One head turned from the other. "Oh, hey, Eli. Great! You're here." And the two floating heads moved languidly to the side. Vince was the first one to climb out.

He emerged completely and utterly naked.

Marnie sucked in her breath—her first instinct was to look the other way, but then good sense took hold—she was standing near a naked Vincent Vittorio and she wasn't going to *look*? Like hell!

She looked. *Wow.* That was so disappointing.

Vince grabbed a towel and wrapped it around his disappointing self, and Marnie looked away. Only her gaze landed on Eli, who was looking at her with one eyebrow of his arched high above the other. Marnie shrugged, her hands out, palms up, in the international sign of *what?*

But Eli's brow came down into a V, and in a huff she turned away—just in time to see Vince give Olivia a hand up. She rose out of the water gracefully and strolled with her Brazilian bikini wax to a chaise to get a towel.

Marnie looked at Eli.

Eli was looking at Olivia.

But when Olivia picked up a towel, Eli glanced at Marnie and smiled. She gave him a slight frown, just as he'd given her moments ago. But Eli merely winked as Vince walked into their midst, shaking his head and scrubbing his fingers against his scalp to make his hair stand tall.

Marnie noticed that without his boots, he was even shorter than she'd previously thought, and once again, she was made to feel like an amazon next to another human being.

"Say listen, Eli, I'm glad you could drop by," Vince said, lifting a couple of fingers to Marnie, which she guessed was his way of saying hello. "I think we've got a little problem."

"Oh yeah?" Eli asked nonchalantly, as if he didn't know they had a problem already, and its name was Marnie Banks. "Why don't we sit down and talk about it?" he suggested.

"Yeah, come on," Vince said, and he and Eli started toward the loggia.

"Hi, Marnie!" It was Olivia, who'd arrived at the group powwow now that she had a towel wrapped around her tiny little body. "I love your dress. That's so cute—where'd you get it?"

As she was not about to admit she got it at Ross Dress for Less, Marnie said, "You know, I don't remember. But thanks." Her smile was only halfhearted, because she was certain Vince had already begun to tell Eli he didn't want her on the job anymore.

"We should go shopping at this cute place I know on Montrose. I think you'd really like it," Olivia said as she wrung water out of her blond tresses.

"I'd love that," Marnie said weakly, knowing that Olivia was just being polite. Olivia would not shop with her after they fired her.

"Come on," Olivia said, linking her little kiddie arm through Marnie's. "I've got an oatmeal shake in the fridge. You want some?"

"I, ah…I don't think so," Marnie said, but allowed Olivia to tug her into the loggia. She pointed to a chair Marnie could sit in, and walked around to the other side of the bar, bent down, then popped up again with a big pitcher full of oatmeal. Really. It was *oatmeal.*

"Eli, you want an oatmeal shake?"

"I'll pass, thanks."

"Marnie?"

"I'll pass—"

"No you won't. You'll love this stuff," she insisted and poured two glasses, and smilingly handed one to Marnie.

"So where are we at, guys?" Eli asked, leaning up against the bar, and for a split moment, Marnie imagined him in a saloon, a six-shooter at his side, his hat pulled down low.

"Look, I'll just get right to it," Vince said, settling in a chair and crossing one leg over his knee so that Marnie had an almost unobstructed view of his less-than-impressive genitalia. "You're not going to like this, but I think we need to make some changes."

Oh boy, here it came. *I want you to fire her ass, Eli. She's meddlesome and she's not that good a wedding planner.*

"Like what?" Eli asked, appearing completely unconcerned.

"We want to get that arch up there," Vince said, and hadn't finished his sentence before Eli was moaning. "Hey, I know it's a big deal, but Livi really wants it, and I'm willing to pay for it. Besides, I figure we're trucking up china and linens and…and what else was it?" he asked, looking at Marnie.

"The lighting equipment?"

"The *lighting* equipment?" Eli echoed.

"Yes, Eli," Olivia said. "Rose and amber lights will make everything so pretty. Everyone does it."

Eli looked, predictably, unconvinced.

"So anyway," Vince said, "I figure we got a couple truckloads on their way up, and I think we just strap that arch on the back of an eighteen-wheeler and haul her up there, too."

"Vince," Eli said, not looking quite so calm and collected now. "It's a logistical nightmare."

"Yeah, I know," he said apologetically, and glanced at Olivia, who smiled sweetly at him as she sipped her oatmeal shake through a straw.

"That's really going to cost us time and money," Eli added.

"Not a problem. I've got nothing but time or money when it comes to Livi."

"You're so sweet, Vince," Olivia said, and beamed at Marnie.

Marnie smiled back, wondering what happened to the reasonable guy she met a couple of days ago who said they weren't going a dime over a million five.

Eli sighed. "Okay," he said. "But on a couple conditions: you plan on setting up a pavilion tent in case of rain, and you hold the invite list down to a manageable number. No more than two hundred."

Vince looked at Olivia. Olivia looked at her oatmeal and shrugged. "Deal," he said.

"I'm glad that's settled," Eli said, and stood up. "You need to chat with Marnie? I can get a cab."

"Oh, that would be great. I wanted to talk about the tables," Olivia said.

"No problem." Eli gave Marnie a very self-satisfied smile. "I'll call a cab, then. Marnie, you want to walk me out?"

That was it? The whole big breakup and Marnie-is-so-fired was over like it never happened in the first place? "Right," she said uncertainly.

"Just come on back here when you're ready," Olivia said, who had moved to sit on Vince's lap, seemingly unaware that her towel was slipping.

Marnie thankfully put aside her oatmeal shake and walked out with Eli.

At her car, she asked, "Are you sure you want to take a cab? I could drive you—"

"Ah, no," he said instantly. "No thanks. I think I prefer to take a cab." He pulled his cell out of his pocket. "I gotta couple things I need to do this afternoon, but maybe we can catch up later."

"Sure," Marnie replied, her thoughts still on Olivia and Vince. "I don't believe it," she said, shaking her head. "Do you believe it? It's over, just like that. The whole ugly scene is over. It's like it never happened."

"It didn't," Eli said with a grin.

But Marnie shook her head again, ignoring Eli's amused smile. He might be used to the roller coaster they were on, but it still baffled her. As he called for a cab, she dipped into her backseat and pulled out her wedding organizer. When she stood up again, Eli had put the phone away and was standing there with his weight on one hip, his arms folded across his chest, looking very sexy in a very Texas way. "So... you think you can finish up here? Or will Vince's package hold you spellbound all afternoon?"

Despite her instant blush, she laughed carelessly. "If I didn't know better, I'd think you were jealous."

"I wouldn't know—I didn't look. Should I be?"

"Well, that's very hard to say," she said, her smile going deeper. "I don't have many other, ah, *packages*, as a point of comparison."

He gave her a very lopsided, sexy smile. "That's a shame."

It was a shame, all right. And here he was, this splendid specimen of man, giving her warm fuzzies again. If there weren't such a tropical heat climbing through her at the moment, she'd remember that he was a little on the schizo side. But damn, the heat he generated in her was a surprisingly nice feeling—so nice, in fact, that Marnie impulsively forgot everything he'd said about poking earlier and shifted her weight to one hip. "We had a bet, you know."

"I know."

"So?" she asked with a smile as she absently jiggled her keys. "Are you ready to name your prize?"

The grin in his eyes made her melt; he glanced down the drive. "Nah...not just yet," he said, and glanced at her from the corner of his eye. "I think I'll save it for later. When we catch up."

"Great. Gives me something to look forward to."

Eli smiled and stepped toward her so that they were standing almost toe-to-toe, and let his gaze casually slide down the length of her and up. "Try not to kill yourself driving, all right?"

"I'm the safest driver on the road."

"That's highly debatable. Try not to hurt yourself ogling Vince, either."

She laughed lightly. "Can't make any promises—the dude sort of lets it all hang out."

Eli grinned, let his gaze dip to the halter of her dress, and another shot of fire went right to her groin. As if drawn by a magnet, Marnie stepped closer to him. Her breasts were just a hair's breadth from his Tommy Hilfiger shirt.

He lifted his gaze from her dress, looked at her with mild curiosity, and touched the tip of her nose. "What do you think you are doing, coppertop?"

"Honestly, I'm not really sure."

"I think you're trying to lead me down the path to debauchery."

"Maybe I am," she said, lifting her face to his. "Do you have a problem with debauchery? Afraid it will get under your skin?" Before Eli could answer, however, some fool cabdriver chose that precise moment to honk his damn horn and ruin The Moment.

Marnie closed her eyes and sighed, but Eli laughed low. "That's a sign," he said, and shifted away from her. "So...you think you can keep a lid on it today? Or are you aiming for more air time?"

"Dude, I have got it under control," she said breezily, and hoped he knew she meant the wedding, because at the moment, her body was out of control, on a little vacation from her good sense, radiating toward Eli and inviting him in for a drink.

Another blast of the stupid cab ruined it for good. "Call me when you're through here, okay?" Eli said, and with a sly wink he sauntered down the drive toward the cab, his butt a moving work of art.

Marnie watched him walk, and had an image of him wearing chaps and walking with a lasso over his arm... and as he followed the curve of the drive and disappeared behind some shrubbery, she told herself to stop drooling. Besides, she had a naked Vincent Vittorio to look at inside.

She made surprising progress that afternoon, nailing down a lot of details, including the food (lobster), the music, and the decorations. Olivia liked the idea of the bowls of floating stars, but was insistent on crystal bowls. Baccarat crystal bowls, to be precise. And then she thought it would be lovely if each guest could take home a little Baccarat crystal bowl as a memento. "Do you think you can round up a couple hundred?" she asked Marnie in all innocence.

"I'll see what I can do," Marnie responded, trying not to think of the expense.

They talked about table arrangements and a stage for the music and dancing, and about the professional guests, the photography, and of course, the bar. They talked about a gown, too. Olivia had already talked to a new designer who was going to make a gown just for her. Marnie was slightly disappointed because she had wanted to shop for a gown with Olivia. Olivia promised to make it up to her with a shoe-shopping date in the next couple of days. "Saks," she said. "They'll give me an exclusive look."

Marnie had no idea what that meant, but it sounded fabulous.

By the time Marnie left Vince's house, she was satisfied that she finally had a handle on the event, and felt confident that even with the cost of getting the arch to Colorado, she could manage this affair for a million five.

Somewhere on Sunset Boulevard, she dialed Eli's number and told him she'd made significant progress.

"Where are you?" he asked.

"On Sunset, coming up on the 101."

"You're near my house," he said. "Take Laurel Canyon and come on up."

Was he asking her over? Was he asking her *in*? Marnie grinned. "You want me to come to your house?"

"Why not?"

"No reason," she said, beaming like an idiot. "Are you going to feed me?"

There was a moment of silence on his end. "Sure, I'll feed you," he said. "Let me give you directions."

As it turned out, Marnie knew exactly where he was— in a very swank part of the Hollywood Hills—and told him she'd be there in a half hour. She clicked off the cell phone, grabbed the wheel of her BMW, and cheerfully darted around another bus. "I don't know what you think you're doing, Marnie Banks," she chastised herself aloud, then laughed.

It was pretty obvious. Ever since that night with Bingo, she'd been developing a large-size crush on Eli. The sudden urge to know him in a less than professional but very biblical manner was not really like her, but hey, she hadn't been attracted to a man in forever. Eli was an exceptionally good-looking man, and really, she was having all these great cowboy fantasies about him.

Somewhere from the time he'd awakened her this morning to this latest phone call, she'd come around to her what-the-hell philosophy, as in, what the hell? It wasn't like she was angling to sleep with her client or anything, for chrissakes. Okay, so she was fantasizing about doing her boss, which really wasn't kosher, but then she rationalized it all away by acknowledging that she'd never flirt like this if this were a *real* job. Since this was just a little short-term gig, where was the harm?

The harm was that this little short-term gig could make or break her career as a wedding planner to Hollywood. This was the guy who would pay her and then recommend her. Fine. Did it necessarily follow that if she had a fling with him, he'd not recommend her? "That does not necessarily follow, no," she said firmly to herself. "Anyway, probably nothing will come of it," she added to the rearview mirror as she checked her lipstick. "He's probably being polite." She could handle that. If nothing came of it, she would still enjoy a big flirt and some very hot cowboy fantasies.

Her mind made up, Marnie pulled into a little package store and went in for a bottle of very nice wine. Couldn't hurt to grease the wheels in her favor, now could it?

CHAPTER THIRTEEN

Eli figured it was Marnie he heard squealing to a stop at the curb and went to the front door to have a look. Yep. Her, all right. His house was built down the hill a little, so he could stand in the covered porch of his entry and watch her long legs unfold out of the BMW, then her tush as she bent over and retrieved something from the backseat, which he hoped to God wasn't that pink book she carried around. He'd had enough talk of weddings to last him a good long while.

Her arms full, Marnie bounced down the steps to his door and looked surprised when she saw him leaning up against the jamb. She smiled her big, infectious smile. "Hey."

"You found it all right."

"Of course." She held out a bottle of wine, still grinning. "I also found the package store."

"Thanks," Eli said. "You shouldn't have."

"Yes, I should have. I practically invited myself for dinner. The least I could do is bring some wine."

"That's right, you did say feed me, didn't you?"

"I did. And now that I have given you the wine to atone for my atrocious manners, you should invite me in."

He smiled, stepped to one side, made a grand sweeping gesture to the door, and indicated she should proceed.

"Thank you," she said, and flashed a pert little smile as she walked past him into the small foyer of his house and deposited her purse on the antique bench there.

"*Wow.* This is so cool, Eli!" she exclaimed as she walked into the living area from the foyer. "I never had you pegged for the hacienda style."

"No? How'd you have me pegged?"

"I don't know, something...really square," she said, making an outline of an invisible square with her hands. "Boxy."

"I think I should be offended," he said cheerfully as Marnie walked deeper into the living area.

She looked down at the saltillo tile, and up at the low-beamed ceiling, and then at the overstuffed furniture scattered about, the Mexican rugs and earthen pottery and the Mexican-style fireplace. "Damn," she said appreciatively, looking at a painting above the fireplace. "You've been holding out."

"How so?" he asked, walking from the living room into the kitchen, which was separated by a long bar covered in blue Mexican tile.

"Because this is really a fabulous place and you obviously have a flair for decorating. It's so cozy. And you are not a cozy kind of guy."

Eli laughed.

"All this time I thought you lived in a truck," she said, stepping into the dining room. "You know, the lonesome cowboy scene."

She had the lonesome part right, but he liked it that way. It was easy. Less complicated. No one stood him up at the altar.

"I mean, I am *really* surprised."

"Hey," he said with a laugh. "I'm not *that* bad."

"Yes, you are," she said earnestly.

He chuckled, put the wine on the countertop, and looked for a corkscrew.

Marnie moved to a bar stool and sat directly across from him. He heard the *plop* of her shoes against the tile as she kicked them off. "I guess it's okay if I make myself at home?" she chirped.

"Could I stop you?" he asked as he poured her a glass of wine.

"No."

Eli smiled and handed her the glass.

Marnie sniffed it, swirled it around in the glass, then slowly sipped it. Her face lit up with pleasure. "Not bad."

He poured a glass for himself, sipped it, and thought it tasted like all the wine he'd ever drunk, and wondered if it would be all right to put it aside and get a beer, or if Marnie would get her feelings hurt. He figured her to be a little sensitive and decided to choke the stuff down.

"So," he asked, "did you manage to get anything done today, or were you too distracted by Vince's balls?"

"Ha ha. As a matter of fact, he put on shorts and deprived me of the opportunity to study his balls further. I did, however, have ample opportunity to study Olivia's breasts. Her towel just wouldn't stay put."

"Oh?"

"Pull your eyebrows down from your forehead." Marnie laughed. "There was nothing too exciting."

Actually, Eli knew that. Give him a woman with Marnie's breasts any day.

"I got a lot done today," Marnie continued. "Olivia and I have some shopping to do, but the rest of it I can handle on my own. You are now free to commence canyoning with your movie star friends."

"That's great," Eli said, and lifted a glass in a victory toast. "But they're not my friends."

"Why not? Don't tell me they get under your skin. They're really nice people."

What she didn't know wouldn't hurt her—she wouldn't be around them long enough to watch them morph into assholes. Besides, a beaming Marnie was lifting her glass in a toast.

"To me," she said. "I am a kick-ass wedding planner."

"And modest, too."

She laughed. "Let's toast to no more surprises."

"I'll definitely drink to that," Eli readily agreed. "Speaking of which…what's the lighting going to set us back?"

"About fifty thousand," Marnie said cheerfully. "But don't worry. I'm working on a final budget. We can squeeze everything in. Even the arch."

"I don't think you've factored in the costs of transportation," he warned her.

"Oh, but don't you?" she asked pertly. "As a matter of fact, Cooper is helping me with that." Obviously pleased with herself, she sipped her wine and then beamed at him so brightly that he could feel it all the way to his toes. "*Cooper* is very helpful. And very good with numbers."

Coop was good with nice long legs. Eli made a mental note to give him a call later and tell him to keep his mitts off the wedding planner.

"So what's for dinner? I'm starving."

The girl was not shy. Eli liked that. "How about salmon?"

"*Oooh*, salmon."

He laughed. "I'll take that as an okay." You never had to guess what Marnie was thinking. Now Trish…he was always trying to guess what she was thinking. He used to have the feeling that she was doing the actress thing and practicing different moods and expressions on him, because he never knew which way the wind was blowing. Marnie? It was always blowing, that was for sure, and he smiled to himself as he walked to the fridge and started to pull stuff out.

She got quiet, which was very unusual, and he glanced over his shoulder to see what she was doing. She had pulled out a scrapbook he'd been working with and was studying the photos. TA made scrapbooks of their stunts so they'd have an idea of what the stunt setups looked like. When they were in the planning stages of a new script, they looked back to the things they'd done for ideas and tips.

"Wow," she said, pointing at a picture. "That's huge."

The only bad thing about the scrapbook was that there were lots of pictures of him in there doing something extreme. Eli couldn't stand it—he moved to the bar and leaned over to have a look. "Oh yeah, that," he said, and walked back to the counter next to the fridge.

"Oh yeah, that? *What* that?"

"Vin Diesel movie. It was pretty intense." It had been more than intense. He'd almost killed himself on that set, flying through the air in futuristic war gear and slamming into a brick wall instead of landing on the hay bales like he was supposed to have done. He'd gotten a nasty concussion for it.

"What's your favorite stunt?" she asked as she flipped through the pictures.

He thought about that for a minute. "I guess the *Matrix* films," he said.

"Really?" She looked up. "You did those?"

"You look surprised."

"I am, I think," she said, looking thoughtful. "I mean, I know you're a stunt coordinator. I know you do extreme sports. It's obvious just looking at you that you're athletic—"

It was? He inadvertently looked down at himself.

"But I just can't *picture* you doing it. You don't seem like the kind of guy to go flying through air and spinning and twirling. You seem too…uptight for that."

"Uptight? I'm not uptight," he protested.

"I think you are—at least a little," she said breezily.

Okay, she had him. He grinned. "Maybe a little. But I love the thrill of those big movie stunts. It's exhilarating. It's the best kind of sport there is."

She smiled alluringly, and slowly closed the scrapbook. "I know an exhilarating sport I'd like to try," she said huskily.

Eli's male antenna went straight up. He turned and faced her fully. "And what sport would that be?"

"Canyoning," she said instantly. "It sounds like a blast." She picked up her wineglass, slid off the bar stool, and padded into the kitchen to check out what he was doing. "I could really get into canyoning."

"No," Eli said.

"Why not?"

"Too many liability issues."

"I swear I won't hurt myself. I'm pretty athletic. I can do it."

"Marnie. You couldn't even climb a rope, remember?"

"Hey, that's not fair. I wasn't prepared for that. I'll learn how before we go, I promise."

"Nope. Not this time," he said, and threw onions into a pan.

"Eli," she cried. "Come on," she said, a little softer, and when he turned around, she was standing right there, the wineglass in her hand, her maple eyes sparkling. "Come on, dude...wouldn't you have fun sliding down some slippery little slope with me?"

Okay. Eli was not exactly a novice when it came to women coming on to him—it happened more than he cared to admit. But there was something about this woman that was really stirring his blood, and he wasn't certain if he liked it or not.

But he did like her neck, he thought, glancing down at the long, slender column. And her breasts, round perky things that were, at the moment, peeking up at him through the fabric of her dress. And he liked her smile a whole lot, he thought, lifting his gaze from her boobs to that pert mouth, and that cute little nose, and those giant maple pancake eyes with dark lashes.

So what was it again that he didn't like? She was a damn good-looking woman. She was giving off all the signs of wanting to do him. His wanker was voting yes. So what the hell was his problem?

Oh right...he *liked* Marnie. That's what was wrong with this deal. No, really, he liked her a whole lot. What he didn't like was going anywhere near liking her. No way, not again. At least not yet. He still hadn't figured it all out.

Unfortunately, Marnie had other ideas. They seemed to have created one of those highly charged instances that made a guy's hair stand up on the back of his neck, and to make matters worse, she moved closer. He could feel some very sexy vibes coming off her body. "Do you think I'm being too forward?" she asked in all seriousness.

"Yes."

"Oh," she said, and smiled like she thought that was a compliment. "So...do you mind?"

"Honestly?"

"Honestly."

"I'm not sure," he said. But he didn't move. Not even an inch.

Marnie grinned and lifted her hand and poked him through the open collar of his chest. "For the record, I don't usually come on to guys."

"Then why are you?"

"Because, Eli McCain, there is something about you that just begs for it," she said softly, and rose up on her toes, lifted her face, and very lightly, very easily, pressed her lips to his.

It was just a feathery little kiss. But it struck like a bolt of lightning, in every vein, in every neuron. And as he was getting used to the idea, Marnie caught his collar in her hand and pulled him closer as she pressed her lips a little more urgently against his, flicking her tongue against the seam of his lips.

It was very disturbing to Eli to learn that his defenses against the female sucked. He had absolutely nothing to work with, not even a whimper of protest. In fact, all his pure male offense suddenly revved into overdrive, and he slipped his arm around her waist and pulled her to him, angling his head so her plump little tongue could go wherever it wanted. His personal body throttle liked her tongue, too—it immediately sprang to attention, inching its way up to his belt line, hoping for a peek.

The sound Marnie made in the back of her throat woke up the rest of him, and he realized, as the knife he was holding clattered to the floor and he twirled Marnie around and pushed her up against the fridge, that he hadn't felt all his parts come together in such teamwork in a long, long time. He was feeling them now, all right, in full glory, up and alert and ready for action.

His hands were roaming her body, caressing full breasts through silky fabric, then down to the taper of her trim waist, and the flare of her hips, the meaty bottom where his fingers dug into her flesh. Their tongues tangled in her mouth, and he felt the smooth veneer of her teeth, tasted the oak flavor of the wine she'd been drinking. His senses were filled with her scent—like roses, he thought, like a bed of fucking roses.

Eli pressed against her, and Marnie pressed back, undulating a little against his fly, rubbing Junior into a tizzy. Eli reached over and turned off the burner where the onions had gone past caramelizing to black bits, and forgot about them, forgot about the knife on the floor, forgot about arches and canyoning and everything but the feel of a beautiful woman in his arms. He was one step away from pulling

JULIA LONDON

the thin string of her dress and taking her right there, next to the salmon, when a thought suddenly swam up from the depths and gasped desperately for air.

He didn't *want* to do this. He really liked Marnie, so he really did not want to date her or fuck her or otherwise get involved. He'd made that vow to himself, and he was not about to break it just because Junior wanted a piece of the action.

He suddenly lifted his head. As he was not the type of guy to end this sort of encounter, he really wasn't very good at it. Marnie's hand slid down his chest and dropped lifelessly to her side. Her head lolled back against the stainless fridge, and her copper hair was everywhere. Her eyes were closed, one leg was hiked up, and her lips were stretched into a very happy little smile.

That smile did not help him to bow out of this in the least. If anything, it pushed him over the edge. "*Now* who's begging?" he growled.

Marnie opened her eyes. "Some things are worth begging for," she said, and planted her lips on his again.

There was no going back. Junior took over his thinking, and the next thing Eli knew, he'd pulled that tiny little string and her dress slid down, so that her breasts were exposed and looking right at him. He grabbed her by the hips and lifted her up to the countertop and took one perfect breast in his mouth.

Marnie arched her back and thrust her breast into his mouth, and then her hands were in his hair, and she was making these deep little sounds that indicated she was having a good time, and rubbing her bare legs against him. Eli's hands were running wild over her body, over her

156

bare breasts, up her thighs, between her thighs. Marnie's breath was coming harder, and she dropped her hands to his shoulders, then to his shirt front, and when Eli lifted his head from her slightly-better-than-perfect breasts, she caught him in a kiss and began to undo the front of his shirt.

Her hands slipped inside to his bare skin; her slender fingers slid over his nipples, then down his sides, her fingernails leaving an excruciatingly arousing trail across his skin. Eli deepened his kiss, caught her bottom lip between his teeth, and then suddenly let go, pressed his forehead to hers. "I'm not taking you canyoning with us. Got it?" he asked breathlessly.

"Got it," she said, and slid her hand down his pants to feel one of the biggest hard-ons he'd ever had in his friggin' life. "Do you have a condom?" she whispered.

Oh yeah, he had a condom, and fortunately for both parties involved, he was still in the habit of carrying one in his wallet. In a flurry of clothes and wine and slithery little dresses that made a pool on his kitchen floor, the two of them ended up naked in his kitchen, with Eli's fingers sunk deep in the soft folds of her flesh, sliding deeper still. Marnie's hands had found him, too, and now he was to the point of bursting.

He suddenly lifted her up; Marnie instinctively wrapped her legs around his waist, and he carried her like that to the living room, sat down on his red leather couch, and buried his face between her breasts again. "Marnie—" he started, but she stopped whatever he would say by filling his mouth with her breast. Her knees were on either side of him, and she slowly lifted herself up and started to slide down his cock.

"*Oh God,*" he groaned as she slid down on him. It had been a million years or more, it seemed. The feel of her body was making him insane, but Eli held on and began to move with her. He lifted his face, looked up at her...and saw something there he didn't want to see, something deep in her eyes that lit a fire way down inside him, way down, in a place buried deep beneath all the baggage and years and locks he'd put on it to keep it from getting out. How she'd done it, he had no idea, but Marnie had a bead on him, and as she began to move faster, her bottom lip between her teeth, that spark in her eye seemed to grow brighter and brighter.

Eli suddenly moved and flipped them over, so that she was on her back on the red couch, and he on top of her. Marnie giggled and put her arms around him. Eli reached between them and stroked her as he began to push deeper into her. She stopped giggling then. Her head rolled to one side, her copper hair went everywhere and she let out a growl of pure pleasure as she came.

It was all the encouragement Eli needed—he was into her now, his arm around her waist holding her hips steady so he could reach as far inside her as he could get. And all the emotions he'd kept bottled up, all the desires he'd left unattended, all the fears he'd let his mind create began to bubble up, mixing into one amazing deadly bubble. With a growl of his own that would have put a lion to shame, the bubble burst and he came.

He was instantly reduced to a quivering mass of flesh—there was nothing left inside him. He closed his eyes and pressed his forehead against her shoulder; Marnie wrapped her arms around his head and sighed contentedly. They remained like that for a few moments until Marnie's stomach began to growl, and she started to giggle again.

Eli carefully dislodged himself, and they cleaned themselves up, found their clothing scattered all over the kitchen, and dressed.

He noticed Marnie had a very rosy flush about her as she freshened their wineglasses, and she began to talk as he threw out the burned onions and tried again. He didn't even mind the chatter as they made dinner together, for it was engaging chatter. They kept bumping into each other as they moved about the kitchen in their quest to prepare the meal, laughing and talking like a pair of old lovers.

They dined on his terrace overlooking the valley, on an old, low, and heavy wrought-iron table he'd picked up in Mexico. He had it between two padded chaise lounges, and on those nights he sat out here and ate frozen pizza, he found it to be the perfect height. They ate salmon and asparagus and watched the lights of LA twinkle below them.

"Did you plant all these?" Marnie asked.

He looked at the giant clay pots planted with bougainvilleas and topiary ficus trees. "Yep."

"Dude," she said, smiling at him over the rim of her wineglass. "You just keep surprising me. You're not anything like the hard-ass I thought you were." She looked up at the open porch covering, through which he'd strung little white lights amid the ivy vines. "It looks like stars."

He glanced up. He'd never really thought of it that way, but they did sort of look like stars.

"This is like an oasis, isn't it?" Marnie asked. "A very nice and quiet place where you go to get away from it all. I bet you spend a lot of time here, contemplating the universe and your navel, right?"

That was pretty perceptive of her and made him feel a little uncomfortable, because he *had* spent a lot of time there, especially after the Trish disaster.

"So," Marnie said, putting aside her plate and turning onto her side in the chaise to face him. "Did you come up with a prize?"

"A what?"

She laughed. "A prize. Remember? If Vince and Olivia were still together, you got your pick of prizes."

"Ah," he said, smiling. "As a matter of fact, I did."

"I hope it's something fun," she said, drawing a circle on the arm of the chaise with her fingernail. "Something along the lines of what we did earlier would be nice."

Eli chuckled. "Actually…it involves another woman."

Marnie stopped making a little circle. She slowly lifted her gaze, and as the multitude of possibilities flashed before her eyes, they grew to the size of saucers. "Are you saying what I *think* you are saying?" she finally squeaked.

"I doubt it," he said, laughing at her conclusion. "I like females, but I do better with only one at a time. But I need your help. I've got a friend who needs some new clothes for school."

"For school?" she echoed. "How old are you, anyway?"

"Thirty-eight. And my friend is twelve."

Marnie opened her mouth. And there it stayed, gaping open, as she tried to figure that one out.

"So that's what I want for my prize," he said, enjoying himself. "I want you to help me shop for a twelve-year-old."

Marnie closed her mouth, and for the first time since he'd met her, she was speechless.

CHAPTER FOURTEEN

Two days later, Marnie decided that Eli McCain was either a big jerk or the most mysterious tall, dark, and handsome type she'd ever run across in her thirty-four years on this earth. She just wasn't sure which.

She had thought, after the awesome, unexpected little tryst between them, that they had passed to a new phase of their relationship, that they had gone from merely working together to something decidedly friendlier. She had convinced herself it was okay to date him, that a little gig like this didn't necessarily have to have the same rules as a real job, and it was perfectly all right to dip her pen in the company ink.

Since that fabulous night at his house, when she'd left him standing on his front porch leaning up against the split-beam post, one leg crossed over the other, his arms folded over his chest, watching her walk away with that quiet, sexy smile of his, she'd thought of nothing else but him.

And she hadn't heard a peep.

He had not called her.

What planet was this guy on, anyway? Hell yes, she'd assumed he'd call her! After all, they'd done it, and it had been fantastic, and she really believed that if two people did it and liked it, then it was the guy's place to call, even if it had been her idea to do what they did.

But Eli didn't call.

She told herself he was busy, and she made herself busy, too, making sure the chairs and linens would be shipped on time to Durango, Colorado, and that Holland had thirty thousand white roses and that there were two hundred Baccarat crystal bowls in LA.

But when Eli still had not called, Marnie was a little pissed. She figured he at least owed her a phone call to see how the plans were going, but *nooo*, Hollywood Hotshot couldn't be bothered. He was too busy being an important stunt guy for the movies to actually pick up a phone.

She was so baffled and pissed that she even ran it past Olivia when they went to interview Rhys St. Paul, the chef Olivia wanted.

"Let me ask you something," she'd said in the back of Olivia's limo. "If you sleep with a guy, and it's great, and there is the usual, 'hey, talk to you soon'...whose responsibility is it to call?"

"Are you kidding?" Olivia asked, blinking her big blue eyes in shock. "His."

Exactly.

So when Eli did deign to pick up the phone on the third day, Marnie tried not to act breathless and relieved and giddy, and tried to be very cool and laid-back about the whole thing, Hollywood style. "Oh, hey, Eli," she said, as if she had to recall who he was. "What's up?"

"Hi, Marnie. I was going to ask the same of you."

"Oh nothing," she said, as she made big black circles on a piece of paper. "Just working the wedding."

"Anything I need to know about?"

"*No*," she said, perhaps a little too sharply. "Well...Olivia and I hired the chef. He's going to do the wedding and the cake. You remember, you were concerned about the cake budget," she said, stabbing her pencil on the paper with the words *cake* and *budget*.

"I remember. So this is a good thing, right?"

"It's *all* good," Marnie said, sneering into the phone.

"Great. So you ready to help me out with that shopping?"

And that was how she wound up at Fred Segal, shopping for outrageously expensive clothes for a twelve-year-old. She picked up a pair of jeans and held them up.

"How much?" Eli asked.

"Five-fifty. Pretty pricey for a kid who will probably grow out of them in a couple months."

"Nah," he said. "Give them to me."

Marnie lifted a brow in surprise and handed him the jeans to add to the mountain of skimpy tees and skirts and jeans and sandals and anything else a twelve-year-old girl might conceivably want in her lifetime.

"So where is this friend of yours, anyway?" Marnie asked suspiciously. "Why isn't she here?" He'd told her the girl was the daughter of a friend and that he was helping out, but she was beginning to wonder about that. Friends didn't help out with clothes like these.

"Because she lives in Escondido, and it's too far to drive between soccer games."

"Escondido. How do you know a kid in Escondido? Did you come up from Texas that way?" she asked, picturing him riding through New Mexico and Arizona and California on horseback, his saddlebags stuffed full, his bandana around his nose, his clothes stained and dirty. The image gave her an unexpected little shiver of delight.

"Very funny," he said. "No, nothing like that. Her father was one of our stunt guys. He died a few years ago."

"Oh." She shut up. For a moment, anyway. "How did he die?"

Holding up the jeans to inspect them, Eli looked at her from the corner of his eye. "A stunt."

"Geez, I didn't know people died doing stunts."

"They don't, usually. Not unless someone is careless."

"Ah, I see," she said. "The guy was careless and killed himself, and you feel sorry for his daughter."

"That's close," Eli said. "Except I was the one who was careless and the guy died. And I do feel bad for his daughter. I guess this ought to do it," he said, looking at the pile of clothing he held.

She could not have possibly felt smaller if she'd been an ant. "Eli, I'm sorry."

"No need," he said, and walked to the front of the store to pay for the mountain of clothes he was holding.

After he'd paid for the clothes, Eli drove her home. When he pulled in her drive, he got out and came around to her side of the truck and opened the door. Marnie slid out, leaned against the arm of the open truck door, and looked up at Eli.

"Thanks," he said. "I really appreciate the help. I would have been lost trying to do it on my own."

That was putting it mildly. "No problem—I love to shop," Marnie said.

"I got that impression," he said with a grin. "So…thanks, Marnie." He moved so that she could step away from the truck.

But Marnie didn't move. Marnie's mouth operated solo again. It was a fact that tact and timing had never been her strong suit. "Eli…are you ever going to call me?" she suddenly blurted.

The question obviously surprised him. "I called you today, remember?"

"I know…but I mean…you know, to like…" Okay, what did she mean? Not get married, hell no. Date? Maybe…the jury was still out on even that, wasn't it? What about a drink? It didn't even have to be alcohol—just coffee? At least some acknowledgement she existed?

"Like…*what?*" he prodded her.

"I'm starting to think you don't like me," she said, and instantly despised her immature self.

Eli smiled. His gaze drifted down to the tips of her newly pedicured toes. "You're dead wrong about that. I happen to like you a whole lot."

She brightened instantly. "You do?"

"Of course I do. Would I ask you to shop for Isabella if I didn't like you?"

No, he wouldn't have done that, she supposed. But that left her with the worst possibility. "Well, then…maybe you didn't like my, ah…*company* the other night."

Eli blinked. Then he laughed and tenderly touched her cheek. "Girl, I'd be gay if I didn't like your *company*. Are you nuts? It was fantastic."

"Okay," she said, feeling enormously relieved. "All right, then. I just thought…you know, that we might get together for a drink, something like that."

Eli nodded thoughtfully. Blew out his cheeks. Looked at the ground. Then up again. "You know what? We'll do just that…when I get back from Florida."

"Florida?"

"There's a hurricane moving toward Florida. We're going to jet down and do some kite surfing while the winds are up. I'll be gone for about a week."

"You are going to kite surf on hurricane winds?" she repeated, just to make sure she'd heard him correctly.

He nodded, as if that were a perfectly reasonable thing to do.

"Oh," she said, feeling very confused and very stupid about kite surfing. "Florida."

"Hey," he said, and put his palm against her cheek, making her look up. "The minute I get back I'll give you a call. We'll have that drink."

He looked very sincere, she thought, but something somewhere nudged her consciousness. Something said that a drink was not very comfortable for him. Something said that he was trying very hard to be nice.

All of a sudden she felt very foolish. "Sure." She would have liked nothing better than to crawl beneath his truck and think a minute.

"If you need me in the meantime for the wedding, just give me a call, okay?"

"Right," she said, looking everywhere but at him.

"If you can't get me, you can always get Cooper. He's not going this time," Eli added.

Unfortunately, crawling beneath his truck was not an option. "Right, right," Marnie said and slipped away from his hand, around the open truck door, and walked toward the front of the truck. "So," she said, walking backward now. "Have a safe trip."

He perched his arm on the open truck door. "Marnie? Are you all right?"

"I'm fine," she insisted loudly, and smiled to prove that she was. And she *was*. She'd had fabulous sex with a gorgeous guy she thought was unique and kind in a very unkind town. But that didn't mean they had to suddenly change everything and start dating. They were adults. They'd had some fun. Now on with the show—she got it. She'd read the latest dating books going around. He just wasn't that into her.

"Okay," he said, looking terribly unconvinced. "Behave while I'm gone, will you?"

"Oh, Eli," she said, and laughed, then waved, turned around, and jogged up to the front door. But she didn't manage to get in before she heard her dad come out of the garage and say, "Is that you, Eli? Hey, how are you?"

She didn't look back, just walked in and shut the door, then stood there a minute, trying to catch her breath. She wasn't exactly sure when her heart had started racing, but thought it was right around the moment he touched her face. Her mind was flooded with the feel of his hand on her body, and the intensity of that feeling surprised her. She closed her eyes.

"Marnie? Are you going to stand at the door all day?" her mom called, and she realized, given the amount of secondhand smoke in the house, that the book club was meeting. She groaned softly, pushed away from the door, and walked to the door of the dining room, where the ladies were gathered.

"Hi, honey," Mom chirped.

"Hi, Mom. Hi, everyone," she said, waving lamely.

"Oh, sweetie, you don't look very happy," Mrs. Farrino said.

"No?"

"No. It wouldn't have anything to do with that hunk out there, would it?" she asked, and the others sniggered. Marnie glanced at the dining room window and realized they had seen the whole exchange.

"Who, him?" She rolled her eyes and flicked her hand at the door. "I don't think so."

"Hey, Marnie, what do you know about Jude Law?" Mrs. Campbell asked.

"I don't know anything about him."

"Oh, that's too bad. I have a good friend whose friend's daughter went out with him and got the wham, bam, thank you ma'am from him."

"Honestly, Bev, are you still going on about that? Of course he did that to her. Did your friend's friend think there would be wedding bells or something? These movie people move from one person to the next and they don't look back," said Mrs. Donaldson.

"And I guess you know so much about it based on your own movie career, Alicia?" Mrs. Campbell shot back.

"Am I wrong, Marnie?" Mrs. Donaldson insisted. "These Hollywood types go through sex partners like water unless they land some huge superstar. Am I right?"

"I, ah…honestly, Mrs. Donaldson, I don't know," Marnie insisted as her stomach slid down to her toes. "And I really don't know anything about Jude Law." But she did know about Eli. She knew right that very moment that it had just happened to her. Of course that was what happened to her. Eli had probably slept with more starlets and makeup girls than he could probably count any longer, and here she was, stupid little wedding planner, thinking it could actually turn into something more.

In the moment of her epiphany, she dropped her purse.

"Marnie, what is the matter with you?" Mom asked when her lipstick came rolling across the floor.

"Nothing, Mom," she said and bent to pick it up.

They flew out on the company plane, Jack at the helm and Michael as co-pilot. That left Eli in the back, presumably with a script to read, and in the hopes of actually accomplishing something, it was on his lap. But he wasn't reading the script. How could he? Marnie's smiling face kept dancing before his eyes.

He sighed, rubbed his eyes, then tried to focus on the script again.

No use. He couldn't stop thinking about how disappointed she'd been when he'd left. Damn it, this was exactly what happened when you let your guard down and slept with good-looking women. There were suddenly too many expectations, too many rules popping up like prairie dogs all around you.

Okay, right, there were too many expectations, but if he was honest, he'd admit he hadn't felt quite like this since Trish. But even still, this wasn't the same as it had been with Trish, not by a long shot. With Trish, there'd been a physical thing going on—he'd felt like he'd been hit with a two-by-four the first time he'd clapped eyes on her. It had started off as an instant, gotta-get-in-her-pants thing. Clicking with her afterward had been the icing on the cake.

Or so he'd thought. Apparently, he had been doing more clicking than Trish.

With Marnie, it was something that had started inside him and had worked its way up to the physical. And that was not to say that he hadn't thoroughly enjoyed their little romp. Nope, it had been pretty spectacular when he thought about it. Which he did quite often. But in the beginning, he'd thought she was a fine-looking woman—but it hadn't been the two-by-four-between-the-eyes good-looking. His physical attraction to her had grown over time. And then *wham.* Right in the sack.

Stupid, stupid, stupid.

What was he going to do with her now? Women, for the most part, could not do a one-time shot, he knew from experience. And while he'd enjoyed their romp, he was not ready for a relationship. There were still days he couldn't get out of bed without feeling like a putz. That putz feeling had been joined by an equally bad feeling in the pit of his stomach that this was not the right thing to do, that it would end badly.

There were only two ways this could go—if it was great with Marnie, then eventually she'd want something more permanent. She was a wedding planner, for chrissakes. But he could not go there. He'd gotten the universal cosmic sign that long-term relationships and marriage were not his thing.

That left this thing with Marnie going south, and it could go south in a heartbeat. They might even have a few fun times before it went south, but then one of them would piss the other off, and really, he was not in a position to risk potentially the biggest gig of TA's existence because he'd left his dirty socks on her floor or something like that. No, ethically, he really couldn't go there.

There was nothing to be done for it. He felt himself shrinking up, turning into a tight little ball, and he knew that he had to go back to LA and tell that very attractive, vibrant, and funny woman that they'd had a fling, but that was all there was to it.

He was not looking forward to it in the least, and he made a mental note that crap like this was a very good reason why he should keep his pants zipped.

CHAPTER FIFTEEN

Olivia was seriously starting to drive Marnie nuts. She called several times a day, almost always in a crisis, and almost always in her *Wonder Girl* suit. "Can you come to the set?" she'd beg.

Today she had called between scenes to say, "I just don't think the starlight thing is going to work."

Yeah, well, the starlight thing had to work. They'd ordered linens and crystal and Olivia had insisted on buying all those Baccarat crystal bowls in which they intended to float the star candles. Marnie had spent hours working with a floral designer and stage manager to learn how to suspend hundreds of white rosebuds from the top of the black reception pavilion ceiling to simulate stars. How could it not work?

So Marnie had driven to the set and argued with the security guy for thirty minutes—again—until he finally consented to call Olivia (and the fact that Olivia or Lucy, for chrissakes, couldn't leave Marnie's name at the goddamn gate was really beginning to annoy her).

Predictably, Olivia was in the trailer with Lucy, the assistant who did very little assisting as far as Marnie could see.

"I just think it's been done to death," Olivia said as she lay with a cloth over her eyes between takes. "My second cousin Irene just did starlight."

"But she didn't do starlight like *you're* going to do starlight. Think of the canopy of hundreds of tiny little stars that are actually rosebuds. How cool is that?" Marnie tried.

"Yeah, you're right...but Irene will think I am copying her."

"Is she invited?"

"No."

"Then she won't know."

"How can she not know? The press will be all over it."

"No, no, Olivia, no they won't. Remember—that's why you hired Thrillseekers Anonymous. Your privacy is pretty much guaranteed."

Olivia considered that for a moment. "I guess you're right. Okay. We can do starlight. But I'll tell you the truth, Marnie—I'm starting to have a bad feeling about this whole thing."

"Pre-wedding jitters," Marnie said confidently. "Everyone gets them. You'll be fine. You're going to spend a week with Vince in the rugged beauty of the Colorado mountains, and then you are going to marry him under an arch and the stars. It will be gorgeous."

"It will be gorgeous, won't it?" Olivia asked hopefully. "What do you think, Lucy?"

Lucy turned a stunned look to Marnie, then to Olivia. "I guess it sounds okay."

Marnie frowned at Lucy. Lucy shrugged and went back to studying her phone. She was always studying her phone or her iPad. Marnie was beginning to suspect it was secretly a mirror.

"Well," Olivia said, lightening up a little. "If Lucy likes it, I guess I'm all right with it."

If Lucy likes it? The same woman Olivia refused to give even the time of day?

"That's great," Marnie said and stood. "So I need to run. I've got to work on getting the roses into the US Is there anything else?"

"Just one more thing," Olivia said. "I changed my mind about the music. Pop seems so…unweddingish. I think jazz would be good. Do you think jazz would be good?"

Marnie gripped her purse so tightly that her fingernails sunk into the leather. But she forced a smile to her face. "Did Irene have a jazz band?"

Olivia wrinkled her brow. "No. I think it was a rock band."

"Then I think jazz would be terrific. One jazz band, coming up," she said jauntily as she inched toward the door. "I'll speak with you later, okay?"

"Oh, Marnie," Olivia said. "I want to go see my spiritual advisor later after I'm done here for the day. Will you ride along? I was hoping we could chat about the bar. I've been thinking, and I'm not really comfortable with the wine selection."

She was never going to make it as a wedding planner to the stars. *Never.* If all of them changed their mind this much, she'd have to get a rope, string it from the crane they had outside to fly *WonderGirl* around, and jump.

"Marnie?"

"Sure. Just give me a ring when you're ready," she said, and grabbed the trailer door and pushed it open before she exploded. "Bye!" she called, but she was already out the door.

She marched to her car, threw her purse in, revved the engine, and tore off the studio lot. What had ever possessed her to be a wedding planner? If she ever got to have her own wedding, it was going to be so simple—a potential husband, a potential pastor, and some really great shoes. Period.

Her cell phone rang; with a grimace, she picked it up, punched the little phone icon, and said, "Did you forget something?"

"I don't think so."

Eli. Marnie's heart jumped up a notch, and she yanked the wheel into the commissary parking lot to talk. "Hey! How was the kite surfing?"

"Fabulous. It's the only way to go. Hurricane-force winds can really give you some loft."

She tried to picture him surfing wind but could only see him in chaps.

"So what's going on at wedding central?"

"Well," she said cheerfully, "Olivia has changed her mind about a number of things, like the theme, and the music, and the food. But she hasn't changed her mind about the flowers, God no—she still wants thirty thousand white roses from Holland flown in. But hey, I have found a supplier in Amsterdam who will make it happen."

"Wow, that's really great. Personally, I'm happy for all the people of Holland—it will probably boost their GNP by a thousand percent."

Marnie laughed.

"So...listen, we were going to have a couple drinks, weren't we?"

"Yes, we were," she said, grinning broadly.

"I know it's short notice, but how about tonight?"

"Tonight would be *great*," she said, and she meant it.

"I'll pick you up around eight, then," he said.

"Great. I can't—" Whoa. She almost said, "can't wait to see you," but caught herself just in the nick of time.

"Pardon?"

"Can't get away before then, but eight will be fine."

"Cool. See you then," he said, and hung up.

Marnie closed her phone. "Dude. What the hell was *that* about?" she asked herself and drove on, picturing Eli with his spurs on, kite surfing. Except that he looked sort of stupid doing that, so she switched gears to how in the hell she was going to find a famous jazz band on such short notice.

Several hours later, Marnie knew a moment of panic when Olivia's limo driver dropped her off and she saw Eli's truck in her parents' drive. She'd thought she'd be back by seven, but *noooo*, Olivia had to have a private treatment with Ari, the spiritual guru who boinked movie stars in the backroom of his salon.

"Little Sunshine," he said to Marnie when he'd finished gazing meaningfully into Olivia's eyes. "You seem, like, really stressed out."

"Do I?" she asked, feeling very self-conscious. Ari had some pretty sharp eyes for a spiritual dude. And an excellent memory.

"Little Sunshine, you do not understand that *rhythm* is the basis for life—not forward progress."

What the hell was that supposed to mean? But she said only, "Oh," as she was not, fortunately, dumb enough to encourage him. And besides, Olivia was tugging at his siesta shirt. "Ari, come on. I'm in a hurry."

Olivia was not in *too* big a hurry as it turned out. By the time she'd finished getting a pike of spirituality pumped into her, it was already seven o'clock, and then they were stuck in traffic on the way back to Marnie's, which gave Olivia plenty of time to review the wine list in great detail. All California wines were to be served, she'd decided. Nothing French. *Cool,* Marnie thought. That would make it easier. But then Olivia said, "But maybe some Chilean. But if I serve Chilean wine, then I'll have to include some Australian and Italian, don't you think? And so what is the purpose of not serving French in that case? Maybe I should go only French," she said, and put a finger to her lips, tapping thoughtfully.

It was enough to make Marnie's head pound, but by the time they arrived at her house, they had come all the way around to Californian, because Marnie had insisted it was the thing to do, seeing as how she and Vince were from California.

"Well, he's actually Canadian, but no one knows that," she informed Marnie.

"Canadian. Great. So listen, you won't change your mind, will you, Olivia?" Marnie asked. "We're sort of running out of time to get all this together."

"I won't," Olivia said, crossing her heart, then suddenly lunged across the back seat and hugged Marnie tightly. "You're so good to me, Marnie. I feel like I've known you forever."

"Really?" Marnie asked with a grin. "Thanks." She got out and leaned down to say good-bye, but Olivia's brow was furrowed. "You know what? I didn't think we should serve

German or Spanish wines. Should we? Oh Jesus, this is just too hard! Look, I'll call you tomorrow and let you know."

Marnie's smile froze. "Okey-doke! Okay. Just…let me know," she said, and with a little wave, she shut the door with a little too much force and watched the limo drive away. "You better let me know by the end of the week, girlfriend," she muttered. "Whatever happened to '*I'm not a wedding person?*'" she added in a mocking voice. With a sigh, she turned around—and saw Eli and her dad walk out of the garage together.

Eli was holding a power saw and her dad had a piece of wood shaped like an S.

"Hi!" she called, walking up the drive. Maybe it was her silly imagination, but it seemed to Marnie that when Eli looked up and saw her, a warm, gut-tingling smile instantly spread his lips and ended in two deep dimples. Marnie felt herself smile back. Except hers, she feared, was big and dopey.

"Hi, honey," her dad said when they met in front of Eli's truck on the drive. He was a full head shorter than Eli and looked half his size. "Eli was helping me with a project. He really knows his way around the power tools."

Eli winked at Marnie as he walked past her to put the saw thing into the big steel storage chest in the bed of his truck.

"Well, I guess I better get back to work and let you two go do whatever you're going to do. Thanks for your help, Eli," Dad said.

"No problem, Bob."

Bob? Dad patted Marnie's arm. "See you, sweetheart," he said, and turned and walked up the drive to the detached garage.

She waited until her dad had disappeared into the garage and said, "Thanks for helping...Bob."

"No problem. We had a good time cutting stuff open."

"I can only imagine. So listen, I'm just going to run in and freshen—"

"*Mar-neeee!*"

"Oh God," she said, and closed her eyes, buckled her knees, and swayed backward as she let out a couple of fake, but dramatic, sobs. "I can't take Mrs. Farrino right now!"

"Marnie, honey. Invite your friend in!" Mrs. Farrino shouted.

Eli looked over Marnie's head, smiled and nodded, but said through his smile, "Just get in."

"What? I have to go in—"

"No you don't. You look fantastic. Just turn around, wave, say hi, and get in," he said, and opened the door of his truck.

Marnie twirled around. "Hi, Mrs. Farrino. Tell Mom I'll be back later, will you?" she called, and did not wait for an answer but dove into Eli's truck. He shut the door behind her, jogged around to his side, gave Mrs. Farrino a wave, and was in with the motor started before Mrs. Farrino could beat a path down the walk. They backed out into the street and sped off, laughing at Mrs. Farrino's look of defeat.

Eli drove to Redondo Beach and a place he knew there, he told Marnie, that specialized in margaritas and martinis. On the way, she filled him in on the details of the wedding— a little proudly, too, as she had accomplished a great deal in his absence. Eli looked suitably impressed.

At the restaurant they sat outside, side by side on Adirondack chairs, enjoying a cool ocean breeze, sipping apple martinis, and nibbling on shrimp. It was a little cool for the tank top Marnie was wearing, so Eli got a jacket from his truck. She really liked that about Eli—he was such a cowboy gentleman. And she liked his jacket. It was suede and smelled like him.

"So tell me about kite surfing," she suggested as they dipped their shrimp into cocktail sauce. "I've only seen pictures of it. It must be totally cool."

"It's a rush like you never had," he said, holding up two fingers to the waiter to signal two more drinks. "Imagine flying through space," he began, and sat back to tell Marnie about his trip. She was amazed how the adventure lit him up—he was so enthused by it that she couldn't help but be excited by just the prospect of it.

"It sounds fantastic," she agreed when he had finished.

"It is. You should try it sometime."

She snorted into her martini. "You won't even let me go canyoning. You're going to let me kite surf?"

For some reason, Eli's smile faded a little, and he looked toward the water. "We've got a couple French dudes who want to try it," he said, as if he hadn't quite heard her. "The trick is getting them over here when there is a hurricane offshore. Those things can turn and go in a different direction in the space of twenty-four hours."

He talked a little more about it, but Marnie wasn't listening very closely. She was beginning to feel very mellow sitting outside at dusk, wearing his jacket, listening to faint tropical tunes drift out from the restaurant.

She liked hanging out with Eli. On an evening as beautiful as this with a cool ocean breeze, it seemed natural and right. She could imagine them doing this for years to come.

Maybe they'd make it their own little tradition. They'd come down here on their anniversaries and big occasions, and they'd sit in these exact same chairs, and they'd say things like, "Remember the time we came here? You'd just come back from kite surfing Hurricane Jane..."

"Marnie?"

She jerked her attention to Eli. She hadn't realized how far down in her chair she'd slid and quickly sat up. Eli was smiling. "Where'd you go?"

"Ha ha," she said with a sheepish smile. "I was just thinking that it's really nice down here. You know, it's funny— I've lived in LA all my life, and I hardly ever come to the beach. I take nights like this for granted."

"We all do, don't we?" he asked, and shifted his gaze to the ocean.

Marnie perused his fabulous profile, his strong chin, the depth of his arm and shoulder, and impulsively put her hand over his. "I don't want to take any more nights like this for granted, Eli. Do you?"

But the moment the words were out of her mouth, she felt the stiffening in his hand and a lot of really bad vibes. And then he did the thing that signaled a huge, giant blunder. He sighed. A really soft, really sorry sigh. "Marnie," he said low, and turned to look at her.

She was about to get a jumbo brush-off. "Oh shit," she muttered and, yanking her hand free of his, sat up. She could be *such* an idiot sometimes.

"Listen, Marnie—"

"Hey, I think you misunderstood me, Eli," she said, laughing a little loudly, her mind frantically racing around her plan to save face. Except that she had no plan and came to her feet.

"Oh," he said kindly. "Okay." And he stood up, reached for his wallet, and threw some money on the table.

"No, not okay," she said, already walking to the door. "You *so* have the wrong idea—"

"It's okay, Marnie."

It's *okay*? There was something about the way he said that, like he didn't think he had the wrong idea at all but was getting off the hook. And for some reason, that made her mad. Actually, come to think of it, it made her furious. There had been *two* people on that red leather couch, both enjoying it, thank you, and as she sailed out of the restaurant, marching to the parking lot, she got even madder.

"Marnie," Eli called from behind her. "Wait up!"

"It's freezing," she said, and kept her legs moving at a furious pace, her face flaming with the humiliation of getting a brush-off and him knowing that she knew that he knew that she *knew* she was getting the brush-off.

Eli caught her arm when they reached the truck and spun her around. "Marnie, please don't be upset."

She laughed at that absurd suggestion. "Jesus, Eli, who's upset?" She laughed again. "What...you think I'm upset? I'm not upset, Eli," she said, and smiled brightly into his blue eyes.

But he wasn't laughing. He was frowning a little, as if he didn't know what to make of her.

"Look, I'll be honest here," she said, in spite of having no intention of being honest, "what I was trying to say..." She paused with a slight wince, put her hand to her nape, and rubbed it a moment. "Is that I don't want to hurt your feelings." HA! Turn the tables. Brilliant!

Eli blinked. He even moved back a little and squinted at her like he couldn't make out what she was saying. "Beg your pardon?"

Too bad she didn't have a piece of paper so she could spell it out for him. "I don't want to hurt your feelings, Eli," she said, smiling sweetly, "but I don't think it's a good idea if we...*this*..." she said, motioning vaguely to the both of them, "goes anywhere. I mean, what happened was fantastic, it really was. But...it was really just a...a thing."

Damn him if he didn't look confused. He shook his head, squinted again, then braced one arm against the truck, beside her head, so that she couldn't really escape him if she wanted to. "So let me get this straight," he said, his blue eyes piercing hers. "You're saying that our little deal the other night was just a *thing*?"

Marnie puffed out her cheeks for a moment, then nodded.

He reared back, put his hands on his hips, and stared at her. "That's not very nice."

She shrugged. "I like you, Eli, but I don't *like* you like you, if you know what I mean—"

"Oh yeah, I know what you mean," he said, his brows dipping into a frown. "I, too, was in the seventh grade once."

"Come on," she said. "I just don't think it's a good idea if we, you know...get into anything here. This is a working relationship, and I think we need to keep it that way. I hope you can understand that."

His frown went deeper. "Oh, I can understand it. I understand it all too well. In fact, I was going to suggest the same to you."

Ha! He *was* going to dump her. Even though she had scored with a preemptive dump, the idea that he was going to dump her turned her fury up a notch. "You were going to *dump* me?" she demanded, folding her arms across her middle. "So you make a habit of sleeping with women and then dumping them?"

Now he really looked confused. "I…what happened to '*It was just a thing*'?"

"That doesn't give you license to just dip your wick wherever you want."

"But it apparently gives you license to invite all the wick dipping *you* want," he shot back.

"You can't tell me what to do."

"I'm not trying to tell you—"

"I am a grown woman, and if I want to have a thing, that is my prerogative, and okay, I don't do it very often, and really, Eli, it was pretty spectacular in my book, so don't get me wrong, I'm not complaining, but upon further reflection, it occurs to me that maybe it's not the best thing I could be doing because you know how you are, all moody and weird and—"

"*Marnie*," he said, and abruptly put his big rough hand to her face and cupped her cheek.

She gulped. "What?" she asked weakly, already lost in his blue eyes, already picturing them above her, already regretting that it really wasn't going any further.

"Shut up," he murmured, and his gaze had gone soft and dipped to her lips.

"Okay."

She had no idea what she was thinking, or even how it happened, but he seemed to reach for her at the same time she impulsively flung her arms around his neck and held tight, kissing him with all her might, meeting his lips and tongue and pressing tightly against him.

Eli gathered her up in his arms, actually lifted her off the ground. He pushed up against the truck and she could feel him hard against her belly, could feel the power in his arms as he held her. She took his head in her hands, curled her fingers into his hair, and kissed him with a desire that billowed up in her and spread out to her limbs.

Eli groaned into her mouth and proceeded to kiss the breath right out of her, then slowly lifted his head, let loose his grip of her so that she slid down his body until her feet hit the ground. He said nothing, just gazed at her, smoothing her hair back from her face and kissing her forehead, then the bridge of her nose. And then he stepped away from her and opened the passenger door.

They rode home in companionable silence, Marnie smiling quietly, her hand in his. When they arrived at her house, he met her at the front of his truck. His blue gaze roamed her face and a strange little smile lifted one corner of his lips. He gave her a light, tender kiss, a squeeze of her hip, then stood back and watched her walk up to her front door and disappear inside.

It wasn't until much later after she'd bathed and tied her hair in a knot and had settled at the kitchen table with a bowl of ice cream and the wedding budget before her that she stopped to wonder if she'd actually been dumped or not.

CHAPTER SIXTEEN

Eli kicked himself all the way home. That kiss was definitely not supposed to have happened, but dammit, she'd looked so mad and cute and oddly vulnerable during her speech that he'd slipped.

Okay, all right. He was having a little more trouble than he'd bargained for in keeping his distance from her. Well, sure—she was a very appealing woman. But she wasn't the first appealing woman he'd ever known, and he usually had a little more self-control. Tonight, he'd proven his deepest fears—that he was a complete putz of a man who could be easily sucked in by *cute*.

Jesus.

Trish never did cute, he had to admit. She used tears to get her way, and it always felt like a sucker punch, because Eli was not the sort of man who dealt very well with a woman's tears. They always made him feel frantic to do something to stop them.

He usually didn't have any trouble when a woman was arguing with him, either, but Marnie, hell—there she was, talking a mile a minute, the fire in her eyes getting brighter and brighter as she tried to cover her disappointment, and he had felt that panic to make her stop. Frantic enough to kiss her. For a really long time.

Long enough to make him ache to be with her again. *Goddammit!*

He drove recklessly, screeched to a halt in his drive, walked into his house, and threw his keys at the Mayan bowl where he usually kept them, missing the bowl and hitting the wall instead. He stalked into the kitchen, flung open the fridge, grabbed a beer, and kicked the fridge shut. And then he went out onto the terrace to sit under his trellis and stare glumly at the lights of the valley.

The best thing to do was lay low. He had a little less than two weeks before he and Vince and Olivia and Cooper took off to do the canyoning in the San Juan Mountains. After that, the wedding, and directly after that, thank God, the Amazon trip with the Japanese. He needed the Amazon trip to clear his head and get it on straight.

So three weeks max, and then it was over. Just like that, she'd be history. He could go on with his life, she could go on with hers, and they'd both be a whole lot happier doing it.

Three weeks. He could do three weeks standing on his head. Well...unless she argued. Or cried. Or smiled that big moon smile at him. No, no, he could handle it, he could do this. He was not ready for a relationship, and he really wasn't ready for Marnie, no matter how appealing she was.

Seriously. He wasn't.

He took a swig of beer and absolutely refused to listen to the little voice inside his head telling him he was a big fat coward and a really bad liar.

Marnie didn't hear from Eli the next day, but she was far too busy to think much about it, because Olivia had a dress crisis.

As in, she absolutely despised the dress she'd commissioned from the new hot designer Ming Xioong. Ming had made the dress based on Olivia's exact specifications, and Ming had delivered. Marnie thought the gown was gorgeous.

"It looks like a potato sack!" Olivia wailed over the phone.

"But Olivia," Marnie tried, "she *hand-sewed* it. And she embroidered it."

"I don't care if she picked the silk and spun it. It's horrible and I am not paying twenty thousand dollars for that rag."

For starters, Marnie didn't think that you *picked* silk, but she set up an emergency meeting with Ming for the very next day, which she managed to squeeze in between her emergency meeting about the reception pavilion and the emergency phone conference about the antique altar Olivia now wanted.

Together, Ming and Marnie convinced Olivia to at least try on the dress. Olivia tried it on, stood up on the little platform before three floor-to-ceiling mirrors, and cried.

"You can't see it?" Olivia demanded tearfully when Marnie asked her what was wrong with it.

"I swear to God, I don't see anything," Marnie said. "You look absolutely gorgeous."

"No, I don't! Just look at this," she wailed, gesturing lamely at her chest.

Ming and Marnie looked at her boobs, then at one another. Suddenly, everything was clear. "So…you don't like the bodice?" Marnie asked carefully.

"Would *you?*" Olivia snapped.

The problem was that Olivia was less than well-endowed in the chest area, and Marnie wondered, with all her freakin' money, why Olivia hadn't gotten on the breast-enhancement bandwagon like the rest of LA But she hadn't, and the result was a bodice that didn't hang exactly right. It had nothing to hang *from.*

"I see this all the time," Ming said knowingly. She disappeared into another room, and then reappeared with a padded push-up bra. "Put this on," she said to Olivia.

"I am not going to wear artificial enhancements," Olivia said stiffly.

"You can have one or the other," Ming said matter-of-factly. "If you wear the push-up, I can make some adjustments and you will look beautiful. If you don't want enhancements, then this is the best I can do, and you still owe me twenty thousand dollars."

Olivia looked at Marnie. Marnie mouthed, *Wear the push-up.*

"Fine," Olivia huffed, and stepped off the podium, snatched the bra from Ming's hand, and went into the dressing room.

She reappeared a few minutes later and looked as if she was seeing the gown for the first time. She beamed at her reflection in the three-way mirror. "This is *so* much better," she said, as if she had thought of the bra herself, and caught Marnie frowning at her. "You just don't understand how stressful this all is, Marnie."

Actually, Marnie thought she had a pretty good idea of how stressful it was.

Olivia turned one way, then the other, admiring herself. "Wow. I look fantastic. I love wedding gowns. They're so beautiful. Do you ever think about getting married, Marnie?"

That question certainly caught Marnie off guard.

"Every woman thinks of getting married," Ming scoffed when Marnie didn't answer right away.

"Sure, I've thought about it. Sort of," Marnie said.

"Omigod," Olivia said, her eyes going wide. "I don't even know if you have a boyfriend. I can't believe I never asked you that," she cried. "I mean, I know about the guy who slept with you and never called you again, but I never thought to ask about a boyfriend. How terrible of me—*do* you have a boyfriend?"

Marnie could feel herself coloring and looked sheepishly at Ming's invoice (which Ming had shoved at Marnie the moment they entered her studio).

"Uh-oh," Olivia said as Ming began to pin her gown. "This is awkward. I shouldn't have brought it up."

"No, no," Marnie said with a laugh and a wave of her hand. "There's a guy," she said with a sheepish laugh.

"Oh?" the Olivia and Ming chorus asked at the very same time, and both of them stopped what they were doing to look at her.

"Sort of," she said. "I mean, we've been…close. But then, not so close."

"Ah," Olivia said, nodding sagely. "*That's* the guy."

"Did you sleep with him?" Ming demanded.

Oh man, this was awful. "Maybe."

"No maybe to it. Either you did or you didn't."

"She slept with him. But he never called her, can you believe it?" Olivia volunteered.

"Bastard!" Ming spat.

Clearly, she was going to have to discuss this, and Marnie put the invoice aside so she'd have her hands free to talk. "Okay, he did call. Eventually. But here's the thing—neither of us meant for it to happen, but it did. And it was fabulous. Fantastic!" It was indeed the highlight of her sexual life thus far. "We'd been sort of building this friendship, and it happened, and honestly, he seemed really into it. But the next time I saw him, he told me he didn't think we really ought to go there for a lot of reasons, which, okay, I could understand. But then he kissed me. And it wasn't a good-bye kiss, either. It was a *kiss*."

"Asshole," Ming said with a flick of her wrist. "Men are such chickenshits. They don't like to fall too hard or too fast, and when they do, forget it. They try and act like nothing happened, that it was only you and not him, blah blah blah. But he won't be able to keep that up if he's really fallen for you. He'll come crawling back with some lame excuse."

"Really?" Marnie asked hopefully. "You think?"

"Bullshit," Olivia opined. "He got what he wanted, and now he's done. Don't kid yourself, Marn," she said, studying her hair in the mirror as Ming pinned her gown. "Men are beasts. They will do or say anything for a fuck."

"Really?" Marnie asked, slumping in her chair.

"Really. Forget him. He doesn't deserve you anyway."

"Don't listen to her," Ming said. "He's getting his nerve up."

"He's not getting his nerve up. He got his dick up and now—*Ming*!" Olivia cried. "You *pinned* me!"

"Sorry!" Ming said, and yanked the pin clear of Olivia.

Marnie put her fist on her chin and moped.

With the dress crisis resolved, she returned home to work from the kitchen table. Only she didn't get much work done, because she couldn't stop thinking about what Olivia and Ming had said. It was sort of hard to argue that Eli had been after only one thing, especially when she'd done the initiating. But neither could she buy the theory that he'd fallen fast and hard.

She didn't know what to make of it, and sat with her feet propped on one of her mom's silk-covered dining chairs, drumming her pen against the table.

"Marnie, honey?" Mom asked, poking her head out of the kitchen. "Could you stop that, please?"

"Mom," Marnie said, tossing her pen aside and dropping her feet. "Tell me what you think of this. I have this friend who is sort of seeing this guy, and things got a little close between them, and they ended up sleeping together. Then he did a one-eighty and said he didn't really want to date her. But...but then he *kissed* her."

"Are we talking about Eli?" Mom asked cheerfully.

"*NO!*" Marnie cried. "We are so not talking about Eli."

"Because I think he is very fond of you," Mom blithely continued. "But I wouldn't put too much stock in a kiss."

"Why not?" Marnie demanded testily.

"Men don't like confrontations with women. They'll do just about anything to keep from having one. Kissing is an avoidance technique. What do you think about stroganoff tonight? I haven't made my stroganoff in a long time."

"Stroganoff is fine," Marnie said absently.

"Don't worry about Eli, honey," Mom said.

"Mom, it's not Eli," she insisted, and in a huff, gathered up her stuff. "I'm going to work in my room."

"Okeley-dokeley!" Mom sang after her.

Marnie didn't get any more work done there, either, and after pacing her floor, stepping over clothes and bridal magazines and more clothes in an attempt to pace, she finally got annoyed enough that she picked up the cell phone to call Eli.

Wait. The damn thing was off. Christ, he'd probably been trying to call her all day and she'd had it off. She turned it on, waited for it to power up, then noticed she had a single message. "See? He called me," she announced to Bingo, who was lying on a pile of her dirty laundry, and retrieved the message.

"Marnie…"

She grinned with delight at the sound of his voice.

"I'm leaving for Colorado in an hour. They've had a wildfire that screwed up our canyoning route, so I'm going to go and redesign it. So listen, Jack is going to fly you and the chef dude up a week from Thursday. All you need to do is get you and the chef to the OC airport that Thursday morning around nine. Okay. See you."

The message clicked off. Her grin faded. Confused, Marnie stared at the phone. He was *gone?* Just like that? If he'd really wanted to talk to her, he could have called her house. Okay, but maybe he'd been really busy. Maybe all the guys had been standing around, and he couldn't really say anything like…*great kiss,* or *you rock.*

Damn. Part of her thought she was still getting dumped. Another part of her said he wouldn't have kissed her like that if he was really dumping her. Another part altogether said she hadn't eaten since this morning, and she was starving, but she wasn't ready to carbo-load on stroganoff.

She showered, changed clothes, picked up her purse, and headed out.

"Marnie," Mom called, waving a hand at her from the front room as she walked to the door. "Come here for a minute, will you?"

The book club was meeting, and Marnie sighed to the ceiling and reluctantly walked into the room, fanning the smoke from her face as she did.

"I was telling the girls about your friend," Mom said with a not-too-subtle wink.

"Mom," Marnie said through clenched teeth. "That was between me and you."

"And I think we're in agreement. He probably doesn't want to date your friend."

She forgot her embarrassment. "Really? Did you tell them that...you know, a good time was had by all?"

"I did."

"The thing is, Marnie," Mrs. Farrino said, pointing a cigarette at her, "if he really wanted to date her, he'd be calling her and sending flowers and trying to get in her pants again. But if he hasn't called her, and he even *told* her he didn't want to date her, it doesn't matter about the kiss. She should move on. He's just not that into her. I saw it on Oprah."

"I saw it, too," Mrs. Campbell said, "and I think we should read that book for our book club."

"Bev, honey...we don't read," Mom said.

Mrs. Campbell shrugged. "Well, anyway, I don't think it's quite that simple, Marnie. I think sometimes men get hit over the head by a woman and they don't know how to act. They are basically chickenshits."

So to sum up, today she'd had two votes for chickenshit, three for asshole.

"Dal is a chickenshit, Bev, but most men aren't your husband," Mrs. Farrino said.

"Hey! I resent that. In Dal's day, he was very decisive."

"Don't listen to them, Marnie. If this man wanted to be with you, you'd know it, because it's all right here," Mrs. Donaldson said, tapping her chest where her heart was.

"Thanks," Marnie said, smiling weakly, aware that her heart was feeling a little empty at the moment. "I'll tell my friend what you said."

"You do that," Mom said sweetly, and the others exchanged a look and a snicker.

Fabulous. By morning, it would be all over the neighborhood that Marnie had been dumped, poor dear.

She spent the next several days in a whirl of activity and frustration, trying to tie up all the loose ends of Olivia and Vincent's wedding. The Chiavari chairs she had ordered had been scheduled for the wrong ship date. The BBJ linens to cover said chairs and tables and tent poles could be shipped to Durango, Colorado, with time to spare. But getting them from Durango to the lodge was another issue.

The security team Cooper had hired had a scheduling conflict, and the three hundred bottles of Cristal champagne Marnie had ordered were lost in transit somewhere. She still had two interviews to conduct for the professional guests Olivia wanted, plus Olivia's hairstylist and makeup artist had left several messages, demanding more information on the climate in Colorado.

JULIA LONDON

Furthermore, the lighting was coming from Denver, and she could not get the driver on the phone. She left message after message, and missed two of his calls, which essentially said, "Hey, don't worry, be happy. I'll show up."

She figured he'd show up. The big question was *when?*

And last, but certainly not least, the tent guy called her to say he'd made his way up to the lodge and had done some preliminary work. "I gotta tell ya, Miss Banks, this is a tough one," he said, and she could practically hear him scratching his head on the other end of the line. "Either you put up two tents to accommodate the guests, or you build some sort of staging to even the ground out. The thing is, the lodge is in the mountains, and it's not like ya got a level playing field up there."

"Two tents?" Marnie cried. "Where would the band be?"

He didn't answer for a moment. "Good question."

"Okay, how much to build the staging?"

He did some quick calculations, and gave her a figure that gave her a headache. She was barely managing to hang on to the million five budget as it was. But she couldn't imagine having the reception split into two tents. "Do it," she said with great authority, and hoped to hell no one came after her for the extra ten grand this guy was going to want when it was all said and done.

In between the actual logistics of setting up this wedding, Olivia was getting increasingly frantic. Marnie had told her, pleaded with her, insisted that she would handle every aspect of the wedding and Olivia did not have to worry about a thing.

But Olivia was worried about everything, and her tone got increasingly sharp the closer to the departure date they got.

196

"Marnie, you must make sure my gown is protected!" she insisted rather shrilly on the phone.

"Of course I will, Olivia, you can trust me."

"What about my other things? What about my wedding shoes?"

"I'll tell you what—I'll come to your house, and we can pack everything up so you can be assured that I've got it."

"Why? Why can't you and Lucy do that?" she asked irritably.

"We can, of course we can. I just thought you might feel better if you saw it with your own eyes."

"Nothing is going to make me feel better, Marnie," she said. "What about the beluga caviar? Did you verify that it's Iranian? Because if it is Russian, you can tell Rhys to fucking stick—"

"It's Iranian," Marnie interrupted. "Hey," she added cautiously, "is everything cool with you and Vince?"

"Of course it is," she snapped. "Why wouldn't everything be okay? Have you heard something? If you've heard something, you better tell me right now."

"I haven't heard a peep, Olivia," Marnie said quickly. "I was just checking."

By the time Olivia and Vince left with Cooper for their canyoning trip, Marnie was a worse basket of nerves than Olivia.

Marnie almost lost it when Rhys, the chef they had hired for the cost of buying a small nation, phoned a couple of days after Olivia left to tell Marnie that he did not fly.

"What do you mean you don't fly?" she asked, gripping the phone so hard that it was a wonder she didn't shatter it.

"Just that. I do not fly. I'm quite afraid of flying, actually."

"You obviously flew to Los Angeles from Ireland," Marnie pointed out, trying desperately to sound light and carefree.

"But I did not care for it."

"Rhys," she said sternly, "there really aren't a lot of options. I don't know if we can get you to Colorado on time if you don't fly. But you mustn't be afraid because our pilot is one of the best in the world. He was trained by the Air Force, and he has flown all sorts of—"

"I really couldn't possibly care if he's flown to the moon and back, Miss Banks. I do not fly."

Marnie glanced at the calendar and glared at it. Three days. She had all of three days to convince this moron he was going to fly to Colorado or ruin everything. There was no time for the kid-glove treatment.

"Now then," Rhys blithely chatted on, "I shall inquire as to the availability of train or bus passage, but I rather prefer a car."

"No," Marnie said evenly.

"No?"

"*No*! You are going to fly, bucko. You are going to fly if I have to come over there and personally put you on that heli-copter. You signed a contract, and you are *not* going to muck this up for me. This is my *one* shot to make it in this business, and I have already endured enough with my celebrity clients changing their minds a dozen times each day! Do you real-ize we are on our fourth band? Our *fourth band*! And Olivia still isn't happy. Do you have any idea what it takes to get some giant freakin' arch to Colorado? You can't just stick one of those things in your suitcase, right? And the linens have to be back in Denver the Monday after this gig, like I could *possibly* come down from the mountain that soon, and you are so going to fly."

Rhys said nothing for a long moment. He cleared his throat. "I suppose I could take a pill or something, couldn't I?"

"Yes, Rhys, I really think you could take a pill or something."

"Very well, then. Thursday morning it is."

"Thank you!" she all but shouted, and slammed the phone down.

It rang instantly, and she glared at it. "Uh-uh, sucker. No way," she muttered, and clicked it back on. "Look, Rhys, I will personally take you to the doctor if that is what we need, but you are not getting out of this at this late date. You should have spoken up weeks ago when we first met."

"Who is Rhys?"

Marnie gasped. "Eli!" she cried.

"Hey Marnie, how are you?" he asked, his voice coming in delayed over tiny little bleeps in the connection. "And who is Rhys?"

"A demanding chef. So where are you?"

"Somewhere in southern Colorado," he said. "There's no reception in the—reached a peak today, and—how's everything going?"

The connection was pretty bad, and she struggled to make out his words.

"Great. Everything is under control. Why are you asking? Did Olivia put you up to this? Is she still worried?"

"Is Olivia worried?" He laughed again. "If she is— word about it. Nope, I called all by myself to make sure everything was cool and you were—"

He had called her from the mountains. He had thought of it all by himself. "Everything is fine," she assured him.

"So listen…before I lose this connection—say I know I left a little—"

"What?" she cried, poking a finger in her free ear to better hear him over the static.

"I said I left a little abruptly."

"That's putting it mildly."

"Yeah…well, I've been waiting—place—so I could call and tell you that I'm really—"

A weird beep and then nothing. *Nothing!* The connection was lost, and with a shriek of frustration, Marnie banged the phone against the table then put it back up to her ear. "Eli? *Eli!*"

All she could hear was a strange clicking noise. She'd lost him. *I've been waiting—place—so I could call and tell you that I'm really*…what? WHAT? Sorry? Relieved? Stupid, a moron, mean, in love?

"*Augh!*" she cried and cursed the heavens that ruled cell phone transmissions.

CHAPTER SEVENTEEN

After four days of canyoning with two preening peacocks who alternately fought, then made love so loudly that it sounded staged, Eli was exhausted, hungry, and not in a very good humor.

Personally, he couldn't wait for the next meeting of TA, so he could announce that if any of them ever booked a wedding again, he'd personally wring their necks before he jumped off a cliff to break his own. After this week, he was certain Coop would join him in that—Olivia had turned out to be a huge whiner, her voice getting more shrill with each passing day—*the water is too cold*, and *that's really high*, and *I may hurt myself* and *I'm not packing anything out* was all he heard from that woman's lips for four days.

But they had done it, had canyoned down some of the coolest waterfalls and ravines he'd ever seen, had climbed up through aspen forests and walked through tiny dales brimming with flowers, had scaled northern faces, had camped under stars so bright and close it felt almost as if he were somehow suspended in the galaxy.

Now they were at the Piedra Lodge, about two thirds of the way up San Miguel Peak, where there were people and separate rooms and Eli could at last put some distance between him and the two stars.

Apparently, they wanted some distance from him and Coop, too, because they disappeared into their suite the moment they arrived, claiming fear of being discovered by paparazzi.

On that front, things looked pretty good. The security team seemed to be holding down the fort, even with trucks arriving almost hourly delivering tents and linens and two huge snowblowers, which were, oddly enough, accompanied by two hundred pounds of feathers.

Feathers.

He did not recall feathers being on the manifest of crap coming to Colorado, and was awaiting Marnie's arrival so she could explain it all to him.

That wasn't entirely accurate—he was awaiting Marnie's arrival, period. He'd missed her smile and her pancake eyes and her exuberance, and after spending six days with the world's whiniest woman, a cheerful Marnie Banks would be a welcome addition to this gig.

He thought of the day he'd called her. He'd wanted to talk longer, but the connection was so poor. He'd wanted to hear her laugh, but had been cut off too soon. And he wasn't certain what she'd heard from him. Especially the part about being sorry for leaving without speaking to her. That part, he'd have to tell in person.

If she ever showed up. She wasn't yet at the lodge.

Jack and the chef guy, a huge mountain of a man, had already lumbered in, carrying three huge coolers, a very large clothing bag, and a smaller briefcase that the dude held tightly to his chest. "Utensils," he had disdainfully articulated when Eli asked.

Utensils? Eli figured the guy could have borrowed a spatula from the lodge, but what did he know? The man waddled off to the bar, mopping his brow, proclaiming to one and all that if he didn't have a bourbon neat, he'd perish, for apparently he had been unnerved by the flight to Durango and the drive up "all those ridiculously winding roads."

"Where's Marnie?" Eli asked Jack.

"I gave her a Jeep. She had to check on some stuff. This is a great place," he added, looking around. "Reminds me of Mexico."

The lodge was a great old place. It was an adobe structure with rustic beams and decor that had made some taxidermist rich. The pine plank wood floors were covered with thick rugs, and three elaborate stonework fireplaces kept the lobby warm. Everywhere a person looked were works of art, including pottery and painting. Each guest room had a spectacular view of the San Juan Mountains, private fireplace, Jacuzzi, and authentic bearskin rug.

TA had booked the entire lodge for the weekend, and every room would be occupied. In fact, once the guests started to arrive, there would be no room for Eli and Marnie, the chef, or the happy couple. The plan was for them to stay at the wedding site, about a thousand vertical feet up from the lodge, a quick four-wheeler drive up an old mining trail. On the day of the wedding, the guests would be ferried up on the back of four-wheelers by local boys who would be paid a small fortune to keep quiet about who their passengers were.

Once there, the guests would walk across an old wood-and-rope bridge that spanned a very deep but narrow ravine that looked like a gash in the mountain, formed by centuries of snow runoff. After crossing the swinging bridge, they would hike up to a small meadow on the banks of a smaller alpine lake, where an old cabin, left over from the heyday of silver mining, had been converted into a very exclusive and private retreat for very rich people.

That is where they would watch the two biggest American stars exchange their vows beneath a plastic model of the Arc de Triomphe. And then the party would be ferried back down to the lodge, where a huge, elaborate reception would take place.

Eli still hadn't figured out how or when the feathers came into it.

He and Jack were trying to decide where to put the damn feathers when two effeminate men walked into the two-story lobby and openly grimaced at the sight of an elk's head hanging above the reception desk.

"Little early for guests," Eli muttered, nudging Jack, who looked up as the two men approached them. Eli was the first to extend his hand. "Eli McCain," he said. "This is my partner Jack Price."

"Oh!" the shorter of the two exclaimed, lighting up. "Are you a professional couple, too?"

Jack and Eli exchanged a quick look of shared horror.

"Professional guests, he means," the taller man said on seeing their expressions, and calmly removed his mohair coat. "Dancers, maybe?"

"Whoa," Jack said instantly, throwing up a hand. "We are *not* dancers."

"And guests aren't to arrive until Friday," Eli added quickly.

"Oh, we're not *those* guests," the first man said, openly checking Eli out. "We're professional guests. We were asked to arrive early to discuss the arrangements with Marnie and then, naturally, be on hand when guests start showing up."

The notion of *professional* guests left Eli speechless. A quick look at Jack, whose mouth was gaping open, told Eli that he had no clue what a professional guest was, either. "Ah...Marnie hasn't arrived yet," Eli said, unable to think of anything else.

"No problem. We'll just wait in the bar," the first man said. "There is a bar, isn't there?"

Eli pointed to a stuffed bear on their left. "Just past Old Smokey."

"Thank God," the taller one said, and away they went, smoothing their perfectly coiffed hair and recoiling from the various heads of game that hung from the walls.

"What the hell is a professional guest?" Jack demanded.

"Hell if I know," Eli said and wondered when Marnie was going to get here and explain it to them.

Marnie was running late. She was enjoying the beautiful scenery as she leisurely drove the two-lane winding road, which, several signs noted, was closed during winter months due to snowfall. Marnie had been to Europe, and she had been to New York and Texas, but she had never seen the United States between the two coasts and it was breathtakingly beautiful. In the distance, the trees on the mountains looked like the stubble of a man's beard, but up close, they were tall and majestic, towering up so far that they squeezed the sun from the sky. Some were so steep that it looked as if God had knifed off a piece, shearing them off so that He could put them side by side.

And now, here she was, seemingly the only one in the world—well, save the RV she had passed a couple of miles back—winding up and up to what seemed like the sky. There was absolutely no one in these mountains. No buildings, no signs. Nothing but a lot of signs warning drivers of cows crossing the road. And cows. *Lots* of cows. Who knew cows could live this high? Wasn't someone worried the cows would be eaten by bears?

Up and up Marnie wound, the Jeep slowing on steep grades. Just when she began to fear she was lost, she found the turnoff to the lodge. She turned left and drove past a field of cows munching on yellow and pink flowers.

She was smiling when she drove across the cattle guard that marked the entrance to the Piedra Lodge. After a short and bumpy ride up a gravelly road, the lodge suddenly appeared before her, built up the side of the mountain with varying levels, so every window had a view of the spectacular surroundings.

The only thing that marred the vista was the dozens of four-wheelers and Jeeps and big crates scattered about the grounds. The site of them jarred Marnie from her trip through the wilderness. It seemed criminal, somehow, to have brought civilization and dropped it here.

She parked her Jeep next to several others and grabbed her backpack and organizer. She'd get her other bag later. At the moment, she was too busy filling her lungs with mountain air. Was anything more invigorating?

Eli saw her before she saw him—her good looks were hard to miss among all the workers who had gathered to erect the massive reception tent behind the lodge.

She looked fantastic—she was wearing skintight hiking pants, a T-shirt that just reached her belly button, and a hooded sweatshirt. Her hair was pulled back into a thick coppery ponytail, and on her feet were all-trail shoes. The girl looked like she was going to hike to the top of San Miguel Peak and kick its ass before dinner.

Her face lit up with a smile when she saw him, he was happy to note, and she waved, as if he hadn't seen her. He actually waved back. Marnie walked across a plank of flooring the workmen had put down. "Hey," she said, grinning broadly, all but skidding to a stop in front of him.

"Hey," he said, grinning a little himself.

Her brows dipped a little over her beaming smile. "Wow...you don't look so good."

"Thanks."

"I'm sorry." She laughed. "You just look really tired. Rough trip?"

He was tired. And he hadn't had a chance to shave or clean up since he'd arrived. "Nah, it was all right. What about you, coppertop?" he asked with a grin. "You look like you're ready to do a cross-country trek."

"Too much, you think?" she asked, looking down at her outfit.

"No," he said, his gaze sweeping her curves. Man, he liked her curves. "Just perfect," he said honestly, and received a warm and grateful smile for it. "So you want to see where it's all going to go down?"

Her eyes instantly lit up. "Yes!"

"Okay. Just a couple questions first," he said, and put his hand to her elbow, turned her around, and pointed to the snowblowers.

"Oh great!" she exclaimed. "They arrived a day early."

"They came with two hundred pounds of white feathers."

"Two hundred pounds." Her brow wrinkled. "That sounds like a lot of feathers."

"It *is* a lot of feathers. What I'm wondering is why we have even one feather?"

"Oh," she said, digging in her backpack and withdrawing a small notebook, "they're for ambiance."

She said it as if that would be obvious to even the biggest moron. He guessed he was the colossal moron, because he couldn't see how feathers and ambiance went together.

Apparently, she saw his confusion. "You know… ambiance at the reception," she said, as if that helped anything, and flipped open the notebook. "We'll be gently blowing white feathers over everyone to simulate falling snow."

Okay, he would *never* have guessed that. "What?"

Marnie didn't answer—she was too busy staring at her little notebook. "Not *two* hundred pounds! A *hundred* pounds! How could they make that mistake? Tell me something," she demanded of Eli. "Do I have a funny accent? Do I speak with a lisp? Do I not e-nun-ci-ate clearly enough?"

"Not that I've noticed."

She groaned heavenward for a moment. "Oh well," she said, abruptly cheerful. "Feathers are not that expensive. That's only a couple hundred dollars extra."

"For feathers."

"Yes, for feathers. They're not expensive, but they're not free, either," she said with a wink, and stuffed the notebook into her backpack.

"So...let me see if I've got this," Eli tried, looking thoughtful. "We have about four hundred bucks worth of feathers—"

"That's right."

"And we rented two industrial blowers to blow them?"

"Yep," she said, rising up on her toes and down again in a very proud fashion.

"And the snowblowers set us back...how much?"

"Two fifty. A day. Each."

"Ah," Eli said, nodding. "So we're spending two grand to blow four hundred dollars worth of feathers."

"Oh stop," she said, and playfully poked him in the chest. "You're just giving me a hard time. So come on, let's go see where this thing is going down," she said with a snap of her fingers and a little sway of her hips.

Eli couldn't help himself—he chuckled and shook his head. "Come on."

"Great. I'm dying to see it," she said, and marched her fine butt out to the drive, passing him on her way to the row of Jeeps.

Eli stopped and, hands on hips, watched her march all the way to the Jeep she'd apparently parked. "Marnie?"

She whirled around. "Yes?"

"Over here," he said, pointing to the four-wheelers.

Her gaze shifted to the four-wheelers. "How cool!"

A person had to like that about Marnie—she was easy to amuse.

He had her get on the four-wheeler first, then straddled it in front of her, easing back between her legs. He couldn't help but be reminded of another, more intimate moment he had been between her legs, and when Marnie slipped her hands around his waist to hold on, he had to grit his teeth to keep from wallowing in that memory like a pig in slop. He'd just spent more than a week getting her out from under his skin, and he wasn't going to let her creep back in there just because she was damn good-looking and pleasingly soft.

They drove up through thick stands of pines and spruce and aspen trees and occasional cottonwoods. Purple thistle grew alongside the old road between fuzzy pink flowers and thousands of little white and yellow flowers. When they reached the old rope bridge, Eli shut the four-wheeler off, and Marnie climbed off the back.

"Listen," she whispered.

Eli listened, thinking she might have heard an elk crashing through the forest. "What do you hear?"

"Nothing," she said, turning around to him, beaming. "Nothing but the wind in the trees and rushing water. It's fantastic, isn't it? It's like we're the only two people on earth."

Her smile seeped into his veins, and he felt slightly awkward because of it. He motioned for her to follow him. They walked up a short distance to the rope bridge. Eli went first, calling over his shoulder for Marnie to grab both sides of the rope rail before she stepped onto the planks, moving easily across. He then turned around with the intention of helping Marnie off.

Only Marnie had not started. Marnie was gripping the rope rails and staring wide-eyed down to the bottom of the ravine.

"Don't look down," he suggested.

"I can't help it. This doesn't look very sturdy," she said from the other side.

"It's fine. Just look at me and come across."

She didn't exactly look at him, she glared at him, and gripping the rope railings, she slid one foot out onto the planks, and then another. And then she was running across in little tiny strides. With a shriek, she flung herself at Eli when she reached the last plank; he caught her before they went tumbling to the ground.

Marnie clutched the fabric of his shirt tightly and stared up at him. Her heart was pounding so hard he could see the leap of her pulse in her throat.

"See?" he asked. "It wasn't so bad."

"Speak for yourself, Paul Bunyan," she said, and let go of him. She straightened her tee, smoothed the loose hair from her eyes, and put on a bright smile. "So where is the arch going?"

With the feel of her in his arms still rattling around inside him, Eli pointed, and Marnie walked on, up a steep trail and around a boulder that protruded from the steep face of the mountain onto the trail, over trees that had fallen across the seldom used path, and then up a rocky slide until the trail opened into an alpine meadow.

"Omigod," Marnie said between gulps of air.

It really was spectacular. The cabin was set beneath a stand of spruce trees, the outhouse ten feet away and connected by a covered walkway. The tiny lake glistened in the afternoon sun, and while the meadow was hardly large enough for more than a few tents and a fake arch, it was covered with flowers and tall yellow grass that looked like wheat, over which enormous butterflies flitted in and out.

"It's fantastic!" Marnie exclaimed, walking forward. Eli joined her, and together they walked to the lake and looked at the fish swimming there. Eli pointed out some of the nearby peaks and the glimpse of a village at the base of the mountain range. They walked up to the log cabin, which boasted a spectacular view of the mountains. The porch was graced with two big padded wicker chairs, a marble table, and a small brazier for keeping feet warm.

Eli opened the door, put his hand on the small of Marnie's back, and guided her across the threshold of the honeymoon cottage.

"Oh man, oh man, this is so charming and so romantic." She sighed, looking around at the large, single room. "No wonder they wanted to be here."

Thick beams of wood slanted across the ceiling, and from it hung an old cast-iron circle candelabra. Beneath it were two leather armchairs, directly before a surprisingly large hearth and near a long leather couch. Wood was stacked to the ceiling on either side of the fireplace. A huge and thick shaggy rug covered most of the floor.

On one side of the cabin was a raised platform, on which was a round, king-size bed. It was centered directly beneath a large ceiling mirror, and was covered with quilts stuffed with down. A trunk along the wall of the platform held wool blankets. A small closet had more blankets and linens, two plush bathrobes, and two sets of sheepskin slippers. Another door led to a single bath and sink—and a small heater, to pump hot water into the tub.

In the kitchen was a wood-burning stove and utility sink that had an old-fashioned handle pump. In addition, there was a small but elegant dining area. A wooden chest was actually a very large cooler, where some foodstuffs were stored. The pantry was stocked with china and crystal, and on the pantry door was a wine rack.

"What about food?" Marnie asked, giving the bed a little bounce.

"Breakfast foods are stored here," Eli said, pointing to the chest. "Lunch and dinner are brought up from the lodge. When they are ready, the couple call for it over the walkie-talkie."

"It's very secluded, isn't it?" Marnie asked.

"Very."

She got up from the bed and walked to the hearth, and looked up at an original painting of a snowbound adobe house above the hearth.

"If I ever get married, I'd want it to be in a place like this." She laughed. "Without the arch, I mean...but someplace really special." She glanced at Eli over her shoulder and smiled. "Wouldn't you?"

Funny, but the mere mention of marriage made him feel as if he were standing on a bed of hot coals. "I, ah...don't plan on marrying," he said, and awkwardly put a hand to his nape and looked at the floor. How had she done it? How had she managed to slide back under his skin so quickly?

"Oh no?" she asked cheerfully. "Well, if you ever change your mind, you should consider this place."

He said nothing, just kept rubbing the nape of his neck, feeling terribly conspicuous. Exposed. Transparent.

"Okay," Marnie said, and stretched her arms high above her head. "I better get back." She walked to where Eli was standing, and tipped her face up beneath his to get his attention. "By the way, you can relax. That wasn't a proposal."

"I didn't say it was."

"No," she said laughingly. "But you blanched and almost fainted. So shall we go? I am expecting some professional guests to arrive today."

"Right, yes...and about those guys," he said, opening the door. "What exactly is a professional guest?"

Her eyes widened with surprise, and then her face broke into a wreath of smiles. "Oh, Eli, you make me laugh," she said, and walked out the door, leaving Eli to think he and Jack were the only men on the planet who didn't know what professional guests were.

He locked up and followed Marnie out onto the porch, where she was sitting with one hip on the railing and a delectably rosy flush from the cool dry air. "At the risk of sounding really out of touch with the world, what *is* a professional guest?" he asked again.

"You really don't know?"

"I really don't."

"They are usually men who make sure all the real guests are sufficiently entertained. They dance, they chat, they fetch champagne and cake. They pretend to be guests, but they make sure the party keeps going and that no one has a bad time."

It took a moment for Eli to grasp the concept. After a moment, he said flatly, "You're kidding."

"No," she said, smiling. "Why would I kid?"

"Come on, Marnie, you're pulling my leg. There's no such thing as a professional guest."

"There is too! Think about it—you wouldn't want to shell out this kind of dough for a wedding and then Aunt Cloris has a really bad time, right?"

"I would trust Aunt Cloris to take care of herself," he said, walking down the steps of the porch.

"But what if Aunt Cloris can't get the attention of someone as suave as you, Cowboy? Then what?"

"Then she can talk to Uncle Harry. Are we *paying* these people?"

"Of course." Marnie laughed, bouncing down the steps behind him. "We have two men coming, and they get a five-hundred-dollar per diem, plus room and board, and then a thousand each for the night of the wedding."

Eli stopped so abruptly that Marnie almost plowed into him. He slapped a hand over his heart as he turned around to face her. "No way," he said, shaking his head. "Please don't tell me that we are paying two gay men almost five grand to dance with Aunt Cloris."

"Okay, I won't tell you that," she said, her smile fading. "But we are."

With a heavy sigh, Eli looked heavenward for strength. "How come I didn't know this?"

"It was in the original budget I submitted for your supreme approval, and maybe if you'd call every once in a while, you might know what was going on."

"I *did* call," he reminded her, "and you said everything was cool."

"Because it was. It is. What did you think I was going to say, everything's a mess? That I can't do my job without your oversight? This wedding is right on budget, pal, and by the way, just why *did* you call? To tell me you were really what?" she demanded, her hands going to her hips.

Suddenly, Eli was irritated. He was tired, and confused, and still miffed they were going to pay those jokers five grand to dance with old broads. Add to that a bunch of useless feathers and God knew what else and he was beginning to feel like a jester in Queen Olivia's court.

"Well?" she insisted.

Now that little demand made it worse, because she said it in a tone that implied she had some right to him, that he owed her a phone call, which he did not, and it didn't set too well with Eli. He lifted a heated gaze to her. "I called to say I was counting on you to take charge and not muck this up."

Marnie's eyes narrowed. She angrily swatted at a bug or something that went flying past. "Is that all?" she asked in a voice that was deathly low.

"Yes. Why do you ask?"

"Oh, no reason," she snapped, and suddenly stepped around him, marching toward the bridge. "I guess I just thought maybe you called to assure me that you wouldn't be so rude as to ride off into the damn sunset without telling me so much as to kiss your ass!"

"Riding off into the sunset?" he bellowed. "What the hell does that mean? In case you have forgotten, I left you a message, but at last look, I really don't have to explain myself to you."

"No, you sure don't!" she shouted over her shoulder. "You don't have to do anything but bark orders and pass judgment on other people's weddings. It's a mystery to me why someone as anti-wedding as you would be so involved in this."

This was going nowhere fast. Eli caught up to Marnie as she reached the trail down to the bridge, and stayed on her heels until they reached the bridge. When he tried to help her, she slapped his hand from her elbow. "I can do it," she snapped. "I had to pass wedding boot camp 101, remember?" She grabbed the rope railing, bent over as far as she could, and made her way across like a duck.

Eli walked across, gestured for her to get on the four-wheeler, then got on in front of her, cringing at the feel of her body around his. Goddammit, why did a woman with a mouth like Marnie's have to feel so damn *good?*

He started the thing up and went racing down the mountain, ignoring Marnie's little shrieks of surprise and terror at his reckless driving. When they reached the lodge, Marnie slid off the back before he could turn it off and said, "If it's all right with you, Herr Commandant, I've got stuff to do."

"I don't give a damn what you do," he muttered.

With a *harrumph*, Marnie pivoted sharply and marched back to the lodge while Eli watched the very sexy wiggle of her butt in those tight fleece pants.

She could just go to hell for being so goddamn cute.

CHAPTER EIGHTEEN

The two professional guests, John and Jim, were more than happy to check all the china and ensure it had arrived intact and in sufficient quantities. Because of their help, Marnie was able to do some other work and then join the rest of the group later for dinner. After a plate of enchiladas and a couple of glasses of wine, Marnie followed everyone outside, all bundled up in her brand-new double-fleece jacket, to sit around a large campfire in one of three bonfire pits the lodge maintained on the front lawn.

Sitting in Adirondack chairs and feeling very groovy (since when did a couple of glasses of wine make her feel so mellow?), Marnie tried to engage Olivia in a chat about her canyoning experience, but quickly learned that Olivia wasn't as thrilled with the experience as she had been during the filming of *The Dane*, when she'd let the stunt double do the really hard stuff. "It was the most miserable experience I've ever endured," Olivia avowed. "You won't believe what they expected me to do! Anyway, I don't want to talk about that. Where's my dress?"

"In a very safe place," Marnie assured her. Just like her shoes, about which Olivia had already asked. But as Marnie was feeling no pain (maybe it was a different kind of wine?), she smiled happily at stars that seemed close enough to reach up and grab and convinced Olivia that everything was fine.

When Olivia was certain that her clothes were accounted for, she began to talk about that damn arch (which had likewise arrived today, a familiar landmark looking so oddly out of place), and how she did not like where they intended to put it. "It will ruin everything," she sniffed between sips of her apple martini. I don't *want* it next to the lake. I want it on the other side of the clearing. The guests might have to walk a little farther, but really, after the party I've treated them to, is that too much to ask?"

Actually, Marnie thought asking for the arch to begin with was a bit too much.

"I don't see what difference it makes," Olivia petulantly continued. "It's not like they can't land it on one side of the lake or the other."

"Olivia, will you shut up about that damn arch?" Vince groused.

"If you tell me to shut up once more, Vince, I swear I am going to walk out of here."

"Go ahead," he said. You won't make it to the main road before a bear gets you."

"Omigod, how long are we going to keep the bear gag going?" she groused while Vince and the TA guys laughed. Well, all the TA guys except Eli, the uptight killjoy who had not deigned to come out tonight.

"Sleeping," Michael said when Jack asked.

"Sleeping my ass," Cooper snorted. "I bet he's sniffing around the cocktail waitress."

"There's a *cocktail* waitress?" Michael asked, wide-eyed.

Marnie sort of had the same question, and really, the fact that Eli was hanging out with some chick did not give her a warm fuzzy feeling—it pissed her off. He'd probably argue she had no right to be pissed off. He had, after all, officially stated his position about *them* in LA, even if he did blow it by kissing her, but nevertheless he had reiterated said position, perhaps not in so many words, but in attitude, just this afternoon. Nevertheless, Marnie had to endure several more days of him, and she would really prefer it if he wasn't diddling the cocktail waitress while they were trying to work.

"Hey kid, you want a nip of this?" Cooper asked, and held up a flask to Marnie. "Brandy," he said with a wink. "It'll keep you warm."

"Nothing else will," she said smartly, and grabbed the flask and took a long swallow.

"Careful," Cooper said laughingly. "Remember the altitude. That stuff will go directly to your head if you're not careful."

Whatever that meant. And anyway, Marnie was past the point of caring, and took another long swallow. And apparently several more, because the next morning, she woke up with a raging headache, feeling exhausted and out of sorts and trying to remember how exactly she'd made it to her room last night.

Her mood was not improved by the discovery of a note that had been shoved under her door.

Marnie—be ready with your gear by 11 a.m.
E.

"All right, *Eeeee*," she snapped and headed for a hot shower.

She was waiting outside an hour later with her backpack on her back so that her hands were free to hold up her head. That was where Rhys joined her wearing a baby-blue ski suit in spite of it being late summer. She thought, as he ranted about not having enough time to make the cake, and when would his help arrive, that the suit made him look a little like the Michelin man.

"Are you going to be okay in that?" Marnie finally asked, unable to bear watching him go on about the cake in that suit. "The temperatures get up in the fifties in the summer, but it feels much warmer because we are closer to the sun."

"How do *you* know?" Rhys demanded gruffly. "Have you read as much in your little travel book?"

"Well...yeah," Marnie said, slightly injured. "It's been pretty accurate so far."

"I *must* be here at precisely eight a.m. or there will be no wedding cake!" he insisted loudly.

"All *right*, Rhys," she said irritably and put a hand to her throbbing head. "Just set your alarm and be here at precisely eight."

"And how do you suppose I will set the alarm in a tent?" he demanded.

Oh for chrissakes, what a drama queen. "There is no tent, Rhys. We'll be back here tonight," she said as a boy pulled up on a four-wheeler and gestured for her to climb on. Marnie did not hesitate to do just that. "Just calm down, and everything will be all right!" she shouted at Rhys as they drove away.

Those were, she would muse weeks later, her proverbial famous last words.

When she reached the bridge, Rhys right behind her, several surefooted boys were already there carrying boxes and coolers and God knew what all across the rope bridge. On the other side was Herr Commandant directing the boys, looking disgustingly sexy in a pair of faded jeans, boots, and a lined corduroy shirt over a tee.

Marnie was the first to cross the bridge, slowly and carefully, and when she landed on the other side, she swore she saw his blue eyes crinkle in something close to a smile. "Morning," he said.

"Whatever," she muttered irritably, and was about to make a smart-ass remark, but Rhys was practically weeping with fear on the other side of the ravine. "Just hold on to the rail," Eli called out to Rhys, then sighed, shoved a hand through his thick hair, and pointed to a stack of stuff behind him. "That's your gear," he said to Marnie, stepping past her.

"I have my gear," Marnie said, turning slightly so he could see her backpack.

"I mean the bedrolls and tents for you and the cake man," he said. "You can pitch it next to mine—you'll see it when you get to the clearing...Yes, it will hold you," he shouted at Rhys.

"I can't do it, Mr. McCain! I simply can't do it!" Rhys was sobbing.

"Yes, you can," Eli called, his voice reassuring. "Just hold on tight, don't look down, and walk across."

"A tent?" Marnie said, trying to get the words *bedroll* and *tent* to click somewhere in her brain. "What do you mean, a tent?" she asked.

"That's great, Chef," Eli called out. "Just a few feet more!" And then, in a low aside, "What's the guy's name, again?"

"Rhys. Did you forget to tell me something?"

"Like what?" he asked, watching Rhys.

"Oh, I don't know. That you're fond of the cocktail waitress. That I'm sleeping in a tent. Yep, I'm pretty sure that not once did the word *tent* or *cocktail waitress* come out of your mouth."

He shifted his gaze from Rhys to her. "What in the hell are you talking about?" he asked calmly. "Okay, how's this? You're sleeping in a tent. And I'm not fond of any cocktail waitress that I am aware."

"Since when?"

"Since when have I not been fond of a cocktail waitress? Or since when are you sleeping in a tent? Look, Marnie, there's not enough room at the lodge for everyone coming in today, and there is a lot to be done up here. Chef Boyardee is going to join us up here, too, because our blushing bride must have all her meals specially prepared, and they are moving into the cabin today."

The cocktail waitress was suddenly forgotten because Marnie could only think of sleeping among bears. "You mean we're going to *camp* up here? And Rhys is going to cook for us?"

"Didn't Jack tell you this? Yes, we're going to camp up here. But Chef Boyardee brought food for the stars and himself. Not you and me. We schlubs will eat what the lodge brings up. And not a cocktail waitress—probably one of these guys. So do me a favor and get your tent set up," he said, glancing back at the trail to the cabin. "Jack is flying the arch up here, and we'll need all hands to get it down."

Marnie looked at the tents and bedrolls laid out on the ground. But what about showers? What about *bathrooms?*

Eli reached for Rhys as he neared the end of the bridge and helped him to terra firma. "See? You made it. The bridge is intact and so are you, dude."

"Only by the grace of God," Rhys muttered, and dragged a sleeve across his perspiring brow.

Okay, Marnie was into adventure as much as the next person, but no one had bothered to tell her that she'd be sleeping on the bare ground with strange animals, and it only added to her general irritation. With a heated glare for Eli, she snatched up a tent and bedroll, stuffed them under her arms, and started up the trail to the clearing. Only the tent and bedroll were heavy, and the trail seemed a lot steeper today than yesterday. By the time they reached the clearing, Marnie was laboring as much as Rhys.

This day was really beginning to blow.

In the clearing, one tent was already set up, just as Herr Commandant had said, beneath the trees near the ravine. It was a nice big tent, too, the kind nomad kings from Mongolia probably used. Marnie dropped her stuff next to it, dumped the contents of the tent bag, and out came the tent and several poles. But no instructions. *No instructions!*

She spent a few minutes examining the pieces, which gave His Royal Majesty time to get up to the clearing, carrying a huge box on his shoulders with not so much as a single bead of perspiration on his face. He walked by her and glanced at all the pieces of her tent as he passed. He put the box down near the lake, then turned around and walked back. He squatted on the ground next to the mess she'd made. Then he looked up as the Michelin man lumbered by.

"Do me a favor," he said quietly. "Give Rhys a hand pitching his tent, will you?"

"Help him?" She leaned across the tent pieces and pinned him with a look. "There are no instructions."

"For what?" Eli asked in all seriousness.

"For what! The *tent*, that's what!"

He looked as if he couldn't comprehend those words. "It's just a tent, Marnie. It doesn't need instructions." He picked up one end of the tent. "This is the top. That's the bottom. Here are the poles you put through these tabs," he said. "Got it?"

"I know that," she said, snatching the tent from his hand, but she didn't know it at all. She didn't know it even a little, because the whole time he was across from her, she'd noticed a couple of well-worn areas of his jeans that frankly were strategic and intriguing and infuriating.

He rose back up to his full height and glanced at Rhys. "So...can you, like, wrap this up here?" he asked, gesturing in a wrap-it-up way. "We've got a lot of work to do, and we can't spend the whole day on basic tent assembly 101."

"Oh yeah, I'm sure you've got a lot of work to do in the cocktail lounge," she said and picked up her tent.

He sighed and put his hands to his waist. "Marnie, I don't know what this is about a cocktail waitress, but I have not set foot in the lodge bar. I have been working pretty much round the clock the last few days. So whatever the problem is, let's just move on past, all right? We've got a goddamn wedding to get through."

"Fine. Whatever," she said.

"Great," Eli bit out, and walked on. Marnie stuck her tongue out at his back, admired his butt for the thousandth time, then futzed with the pieces he'd shown her.

"Oh for heaven's sake," Rhys said from behind her after several minutes of her futzing. Marnie glanced over her shoulder—and her mouth dropped open. Rhys had not only assembled his tent, he had already unrolled his bedding and placed it inside the tent. The Michelin man marched to Marnie's side, took the pole from her hand, then the tent. "It's really quite simple," he said with much superiority, and in minutes, he'd assembled her tent. "There you are. You need only to stake it securely, and you will enjoy a good night's sleep."

"Rhys…thanks!" she said with great delight and surprise as she admired her tent. A tent that was, she couldn't help noticing, considerably smaller than the other two it was sandwiched between. She'd been lucky enough to pick up a pup tent.

"You are quite welcome. And for the record, that man was not in the bar last evening, I can assure you, because I was, and I would have definitely taken note of him, along with any cocktail waitress."

"Ah," Marnie said. Wasn't this just grand? Now she felt like an even bigger fool. "Thanks."

"You are very welcome. Now if you would be so kind as to show me the facilities, I really must begin preparing the midday meal for Olivia. She's hypoglycemic, you know."

No, she didn't know, but Marnie was not surprised. Olivia had a little of everything. Money. Looks. Weird diseases and religions.

She showed Rhys the cabin, which he instantly proclaimed totally inadequate for his needs, but he went to work nonetheless, fishing things out of one of the three coolers that had been brought up to the cabin. Marnie left him just in time for the arrival of Vince and Olivia, which, she thought, might as well have been on a red carpet.

For one thing, all the local boys TA had hired were following Olivia with their mouths gaping open. She walked slowly and serenely, smiling beatifically at the mountain peaks that surrounded them, the sparkling lake, the luxurious little cabin. It was almost as if she were filming a scene.

"Marnie!" she called as she glided through the tall grass.

"Hey, Olivia."

"Isn't it beautiful? Isn't it exactly as I described? Look," she said, slipping an arm around Marnie's waist and resting her little head against Marnie's shoulder, "that's where we filmed the last scene. You know, the one where I find Vince dying? I think that was some of my best work. Of course, I was inspired by the beauty of this little place."

"It is beautiful," Marnie agreed.

"I knew you'd like it," she said, smiling up at Marnie, She let go and stretched her arms to the sky. "Oh my, I am so tired. I think I'll rest now." With a very loud yawn, she wandered up the steps to the cabin and disappeared inside.

"Hey," Vince said absently as he jogged past Marnie and followed Olivia inside.

"Hey," Marnie said to his back. She turned around and looked at the meadow. At the moment, two boys were carrying up bottled water and chairs. That reminded her—she had a lot of work to do, too.

She spent most of the day going back and forth between the lodge, carrying up everything Olivia and Vince would need for the actual ceremony (and very carefully, too, as the bridge creaked and moaned and really gave her the creeps)—their clothes, the paperwork. Michael and Jim and John helped her out by checking in everything they would need for the reception, which was arriving as frequently as guests, in big trucks that rumbled up the gravel drive, the screech of their low gears echoing through the mountains.

By midafternoon, the lodge was almost filled with people ready for a party. All the stuff Marnie had ordered had arrived, save the flowers, which would arrive fresh in the morning, and the reception tent had been fully erected, its four peaks mimicking the mountains. Marnie and Michael took a couple of local boys and went over the table arrangement with them—they would set up the tables on the wedding day and then Marnie, Jim, and John would begin laying out linens, crystal, and floral arrangements.

While Marnie reviewed everything with Jim and John, Operation Arch was underway, signaled by Jack's arrival in the helicopter from Durango, where it had spent the night in a hangar. Marnie got a ride back up the mountain from one of the local boys so she could make sure the arch and altar were set correctly.

In the clearing, Eli, Cooper, and Vince were waiting to receive the arch. Marnie joined them to wait, too, idly watching the dark clouds forming behind one of the mountain peaks. "Looks like rain," she said to Cooper, nodding in that direction.

He glanced at the clouds. "Monsoon season. It's typical to get showers in the afternoons and evenings." He shifted his gaze in the opposite direction, where the arch would appear. "Nothing to worry about. The summer storms usually clear out as fast as they come in."

Marnie looked at the clouds. It didn't rain a lot in LA, so she really didn't know, but the dark-purple and midnight-blue clouds looked awfully menacing. But she quickly forgot it when she heard the crackle of a radio. It was Jack on the other end, telling Eli they were ready to bring it up. A moment later, they heard the whir of a helicopter starting up.

The sound obviously woke up Sleeping Beauty, because Olivia came stumbling out of the cabin, squinting at them and the lake, where four bright orange stakes had been planted.

"Oh no," Olivia shouted over the noise the helicopter was making below. "No, no, no, *no!*"

"What is it now?" Vince snapped with exasperation.

"I *told* you! I don't want it there. I want it on the other side of the lake in that beautiful clearing."

"There isn't room enough over there, Olivia," Cooper said calmly.

"Yes there *is.*" she shrieked. "I want it over there."

Cooper, Marnie, and Eli looked at Vince. Vince threw back his head and roared, "Good *God* will someone please burn that fucking arch?"

"I'm the *fucking* bride, Vince! And I don't *fucking* want it there. Why doesn't anyone give a *fuck* what *I* want?" Olivia shrieked the last question so loudly that a flock of birds lifted from the trees behind the cabin. She whirled around and stormed back inside. A scant moment later, Rhys came running out as if he'd seen the Texas chainsaw guy.

"Goddammit!" Vince shouted as the arch rose above the trees and headed right for them. He probably never even saw it—he'd gone racing into the cabin after Olivia. But Marnie saw it, and she stood, dumbfounded, as three hundred pounds of plastic flew right at them.

CHAPTER NINETEEN

Somehow, Marnie, Eli, and Cooper managed to get the arch down. With a lot of grunting and shoving and moving the thing this way and that, they got it anchored and tied down with two bungee lines at each corner.

The sun was beginning to sink behind the mountaintops when Cooper returned to the lodge, catching a ride with the guy who brought food up for Eli and Marnie. After they devoured the food—they were all ravenous—Eli, Marnie, and Rhys sat around the fire Eli had so effortlessly built and listened to the sounds of what Eli said were night owls, distant coyotes, and lynx, until the rising wind drowned them out with the rustling of trees around them...and what the wind didn't cover, the fighting in the cabin did.

Somewhere between the pan-fried steak and crème brûlée Rhys had prepared, the soon-to-be-weds had begun to argue.

Marnie felt dizzy—everything seemed out of sync now. The happy couple fought bitterly, the stars disappeared behind black clouds, and a bone-chilling wind made her headache even worse. She'd had the headache since she and Eli had argued yesterday, but at some point this afternoon, it had begun to pound like a drum.

Rhys turned in, tired and cold and surprisingly happy to wander off to sleep with his coolers, which he insisted on having in the tent with him. Marnie watched him go off, grimacing slightly at the pain in her head.

At the sound of a thud in the cabin, Eli turned and looked at the door. "I hope we didn't fly that arch up here for nothing," he said, wincing a little when the *thud* was followed by the sound of glass breaking.

"Pre-wedding jitters. A lot of brides go off a day or two before the big event," Marnie muttered. "It's to be expected."

"I give it two years, max," Eli said, as the cabin door suddenly opened and a pair of boots came flying out onto the grass below the porch.

Marnie watched the boots roll to a stop. "That's ridiculous—a year at most."

Eli looked at Marnie with some surprise and smiled. Marnie tried to smile, but she couldn't manage it and rubbed her forehead. Eli's smile faded into a look of concern. Oh yeah, right, she thought bitterly.

"What's the matter, Marn? Are you all right?"

"I have a raging headache, if you must know."

"Ah," he said with a knowing nod, shoved a hand into the pocket of his jeans. "Did you ever hear of altitude sickness?"

"Yes, Eli, of course I have," she said irritably. "But we're not exactly climbing Mount Everest here."

"What does that mean?"

Was he kidding? "Mountain climbers who go way up get altitude sickness. Not people like us, just somewhere in the mountains," she said, waving her hand at the somewhere they happened to be.

"Somewhere in the mountains," he echoed and withdrew a tin of aspirin from his pocket and shook out two.

"This may not be Mount Everest, but you came from zero feet above sea level to eleven thousand feet above. Your body is bound to react to the altitude, and that headache of yours is a primary symptom." He took her hand, turned it palm up, and put the aspirin there, then reached for a bottle of water nearby. "It takes the body a couple or three days to adjust to the oxygen deprivation." He handed her the water. "Take the aspirin, get a good night's sleep, and you'll feel immeasurably improved by morning," he said with a wink.

She really wished he wouldn't wink. He was so sexy when he winked, and she could picture him, dipping his hat at her, winking, before he rode off into the Texas wilderness to find his lost brother or something. *"But Sheriff, when will you come back to us?"* *"Aw, now, Miss Banks, don't go waiting on me. I'll come back in the spring…if the Indians and the vermin don't get me first. You take care of yourself and Rufus, Miss Banks."*

Rufus? Who the hell was Rufus? Marnie shook her head. "Thanks," she said and popped the aspirin into her mouth, chased them down with some water. "I think I'm going to take your advice and turn in."

"Well, hell, we're making some progress here," he said with a grin. "You're taking my advice."

"Only because I'm incapacitated. Don't get used to it," she said and stood up, giving him a begrudging smile before walking on.

She went to her tent, grabbed a little bag of toiletries, and headed for the outhouse, conveniently equipped with a pump sink for those poor souls who did not have access to the cabin. When she emerged, she tiptoed around the back of the cabin, but as she neared the corner, she stopped, her mouth agape. Was that *moaning?* The kind that went along with hot monkey love? Dear God, it hadn't been fifteen minutes since the boots had come flying out the door and here they were, going at it again. What was it with those two? Whatever it was, they were definitely getting it on.

Some people had all the luck.

Marnie marched on around the corner and down the path to the tents. Eli was still at the fire, staring into it, his eyes on something a thousand miles from this mountain. Interesting. What was he thinking? What he had to do for the wedding? His next extreme sport? If he should get down to the lodge to meet the cocktail waitress she'd gone on and on about like an idiot?

Maybe he was thinking about all the reasons he'd be glad to be rid of her, she thought petulantly and crawled inside her tent, managed to squirm out of her clothes and pull on her pajama pants and a thermal shirt. She stuffed her clothes and toiletries into her backpack and crawled into her sleeping bag.

Surprisingly, she had no trouble drifting off to sleep. It was as if the stress of the last couple of days had finally caught up with her—plus the fact that her bedroll was nice and cozy and unexpectedly comfortable. And okay, the utter tranquility of the mountaintop was soothing. The wind was like a lullaby, and she felt herself sliding into a deep sleep.

It really wasn't until later—how much later, she had no idea—that the sound of thunder startled her from her sleep.

At the top of the world, stars seem close enough to touch. Thunder also seems a whole hell of a lot closer. Like in the tent with her. Marnie didn't like it so close, and pulled the sleeping bag over her head, trying to muffle the sound of it, but it was impossible. The wind was picking up something awful, and it was obvious the storm was moving toward her, not away.

Cooper had said these storms passed quickly, and she lay there hoping it would rush right by. But then rain began to fall, big sheets of torrential rain, pounding so hard on the tent that she feared it would give way. Still, Marnie was determined not to be a big baby about a storm...until the crack of lightning striking something very nearby scared her out of her wits. She came up like a shot, unzipped the tent, and looked outside into a downpour. The wind was blowing so hard now that it actually lifted one corner of her tent.

With the second gust, Marnie had an image of herself rolling down to the bottom of the ravine, tumbling and crashing into rocks. The next gust convinced her; with a shriek, she grabbed her backpack and darted outside. She was quickly soaked through and freezing—the sting of rain on her face felt more like shards of ice. She crawled the fifteen feet on all fours to Eli's tent. "Eli!" she shouted, and groped for the zipper of his tent. Another clap of thunder on top of her and she screamed.

The flap of the tent suddenly came open and whipped away. Eli was on the other side, reaching for her with two strong hands, dragging her through the entrance and quickly zipping it up again.

"What the hell?" he asked calmly in pitch blackness. "You should have stayed in your tent—you could have been struck by lightning!"

"I know, I know." Jesus, her teeth were chattering.

A flare of soft light startled her; Eli had a small kerosene lamp, just enough light to read by or, in Marnie's case, to get a good look at Eli in his thermal shirt and boxer shorts.

Eli didn't notice—he was too busy frowning at her. With his big hands he pushed her wet hair away from her eyes and behind her ears. He clutched both sides of her head and lifted her face up to his, studying her. "Are you all right?"

"Yes. *No!* The storm is on top of us, and I thought I was going to blow away."

"Yeah, it's a bad one," he said, just as another crack and flare of light shattered the dark around them. He ignored it and rummaged through his bag, pulling out a long-sleeved tee. "Here," he said. "Put this on. You're soaked through."

"No, no, that's okay."

"It's not okay. You could get hypothermia." He thrust the shirt at her. "The pants come off, too."

With a sniff, Marnie reluctantly took the shirt and shifted around as best she could in the tent, took off her shirt with her back to him, glanced over her shoulder to see him watching her intently, then hastily pulled the T-shirt over her head. She glanced over her shoulder again—he had stretched out on the sleeping bag, one leg bent at the knee, obviously enjoying the show. She frowned at him and artfully wiggled out of her pajama pants.

Eli watched her—or her legs, rather—with a look that sent a warm rush of blood through her. But another crack of lightning brought her back to her senses. She glanced fearfully at his tent, expecting it to rip away from the poles. "This is really bad, isn't it?" she asked as the rain beat down on the nylon.

"It's a little freakish," he admitted. He threw open the top layer of his sleeping bag and slid his bare legs into it. "Come on...get in."

Now the warm blood spread to her face. "That's really not a good idea," she said, shaking her head. "We're, ah… we're not going there, remember?"

"You have a better idea? Come on, coppertop—it's freezing. It's not a declaration or an invitation—it's survival."

She might have argued, but it was freezing and another rip of thunder and a gust of wind sent her into the sleeping bag with him.

Eli covered them up, zipping the thing all the way around so that they were snugly ensconced. In deference to their mutual agreement not to go there, Marnie turned on her side, but Eli spooned her, putting his arm around her waist and holding her tightly to him.

The wind was whipping the tent; another crack of lightning struck something nearby, eerily illuminating the world outside, and Marnie scrunched down deeper in the warmth of his bag. "Is it possible this could be a tornado?" she asked.

"No," he said softly, his breath warm on the back of her neck. "Don't be afraid—this will pass. We won't blow away, I promise."

Marnie wished she could believe him, but groaned softly at a succession of thunder and lightning claps. The wind was so fierce that the tent seemed to be sliding along. "We're moving!" she said desperately.

Beneath the cover of his thermal bag, Eli caressed her arm. "We're not moving, Marnie. We're staked down all the way to China."

Staked. Shit! She'd forgotten to stake her tent. No wonder she'd felt the corner lift. She squeezed her eyes shut, could feel a tear slip from the corner of one.

"Marnie?"

She couldn't answer, because if she did, she'd scream.

"It's all right, coppertop," he said soothingly into her ear. "It's all right." And he continued to caress her arm, his hand amazingly soft for one so large and callused. She hoped he'd never stop, that he'd keep caressing her arm, and that if he couldn't do it forever, that he would at least do it until the storm passed. But then his hand went to her hair, stroking it, his fingers carefully moving the wet, tangled tresses from her face.

She wasn't so cold anymore. She could feel her limbs warming, the blood in her swirling around, spreading out in a hot stream. The memory of the night they were together was suddenly the only thing on her mind. The storm raging around them was fading in her consciousness and being replaced by the memory of how it felt to have him cover her body, to move inside her.

The release of her breath was inadvertent, like the leak of air from a balloon, long and soft. Eli draped a leg around her, pulled her into his body, and his hand slipped up beneath the T-shirt she wore. His fingers were rough; the feel of them on her skin ignited her as he rolled the peak of her breast between his fingers and filled his hand with her. That was when Marnie rolled over and buried her face in his neck, surrendering her fear to him.

The rain continued relentlessly, pounding the tent in hard sheets while thunder shattered the air around them. But the storm was only a distant noise to Marnie— suddenly, there was nothing but a rough-and-tumble cowboy and his girl, making love by the light of the campfire, beneath the stars and the shadow of horses. His hands moved expertly on her body, arousing her breasts, then skimming down to her bare leg, and up again, his fingers slipping carelessly and enticingly between her legs and the folds of her sex.

His mouth moved, too, sliding down to the breast he'd somehow managed to bare, and up, to her shoulder, and her neck, and her mouth again, which he filled with his tongue. He nipped at her lips, licked her cheek, and sucked on the lobe of her ear before descending to her breasts again to tease her nipples with his teeth.

All the while, his hands were moving, stroking and caressing her, making her slick with desire, then retreating to more untouched skin. Marnie stopped trying to keep pace with him; her arms moved upward, out of the bag and above her head, and she closed her eyes, let her head drift to one side as he moved so smoothly across her body.

When he came over her, straddling her legs, his cock pressed into her belly, he smiled wickedly at her in the dim glow of the kerosene lamp, and he very adroitly unzipped the bag. "I love the taste of you," he said, nipping at her lips.

"Taste," she repeated breathlessly, incapable of speech.

"Yeah... *taste*," he growled, and moved down her body, his mouth trailing little bites on her skin, his hands moving to her hips. Marnie's knees came up and apart, and as he sank between them, she gasped—his tongue plunged into her deep and hard, then feathered her with little strokes, up and down, circling around, circling and nipping and teasing her until she couldn't bear it. She would die with longing, she was sure of it, so close to release yet so very far from it. And when she thought she would cry out with the agony of wanting it, his mouth closed around her, his teeth lightly nibbled her, and his tongue danced across her clit.

Marnie lifted her hips to him, moving in primal rhythm to his mouth. And then she was falling away, bits of her raining down as she came with atomic force. Her heart pounded with the exertion of the explosion in her, and she gulped the cold mountain air.

Eli slowly made his way up her body, retracing the path of his mouth, his breath hot on her skin. And when he reached her head, he sank his hand into her hair, his fingers reaching for the back of her head, and he slowly sank his cock into her with a long sigh of relief. He moved fluidly inside her, gliding in and out, the rhythm fast and furious as his hand moved through her hair, to her neck, her chin, and her hair again as his tempo increased. When he at last reached his release, he groaned against her skin, his breath hot and his voice deep and roughened with pleasure.

A moment later, breathing hard, Eli slid off her but not out of her—he pulled Marnie to her side, keeping her close to his chest and his warmth.

She pressed her cheek against his shoulder, smiled as he brushed her hair from his face, and thought she'd never felt so safe or warm in her life.

Nor so sated.

Or close.

In that tent, on top of the world, Eli was the only warmth. She loved him. She knew she did, she loved him, and she didn't want anything to move so she wouldn't lose the moment.

At some point, she realized the storm had moved north, and the downpour had slackened to a hard rain. Marnie drifted easily into sleep, knowing that in his arms, the world was safe and impossibly still.

CHAPTER TWENTY

Eli woke at dawn the next morning in something of a panic, first of all, because he'd made love to Marnie last night—mind-altering, killer sex—and second, because waking up next to that woman gave him a boner the size of a pine tree.

He looked at her lying next to him—all leg, strands of copper hair strewn across her face, the hint of a guileless smile on her lips even in sleep. She was beautiful to him. And honestly, did anyone look as sexy as she did in an old T-shirt? It was pretty damn hard not to think about how good she'd tasted and felt and how fantastic that ride in the storm had been.

Hence the enormous erection.

It left him feeling a little scarce of breath, so Eli got out of the tent for some air. Yep, he'd gone and done something stupid, just like he'd told himself not to do. But he was falling hard down a hole, he recognized all the signs of it, and it scared the shit out of him. After being paralyzed these last months by hurt gashed so deep that he once thought he'd drown in it, he was now feeling—and acutely so—a bitter conflict of emotions. It was fear, that gnawing fear of... what? Something. Bits of him were falling away every time he was with her, hard, thick bits—yet she hadn't reached the soft core, that hot, massive thing that kept him shackled.

He felt strangely hopeful, although that pissed him off and made him feel like the putz again. He felt what he thought might be love, too, although he wasn't certain, because he was confused as to what love truly was, but he was fairly sure those were the mewling sounds of it deep inside him. And he felt resentment, too, because he didn't want to feel love—he was too afraid of it. He was too afraid of needing it.

God, he was a mess. Thankfully, no one else was up, and he thought to clear his head with a jog down to the lodge for some coffee. He zipped up his jacket, ran his fingers through his hair with a yawn, then turned...and noticed Marnie's tent was gone.

Just *gone*.

He walked toward the ravine, looking around and behind rocks. When he reached the edge, he looked down and saw something gray. Well, shit. That had been some storm all right—that was Marnie's tent down at the bottom of the ravine. She must not have staked it very well.

He turned around, walked back up the meadow, and noticed for the first time that beyond the tents, there were two pines down that he could see, sprawled across the trail to the bridge. And another still smoking from where lightning had struck and knocked its top off. Even worse, he couldn't see that damn arch. He hurried up a rise in the meadow and stopped in the middle of it.

That damn plastic arch was lying on its back, half in the lake, floating peacefully. It would take them forever to get it up. The antique altar they'd struggled to get up here yes-

terday was gone, too. Eli suspected it was lying beneath the
arch in the alpine lake, and began striding in that direction.

Just as he suspected—tipped over by the arch, just visi-
ble below the surface of the shallow lake.

When he turned around to face the cabin, he saw that
the roof over the kitchen area had been damaged, and part
of it seemed to be missing altogether. He'd need help to get
it cleaned up, and walked on, past the cabin, climbing over
the two fallen pines. But when he reached the bottom, he
stopped. "Oh Jesus," he muttered.

Eli stood there, hands on hips, wondering how in the
hell they were going to fix this. Another massive pine tree
was dangling precariously across the bridge. Lightning had
obviously struck the tree—not unusual at this altitude—but
this tree was a monster. The bridge itself was damaged— the
rope had come undone on one side, which meant that the
bridge, which had seemed to him to be weakening yesterday
with all the traffic across it, wasn't very stable at all today. It
wasn't safe. It was impassable.

Eli moved closer; he could see parts of the bridge plank-
ing below in the river, already being pushed away by the
rushing water.

Damn it all to hell, they were stuck until they could get
this fixed. Even worse, a hot cup of coffee was on the other
side.

This was the last damn thing they needed, the icing on
the goddamn cake. He turned around to go back to the
meadow and get his radio.

When he climbed back up to the meadow, some of
the natives were up and about. In particular, Rhys was
ranting at Marnie, who seemed oblivious to the fat man

as she peered up at the treetops as if she were looking for something.

"Ah, there you are!" Rhys shouted when he saw Eli. Marnie instantly turned toward him and her face lit up with a smile that got him right in the gut.

He tried to smile, too, but Rhys was suddenly in his face. "I've a rather nasty dilemma, sir. I seem to have lost my case of cooking utensils and I cannot possibly prepare the wedding food without it. I shall require a search party."

"A *search* party?"

"Yes! A search party. Those utensils and knives are very expensive and worth thousands of dollars."

"Have you seen my tent?" Marnie asked as Eli calmly considered which planet to kick Rhys to.

"As a matter of fact, I have. It's at the bottom of the ravine...probably next to his utensils."

The fat man blanched. "Oh dear Lord, I think I shall be sick!" he declared dramatically, and went down in a heap, sitting cross-legged on the wet grass, staring in disbelief at the treeline.

"But...how will we get my tent back?" Marnie asked.

Eli looked at her. She blinked her big brown eyes and he could see the situation sinking into her head. Marnie did not pursue her line of questioning any further. "Wow," was all she said.

And then the pristine morning was rent by the wail of a screaming banshee when Olivia emerged and saw her precious arch floating serenely on the alpine lake.

"Calm down, Olivia," he called out to her, and dipped into his tent to grab his radio. When he emerged, Vince had walked out onto the porch wearing pajama pants and a fleece jacket, scratching his bare stomach. "Damn," he said, looking around the meadow. "That was some storm, huh?" He looked at Eli. "It took part of the roof off the cabin."

"This is a fucking disaster!" Olivia shrieked. "There is no way in hell we can get married in the middle of this fucking mess." She whipped around and came marching down the steps of the porch, her blond hair flying, her eyes blazing. "Eli! You need to get someone up here right away. I don't care how many people it takes, but I will not get married in this meadow tomorrow afternoon until this place is cleaned up."

"Olivia," Marnie tried, "we wouldn't dream of having you proceed until we—"

"I am speaking to Eli!" Olivia snapped.

"Olivia, calm down," Eli responded sharply, despising her for being so rude to Marnie. "It's not like any of us got up in the middle of the night and did this to you. It was a bad storm, and we'll do all that we can to fix things."

"You'd *better* fix it," she snapped again, her face going red.

Eli had seen her like this once before, on the set of *The Dane*, when she had brought production to a halt with a temper tantrum over a costume change that had made her look fat. As if it were possible to make anorexia look fat. But she'd been enraged, had stormed into her trailer and locked herself in until the producer and director agreed to her costume demands.

"Like I said, we'll do what we can. But at the moment, we've got a bit of a bigger problem than your goddamn arch. The bridge is impassable."

"Impassable? What does *that* mean?" Olivia demanded.

"It means there is a huge tree lying across it, it is unstable and impassable, and we can't cross it."

"Oh my God!" Olivia shrieked, and whirled around, grabbed onto Vince's fleece jacket, and glared up at him.

Vince stared at Eli, obviously confused. "Then...how do we get down?"

"Helicopter," Eli said. "I just need to talk to the guys. So everyone take a breath, all right? Everything is cool. I'll let you know what I find out."

"This isn't *cool*, this is un-fucking-believable," Olivia yelled. She pushed Vince away. "Rhys, could you please come with me?" she asked, and half ran, half walked to the cabin. Rhys glanced nervously at the others before walking after a tearful Olivia.

"Pre-wedding nerves," Marnie said confidently to Eli and Vince as they watched Olivia run up the steps of the cabin porch and trip, falling to her knees. She shrieked, got up, and ran into the cabin, banging the door shut in Rhys's face. "She'll be fine," Marnie added unconvincingly.

Eli and Vince said nothing, but exchanged a look that suggested neither man believed Olivia would be fine. Regardless, Eli had better things to do than watch Olivia's temper tantrum, and buzzed Cooper. And he buzzed him again. And a dozen times more until he finally got him. "Yo," Coop said.

"Dude, we've got a problem," Eli said.

"You don't even know the half of it," Cooper replied. "We've got no power and half that giant tent is gone and the rotor blade on the bird is damaged."

That was definitely bad news. "So what's Jack going to do?" Eli asked.

"He's going to Denver to get a new blade and a chopper mechanic. And then he's got to get a crane up here so they can replace the blade. We're talking two or three days here."

Eli glanced from the corner of his eye at Marnie, who was standing a few feet away, still wearing his tee, her hair a sexy mess, her boots untied. She looked very appealing. And very hopeful.

"Ah, well…that sort of puts a damper on my plans," Eli said, and turned his back to Marnie and walked away, out of hearing distance. "That goddamn bridge is about to be lying at the bottom of the ravine. Lightning knocked a pine right onto it."

"No shit?"

"No shit."

"Okay. Hold tight. I'll get Jack and Michael and we'll figure out what the hell we're going to do here."

"Just…do me a favor and hurry it up, will you?" Eli asked.

"Right," Coop said, and clicked off.

Eli forced a smile and turned around to Marnie. She had moved closer, waiting for him to speak. He was a little unnerved that he couldn't think of how to tell her the spot they were in. Not to mention any hope she had of a perfect wedding pretty much shot to shit.

"So?" she asked with a smile. "What's going on? They're just sitting down there having breakfast while we are starving up here, right? Ha ha."

Eli shook his head. "Not exactly. They had a little damage down there, too." Did he wince? He hadn't meant to wince. He'd definitely winced, judging by how quickly Marnie's smile faded.

"What sort of damage?" she asked, frowning darkly now.

"Well…they don't have power, for one."

"Okay…and?"

"And, ah…well, it seems that part of the reception tent is gone."

She gasped. "No!"

"Yes."

"No, no, no, not the tent!" she cried, horrified. "All the china and the linens were in there. And the chairs! The chairs and the tables and omigod, omigod, the *Cristal champagne!*" She suddenly grabbed his jacket and yanked him close. "Three hundred bottles of Cristal champagne, Eli. I've got to get down there right away."

"There's no way to get you down, coppertop."

She groaned loudly in agony, shoved two hands in her hair and dragged her fingers through, making it stick out even worse. "But if we can't get down, then how will they get up *here?*" she asked frantically.

Eli tried to smile. He patted her reassuringly on the shoulder. "Don't worry. We'll think of something. We're some pretty resourceful guys, right?"

"You mean we're stuck? We can't get out?"

"Hey, let's not jump to conclusions," he said with a weak laugh. "Just hang tight, and Coop will get back to us. In the meantime, let's go get something to eat. I don't think the lodge is delivering this morning, and that storm caused me to work up a pretty mean appetite," he said with a wink.

Marnie blushed. "That makes two of us," she admitted. "But Rhys didn't bring food for us."

"We'll bribe him," Eli said, and wrapped his arm around her shoulder, pulled her into his side, and led her up to the cabin.

The morning, unfortunately, did not improve for Eli. Rhys was affronted that Eli would even ask about eggs.

"I have no eggs and bacon," he all but spat as he withdrew two perfect quiches from the oven. "I did not bring my kitchen, sir—as you can see there are not proper storage facilities. I brought only what we'd need for six meals: two luncheons, two dinners, and two breakfasts. And tomorrow's breakfast is cheese and bread."

"Dude. You brought three enormous coolers up here," Eli argued. "Are you telling me you don't have a little bit of food to spare?"

With a *harrumph*, Rhys walked to one of the coolers and kicked it open with the toe of his shoe, then stood aside, his arms folded over his chest. Eli and Marnie inched forward to look inside. The cooler was filled with spices and various packages of sprouts.

"That's it?" Eli asked, peering in. "We carried up a cooler full of spices?"

"What do you think is the secret to my cooking? Now if you will kindly step out of my way, I will serve the quiches."

Eli looked over his shoulder. The lovebirds were sitting on the bed, cross-legged, facing each other. Vince was leaning forward, his hands on Olivia's knees, speaking low to her. Olivia was, predictably, crying, and words like *ruined* and *shattered* kept floating up. Eli turned back to Rhys, standing majestically beneath a small patch of blue sky where the roof had torn away. "Look," he said low, "I'll give you twenty bucks for one of those quiches. Give them one, sell us one."

"Are you insane?" Rhys whispered harshly. "Have you any idea how much one of these would bring in LA?"

"Make it thirty," Marnie whispered, nudging Eli in the side as she peeked back at Olivia and Vince.

"Thirty," Eli complained as he pulled out his wallet. "That's highway robbery!"

"You are privileged to even *taste* the food of Rhys." But the chef snatched the bills Eli held up and shoved the small dish at him in exchange.

"You're lucky I don't just take the damn thing," Eli groused. He grabbed Marnie's hand. "Come on," he said, pulling her out of the cabin, "let's eat."

Marnie grabbed a couple of forks from a basket on the kitchen table as Eli pulled her out of the cabin and onto the porch. They parked themselves on the plush wicker chairs on the porch; Marnie gave him a fork, and they balanced the dish on Eli's knee and dug in with the determination of two people who knew their next meal might not come for quite a while.

And they were both thankful for having forked over the thirty bucks a couple of hours later when Cooper called back and asked Eli and Marnie to come meet them at the ravine, because that was when they both knew their next meal could very well be tree bark.

Cooper, Jack, and Michael were on the other side. With Eli on this side, the four of them did a lot of walking back and forth and peering down into the ravine and talking on their radios while Marnie sat under a tree, her head propped in her hands, staring distantly.

They were arguing the merits of climbing over the tree when all four of them heard a snap. "Shit," Jack said, just as the bridge gave way, and its middle section, and the tree, crashed the one hundred yards to the bottom of the ravine and the raging river there. The four of them leaned over to have a look.

"Okay," Michael said a moment later. "We go to plan B. Anyone got a plan B?"

No one had a plan B, and after more pacing back and forth, the four men determined they were really in a pickle. At that point, Jack, Coop, and Michael got on their four-wheelers and headed down to do some more thinking. Eli strolled to where Marnie was sitting.

"So here's the deal," he said, dispensing with any chitchat. "They can get to Farmington to get what we need to repair the bridge, but the repair will probably take a couple days. They can bring in a chopper from Farmington or Durango to pull us out before then, but then everyone will know what's going on up here, and the press will descend like vultures and there probably won't be a wedding. That's the risk we take."

"Are you kidding? Olivia would just as soon leap into the ravine as have the press shooting her stuck up here without benefit of her makeup girl," Marnie said.

Eli grinned at her accurate assessment. "Jack can get us out, but he has to go to Denver to get a rotor blade, and pay someone a small fortune to come up and help him replace the blade. We're talking three to four days in that case."

"Can't we hike out?" Marnie asked, glancing at the ravine.

"Maybe Vince and I could. It's probably twenty miles around, mostly rough terrain and some of it very steep. I don't think the princess and Rhys could make it. Crossing the ravine would require a lot of rapelling, then climbing up, and I don't have the proper gear for that. I could possibly do it, but I can't leave anyone on this side."

She looked again at the ravine and shuddered. She could just see Eli hanging there by a thread and glanced up at him. "So…we're stuck for at least two days, and maybe as long as four?"

"Looks like."

"But…but what about the guests?" she asked, tossing a rock aside. "What about the wedding tomorrow? And the spiritual guy Ari who is going to marry them that I have to pick up from the airport in Durango? What about a *bathroom?*"

"Michael says he can handle the guests, not to worry. He's going to break out some of that champagne you had shipped up, if there's any left—"

"Oh *no*—"

"And the wedding will go down when and how Olivia and Vince want it, considering the circumstances. We can get someone to pick him up, and if we have to, we can bring them down here and have the spiritual guy marry them over the radio."

"All the planning, all the work," Marnie moaned, leaning her head against the tree trunk, her eyes squeezed shut.

"As for a bathroom…I don't know what to tell you, other than there is the outhouse and some very big rocks to step behind."

Rocks? Marnie's head snapped up. "But…but what about baths?"

He shrugged. Rubbed his hand on his nape. "Depending on how the firewood holds out, it may be a cold one."

"Oh. My. *God!*" she cried.

"Hey, it's not that bad," he said, his expression serious but his eyes shining with amusement as he held out his hand to her. "I think you smell pretty damn good."

"Maybe it's not me I'm worried about."

He laughed. "Come on, coppertop—let's go deliver the good news to the rest of the group."

Marnie looked at his hand and then at him. Eli read her mind and lifted one brow above the other. "I think we declared a truce last night, didn't we?"

She suddenly laughed and smiled that brilliant smile he'd missed the last couple of days as she put her hand in his. "I'll say."

Eli pulled her up; she popped up and landed so close to him that their bodies grazed each other. "But it's a truce only until we're out of here," she said, and poked him in the chest. "And then it's back to petty bickering as usual. Deal?"

Eli pushed some of her wild hair behind her ear. "Deal," he said, and affectionately touched his finger to her nose. As they turned around and walked to the cabin to deliver the news to the rest of them, Eli knew that for all his fretting, it was too damn late. He'd definitely fallen. Headlong.

CHAPTER TWENTY-ONE

After they delivered the bad news, there was a lot of loud arguing about it for a couple of hours. Olivia and Vince were adamant that no one find out they were stuck, lest the press have a field day with it. "Can you imagine the headlines?" Vince shouted. "World's Biggest Action Star Stuck on the Wrong Side of a Bridge!"

He glared at Rhys when the man had the audacity to laugh.

Eli wasn't crazy about it, either. "You think we want Thrillseekers Anonymous held out as the extreme sports outfit behind this fiasco?"

"You're all overreacting," Rhys said, as if he didn't mind being stuck on this side of the bridge. In fact, he was busily going through one of his coolers, muttering to himself.

As for Marnie, all she could think of was a bath, and where exactly she would sleep tonight. She wouldn't mind sleeping with Eli, nosireebob...but she sort of wondered where last night's storm had left them—it wasn't a declaration, it was survival. That's what he'd said, and frankly, she didn't know if her heart was strong enough to survive sleeping with him and then not being with him.

As *survival* had not been clearly defined, she was a little leery of sleeping in Eli's tent because she had absolutely no self-control. But then, Rhys was weighing in at about three hundred pounds and guarded that spice-cooler thing with his life, so she figured his tent was out of the question. That left the cabin, and given Olivia's bad mood, which was darkening by the minute, Marnie wasn't sure that was such a great idea, either.

Olivia and Vince were starting to snipe at each other again, too, with Vince blaming Olivia for having to have this "ridiculous, asswipe kind of wedding," and Olivia blaming Vince for "being such a shrimp he couldn't help them out of a bucket."

When Marnie tried to step in to stop the bickering, Vince told her to shut up, and Marnie came very close to punching him. But Eli stepped in before she could take a swing at the shrimp and, standing between Marnie and Vince, said, "All right, folks. Everybody take a deep breath. This bickering isn't going to get us anywhere, so the next one of you who says a disparaging word against another will be the first person we try and build a human bridge with."

He did not look like he was joking. Everyone promptly bowed their heads and glared at the floor.

"That's more like it," Eli said, and was about to say something else, but the bitchfest was suddenly interrupted by the unmistakable sound of laughter in the far distance. And four-wheelers.

"What's that?" Vince asked.

"Dunno," Eli said, looking toward the ravine where the bridge had once been. They all looked at one another and then were suddenly marching toward the ravine.

By the time they hiked down, there were already a dozen cheerful guests on the other side, riding tandem on the four-wheelers, led by Jim and John. By the look of things, they were all having a grand time.

"Who the hell is *that?*" Olivia demanded of Marnie as the professional guests got off their four-wheelers and helped the others off.

"Jim and John," Marnie said. "Our professional guests."

"What the hell is a professional guest?" Vince demanded.

"Shut up, Vincent," Olivia muttered and walked down to the edge of the ravine.

"Hi Livi!" Olivia's mom yelled.

"Mom! What are you *doing?*" Olivia cried, spying her mother in a tight spaghetti-strap camisole and even tighter running pants.

"We're riding around," her mother shouted back. "Oh, Livi, it's so much fun," she squealed, and stared adoringly at her companion, a dark swarthy guy Marnie did not recognize.

"Dear God, she's doing the cinematographer," Olivia whispered, horrified.

"Dear God, they've been drinking," Rhys added breathlessly, still huffing from the hike down from the meadow.

"Livi, we brought you something," Della yelled, and held up a plastic grocery sack. "Can you guess what it is?"

"Where's my manager? Where's Donnelly?" Olivia demanded.

"Oh hell, I don't know," her mom cheerfully returned. "Probably in Durango or somewhere. Don't you want to know what this is? It's champagne! No reason you should be high *and* dry," she said, and the group laughed soundly, as if that were the most hysterically witty comment they'd ever heard.

"You are not drinking the champagne for my wedding!" Olivia cried, horrified.

"Well, what the hell are we supposed to do? You're stuck over there and we're stuck over here. Oh, stop looking like that. We'll just get some more," Della shouted, and handed the bag to the cinematographer. "It's two bottles. We wrapped it in bubble wrap so they won't break."

"Omigod, that shit is two hundred dollars a bottle," Marnie moaned as the swarthy guy walked to the edge of the ravine.

"Shall I throw the bag to you?" he called out in heavily accented English.

"No!" Eli said sternly, but the man was winding up. "Ah, for the love of Christ, he'll never make it."

Eli was right. Four hundred dollars' worth of champagne went flying across the ravine, hit the bank, and tumbled down. They all waited, expecting to hear the sound of breaking glass as it hit bottom. But there was no sound of breaking glass. A cheer suddenly went up among the sots on the other side of the ravine, and they all clamored around to give the swarthy guy lots of claps on the back.

The five stranded members of the wedding party moved forward as one to the edge of the ravine and carefully peered over. As it happened, the bag had caught on a root and was hanging precariously about ten feet down from the edge of the ravine.

"Hey," Della shouted. "We've got chocolates, too."

"Not my Godivas, please say it's not my Godivas," Marnie begged to no one as Olivia's mother produced another bag and gave it to the Italian, who tossed the thing in the air. This time, he was not so lucky—the bag went sailing down to the river below and was quickly carried off. On the other side of the ravine, they laughed again.

"Okay, Livi!" Olivia's mother yelled. "We'll check on you a little later. We're going to ride around the old mining trails. Isn't that great?"

"They're just going to leave us here?" Olivia sniffed as the party climbed back on their four-wheelers and sped off, their laughter drifting back to them over the sound of the motors.

"Your mother is a head case," Vince said.

Olivia gave him a scathing look. "Do *not* start on my mother. At least I have one who doesn't drink herself to death every night."

"Oh, really? I guess she drinks herself to death during the day. God, Livi, you're really a piece of work, you know that?" Vince spat as Olivia turned and began marching back up the trail. Vince was quickly on her heels, ticking off all the things he thought were wrong with her. In the meantime, Rhys had braced his hands against his knees and was leaning over, staring at the champagne.

Marnie looked at Eli, who looked about as miserable as she felt.

When Rhys finally came away from the edge of the ravine, they reluctantly hiked back to the meadow—taking several breaks for Rhys to catch his breath—and got back just in time to hear the cabin door bang shut and see Olivia go flying out, her arms swinging and her stride determined as she strode toward the fallen arch and around it.

"I think," Eli said, "that we should brace ourselves for a very long couple days."

"That's the understatement of the year," Marnie said and walked up to the cabin porch and plopped down in one of the wicker chairs.

Vince joined her a half hour later, coming from behind the cabin wearing a very smug smile.

"What's funny?" Marnie asked.

"Nothing," he said, his smug smile growing even larger. "Nothing at all."

And there they remained—Vince chuckling to himself occasionally—until Olivia came back. It was obvious she had been bawling—her face was red and puffy and her nose was leaking. She walked past Vince and Marnie and into the cabin and slammed the door.

Olivia might have had a bigger audience for her dramatic entrance, but Rhys was napping in his tent as if it were a lazy Sunday afternoon, and Eli…well, Eli was working on the water pump in the bathroom, which Marnie had discovered was not working properly.

He crawled out from underneath the cabin a few minutes after Olivia slammed the door, wiping his muddied hands with a bandana, looking grim. "Got some bad news," he said to Vince and Marnie. "We've got a busted pipe."

"Then we'll just use water from the kitchen," Vince said. "That's what we did last night."

"Won't work," Eli said, shaking his head. "There is only one pipe into the underground well. The water is hand-pumped up to a tank via a single pipe, then fed from the tank into the kitchen and the bath and the outhouse on different tracks with the manual pumps in those rooms."

"I don't understand," Marnie said.

"The single pipe to the tank is busted. The only water we've got is what's in that tank and it looks to be about two gallons."

No water? No *water*? It was enough to bring tears to her eyes. "We have no food and now we have no water?"

"We have water," Eli said soothingly. "We've got two cases of bottled water for drinking and any cooking we do. We just don't have water for bathing."

At last, a real tear slipped from her eye. This was the most miserable experience she'd ever endured, bar none. Well, okay, maybe that time in high school when she'd been depantsed in gym—but she'd never felt so filthy or hopeless as she did at that moment, and she wanted nothing more than to lie down somewhere and cry herself to sleep. Unfortunately, she didn't even have a bed. She had nothing but one last change of underwear. Another suitcase with more undies and clothing for the wedding were in the Jeep.

Marnie folded her arms across her knees and with a groan, laid her head on them. Her first solo wedding was an unmitigated disaster, an absolute nightmare!

"Come on, Vince, let's see if we can find some buckets or pans," Eli suggested.

"Why?" Vince asked testily.

"Because," Eli said calmly, "it looks like rain."

It did indeed rain that afternoon, a slow steady rain that Eli said was unusual for that time of year. But the clouds broke at dusk, and Eli made a fire in the middle of the little meadow with nothing more than a few sticks and a match.

Thank God for Boy Scouts, he thought as he blew on the kindling, because the Lord knew no one else in this group would have known how to do it.

As the late afternoon sun peeked out behind the clouds, Eli convinced Vince and Olivia to join him and Marnie and Rhys at the fire. It was a gorgeous dusk, bright and crisp. The wind had died with the passing of the rainstorm, and everything was so dewy and beautiful around them that the collective mood, it seemed to Eli, had improved a little over the morning.

There were even a couple of smiles at the quips he made about being stuck. Eli began to think they'd be all right, would survive this glitch, when the subject of food came up. Marnie was starving, and asked Rhys for something to eat.

"No. I have nothing to spare," he said quickly and adamantly.

"Oh come on...isn't there something you can give us?" she pressed. "Cheese, maybe? Some crackers?"

"Cheese and crackers?" He pressed his lips tightly together, obviously offended. "Do you know who I am? I am Rhys St. Paul. I do not dabble in cheese and crackers like some short-order cook."

"Well, then surely you have *something* we could eat?" Marnie pressed, unintimidated.

Rhys sighed. "I don't think you understand," he said irritably. "I have prepared a set number of meals. At present, I have one dinner meal left, and one breakfast. The portions are sufficient for two people...not five."

"What is the dinner?" Marnie asked, her brown eyes lighting up.

"Veal with raspberry remoulade and assorted vegetables."

Eli joined Marnie, Vince, and Olivia in a huge sigh of longing.

"There is only enough for two," Rhys insisted, and Olivia gave them a superior little smile.

But Rhys was being battered down by Marnie's imploring look. "Oh very well," he snapped. "I shall make a deal with you of sorts. To the person that can retrieve the two bottles of champagne, I shall reward with a hearty helping of veal and asparagus. The other three may share the second meal."

"But...what about you?" Marnie asked.

"I have provided for my needs."

"That's not fair!" Marnie cried. "What else do you have?"

"It is *my* food," Rhys cried.

"Forget that," Olivia said with a flick of her wrist. "Just how are we supposed to get the champagne?"

Rhys shrugged, put his hands in the vicinity of his waist. "That, as they say, is your problem."

Marnie looked at Olivia. Olivia looked at Vince. Eli could almost hear the wheels cranking in their three heads, and quickly rose up from his haunches. "Wait, wait, wait," he said, shaking his head. "I'm not going to let you guys do something foolish and risk your necks."

"You think you can stop me, Cowboy?" Vince asked. "You think you have the nads to stop me?"

What the hell? The little man thought he could take him? "Vince, come on," Eli said, trying to sound reasonable and not laugh, "You don't want to risk your neck for champagne."

"Like hell I don't. What, you think you're the only stud out here? The only one who can get it?"

"I didn't say that—"

"I'm going for that champagne."

"Fabulous!" Rhys cried with glee. "I would absolutely kill for a bit of alcohol just now." He pivoted around on his surprisingly tiny foot. "I shall commence the preparation of the meal. To the victor goes the spoils."

The moment the words were out of Rhys's mouth, Marnie, Olivia, and Vince were running before Eli could stop them.

Why did he suddenly feel he had stepped into some episode of *Survivor*? Never mind that—someone was going to get killed, and with a sigh, he kicked dirt on his hard-fought fire and went after them.

At the edge of the ravine, there was a lot of bickering. Vince was down on his belly, yelling at Olivia to hold his feet while he tried to reach ten feet down the ravine for the plastic sack. When Olivia got tired of holding his feet, she let go and stood up, leaving Vince to shout angrily as he pushed himself back up while she demanded that Eli bring her a rope.

He wanted to get a rope, all right. He wanted to put her dyed-blond head through it. "What do you need with a rope?" he asked calmly.

"What do you think, Mr. Stuntman? I'm going to rappel down," she said, lifting her chin.

"Okay," he said, nodding. "So let me make sure I have this straight…you wouldn't rappel down the side of a ravine last week when we had the appropriate gear, but you'll do it now with nothing but a rope?"

Olivia glared at him. "Wait a minute, Bucko—who works for who here?"

"I'm not letting you rappel down that ravine on the tail end of a rope."

"Then I'll do it," Marnie chimed in.

Eli snorted at that. "You are *definitely* not going down—"

"What do you mean, I'm *definitely* not going down? Why not? I've rappelled before."

"Oh yeah?" he asked suspiciously. "Where?"

She frowned and looked away. "What does it matter? I've done it. All you have to do is hold the rope and lower me, then help me climb back up. It can't be that hard."

"And if you slip and fall, you fall to your death. Nope, sorry, not going to let you do it."

Now Marnie's brows dipped into a seriously disgruntled V. "*Let* me? And just who made you the boss of me?"

"You did," he reminded her, "the day you signed the contract to do this wedding."

"Oh hell, that is obviously null and void."

"Yeah!" Olivia piped in.

"They've got a point, Eli," Vince said, dusting his pants off.

The three of them stood there, glaring at him, and Eli could see that he had a mutiny on his hands. "Fine," he snapped. "I'll get a rope. Just stay put," he said sternly, and in the interest of surviving, he hiked back to his tent.

When he returned, he ignored them all, tied the rope securely to a tree and easily lowered himself down, retrieved the plastic bag and two intact bottles of champagne, then climbed back up.

Did he get as much as a thank you from the group? Hell, no. Well, okay, a small little chirp of thanks from Marnie, but she was running to keep up with Olivia and Vince, who were running with the champagne as if they'd retrieved it. They struggled up the trail, dashed across the meadow, and were met by Rhys, who was standing regally on the porch, his arms akimbo, peering down at the group. "Who is the winner?"

"I am!" Vince instantly cried, earning a gasp of shock and indignation from Marnie and Olivia.

"That's a lie!" Olivia cried. "*I* got it!"

Marnie gasped again. "I can't believe you two! You're both awful. You know it was Eli who got the champagne."

Olivia whipped around to Marnie so fast it was a wonder her head didn't snap off. "Why are you on *his* side?" she demanded angrily. "He wouldn't even get us a rope."

"Don't be stupid, Olivia," Vince said angrily. "She figures if he wins, she can get half of it by letting him in her pants."

A tiny sound of shock escaped Marnie, and she turned several shades of red. "No!" she cried. "No, no, I just—"

"It hardly matters," Rhys said imperiously. "I've divvied the dinner into four small portions. Now, if someone would kindly hand me the champagne, I should like a very big glass of it."

So would Eli, and he stepped up through the group and snatched the bag from Olivia's hands before she could react. He'd had enough bickering and drama for one day, and by God, he was not missing out on his fair share of alcohol. "Let's make sure we all get a taste, all right?" he said coolly to Olivia, and walked into the cabin with Rhys nipping at his heels.

CHAPTER TWENTY-TWO

Personally, Marnie had not known before today that Cristal champagne was so good. Her only regret was that she'd probably never be able to afford a bottle on her own, so she sipped carefully.

The five of them shared a bottle with their little meal, which was, amazingly, the most tender and delectable veal Marnie had ever eaten. The champagne had helped take the edge off their nerves, so when the rain started up again, they took the second bottle inside the cabin and sat around a roaring fire that Eli built...naturally.

Frankly, Marnie was beginning to wonder if Vince did anything but star in movies. He had yet to lift a finger that she could see—Eli was doing all the work. What amazed her was the amount of work Eli was able to do. The man knew how to do just about everything—repair plumbing, build fires, retrieve bottles of champagne hanging precariously from an exposed root in a steep ravine. It was really very sexy.

Eli *was* sexy. And tonight, while everyone was calm, laughing as they named the worst movies they had ever seen (or, in the case of some, had starred in), Marnie couldn't keep her eyes from him. She kept stealing glimpses of him, sitting a little apart from the rest of them, his head down, lost in thought...until he suddenly looked up and caught her looking at him.

As Olivia went on and on and on about some movie she had starred in where she didn't have a proper trailer, Eli lifted a dark brow in question to Marnie. She smiled softly and lifted her coffee cup of champagne in silent toast. He returned a smile so warm that the corners of his blue eyes crinkled, and he responded by lifting his coffee cup.

She smiled, sipped from her cup, and thought, with an inadvertent shiver, about last night, and how his warm blue eyes had looked then—dark, not light. Bold. Full of desire. Tonight his eyes were full of restlessness and, she thought, a tiny beam of hope. Maybe even affection.

When Rhys announced he would turn in, he startled Marnie by asking, "And what do you intend to do, Miss Wedding Coordinator?"

"Do? What do you mean what is she going to do?" Olivia asked.

"I lost my tent in the storm," Marnie said, trying not to look at Eli. "So, I ah, I need a place to sleep."

"Oh, you poor thing," Olivia cried, her good humor returned with the champagne. "You must stay in here. On the couch. There are some extra quilts and you'll be very comfortable," she said, nodding adamantly.

"Oh. Well, I wouldn't want to impose—"

"Don't be ridiculous. These are desperate times."

"They're not *desperate*," Vince said, tossing back the last of his champagne. "But I don't care. Let her sleep here if she wants," he said with a shrug.

"It's settled then. You'll sleep here," Olivia said, and smiled sweetly at Marnie.

No, no, no, she didn't want to sleep here. She wanted to sleep in Eli's tent. She wanted to feel his arms and legs around her, to feel his warmth and strength seep into her. She glanced at Eli and willed him to say it, to say she would sleep with him.

But he only smiled and winked as he followed Rhys out. *Damn.*

Her good mood effectively ruined, Marnie fetched her backpack and excused herself. She went to the little outhouse and brushed her teeth, washed her face and her body as best she could in the freezing dribble of water that was left, and when she returned to the cabin, the lights were already out. Olivia and Vince were already in bed, and there was nothing but the glow of the fire.

Marnie crept to the small couch. Olivia had left a couple of quilts out for her, and she very quietly laid them out, slipped between them, and turned on her side away from the bed. She closed her eyes, and her mind's eye danced with images of Eli, of the things he had done to her last night, images so clear that her body began to heat…until a familiar noise pierced her consciousness.

Marnie's eyes flew open. She quietly sucked in her breath and held it. *Unbelievable!* It wasn't her conscious dream of Eli making that sound, it was Olivia and Vince. Those morons were actually making love with her in the room.

She curled into a ball and tried very hard not to listen, but really, how could she not? There was no mistaking their heavy breathing, the grunts and groans of lovemaking. And the sucking sounds. Those sounds were perfectly sexy and arousing when performed on *her* body, but when performed by another couple in the room, it grossed her out completely.

And when Olivia said, in a childlike voice, "Come on, baby, give me some of that sweet meat," Marnie practically fell off the couch in her haste to get out from beneath the quilts. She glanced at the bed only once, long enough to see Vince on his knees, straight up, Olivia on all fours, and Vince sliding in from behind.

She rushed out into the cold night air, a quilt around her shoulders, her feet freezing from having forgotten her shoes. She thought about sleeping on the wicker chairs, but it was still rainy and cold and wet, and okay whatever—she knew where she wanted to be. Let Eli think she was a nuisance, but she was *not* going back inside that cabin with those two.

Except that she did remember one thing: There was still a little champagne left in the second bottle. She'd noticed it when she'd put it aside when the party broke up. Marnie glanced at the door of the cabin, then at the tent, and in a moment of determination, she opened the door of the cabin. If the rest of the crew didn't like her taking the champagne, they could vote her off the damn mountain.

She darted inside to the sound of Olivia breathing hard and muttering, "Oh yeah, oh yeah baby, oh yeah," grabbed the champagne and flew out again, and ran in bare feet to the tents, her thumb firmly in the bottle to keep it from spilling.

At Eli's tent, she dispensed with any polite knocking and fumbled clumsily with the zipper long enough to wake him. The flap opened and she fell in, wet and with a bottle of champagne tipped to one side, saved only by her thumb. Eli had already lit his kerosene lamp and was sitting up, his arms braced on his raised knees, the shadow of his beard very sexy, his chest broad and outlined by a tight T-shirt, and watching her with a look of curiosity.

Marnie righted herself. "I have champagne," she said, thrusting the bottle toward him.

He didn't say anything, just smiled that sexy, lopsided grin that made her weak in the knees.

"I know I didn't knock, but it's raining," she said. He quirked a brow. "Okay, I'm definitely arriving uninvited. Again. But the thing is, Olivia and Vince...well, let's just say they are not exactly a shy couple."

He squinted at the bottle. "How much is left?"

"I'd say sixty-five dollars worth."

"Then welcome to my humble abode," he said, and moved his feet so she could sit on the end of his sleeping bag.

Marnie smiled and half moved, half rolled to the end of his sleeping bag and handed him the bottle.

Eli took it, took a sip, and said, "So the happy couple is extra happy tonight?"

"You could say that," Marnie said, and easily fell into a comfortable conversation, telling Eli what had happened in the cabin, making him laugh at her mimicking Olivia in the throes of passion.

They sat across from each other, knee to knee, passing the bottle back and forth, talking like old friends about their dilemma, predicting which of the five would be the first to crumble under the pressure (Olivia getting a unanimous vote), and how long Vince could last without someone to do every little thing for him. They both professed astonishment at how well Rhys seemed to adapt to the situation, when they both would have guessed him to be the first to come unglued.

They speculated about Vince and Olivia, and how two people who were supposedly in love could fight as much as they did.

"It must be the grind of celebrity," Marnie said. "Because they always make up."

"It's the ego of celebrity," Eli countered. "If it were me, I'd skip the fighting altogether and head right for making up." And then he looked at her in a way that made her skin tingle. Jesus, but the man could make her hot just by *looking* at her.

She took another slug of champagne and asked boldly, "So what about you, Eli McCain, man of mystery. Did you ever think about getting married?"

Wow, was that an arctic blast that just rattled the tent, or did the mood suddenly change? Eli's jaw was suddenly clenched tightly shut, and he handed the champagne to her. "Yeah, I've thought about it."

"At least you've thought about it," she said with a self-conscious laugh. "I've never been in a relationship long enough to even contemplate it."

"Really?" he asked, glancing up, the scowl gone.

"Really. It seems that the couple times I thought I had something really good, something or someone would come along to really screw it up."

"Like what?"

"Like? Well, in one case, an old girlfriend suddenly popped back into the picture. You know, 'the one who got away,'" she said, making quote marks with her fingers. "And then there was the guy who was so great and everything between us was great...until he lost his shirt in the stock market. He just announced he was moving to New York one day. And when

I asked him about us, he pretty much said there was him and money, and that was his *us*, and other than that, he had no *us*. Money was his first love. I was an incidental second." A booty call, she thought bitterly. "Yep, that really sucked," she said with an honest laugh. "I could have seen all the signs if I'd only admitted it to myself. But I honestly thought he was the guy for me. It's funny how I can fool myself into thinking someone is right for me, but then he turns out to be the last person on earth I should be with." She laughed.

Eli didn't say anything to that, just looked at the bottle she held. Marnie closed one eye and peered into the bottle, then passed it to Eli. "At least that's what I discovered about me," she said, reverting to her bad habit of talking to fill awkward silence. "But that's been a few years, so I don't think about it much anymore. I just really thought we were going the full nine yards, and it took me a while to get over the realization that he was more interested in money than me. Ouch."

Eli took a swig of the champagne and handed the bottle back to her. "I'm sorry you had to go through that, Marnie. I know that must have hurt like hell."

She smiled sadly. "You cannot imagine."

"How long?" he asked. "How long did it take you to get over it?"

She shrugged and sipped from the bottle. "About six months, which, I recognize, is a pathetically long time to let one dickhead screw with your head."

"Not as pathetic as a year," he said, taking the bottle.

"Ooh, a full year," she said with a soft smile. "That's a long time, too."

With a soft sigh, Eli took the champagne bottle from her. "It's even worse. I was practically standing at the altar."

Marnie's smile faded. Eli downed what was left of the champagne, tossed the bottle aside, and propped his arms on his knees.

How was that possible? How could a woman do that to a man like Eli? If Marnie had a guy like Eli, he'd probably get sick of her always wanting to be with him. "Oh, Eli," she said sympathetically. He was too handsome, too strong, too...*good*. She drew her knees up to her chest, wrapped her arms around them. "Seriously, you were at the altar?"

"Not literally, but a week away," he said with a shrug. "Yep, something on the scale of this wedding—lots of people, lots of money sunk into stupid details like feathers and arches. But it was what she wanted, and at the time, I would have done anything she wanted."

This was not in keeping with the image she had of a man with such a tough exterior. *This* guy seemed very vulnerable at the moment. "So...what happened?"

"What happened was that she was sleeping with another man. An actor, of course. Someone who she thought would be her ticket to fame and fortune."

Marnie gasped. "Omigod, how awful for you. How did you know? I mean, you didn't just...you know, *find* them—"

"No," he said with a snort. "She just called the whole thing off one day after she informed me she was sleeping with someone else without even batting an eye."

"You had no clue? No inkling that things weren't right?"

His eyes went dark, and she could see the clench of his jaw as he thought about it. "None," he said tightly.

Marnie didn't say anything—what could she say? It was too horrible to even contemplate. How devastating it would be, to have your heart broken in such a public and humiliating way. It was little wonder that he abhorred this wedding as he did. At least in her case, she'd never gotten near marriage with Jeff. If Jeff had taken her that far and left her, she would have crumbled into dust.

"I'm sorry, Eli."

"Don't be. I'm like you, coppertop. I could have seen the signs if I'd only opened my eyes. But that's the nature of love, I guess—you're too blinded by it to really know the person you're with."

"At least the people you and I chose. But most of the time, I think love opens up a window in people. Don't you?"

He glanced up at her, his eyes gone cold. "No," he said calmly. "I don't. I don't really know if love even exists. And if it does, I don't know if I think it's possible to sustain it over time."

"Wow, *that's* a little cynical. We all make mistakes, but we learn from them, right? And the next time, love is even better, because we're not as vulnerable as we were the first time it happened."

That earned her a disdainful snort. "You sound like Dear Abby. If you ask me, a person can never really know what's in another person's heart, not without climbing into their skin and looking inside it. And the inability to do that makes every one of us a potential putz."

"That's not true," Marnie retorted. "I don't know everything about you, but I think I know what's in your heart."

"You don't know me," he snorted.

"I do," she insisted. "I know you're a good man with a big heart and that you really do care about people and things, even if you aren't very verbal about it."

"Marnie. Stop the psychobabble crap. You don't know anything about me. You have no idea what's in here," he said, tapping his chest. "A couple rolls in the hay does not mean you *know* me."

That remark took the wind out of her sails. "And what is that supposed to mean?" she asked tightly.

"Just that."

"I know you're not that cold, Eli. I think you have been stung and now you are pushing—"

"Will you *stop*?" he suddenly snapped. "That's the problem with you, Marnie, you just keep talking without ever listening. You don't *know* me. You will never know me, any more than I will know you. We've had some good times, but don't make it into something it's not."

He might as well have slapped her—his words hurt just as bad. She'd never said she expected anything...but she didn't have to say it, did she? Her deeds had said it for her, and he'd seen it. He'd damn sure seen into *her* heart, and had just punted it right out of the ballpark. She dropped her gaze to the bag. "Fine," she muttered.

"Oh for God's sake, please don't be hurt." Eli groaned.

That infuriated her and she jerked her gaze to him. "I'm not hurt, Eli. How could I be hurt if I don't give a damn? Newsflash! You don't know me, either. But I guess you think every woman you sleep with is looking for happily-ever-after with you, right? Yeah, you're such a stud."

"Marnie," he said, but she flopped down on her side and pulled the quilt up around her face where she couldn't see him.

"Is it okay if I sleep here? I really don't have anywhere else to go."

"Yes, of course you can," he said irritably.

"Great. Good night." And she closed her eyes. Squeezed them shut.

Eli sighed. Twice. But he said nothing.

"You're not the only one who has ever been hurt in this life, Eli," she muttered angrily. "You don't get a Purple Heart for having suffered a bad relationship. You pick up and move on."

Eli said nothing. Marnie was too angry to think and hoped tomorrow she could think of something clever and witty to say that would put him in his place. That's what he needed, he needed to be put firmly in his place, the sorry bastard. And just how she'd put him in his place was the subject of the many thoughts that banged around her brain as the rain lulled her to sleep.

Sleep did finally come, because at some point, something—a sound, a movement—woke her. She opened her eyes, wondering what time it was. The rain had stopped, and the moon had come out, judging by the thin ray of light seeping in from the flap of the tent. It was open, because Eli was sitting there, staring out into the meadow.

She came up on her elbows and stared at him. What the hell was he doing? It was then that she noticed she was covered with the sleeping bag. He had covered her in his sleeping bag so she wouldn't be cold.

Oh no, he didn't care one bit, did he?

Stupid man.

Marnie lay down and snuggled deeper into the bag, and drifted back to sleep, the image of a lonely, stupid, stubborn cowboy in her mind's eye.

CHAPTER TWENTY-THREE

The next morning, Eli walked down the ravine so he could get some air—he'd been surrounded by Marnie's scent all night and it was driving him crazy, because he loved the way she smelled. But then he'd been such an idiot and had a knee-jerk reaction that cost him a chance of getting close to her.

God, he wished he weren't such a jerk. Especially and particularly since he really liked Marnie, liked her so much he'd hardly thought of anything else in the last couple of weeks. And since their little foray into storm sex the other night, he'd been aching to hold her again.

But then she'd shaken him up with talk of love and weddings, and a lot of old feelings had come rushing back up, and he felt something old and clumsy rising up in him. He was definitely feeling for Marnie what he'd once felt for Trish, only it was different somehow. Stronger. Deeper. A feeling that was, oddly, way more alive than it had ever been for Trish.

All right, already, Marnie wasn't Trish. No, Marnie was far better than Trish, which made his feelings even more disturbing—he had, potentially, much further to fall. He'd never really figured out what went wrong the last time—

with Trish, he thought he'd done everything right, but in the end, it was wrong, all wrong. He had no idea why or how, but something obviously didn't work right, or Trish wouldn't have done what she did.

None of this would be an issue if he hadn't let his guard down with Marnie. But now that he had—*shit, he'd even told her about Trish*—he didn't like how vulnerable he felt, as if he were flaying himself open so that she could poke around inside him with her finger.

No, he didn't like that at all.

Okay, so he had his baggage...but he didn't have to be such an ass. He wanted to apologize for being so short with her last night. He just needed to find the right moment.

She was still sleeping when he'd left the tent, and he glanced at his watch now. A quarter past nine. He took his radio from his pocket and called Cooper. A few minutes later, he wished he hadn't beeped him, because Cooper told him Jack was having trouble getting a rotor blade up here, and that it would probably be the next day before someone could get them off this side of the ravine and put them on the side of civilization.

"What about repairing the bridge?" Eli suggested as he peered down the ravine at the remnants of the old bridge.

"We've got a crew from Pagosa Springs lined up," Cooper said.

"Really?" Eli asked, a little surprised. He'd learned a long time ago that this part of the world moved a whole lot slower than LA

"Really. They ought to be able to get to it next week. A month at most."

"Ah hell," Eli groaned over Cooper's laugh. "What about food?"

"Ah, now Jack's come up with a solution for that. He's bringing it up to you now."

"Thanks," Eli said. "If you could send up a gun and shovel, too, I'd appreciate it."

Cooper laughed again. "Look, dude, we'll get you out of there," he assured him. "Just sit tight."

"I don't think I can sit any tighter, Coop. And I'd just like to remind you and the other party animals down there that I was the one who was dead set against this deal."

"Hey, trust me, you got the sweet end of the deal, pal," Cooper said amicably. "We're fighting chaos down here. Do you know how much wine and champagne was shipped up here? Do you know how much two hundred people can drink? The lodge sent a truck to Durango this morning to buy out every liquor store they can find. We've been in the middle of party central for twenty-four hours now, and there are no signs of it ending anytime soon. You ever seen one hundred pounds of feathers spread out?"

"You're kidding."

"I am not kidding. They rolled the guy who directed *Love Bites* in those feathers last night, and he's still picking them out of his hair."

Now it was Eli's turn to laugh. "Serves you assholes right for leaving me up here with these egomaniacs," he said, and grinned at Cooper's spicy retort. They talked a little more, then Eli hung up.

He was starting the climb back to the meadow when he heard the sound of four-wheelers, followed by the even clearer sound of maniacal laughter. The party was coming back.

By the time the guests had driven up to the ravine, the stranded bridal party had half rolled, half fallen down the trail in their haste to see what was going on, beckoned by the call of motors and laughter.

Vince, who arrived far ahead of Olivia, asked what was happening. Marnie stood on the other side of Rhys and refused to look at Eli. Her hair, he noticed as she tripped over a rock, was even wilder today than yesterday. In his T-shirt, her fleece jacket, and the boots she refused to lace, she looked like a wild mountain woman.

Olivia stood in front of them all, her hands on her bony little hips, her mouth set in an implacable line.

"They're bringing up some food," Eli said.

"Thank God," Olivia snapped, just as the four-wheelers came into view.

There were at least six of them, and a dozen people fell off the things when they came to a halt, laughing and carrying their morning mugs of whatever, visibly steaming in the crisp morning temperatures.

A very stoic Jack arrived behind them, pulling a small trailer behind his four-wheeler that carried one of Marnie's industrial-size snowblowers. He stepped off his four-wheeler and walked purposefully to the edge of the ravine, took out his radio, and flipped it open as the party guests gathered around behind him.

Eli flipped open his radio, too. "Yo."

"We're going to shoot some sandwiches and apples at you. Tried soft drinks, but that didn't work out."

Eli glanced at the snowblower—as did the rest of the bridal party, seeing as how they had heard what Jack said—and stared at it, trying to process how, exactly, this would work. But Jack didn't give them a chance to ask questions, for he had turned away and was marching through the guests back to the trailer with the snowblower.

"Hi, Livi," Olivia's mother called as they waited for Jack. She was hanging off the cinematographer, waving with her free arm.

"Oh *Jesus*," Olivia muttered.

"Hey," Vince said, peering across the ravine, his arms folded tightly across his chest. "Is that Ari?"

Olivia gasped and looked to where he pointed. "Ari!" she shrieked.

From across the ravine, Ari let his hand drop from the shoulders of a young woman. "Ah, little raindrop. You must have a care, for I detect bad karma," he called out to her.

"No shit," Eli snorted.

Olivia moved as close to the edge of the ravine as she could get, her hands clasped to her chest. "Oh, Ari, I wish you were on this side to help me through this. It's a horrible ordeal. You cannot imagine the conditions under which we are surviving."

"For chrissakes," Vince moaned.

Ari shrugged and looked down at the pretty blonde he'd been handling just a moment before. "You must have strength, little raindrop, for is it not adversity that makes us wiser?"

"Wiser?" Marnie asked Rhys. "Or stronger?"

"Perhaps both," Rhys opined.

"And I shall be here to guide you when you are ready to cross the chasm," Ari continued.

"When you're ready? Is he nuts? We're fucking stuck!" Vince blustered.

"Shut up, Vince," Olivia snapped, and waved at Ari.

"Hey," Vince said, "is that Rebecca Strand he's with?"

Olivia jerked toward Vince, her eyes narrowed. "You blindass fool. Of course it's not her. Why would it be her?"

He shrugged. "It looks like her. If it's not Rebecca Strand, then who is it?" he asked, apparently the only one oblivious to Olivia's ire—although it was hard to understand how he could possibly miss it, the rest of them were blown back ten or fifteen feet by the fire that was blowing out of her ears and nose at that very moment.

"It's Caroline Devereaux," Marnie said helpfully, and got such a scathing look from Olivia that Eli was surprised she didn't melt on the spot. Poor Marnie could have no way of knowing that Vince had once diddled Caroline on the studio back lot during the production of a feature film. He didn't think Olivia knew it, but judging by her ferocious look now, she certainly did.

"Huh," Vince said, nodding thoughtfully. "I haven't seen her since we filmed *Backwards*."

"Who the fuck cares?" Olivia seethed.

Yep. She knew, all right.

And she might have actually obliterated Vince with that hardass gaze of hers had Rhys not stepped between the bridal couple and pointed.

"He's aiming that thing at *us*," he announced. They all jerked their gazes across the ravine.

Olivia's mother was making out with the cinematographer, and a group of about five were gathered around one four-wheeler, passing a flask. Jack and another guy who Eli thought was a lodge employee had pulled the trailer toward the edge of the ravine, and the snowblower pipe that would blow feathers over the guests at the reception was pointed directly at them.

Jack had always been an inventor of sorts, even when they were kids. He was the one who'd rigged the mother of all cherry bombs and blown the fur off Cooper's cat. With a wide grin, Eli went down on his haunches. This was going to be good.

"What precisely does he intend to do with that thing?" Rhys demanded.

"I think he intends to shoot some sandwiches our way," Eli responded, and Rhys looked at him as if he'd lost his mind. But then Jack called out to someone, and a woman in the group of five passing the flask shrieked, jumped off her seat on the four-wheeler, and fished a box from the four-wheeler's basket. Clutching it tightly to her chest, she hurried forward to Jack and smiled a little too adoringly as she handed it to him.

The old boy had obviously been working on more than the snowblower, Eli figured.

The rest of that motley crew gathered around behind Jack, crowding him and the snowblower. The thing was six to eight feet tall, and when Jack proclaimed it loaded, the two professional dancers, or whatever they were, lined everyone up on either side of the thing. Both of them appeared to be explaining something to their respective groups.

"What the hell?" Eli muttered, just as the first apple came flying across the ravine.

It just missed hitting Marnie in the head. "Hey!" she shouted across the ravine as she ducked another apple. A cheer went up from the left side of the snowblower, and Eli turned around, saw that the second apple had hit a tree. They were betting, he surmised, one half getting points for everything an apple did hit, and the other side getting points for a clean drop. More apples came, and as one rolled down to Eli's foot, he picked it up, noticed it had what looked like bite marks in it. The snowblower had a serrated blade, he gathered, to help grind up snow and ice. Or apples, depending on its use.

Jack shot about fifteen apples at them, and once Marnie and Olivia had gotten over their shock at being fired on, they scrambled to pick them up, losing only two to the ravine.

When Jack paused the snowblower, the two professional guests quickly compared notes; a wail was heard from the team on the left as they all reached for their pockets and pulled out a handful of bills. A few minutes later, Jack started the thing up again. The guests quickly resumed their positions and watched as the first sandwich was hurled across the ravine, landing squarely on Rhys's foot.

Rhys bent down and picked it up as the sandwiches continued to fly. "Mmm. Peanut butter and jam," he informed them, and proceeded to open the plastic wrap and eat it.

"Hey!" Vince said. "That's not fair."

Rhys shrugged and continued munching as another sandwich hit him in the shoulder, much to the delight of the team on the left. "If you will only look about, you will notice they have an entire box. I think there is more than enough to see us through."

He was right—they ended up shooting about thirty mangled peanut butter and jelly sandwiches in all. The bridal party did not seem to care—they were starved and had each gathered up armfuls of apples and sandwiches.

When the last PB&J was shot across, Jack turned the snowblower off, flipped open his radio, and gestured for Eli to do the same. "That ought to get you through the next day," he said.

"Peanut butter? That's all they've got down there?" Eli asked.

"That, and a lot of lobster," Jack said. "Okay, gotta book." He clicked off.

Eli and the rest of his castaways watched as the guests settled up their bets with a lot of laughter and high fives, then got on their four-wheelers and drove off with Olivia's mother waving over the top of her head to her daughter.

When the four-wheelers had disappeared, Olivia looked down at her pile of sandwiches. "They're all messed up," she said tearfully.

"For chrissakes, Olivia," Vince sighed wearily. "It's food." And with that, he started the grim hike back to the meadow, munching on an apple.

At the cabin, they sat in silence, each of them eating a couple of sandwiches and an apple and drinking bottled water. No one was in the mood for talking—Olivia kept glaring at Vince, and when Eli tried to make eye contact with Marnie, she refused to look at him.

It was Rhys who finally broke the silence. "What shall we do today?" he asked cheerfully. The man acted like he was on a little camping vacation.

"Oh, I dunno, Rhys." Vince sighed. "Nap? What else is there to do?"

"I had in mind something a little more engaging than that," he said primly. "We're all rather desperate for a bath."

"There's no water, genius," Olivia said.

"There certainly *is* water. Mr. McCain here managed to put out enough receptacles for rainwater to wash with."

The group collectively snapped their gaze to Eli, startling him.

"There's *some* water," he said instantly. "But not enough for baths."

"How much?" Olivia demanded.

"Enough to wash up. For at least a couple people."

"Dibs!" Olivia shouted, jumping to her feet.

"No, no—hey," Marnie stammered, coming to her feet, too. "You can't have dibs. I want a bath, too."

"Sorry, Marn. It's not your wedding."

"There isn't *any* wedding at the moment," Vince reminded her. "And I want to shave. I can't stand hair on my face."

"Whatever, Vince. It's not like you have enough facial hair that anyone can actually notice," Olivia shot back. "And I am *so* not washing after you."

"I've quite a bit of facial hair," Rhys said. "And if you don't mind, I'd like to tidy up a bit."

"Then use the lake," Olivia cried. "That's the only place with enough water for you."

Marnie gasped at her insult, but Rhys was quite unaffected by it. "I will not bathe in that water. It is stagnant and there is a peculiar smell."

"Marmots," Eli said.

The four of them looked at him questioningly. "Giant gophers," he clarified. "They live just above the lake, a colony of them. Their waste is what you smell. It washes into the lake."

"Omigod," Olivia swooned.

"But the real problem we've got is parasites and the paint from the arch, which is washing off and casting a film on the lake."

"Then what are we supposed to do?" Olivia demanded. "We'll have to share the water you've collected. And I'm the bride, so I should get to go first."

"I suggest we draw straws," Eli said calmly. "It's the only fair thing to do."

"I'm not drawing straws," Olivia huffed.

"Then perhaps we might compete for it," Rhys said. "You know, like they do on *Survivor*."

"Are you kidding?" Marnie asked. "How would we compete for it?"

Rhys looked at Eli. So did Marnie, her big maple-brown eyes blinking up at him and making him feel even worse for having been such a jerk to her last night. Olivia snorted, but Vince was smiling and nodding. "Great idea, Doughman. A contest. So think of something, Eli."

Eli frowned. But then he looked at Olivia, pouting because she was not getting her way, and said, "Sure. A contest. How about this—you guys will work in teams of two. Each team will have thirty minutes to drag that altar out of the lake. The first one to get it out gets the first shot at the rainwater. The losers get sloppy seconds."

"That is so lame!" Olivia exclaimed.

"Why?" Eli asked. "We've got to get it out of the lake."

"Why do we have to get it out of the lake? Why can't we just leave it there? It's ruined and I don't want it anymore."

"Because," Eli said calmly, even though he was quickly losing patience with the diva, "we are responsible adults, and responsible adults don't leave trash to pollute the lakes the wildlife use. That's why."

"Get off your soapbox, will you?" Olivia snapped. "You act like a fucking game warden."

Okay, the chick was really riding his last nerve. He bit his tongue to keep from saying what he *really* wanted to say, then said quietly, "You want the rainwater, Olivia? I am the only one who knows where the buckets are."

"I'll do it. I'll do anything to wash my hair," Marnie said, putting her hand to her enormous furball of hair. "But... but what if neither of us can get it out?" she asked. "And how will we choose teams?"

"That's for you to decide," Eli said, and stood up, gathering the remaining sandwiches and apples. "In the meantime, I'll just put these somewhere safe."

The other four eyed him and one another suspiciously.

"I'm not entering some fucking contest to take a bath," Olivia haughtily informed them, and marched for the cabin door. "I'm going to get a nap," she said curtly, and disappeared inside.

"Bitch," Vince muttered.

ALL I NEED IS YOU

That left Rhys and Marnie to eye each other, and judging by the looks on their faces, neither of them seemed too terribly happy with the prospect of hooking up for the contest.

"I think I should like another look at the lake," Rhys said after a moment. "Perhaps it is not too terribly bad for washing."

Marnie watched him walk down the steps and toward the lake, then glanced at Eli from the corner of her eye. She sighed wearily, put her hand to her hair again, then followed Rhys away from the cabin, heading to the tent, her hair bouncing in a tangled ball behind her.

Eli shrugged and went in search of one of Rhys's coolers.

In the tent, Marnie sat cross-legged and tried to pull her hands through the mess of her hair. One thing was certain, if she had to partner with Rhys, she'd never get to wash her hair, because she knew *he* wouldn't get in that water. She'd have to do it, because she had to wash her hair. It was the top item on her agenda. She couldn't stand the feel of it another moment.

She couldn't stand being around Eli and not being with him, either. All day she'd waffled—one moment she was furious with him for being such an ass, but then he'd look at her with that expression of amusement and affection and it would just seep into her and make her ache for him.

Marnie was miserable, and with a moan, she threw herself down on the sleeping bag that smelled like Eli, and that only reminded her that she was falling in love with a

289

stupid cowboy with stupid hangups. Yes, yes, she was falling in love, it was so clear! Not a moment passed that she didn't think of him, and she was watching his every move. She had all the maturity of a sixth-grader. But she couldn't help it. He was handsome and strong and smelled so damn good, like a real man, like a sexy man, and she loved the way his body felt in hers and around hers, and she loved the fact that he was wounded and not a womanizer, and she loved how he managed to keep so calm when everyone else was panicking and how he knew just the right thing to do in every situation—

"*Psst*! Marnie!"

Marnie pushed herself up and turned her head to see Olivia poking her head through the tent. She smiled and climbed through, zipping the tent flap behind her.

Marnie was definitely not in the mood. "What are you doing?" she asked as Olivia crawled to sit next to Marnie's head.

"I have to talk to you," Olivia whispered, peering intently at the tent flap, as if she expected someone to come through it at any moment.

Marnie looked at the tent flap, then at Olivia. "Why are you whispering?"

"*Sssh*! I don't want anyone to hear us." She turned from the tent flap and scooched around so that she was facing Marnie. "Listen, Vince is an asshole. I am so thankful for this disaster, because if I had actually married him, I would have killed myself in a week."

"Oh, Olivia," Marnie said, and put a comforting hand on her knee. "You're just feeling very stressed right now. You're going to marry him."

"I am not," Olivia spat and slapped Marnie's hand off her knee. "I've learned way too much about him, and believe me, it's not good."

This from a woman who was calling out for his sweet meat only last night, Marnie thought.

"So Marnie, we have to stick together."

"Stick together?"

"If we're not careful, Vince will take all the water and leave us to die. He is that fucking selfish. And God only knows how long we can eat peanut butter and jelly before we turn on each other."

Marnie snorted. "Aren't you being just a smidge over-dramatic, Olivia? We're not going to be here much longer. No one is going to die. And if they can shoot peanut butter and jelly, then surely then can shoot something else over here. Lobsters, maybe."

"Oh, excuse *me*," Olivia said, rearing back to her heels. "Beg your pardon, Miss Survivor, but have you heard any helicopters up here?"

"No, but I—"

"And do you think those frozen lobsters will be any good after today? They've got a shelf life. They'll be shooting rancid lobsters at us!"

"I was only kidding. I don't think they will shoot the—"

"Listen, Rhys has some home-baked breads and imported Camembert cheese that he gave me—*sssh!*" She paused, her hand on Marnie's arm, and raised her head like an animal, listening intently for a moment. When she was apparently convinced there was nothing outside, she lowered her head and said, "If you align yourself with me, I will share that bread and cheese with you."

"That's very nice, but why don't you just share it with everyone?"

"Are you kidding? There's not enough for everyone. Listen, all you have to do is help me get that altar out of the water, and I'll give you a hunk the size of your head," she said, looking curiously at Marnie's hair. "I don't want Vince to win, and I don't think Rhys can. If *we* get it out, not only will we get the rainwater, but we will be eating *real* food instead of that stupid peanut butter crap. Jesus, you pay a million plus for a fucking wedding, and you think the least they might do is shoot something good at you!" she exclaimed with great frustration. "So what do you say?" she asked, leaning closer.

Marnie did like the idea of that rainwater. So much so that she said, "Okay. If I can go first with the rainwater. I really, *really* want to wash my hair."

"Of course," Olivia said brightly. "I wouldn't have it any other way. So come on out when you're ready and we'll announce our team."

"But...what about Vince and Eli and Rhys?"

"What about them? They're men. They can go a lot longer without washing than women," she said blithely. "But I am not stepping back into civilization smelling like a cow."

There was something in Olivia's blue eyes that seemed a smidgen off sane, and Marine had a moment of doubt that she was doing the right thing. But Olivia was already moving. "Okay!" she said, crawling toward the front of the tent. "I'll see you at the cabin." And with that, she unzipped the tent flap and went out.

Forming an alliance with Olivia was fine, Marnie supposed, but Olivia had forgotten one thing—how in the hell did she think the two of them would get that altar out of four feet of water? Whatever—Marnie would give it a shot. It wasn't as if she had anything better to do. Her mind made up, she reached for the tent flap at the same time Eli opened it and came in.

Marnie reared back on her heels.

"Hey, coppertop," he said.

"Hey," she said, eyeing him coolly and reminding herself not to act like a fool.

"What's up?"

"Resting."

He nodded and scratched his beard, which was, she had to admit, too damn sexy. "So listen, Marnie...I ah...I owe you an apology."

She blinked with surprise. All right, then. Stupid Cowboy had morphed back into Sexy Smart Cowboy. "Oh. Do you?" she asked, trying not to smile.

He smiled, though. "I do."

Damn that smile of his. It reduced her to mush every time. Marnie couldn't help but smile, too, and absently fingered the tail of his long-sleeved T-shirt she'd been wearing. "I sort of thought you'd see it my way."

"I didn't say *that*," he said. "But...I said some things I wish I hadn't said."

"Such as?"

"Such as..." he sighed as he pushed his hand through his hair and laughed low. "I don't think you talk too much."

"Ooh," she said, quite pleased with his admission. "Well, that's really great of you to say. Frankly, I didn't think you meant it because I really don't talk that much. I mean, when I have something to say, I'll say it, but I don't go on and on just to hear myself talk like some people, not by—"

"Marnie," he said, putting his hand on her knee and sending a little bolt of lightning into her groin.

"Oh," she said, and laughed as she glanced at his big hand on her knee. She'd really like that big hand to be other places. "So…is that all?" she asked.

"Is that all?"

"I mean…isn't there anything else you'd like to say?" she coyly suggested, punching him lightly in the shoulder. "Like, maybe, you didn't mean to be such a jerk, but it's a painful topic for you, and you sort of reacted from a bad place?"

Eli gave her a lopsided smile. "I would never put those words together in a sentence, but yeah, I'm sorry I was a jerk. You didn't deserve that."

"Well, now you're just making me happy," Marnie said, and leaned forward, so that they were almost nose to nose. "You're excused," she murmured, and kissed his mouth.

"Hmm," Eli said. "I think I like being excused." He put his hand to her hair and gave her that look of affection that Marnie loved. "Excuse me some more, why don't you?" he asked.

"I can't," she said, leaning back. "I have to fish an altar out of the lake so I can wash my hair."

"With who?"

"With Olivia."

"Olivia?" He laughed. "You should have gone with Rhys. Olivia doesn't do any heavy lifting."

"No, it was all her idea," Marnie said, and started to move past Eli. "She's definitely going to help. She doesn't want Vince to win."

"Wait," Eli said, catching Marnie's arm. "What do you mean, her idea?"

"Her idea to be partners because she is mad at Vince. I help her, and if we win, she shares her bread and cheese and I get to use the rainwater first."

"How did she get bread and cheese?" Eli asked, shaking his head. "Listen, don't align yourself with Olivia. She's bad news."

Okay, here they went. Sexy Cowboy had turned into Mr. So Not a Wedding Consultant. "Thank you, but I *think* I know my bride." Rule number one for the successful wedding planner: Know your bride. Duh.

"I don't think you do," he said. "Olivia is the kind of girl who will cut you the first moment you aren't useful to her."

Okay, apology for being a jerk aside, Eli was treading dangerously close to being a jerk again. "That's not very nice," she said.

"I don't mean to be a jerk, Marnie—"

"Seems to me you've got it down to a fine art."

He frowned. "I just know her."

"Really?" Marnie said, pushing past him. "I don't think you know her at all...unless you crawled inside and looked, right?" she said, throwing his words back at him. She rolled out of the tent and went in search of Olivia, more determined now than ever to win.

She found Olivia sitting on the porch with Rhys and marched up the steps, stood in front of the megastar, and said, "*Game on.*"

"Yippee!" Olivia cried, and jumped up. "I can't wait to tell the idiot," she said, and skipped into the cabin.

CHAPTER TWENTY-FOUR

On the edge of the water, Olivia and Marnie argued about how best to proceed and finally decided they needed Eli's rope. He was more than happy to provide it—he stood with his weight on one hip, his arms crossed over his chest, watching them with the same interest with which he might watch a round of bull riding. Marnie pictured him doing just that, the smug bastard. But why did he always have to look so damn good, even when he was annoying the hell out of her?

Her lack of focus was probably why Olivia won the argument. "I'm too small," she said, pushing Marnie toward the water. "Look how tiny I am and how big you are. You have to do it."

It was hard to argue with that—Marnie did indeed tower over the diminutive star. So she waded into the lake, whimpering with each step as the ice-cold water seeped into her clothes and touched her skin. They had decided—well, Olivia had decided—that Marnie should wrap the rope around the altar. Then they'd both pull it upright, and together they'd move it to shore.

"You sure you want to do it that way?" Eli called from the bank once Marnie was already up to her knees in ice-cold water.

Hell, no, she wasn't sure, but it was a little late now, wasn't it? She gave him a withering look, then shifted her gaze to the altar. It was submerged only a foot or so from the edge of the lake. She leaned down and put her arms in the water, too. "*Yikes, yikes, yikes,*" she whimpered through chattering teeth. The water was so cold she could hardly feel the rope in her hands. It didn't help that the legs of the damn Arc de Triomphe were bobbing around her and knocking into her.

"Don't do it like that," Olivia said from her dry and much warmer spot on the edge of the lake. Marnie bit her tongue to keep from telling Olivia to jump out here and do it herself, and kept struggling to get the rope under the altar.

"Marnie! You're going to mess it up," Olivia cried.

"Then how the hell should I do it?" she asked sharply.

"God, you don't have to cop an attitude. I'm just trying to help."

Marnie paused to glower at her and noticed that Rhys and Vince had wandered down to watch.

"It might go a lot faster if you'd just use your hands," Eli said.

Great. More free advice. "Thanks for the tip, Popeye, but it's too heavy," Marnie shouted.

"It only weighs about fifty pounds," Eli said.

Marnie glared down at the stupid altar that they had to have flown in especially for Princess. Behind her, the plastic arch bumped her in the butt, and Marnie leaned down, grabbed the edges, and gave it a yank. It came up with a little bit of force. Dammit! She glanced over her shoulder— Eli had lowered his head and was laughing. *Laughing.*

"Fine," she shouted. "At least I win." She wrapped her arms around the stupid altar and dragged it out of the water. When she reached the edge, Olivia gave out a "Woo-hoo!" and did a little victory dance around Vince. Marnie let the stupid thing fall over; Eli wrapped her in a quilt. "You need some dry clothes."

"Really?" she snarled, and yanked the quilt tightly around her, ignoring Olivia's victory dance and taunting of Vince, ignoring how Eli picked up the altar, hoisted it onto his shoulder as if it weighed nothing, and walked away with it, leaving a trail of alpine lake water behind him as he went.

The rest of them followed Eli, Olivia shouting after him about the rainwater. "Thanks for all your help," Marnie muttered, and marched in the opposite direction, toward the tent, squishing with each step.

It took some doing to get out of her wet jeans. She was so cold she could barely make her fingers work, but she did eventually manage to squeegee herself out of them. She pulled on a pair of sweats, a camisole, and a dirty sweatshirt, then searched forever for dry socks. She donned two pairs, as her boots were waterlogged. When she had finally dressed, she made her way out in her socks, carrying her waterlogged boots to dry in one hand and her toiletry bag in the other.

At the very least, she was finally going to be afforded the luxury of washing herself and her hair. The very thought made her smile brightly.

She found Eli at the fire ring where he'd built another roaring blaze from nothing but some twigs and a lighter. He smiled as she walked up, took her shoes from her without a word, and put them near the fire to dry.

"Thanks," Marnie said. "When do I get to bathe?"

"I brought the rainwater up to the cabin. You should be good to go," he said with a smile.

"Great. I'll see you later when I'm squeaky clean," she said, and walked on to the cabin.

When she stepped inside, Vince was lounging on the couch, eating another peanut butter and jelly sandwich. Olivia was sitting on the bed, wrapped in one of the thick terry robes with a towel piled high on her head. Even so, it took a moment for Marnie to understand that Olivia had cheated—she'd reneged on her word and had gone first.

"Olivia!" Marnie exclaimed. "You promised I could go first."

That seemed to startle Olivia; she blinked up at her and looked around the room. "Well...you were taking so long."

"That's because it is very hard to get soaking wet clothes off when you are so cold you can't feel your fingers," Marnie cried. "But still, you promised."

"*Sor-ree*," Olivia said as she rubbed lotion on her feet. "It's not that big of a deal, is it?"

Yes. Yes, it was a very big deal, and Marnie was really pissed. With a snort of disdain for Olivia, she walked through the cabin, on the way to the bathroom.

"Ah...hello?" Vince said, but Marnie was in no mood to ask permission for water that was supposed to have been hers to begin with, and quickly reached the bathroom door and flung it open before the shrimp thought to call her back.

She didn't know who shrieked louder, her or Rhys. "Excuse me, the bathroom is currently occupied!" he screeched, trying to cover himself with a towel.

Marnie threw a hand up over her eyes. "What are you *doing*?" she screeched back. "That is *my* water!"

"Oh dear. Marnie, love, I've left you a big hunk of bread and some imported Camembert cheese on the dining table. It's from France. Why don't you have a bit and we'll talk when I am through here?"

"*Cheese*? You think to appease me with cheese?" Marnie exclaimed, her eyes still covered. "You cheated, Rhys. I got you this gig and you *cheated* me."

"Would you kindly close the door?" Rhys snapped. "It's rather cold."

Marnie slammed the door shut, whirled around, and marched into the main room of the cabin to Olivia, glaring furiously at her, arms akimbo. "What the hell, Olivia? You promised me."

"Marnie, Marnie," Olivia said, casually drying her ears. "I know I did, but you were in the water, and it just seemed that you had already had your bath."

"I did not have my bath. There was no soap. And it stunk. And there was a giant arch bumping against me! Jesus, Olivia, how could you be so mean?"

"She wrote the book for mean, kid. Have some bread and cheese and get over it," Vince suggested.

"Just shut *up*, Vince!" Olivia cried.

"I wanted to wash my hair!" Marnie exclaimed. "I went into that freezing lake on the promise that I could wash my hair, Olivia. You made me think we had an alliance, but you really had one with Rhys and you used me to get the water."

Olivia sighed and shrugged. "Survival of the fittest, Marnie. Survival of the fittest."

"*Aaaiieee!*" Marnie shrieked, and bolted for the door. "That's *it!*"

"Oh, honestly, Marnie. Stop making such a big deal about everything. You did get cleaner in the lake," Olivia said as she stuck the tip of the towel in her ear and dried it.

"Take the cheese," Vince coaxed her.

"I'll tell you what I'll take," Marnie said, and tried to think of something profane to take, but couldn't because she was so insanely mad, and with another shriek, she stormed out of the cabin and off the porch, stomping toward the fire with every intent of picking up a burning log and setting fire to the towel on Olivia's head.

"What's the matter?" Eli asked as she bounced to a halt at the edge of the fire ring, her chest heaving with her pant of fury. "Marnie?" he asked, leaning forward a little to look at her.

What was the matter? *What was the matter?* Everything was the matter! Every little stupid thing was hugely the matter. A tear of frustration slipped from Marnie's eye. And then another.

"Oh shit, what's wrong?" he asked, his voice full of alarm now.

"*They double-crossed me!*" she wailed. "They tricked me into going into the lake, and then they used the rainwater. And they tried to give me cheese to make up for it," she said as the tears suddenly poured from her eyes. "Oh God," she said, and pressed her hands to her face. "Oh God, I can't believe I'm crying. But I just wanted to wash my *haaaair.*"

"Ah hell," Eli said softly. "Marnie, don't cry."

"I don't want to cry. But I can't help it." And the tears of frustration began to flow.

Eli was suddenly at her side. He enfolded her in his arms, pressing her face to his shoulder. "Don't cry, Marnie, don't let them get to you. We'll be out of here in a day or two, and you can have all the baths you want."

"No," she wailed. "I wanted it *now!*"

Eli patted her on the back, held her tightly to him, and let her sob her frustration a few moments longer. But then Marnie got mad and pushed away from him, dragged the back of her hand across her nose. "You were right," she said hotly. "The woman cannot be trusted."

Eli nodded knowingly.

"That's my problem, you know it? I always trust people. Why do I trust anyone?" she demanded.

"I don't know about writing off the whole human race, but Olivia Dagwood should definitely be on your list," he agreed, and pushed a twisted strand of hair out of her eyes and behind her ear.

"Oh, she's at the very *top* of my list. Slot A-1." More tears slipped from her eyes.

"No, no," Eli murmured, and slipped two fingers under her chin and lifted her face up to his, made her look at him. "You know what? You deserve something special tonight."

"Like what?" she asked with tearful self-reproach. "*Two* peanut butter sandwiches?"

"Better than that. Look up there."

Marnie looked to where he was pointing and gasped. In a spruce, about halfway up, was an ivory object. Marnie squinted. "Is that...is that what I think it is?" she asked, fearful of the answer.

Eli nodded.

"How in God's name did Olivia's wedding dress get up there?"

Eli sighed. "Vince."

Marnie's heart leapt to her throat. "We have to get it down. That's an original. A *twenty-thousand-dollar* original," she cried, pushing Eli toward the tree.

"Not so fast," he said, and with a wink, he started for the cabin.

"Hey!" Marnie cried, twisting around. "Where are you going?"

Eli paused, glanced over his shoulder and smiled. "Just hold tight, coppertop," he said, and walked on.

Eli remained calm, but he was quietly seething for Marnie. It was one thing for Olivia to pull those little tricks on her own retinue, but to do it to Marnie, well…for a man who worked with superegos and unreasonable people for a living, he had finally reached his breaking point. Marnie didn't deserve this—the woman had a good heart, was as earnest as she could possibly be in doing a good job by these losers. If anything, she deserved a night at the Ritz to make up for the shabby way they had treated her.

If there was one thing Eli could not abide, it was meanness. Not in anyone.

He walked into the cabin, into the middle of the room, and sat on one of the leather chairs. Olivia smiled at him. Vince didn't look up. And Rhys, the fat, double-crossing bastard, was spreading cheese on a slice of bread.

"What's going on, Mr. Stuntman?" Olivia asked sunnily.

"We're gonna have another contest," Eli said.

Olivia instantly shook her damp head. "I don't want to do any more contests."

"I just bet you don't. But now that you've managed to have everything your way, we're gonna have one more."

Olivia's eyes widened at his tone. "*Excuse* me? I really don't know what that is supposed to mean, but let's not forget who employs who here, all right?"

"Let's not forget there's only one of us who can get us off this mountain," he coldly reminded her. That pushed her back—Olivia's eyes rounded, and her lashes fluttered a little, but she slowly leaned back, regarding him closely.

"So...what do you have in mind, mountain man?" a clearly amused Vince asked, stretching his arms high above his head.

"Let's agree on the stakes first—the winner gets this cabin for a night."

"No way," Olivia snorted. "I'm not sleeping in a tent."

"We don't know how long we're going to be here. It seems only fair to rotate the only true sleeping quarters we have. Think of Marnie—she doesn't even have a bed."

"Doesn't she?" Olivia sniffed.

"So what is the contest?" Rhys asked.

"Come on out and I'll show you," he said, and walked outside. Vince and Rhys were right behind him. Olivia reluctantly followed a moment later. He pointed to her gown hanging from the spruce. "The person who can get that down wins the right to sleep in the cabin tonight."

Olivia shrieked and whirled around, striking Vince in the chest.

"What?" he demanded, palms up. "You ruined my boots and you said it was off. I didn't think you'd need it."

"You sorry bastard!" she cried.

"Ridiculous contest," Rhys said, ignoring Olivia's tantrum. "One must merely climb a tree."

"It's not as easy as it looks," Eli said.

"Vince can climb it," Olivia snorted. "He put it up there."

"No, I threw it."

"Omigod, Vince! That dress is worth thousands," Marnie cried. "It was made especially for Olivia. It's hand- beaded. It's an original."

"Who cares?" Olivia cried. "I'm sure as hell not wearing it, and I'm not climbing the fucking tree for it, either."

"Then I will," Vince said cheerfully. "I want the cabin tonight."

"That's great, Vince, but you're not getting it," Olivia said angrily.

"I do if I climb that tree. And then *you* can find another place to sleep."

"Don't be so stupid, Vittorio," she retorted with a roll of her eyes.

"Personally, I do not mind the tent," Rhys said, and stuffed a piece of bread into his mouth. "It's rather refreshing," he added through a mouthful.

"Great. We'll count you out," Eli said, rising.

"Well, *I'm* certainly not going to do it," Olivia reminded them.

"Then I'll make sure my tent is tidied up for you," Eli added.

"Fuck that," she said, glaring at him. "I'm not sleeping in a goddamn tent."

"So what, it's you and me, Eli?" Vince asked with a grin. "You're on, pal. Let's go."

"And me," Marnie cried.

"Me first," Vince said, and started for the tree, but Olivia suddenly darted in front of him.

"Vince, baby, I didn't mean it was over," she said, smiling prettily. "I was just upset about everything. This has been a disaster. But I didn't mean it, okay, baby? I can't sleep in a tent."

"I know, baby," he said. "That's why I'm going to go do this for you. Eli's right—it's only fair that we compete for it, and I'm going to compete for you. I wouldn't dream of letting you sleep in a tent. I wouldn't dream of letting you sleep anywhere but a nice, comfy bed while the rest of us sleep on the hard cold ground." And Vince smiled the smile that made his movies gross thirty million on opening night.

Olivia looked confused by his smile. "Oh," she said uncertainly. "Okay."

Vince grinned at the rest of them. "Well, come on, kids. Let's climb a tree."

The climbing, as it turned out, was very anticlimactic. Vince didn't even try. One leg up, and then he was down. "That's just too high for me," he said.

"*Augh!*" Olivia cried. "You are such a bastard!"

Eli had thought Vince would at least give it a shot. He looked at Marnie. "You're up, coppertop," he said.

And Marnie tried. She made it about halfway to the dress, carefully pulling herself up through the sticky, pointy limbs, until she began to whimper. "My arms are giving out," she cried, and let Eli help her down. He had counted on her failing. The girl was full of spunk, but she was exhausted and not quite strong enough.

Once Marnie was down, Eli went up, grabbed the dress, and swung down in fifteen minutes. He landed to applause from Rhys and Vince and Marnie. Olivia was pouting. The dress had been rained on, and it was wrinkled, and there were a couple of snags in it, but it looked almost salvageable. "Thank God," Marnie said with a sigh of relief.

Olivia snatched the gown from Marnie's hands, pivoted on her heel, and marched inside.

The rest of them returned to Eli's fire and stood around it for a while.

"Damn, it looks like more rain," Vince said at one point, looking up as the sun slipped behind a rain cloud. The distant rumble of thunder confirmed it. "Great. Not only does the bitch get to sleep in a tent, but she gets to do it with a storm passing over us. I can't wait to tell her," he said, and with a laugh, he started for the cabin.

Rhys looked up at the sky and at Vince's departing back. "Frankly, I don't believe he ever meant to try for the cabin. I think he's quite through with her," he mused, and followed Vince.

Marnie looked at Eli. "Do you think that's true?"

Eli shrugged a little. "She does seem to be wearing a little thin on everyone." A shriek and the sound of a large crash in the cabin startled them; Eli grinned. "Maybe sooner rather than later." He laughed and looked at the sky. "It's going to let loose any minute now." He started kicking dirt on the fire. Marnie helped him, and when they had put out the flames, he grabbed her boots and they hurried to the cabin.

Vince and Rhys were seated before a fire at the hearth eating sandwiches when Eli and Marnie came in; Olivia was on the bed, her arms folded over her chest, pouting.

"A fire," Marnie said, moving to stand before it. "Vince, it's perfect."

"I beg your pardon, but I am responsible," Rhys said. "Peanut butter sandwich?"

"Thanks," she said, taking it. Rhys held up one to Eli, which he gratefully took, along with a bottle of water, and joined Marnie in front of the fire. The four of them— Olivia was still pouting—made small talk while they ate sandwiches and apples. Every once in a while, one of them would walk to the door and open it to peer outside, then close it again, when it appeared the rain was not abating.

Beneath the damaged roof Eli had patched, they had several pots lying around to catch the tiny streams of rain that came in. Periodically, Eli would pour the water into a kettle.

When the rain did at last pass over them, and the stars came out, Eli quietly left the cabin during a lively discussion between Olivia and Vince about a script she obviously loved and he despised. As he stepped out, Olivia called Vince stupid and moronic, and he responded by calling her a bitch.

When Eli returned a half hour later, he had a flashlight in one hand and Marnie's backpack in the other. "I'm beat," he announced. "Time for you all to go home."

Olivia turned big, sad eyes to Vince. Vince rolled his eyes.

Rhys stood up, took one last peanut butter sandwich, and sang out good night. Vince stood, too, and frowned down at

Olivia, who was sprawled in one of the leather chairs before the fire. "What?" she said weakly.

"Come on. Eli won. He gets the cabin."

Marnie stood, but Eli put a hand on her arm to stop her.

"It wasn't really a contest," Olivia whined. "I didn't agree to it, and I paid for this cabin."

"I'll reimburse you," Eli said.

"I'm not going," she said, and tossed her head.

"Jesus H. Christ," Vince shouted. "Would you, just once, think of someone besides yourself? I am so sick of your shit," he bellowed, and grabbed Olivia's arm and yanked her up to her feet. "Put some shoes on."

"Who are you kidding?" Olivia said sharply, yanking her arm from his grasp. "You think *you* can make me? What a joke."

She said it with such disdain that Eli thought Vince would strike her. He didn't strike her, but for the first time since they had walked into this meadow, Vince lifted a finger. He lifted all ten of them and firmly grabbed Olivia, slung her like a sack over his shoulder, and pushed past Marnie. "I swear, Livi, you are on my last nerve," he shouted as Eli calmly opened the door for him. Out they went, Vince marching stoically on, Olivia screeching at him to put her down.

The last thing they heard was Vince roaring at Olivia to shut up, followed by, "I hate you, Vincent! I hate you so much!"

Eli shut the cabin door and smiled at Marnie. She looked so bedraggled—even a twig was stuck in her hair now—that Eli couldn't help laughing. He'd never seen a more charming woman in all his life, and moved to where she stood, trying in vain to smooth one side of her hair. "I've got something for you," he said. "Wait here."

He walked out the back door and picked up the kettle of rainwater he had saved for her. It was full. Coupled with what was in the kitchen and the two buckets he'd put out back, he thought there might be enough for a shallow bath. He returned to the cabin, walked to the hearth, and hung the kettle from a hearth hook, left over, presumably, from the days when this was someone's home.

"What are you doing?" Marnie asked, watching him closely.

"Giving you a hot bath," he said, and laughed when Marnie squealed and clapped her hands with delight. In the kitchen, he grabbed two of the pots and brought them back to the hearth. "There's not enough water to run through the bathroom's heating element, but there's enough to heat and pour into the tub the old-fashioned way."

They stood side by side, anxiously watching the kettle and willing it to boil. When the water began to sizzle, Eli took the kettle from the fire to the bath and poured it into the tub.

"Get ready," he said. "I have enough for one more kettle, and that should be enough for a shallow bath."

"Oh, Eli," Marnie said, throwing her arms around his neck. "I think I love you!" She covered his face with kisses, then abruptly let go, grabbed up her little bag, and hurried to the bathroom.

Eli swallowed down the admission he felt on the tip of his tongue: *I think I love you, too.*

When he returned with the second kettle full of water, he walked into the scent of lilacs. Marnie had poured a small bottle of soap into the tub. He poured the water, went out, and returned with one of the thick robes Olivia had worn and a towel, both of which he hung on the hooks provided. "Have fun," he said and moved to close the door behind him, but Marnie stopped him with a hand to his arm.

"Eli...thank you," she said. "I know it sounds silly, but this means so much to me."

He smiled and wrapped his fingers around hers, squeezing them lightly. "I know," he said. "Don't let it get cold," he added and let go of her hand.

He shut the door behind him and returned to the main room of the cabin, a silly grin on his face. As he stood before the fire, his hands on his hips, his grin settled in. It made him feel good to see her smile like that.

Damn good.

Too damn good.

CHAPTER TWENTY-FIVE

Eli definitely hid a softer side, and the more Marnie was around him, the more glimpses of it she was seeing. As she luxuriated in her three-inch bath, she mulled over how he came off as a tough, no-nonsense kind of guy, the lonesome cowboy in an urban jungle, but in reality, he was very tuned in to the people around him. And he was a very resourceful man. Was there anything he could not do?

But what she liked most of all was that he was, in his own uniquely gruff way, very caring of her.

How frustrating it was that she'd see these pieces of him and feel that she was getting closer to him, and then the walls would come up and shut her off. She kept thinking back to last night, when he had gotten so angry with her. She had forgiven him that outburst today, because she understood that he'd been wounded. Lost loves could really mess with a person's head.

What bothered her was that he hadn't moved past it.

Whoever the bitch was that had jilted him so heartlessly had done a damn good job of it—the man was absolutely terrified of love.

That really sucked, because she had fallen in love with him. Soaking in a bath he'd made for her after winning her this cabin, which was probably the nicest, sweetest thing anyone had ever done for her, she would admit that she had, wholeheartedly, fallen in love with the lonesome cowboy. Which was why she really couldn't abide his erecting walls when she got close.

Eli needed help letting go of the past. Marnie was all for helping—she just wasn't sure how. That sort of damage was well out of her realm of experience. But instinctively, she knew she could not be the one to hold back.

So when Eli knocked on the door and said he had more water, Marnie smiled and called for him to come in. He opened the door and poked his head inside and seemed slightly taken aback that Marnie had made no attempt to cover herself. He stood in the doorway, holding a bucket of steaming water, his blue eyes greedily taking in every inch of her.

She sat up, gripping the sides of the old claw-foot tub. "Would you pour it on my hair? I don't think I got all the soap out."

A corner of his mouth tipped up. Being the man of few words that he was, he walked in and took a seat on the edge of the tub. Marnie couldn't see him, but she could feel his hand on her hair, his fingers sliding through the wet tresses, then his hand on her shoulder, moving her wet hair to her back, his fingers trailing lightly down her neck.

"Ready?" he drawled behind her.

Marnie nodded. The stream of hot water caught her off guard; she arched her back, dipped her head back and closed her eyes as he poured water through her hair, using his hand to help the rinsing along, lifting her hair and guiding the water over it. When he had finished, he put the bucket down, slowly lowered her hair, then laid his hands on her shoulders, massaging them, caressing her arms, her chest, her neck. His touch was tender and lingering, and Marnie knew that even though he fought the desire to love her, he couldn't quite distance himself, either.

She closed her eyes, leaned her head against his hand, and murmured, "Thank you."

"You're welcome." He ran his hand over the top of her head, stood up, and walked out without looking back. Marnie leaned back against the smooth curve of the tub, her fingers curling around the ends of her hair, her imagination running wild with an image of her in the back room of some saloon, her handsome cowboy bathing her, his hands running up and down her body...

She emerged from the bath a few minutes later wrapped in a thick terry robe, her hair wrapped in an even thicker towel. The cabin was dark, save for the light of a roaring fire, and Eli was seated in one of the two leather chairs facing the hearth. On a small granite table between the two chairs were a bottle of champagne, a heel of bread, and about two ounces of Camembert cheese.

Marnie grinned. "You are a miracle worker. Where did you get champagne?"

He smiled and poured some into a fine crystal flute. "Our illustrious couple was holding out. It was under the bed with some other things they apparently meant to trot out for the ceremony, including these flutes."

Marine picked one up and looked at the tiny stamp on the bottom. "Waterford," she said. "Someone's bridal gift." She handed the flute to Eli, slid into the chair next to him, tucked her feet under her, and took the full glass he offered. "This is such a treat," she said, and lifted her glass in a mock toast. "You are obviously a man of mystery and surprises."

"I don't know about that," he drawled. "But I figured you'd endured enough in the last few days. You probably didn't bargain for this when you signed on with us."

"That's putting it mildly," she said with a wink. "Yet, in a strange and kooky way, it's been kind of fun."

Eli snorted, but Marnie laughed. "A bath and clean hair has done wonders for my outlook," she said, and put aside the flute of champagne to spread some cheese on the bread. "I've been making a list of all the things I have learned on this trip," she said, handing a piece to Eli.

"Like?"

"Like...never let a bride talk you into a plastic arch. Don't leave home without extra underwear and protein bars. Don't trust anyone who is either hungry or dirty."

"Stake your tent," Eli added.

"Stake your tent." Marnie laughed and clinked her glass to his, sipped her champagne, and looked into the fire. "I also learned that some people are not what they seem."

"Ah," Eli said, lifting his glass. "So you've got the Supreme Drama Queen's number."

"Oh yeah," Marnie said, nodding adamantly. "But I was talking about you."

"Me?"

"Mm-hmm. You're not at all what you seem."

"How so?" he asked, looking at her fully now.

"Well," she said with a smile, "you are, in fact, a lot nicer than you appear."

"Damn, that hurts," he said with a grin as his gaze dipped to the V of her robe.

"No, it doesn't," she said, putting her champagne aside and moving her feet from beneath her. "I think you know that you come across as a tough guy, but you're really a big fluffy marshmallow inside."

"Ah, now, that's not right," Eli said, and began to shake his head, but Marnie was already moving to her knees on the rug at their feet, slipping between his legs and bracing herself with her hands on his thighs.

Eli cocked a curious brow as he put his champagne aside. His eyes were dark, roaming her face, her hair, her décolletage, and murmured, "What are you doing now, coppertop?" as he fingered a damp strand of her hair.

"I don't really know," she said, and leaned forward, so that her face was only inches from his. "I just wanted to say that...what happened to you? She's definitely the big loser," she said, and tilted her head up, kissed his cheek. "You're a good guy, Eli, a really good guy with a heart of gold and you deserve to be happy. But I think you hold yourself apart because you are so fearful of being hurt again—"

He squirmed beneath her hands and tried to speak. "No—"

Marnie instantly pressed two fingers to his lips. "You can't fool me," she said quietly. "You are afraid, it's obvious. But you don't have to be afraid with me because I would never hurt you, Eli. I'm just so sorry all of that happened to you," she said, and lightly kissed his lips. "You really didn't deserve that."

He caught her face between his hands and smiled salaciously. "So what do I deserve?"

"Better," she whispered, and kissed him again, then slid her mouth to his chin and his neck.

Eli put his hands on her shoulders and let them slide down her arms. Marnie slipped her hand beneath his thermal shirt, pushing it up as she ran her hands over the hard wall of his abdomen to the mounds of his pecs. Eli sighed as her fingers flitted over his taut nipples before pushing his shirt up and forcing him to lift his arms. She tossed the shirt near the fire, then moved back a little to admire his body. He was perfectly formed, she thought, the sort of masculine physique that every woman dreamed of.

How lucky for her that this was not a dream. She put her mouth on his nipple, her teeth lightly around it, and Eli moaned deep in his chest. His hands found their way inside the V of her robe, searching for her breasts, his fingers tweaking her nipples.

"Are you sure about this?" he asked roughly as she moved to the second nipple and bit it lightly. "You just bathed and I haven't been so lucky."

"I don't care," she said. "I love the way you smell." And it was true that the heady, masculine scent of him was seeping down into her groin, between her legs.

As he filled his hands with her breasts, she let her hands slide down his torso to the top of his pants. She unfastened them and pulled them open—and discovered that the man was not wearing any underwear. His erection was straining against the fabric of his pants, hard and thick. Marnie slipped her hand around him and slowly slid up, then down. With a groan, Eli massaged her breasts in response.

Marnie freed him from his pants. He closed his eyes; his head lolled back against the chair as she moved her hand down to the dark patch of hair and up again.

"Wait a minute," he said, lifting his head and putting his palm to her cheek. "You're not trying to bribe the last PB&J out of me, are you?"

"No," she said, and leaned down to touch the tip of her tongue to the swollen head. Eli flinched. "I'm after something way better than that."

"You want my tent? You can have it," he said a little breathlessly. "Name it, girl—whatever you want, it's yours."

She smiled, bent her head again, and her hair surrounding her, she took him into her mouth. Eli's entire body seized and he moved, lifting up, pushing his pants down to give her better access. Marnie was not the most experienced woman in LA, not by a long shot, but she knew instinctively what to do, and slid her mouth down the shaft of him while she cupped the taut sacs beneath, squeezing lightly, sucking tightly. She moved on him, her lips sliding, sucking and nipping, taking him as deep as she could and rising up again until he was groaning with pleasure. He caught her hair in his fist, moved it aside so he could watch her. When she let go of his cock and took a testicle in her mouth, he made a guttural sound of pleasure and grabbed her arms, holding her tightly.

"If you keep this up, there will be nothing left for you," he said, and forced her head up. He opened the palm of her hand, placed a condom in it.

Marnie smiled and artfully dressed him in it, using her fingers and her mouth to put it in place. Once it was secure, Eli grabbed her beneath her arms and easily pulled her up, onto his lap, and said in a lonesome cowboy drawl, "Ride me, baby."

Marnie rode him, all right, sliding down onto his shaft while his hands cupped her breasts. He was moving beneath her, meeting her thrusts with a powerful updraft of his own. And then, without warning, he slipped an arm around her waist and rose up, holding her, then easily lowering both of them onto the rug.

Her robe fell open; Eli gathered her arms in one hand, holding them high above her head, and gazed at the full length of her. She was beautiful, he thought, all soft flesh and curves. Gorgeous.

She smiled up at him as his gaze greedily roamed the naked length of her, lingering at the reddish spring of curls between her legs. "What are you doing?" she asked. "You're not trying to get the last PB&J out of me, are you, cowboy?"

Eli looked in her eyes, the big pancake eyes that he had come to long for, and smiled warmly. "It ain't your PB&J I'm after, coppertop," he said, and lowered his mouth to hers, slipped his tongue between her lips, and kissed her deeply. With his free hand he lazily felt her body, skimming every curve and the soft patch of hair, taking in her scent, the silken feel of her skin. He shifted his mouth to her neck, nuzzling her, and down a little farther, to her breasts, the round, succulent mounds of flesh with the small, dark nipples. He took the peak in his mouth, tweaking it with his teeth as she had tweaked him, sucking lightly, feeling her body rise up to meet his, hearing her little gasps of pleasure that had the effect of making his cock, impossibly, even harder.

His hand slipped to the curls between her legs, between the folds. She was slick and wet, and the earthy scent of her desire made him crazy. A switch deep inside him was suddenly kicked on, and he was impatient to be inside her again. He slipped one finger in deep, felt her clinch around him, then slipped another inside her while he attended to her clit with his thumb, and began to move his fingers in primal fashion.

Marnie's eyes were closed, her brow creased with her concentration on his attentions. The skin of her breasts was pink from the lingering heat from his mouth. She looked, he thought wildly, as beautiful as any woman had ever seemed to him, and he suddenly, desperately, needed to be inside her, to thrust deep inside her, to touch her. He moved on top, his hands and fingers working maniacally, bringing her closer and closer to release. But when she began to moan, he withdrew his hand and slid his cock into her.

Marnie gasped and her eyes fluttered open; a smile of pure delight spread her full lips. She reached up, touched his face. "I'd really like it," she said breathlessly, "if you would just...*fuck* me, Eli."

The power of those words sent him soaring. He was suddenly thrusting hard into her, his thumb still moving against her. Marnie lifted her hips to him, put her hands to his nipples and squeezed them hard, adding to his burgeoning pleasure. She was slick and hot—he moved like a madman in her, desperate to reach the core of her, desperate to be part of her.

His jaw clenched, he stroked her, driving her to a climax they could share. Marnie groaned with pleasure; her mouth fell open, her eyes fluttered shut, and she began to cry out, her pleasured sobs of release his undoing. Her body seized around him with her last cry; he could feel a different heat squeeze him as she convulsed in one long wave, and he grabbed her hips, drove into her until he had exploded, too, coming in her aftermath, coming hot and hard and long.

Spent, exhausted, and feeling uncharacteristically tender of heart, Eli lowered himself to Marnie, pushed her damp coppery hair from her face, and kissed each and every freckle there.

After a moment, she opened her eyes and studied his face. With the pad of her thumb, she traced the line of his jaw, felt the stubble of his beard, then slowly rose up on her elbows and touched her forehead to his. "Eli," she whispered, "I have to tell you that I think I really, truly love you."

The admission stung him—he was still breathing raggedly, still feeling extraordinarily tender, but could say nothing. It was as if his tongue had frozen, his brain unable to conjure up the words to respond in kind. He put his hand to the back of her head and drew her up to his shoulder, then lowered them down to lie on the rug. Marnie released a small sight of contentment, her breath warm and moist on his skin.

He was feeling something very strong for this woman, he would not attempt to deny it. But was it love? Did he even know what that was anymore? Did he confuse it with lust?

After a moment, the air grew cold around them, and Eli stirred, made sure Marnie's robe was tightly around her, then donned his thermal shirt. He put two logs on the fire and helped her up to the bed. Before he joined her, he grabbed the champagne and the flutes. The two of them sank beneath the down comforter and quilts to sip champagne.

They said nothing for a time, until Marnie said, "I'd like to request lobsters tomorrow."

He turned and looked at her. "Beg your pardon?"

She was tracing a tiny path on his chest. "When they come with the snowblower, could they shoot some lobsters at us? I don't think I can eat another PB&J."

He smiled and kissed the top of her head. "I'll make them give us lobsters," he said, and lazily laced his fingers through hers. "Marnie," he said quietly. "I'm, ah...I'm not sure..." His voice trailed off, and he hated himself. He was, at the defining moment, unable to summon his feelings into words.

"Not sure...we'll get out of here?" she asked with a wink. "Of course we will. You just have to have faith."

She was, in her own way, sparing him an awkward moment. Whatever he was feeling went deeper as a result; he smiled gratefully and gripped her hand. "Okay," he said softly. "But so do you."

Her dark eyes peered into his, searching for the thing he could not yet bring himself to give. "Okay," she said at last. "I'll have faith, too."

He nodded and slipped his fingers into her hair. His thoughts were jumbled and confused—he wanted to say something reassuring, to let her know he had feelings, that he hadn't quite worked through them all yet. But he'd learned a long time ago on the plains of West Texas that it was best to keep quiet when a person wasn't sure what was going on. So he gathered her hand in his, brought it to his mouth, and kissed her knuckles. Then he let go and kissed her, kissed her hard, with all that he was feeling and could not name.

She made that little sound of contentment when he lifted his head and laid her head against his chest. Wrapped in each other's arms, the two of them fell asleep, the sound of a dying fire fading into the distance.

They were still wrapped in each other's arms the next morning when the whirring sound of a helicopter descended on their little meadow.

CHAPTER TWENTY-SIX

E li almost killed himself untangling his limbs from
Marnie when he heard the sound of the helicopter
above them. He was hopping around with one leg in his
pants, trying to get the other leg in, too, when she sat up,
scratched her head, then looked at him as the sound reg-
istered somewhere in her sleepy brain. "Helicopter!" she
shrieked, as if he hadn't noticed, and was suddenly fighting
the covers to get to her feet, and then, leaping off the end
of the bed, she ran for the bathroom.

Eli shoved his feet into boots and grabbed up his shirt,
marched to the door, and flung it open just in time to see
a couple of parcels drop from the bird above them—he
jumped off the porch and looked up.

It was not a TA bird dropping stuff to Vince, Olivia, and
Rhys, who had run into the meadow, too.

Eli was still standing there when Marnie ran past him.
"Come on, let's see what it is!" she cried, and bounded down
the steps, her copper hair streaming behind her as she ran
to the meadow.

As the helicopter rose up and turned toward the lodge,
Eli caught sight of a man hanging out the door, a wide-
angle-lens camera in his hand.

The press had found them.

His radio went off, and he withdrew it from his pocket, flipped it open. "How'd they find us?" he asked.

"Someone talked in LA. Once they got up here, they didn't have to ask around too hard to find out there was a little problem at the lodge," Jack drawled.

"Damn," Eli said.

"It's pandemonium down here. If they aren't drunk, they're trying to get out before their half-drunk faces are plastered all over the tabloids."

"I don't think our bridal couple noticed," Eli said as the bird came round again and swooped low, getting pictures of Vince and Olivia digging through the packages they had dropped.

"Good news is, our bird will be up in a couple hours. You'll be out of there by early afternoon. Not a moment too soon, either—you're booked on a morning flight to Brazil."

Eli didn't say anything. He'd managed to put the Amazon trip with the Japanese contingent of businessmen out of his mind during the last few days.

"Unless, of course, you want me or Coop to go," Jack was saying. "I don't mind, bro, if you need a break after this—"

"No," he said, cutting Jack off. "I'll go. I committed to them and honestly, I need a little space to clear my head." Did he really? Didn't he know what he wanted?

"Sure," Jack said. "We'll have you back in LA tonight."

LA It seemed like another planet at the moment. He watched as Marnie pulled out a tabloid from one of the packages. The moment Olivia saw it she jerked her gaze up, saw the camera, and shrieked. She snatched the tabloid from Marnie's hand to shield her from the paparazzi above and was suddenly running for the cabin.

Eli closed his radio and went out into the meadow to pick up whatever the paparazzi had tossed down to them.

The five of them sat in the cabin, their nerves frayed by the sound of helicopters buzzing them, looking up at the roof every time one flew overhead, munching on Ho-Hos and bananas, courtesy of the tabloid press. Vince and Olivia were not even speaking—they'd made it quite clear that the wedding was off by calling each other a host of names that made Marnie cringe. Rhys was certain he'd been poisoned by the lake water, given that he'd spent most of the night in the outhouse, and Eli was busily preparing to have them all lifted out in a matter of hours.

Marnie was the only one who was smiling as she ate her Ho-Hos, but then again, she'd always been a huge fan of the chocolate treats. Not that the Ho-Hos were at the root of her frighteningly good mood, really—it just seemed as if the air was just a bit crisper, the sun a bit brighter, and the company she kept not nearly as odious as they really were. And even though Olivia was being a monstrous horse's ass, Marnie didn't even care.

When the TA helicopter finally came and they were deposited at the lodge, Marnie was the only one who was not rushed into the waiting hands of some handler, the only one who was not put in front of a camera or microphone to talk about how the hush-hush wedding of the century had disintegrated into a true episode of *Survivor*.

No, Marnie was shown to what remained of the reception tent and left to sift through all the stuff that had been ordered for the wedding of the century, to get it ready to be returned. Outside the tent was sheer chaos—the press was everywhere and frantic celebrity guests were sneaking away from the lodge. Vendors and lodge personnel looked shell-shocked. Marnie wandered around the madness, dressed in a clean pair of terrain pants and jacket, her hair buried under a baseball hat, calmly thinking amid the chaos about the enormity of what had happened between her and Eli.

It was huge, wasn't it?

In the half of the reception tent that was still standing, amid tables and chairs that some kind soul had stacked and moved out of the elements, Marnie searched through the debris in the wake of a couple of days of hard partying to inventory the linens. She didn't care that it looked as if all the champagne was gone. Nor was she particularly perturbed that some of the Baccarat crystal bowls had been used for ashtrays.

Nope, Marnie was too busy waxing romantically that she and Eli had crossed some invisible barrier. There was nothing to hold them back now—they'd been freed from the past, from their working relationship, from the secret insanity of this wedding. Marnie didn't even care that her one shot at big-cheese wedding planner stardom had been effectively dashed when Olivia's publicist had informed the gathered throng of press that Olivia Dagwood had no plans to marry anyone, and that she and Vincent Vittorio were merely friends.

No, this afternoon everything was looking rosy and beautiful, and as Marnie folded a tablecloth that had been used to wipe something brown with, she pictured herself with Eli riding on horseback through a mountain meadow. Maybe in matching chaps. Yep, she was pretty certain Eli was The One, the man she would spend the rest of her life with. She knew it as well as she knew that she was sitting right in the middle of a sensational *Access Hollywood* taping.

So naturally, she was expecting Eli to confirm there was a "them" when he came walking into the reception tent several hours later, clean shaven and dressed in a fresh pair of faded Levi's and a starched white shirt. Marnie lit up when she saw him, and thought, now that they were off the mountain and essentially clear of their constant companions (who were, Marnie'd heard, already on their way back to LA), that maybe he would be able to speak more clearly about what was in his heart.

She honestly expected him to take her in his arms and kiss her and laugh about the three days they had spent marooned with Bridezilla and company, then offer to drive her to Farmington or Durango where they could hop a puddle jumper to Phoenix and go on to LA together. She expected it so much that she turned toward him with a beaming smile.

But Eli did not gather her in his arms. He stood on the other side of the table and smiled thinly, and Marnie felt the first worm of doubt creep into her heart.

"You doing all right?" he asked, and put his hand to his nape, rubbing it a little in a way she had learned meant that he was uncomfortable.

"Yes," she said, swallowing down a sudden swell of panic in her throat. "Clean clothes, clean body—I feel like a million bucks. What about you?"

"Feeling pretty damn good myself," he said, then lowered his hand, put it on his waist. Then dropped it. Then put it on his waist again.

"You want a drink? There's some champagne left," she said, and forced a little titter that was supposed to be an easy laugh but sounded more like the screech of a night owl.

"No thanks," he said, missing the joke. "Listen, Marnie, I've got to head out tonight."

Now the panic reared up and slapped her. "Head out?" she repeated stupidly. "What do you mean?"

"I've got to be on a plane to Brazil in the morning. I've got another gig lined up with some Japanese businessmen who want to do the Amazon."

"Do the Amazon?" she echoed, and mentally stomped her foot, wishing she could find her tongue instead of repeating everything he said.

"A raft float and then a hike into the jungle, basically. So I'll be incommunicado for a while."

"Oh," she said weakly as her heart slipped from its sky-high perch. "So…" She had to pause and screw up her courage to ask the obvious, folding the tablecloth into an even smaller square. "When will I see you again?"

"Ah…I, ah…I can't say for sure," he said quietly.

She tried to smile, but it was impossible to do so when she was trying to make sense of what was happening. "Don't they have phones in Brazil?" she asked, and risked peeking up at him.

Eli wasn't any better at forcing a smile. "Sure they do," he said. "In some places. I'll give you a call when I can."

"Oh. Well. A call," she said.

Eli surprised her by leaning across and putting his hand on hers, stopping her from folding the tablecloth once more. "I think it's folded," he said, and Marnie noticed that she had folded it into a towering square. She put it aside, folded her arms across her middle, and looked at him.

"I'll give you a call when I'm able, okay?"

She nodded and waited a moment, waited for him to tell her how much the last few days had meant to him, how he would miss her. But when the words didn't come, she began to doubt her sanity, to wonder if perhaps the whole *we're trapped!* atmosphere had led to the best sex of her life. Was it nothing more than that? Marooned sex? Not the ride-off-into-the-sunset sex she had believed all afternoon, shivering with delight each time she thought of it? Was Eli right, and she'd confused sex with love?

"Marnie," he said.

She pressed her lips together.

"I'll call you."

"Great!" she said, and forced a smile. "Give me a call when you get back to LA and we'll catch up. So…how am I supposed to get out of here?" she asked, picking up another linen. "And I'm still getting paid, right? I mean, you guys aren't going to hold that freak storm against me."

"Of course not. Michael will take care of it when you get back to LA I just assumed you'd have enough to do here to keep you a couple days."

"Right, right," she said, and picked up another table-cloth. "Lots to do."

Eli sighed and shoved his hand through his hair, and she realized she missed his growth of beard. "I'll talk to you, coppertop."

"Okay," she trilled. Eli smiled sadly and started to turn away, but Marnie couldn't let him go, couldn't let him walk out of this tent without knowing what had happened between last night and today. "Wait."

He stopped and turned halfway toward her. Marnie dropped her tablecloth. "Is that all there is, Eli? After...after such a fantastic night—*nights*—together, the best you can do is say you'll *call*?"

He gave that a thoughtful nod and looked at the floor a long moment. "I'll be honest, Marnie. I don't know what to think," he said, lifting his gaze. "I'm not really sure where my head is at right now."

"Oh," she said, nodding smartly. "I guess that means you're just not that into me."

"I didn't say that."

"You didn't have to." Did he think she was naïve? She'd read the book, along with the rest of America. Oh yeah, she was a great bang when they were stuck on a mountaintop, but in the real world? God, she hated him in that moment and looked away from him. "Whatever, Eli. Have fun."

"Look, Marnie, I've got to get back to LA and be on a plane first thing in the morning. I haven't had time to think through everything that has happened with us, and the only truly honest thing I can say at this moment is that. . . I don't know. I just don't know what I'm doing, I don't even know what I'm *capable* of doing. And I don't want you to think there's going to be something between us if I can't live up to my end—"

"This is just fucking fabulous," she snapped.

Eli frowned and rubbed his nape once more. "I never said—"

"I know, Eli, you never said anything. That's the difference between me and you, right? I do all the talking. You do all the taking."

"Marnie…" He sighed. "Just let me call you, all right?" he asked. "I don't have time to have this conversation right now. I've really got to go."

"Fine. Go," she said, and turned around, away from him, willing him to leave, to go so far away that she'd never have to lay eyes on him again, and began to fold her tablecloth with a vengeance.

Eli started to walk away. But then he pivoted and walked around to Marnie's side of the table. She ignored him, kept folding her tablecloth. He leaned to his side, put his hand against her cheek, his big rough cowboy hand, and she crumbled. She closed her eyes, leaned into his hand, and let him turn her to face him.

Eli pressed his forehead to hers. "Have faith, remember?" he whispered, then kissed her. It was a tender kiss, a sweet untangling from what they'd shared on the mountain. He lifted his head, kissed her forehead, then dropped his hand and turned away, striding out of the reception tent.

Marnie waited until he had disappeared into the fading light of the day before she lifted her hands and tried to stab the tears of frustration back into her eyes before they fell.

CHAPTER TWENTY-SEVEN

In a village of no more than one hundred souls deep in the jungle of the Amazonian basin, Eli traded soap, a package of cheese, and an LA Lakers T-shirt for an insect net and paper and pencil. That night, after he and Cooper had settled their Japanese wards (who had been quite titillated by the sight of two very large caiman lizards on the edge of the village), Eli made his way to a thatched roof hut made of walking palms where he and Cooper would sleep.

It was the first real bed he'd seen in two weeks, and it was a hammock.

Eli didn't care; he climbed into the hammock, exhausted from the energy required to float the Amazon with fifteen men who did not speak the slightest bit of English, or, it seemed, possess even the most basic of outdoor skills. His days had been filled with hiking and herding and floating, and this village was the first opportunity they'd had to really rest. They'd be here twenty-four hours to rest up before hiking deeper into the rain forest.

With a candle on the wall providing the only light—the village did not enjoy the wonders of modern electricity— and two parakeets hopping around below him, Eli picked up the paper and the pencil and wrote:

August 12 Dear Marnie

He stopped, squinting at the words. Too formal, wasn't it?

August 12 Dear Marnie
Hey, Coppertop, how are you? I am in the middle of the rain forest in Brazil.

He paused again, tapped the pencil against the paper and sighed. He was not exactly the corresponding type. He could count on one hand the letters he'd written in his life—they'd all been when he was six, written to his mom when he was away at camp for the first time. Now that he was an adult, he had no idea how to go about it.

What he wanted to say was that he missed her, and he'd been doing a lot of thinking, and he was thinking that he really was...in love with her.

I miss you. I can't think of anything but you. We float down the Amazon and all around us are jaguars and pink dolphins and macaws and anacondas, but all I see is you and your smile and those long goddamn legs. I wish you were here, I wish I could hold you. I wish I weren't so damn tongue-tied and could say out loud that I think I love you, too.

Ah hell, he sounded like a kid with his first crush, all sappy and pathetic.

It had been three weeks since he'd left her standing in that tent in Colorado. She'd probably gone on to her next gig by now and after the way he'd left her, she'd probably gone on with her life. Who could blame her? He was a putz, a big fucking chicken, quack quack, and he suddenly felt like an even bigger fool. What did he think? Some love letter written in a village with no post would fix things?

He folded the paper, stuffed it into his all-terrain pants, the pencil, too, and put his arm behind his head for a pillow.

He needed to sleep.

In her new tiny little apartment in Van Nuys, Marnie spread her portfolio on the little kitchen table to show to Miss Emily Buckholtz, the bride with a shoestring budget and a need to be married in three weeks' time. It wasn't exactly the wedding Marnie had hoped for, but it was work.

"Ooh," Emily said, her little green eyes going round. "Is that who I think it is?"

"Yes," Marnie said with a smile. "That is Olivia Dagwood and Vincent Vittorio. But you know these Hollywood stars—they called off the whole thing at the last minute." Too bad, too, because it really would have been a spectacular wedding, if Marnie did say so herself.

"Look, here's her gown," she said, turning the page, and tried to block the image of it dangling from a tree.

"Omigod, I would *kill* for a gown like that!"

"I don't think a Xioong original fits within our budget," Marnie said with a laugh.

Emily Buckholtz looked up, her eyes wide as saucers. "How much did it cost?"

Marnie leaned forward and whispered in return, "Twenty thousand." Emily gasped. Marnie nodded. "I know a place where you can get one off the rack that looks almost exactly like it for a very reasonable price."

"Really?" Emily asked, looking hopeful.

"Really. Betty's Bridal Discount. We can go later and check them out if you'd like."

"Oh, I'd love to."

Marnie smiled and turned the page to show her the linens they would have used when the phone rang. "Why don't you look through here a minute," she suggested and picked up her phone. "Hello?"

"Hi, honey!" Mom trilled on the other line.

"Mom, I'm in the middle of a meeting. Can I call you back?"

"I finally found a reason for you to come home to visit, Marnie," Mom said, ignoring her.

"Okay, but can it wait?"

"Sure. A letter came for you from that outfit you were working for, Thrillmakers."

Marnie's heart dipped, and she unconsciously gripped the phone a little tighter. "Thrillseekers. A letter, you say?" she asked weakly.

"Uh-huh," Mom said in a singsong way. "A *letter.* Addressed to Miss Marnie Banks."

A letter, a letter...was it from him? Could it possibly be from him? "Okay, okay," Marnie said, glancing over her shoulder at Emily. "Just leave it on the bar. I'll stop by later to pick it up."

"Great. I'm making my famous soy enchiladas for supper. We'll expect you. Toodleloo!" she said, and clicked off before Marnie could decline the invitation to supper.

"This table is gorgeous," Emily said when Marnie returned.

Marnie glanced at the picture she had taken of a mocked-up table to show Olivia what they would do for the reception. "Yeah," she said wistfully, taking a seat. "That would have been fun." She proceeded to tell Emily about the Baccarat bowls with floating stars and the white roses that would have been strung and hung from the tent ceiling to give an illusion of stars, and what Emily might do at a fraction of the cost...but as she talked, she could see only Eli, could think of only Eli.

She'd thought about him constantly since he'd left. For the first couple of weeks, she'd thought each day would be the day she'd hear from him. And when each day passed without a word, Marnie became the master of rationalization and gave him every excuse. He was in the Amazon, for Pete's sake. It wasn't as if he could pick up a cell phone or drop her a line.

But in the back of her mind, a tiny voice would argue, couldn't he, really? Didn't they have mail in Brazil? Phones? Was she to believe that those poor people lived without the basic means of communication with the world? No, no, of course they had mail, and now that he had been gone for five weeks, she had finally come to the conclusion that she'd been dumped. Again.

Or had she? Maybe, just maybe, he really couldn't get hold of her. He'd told her to have faith. Maybe, hopefully, please, a letter from him had arrived. And maybe Emily Buckholtz would quit talking about the sort of wedding she'd always wanted so Marnie could go find out.

The next hour seemed interminable to her, but she smiled and nodded and managed to talk through plans with

JULIA LONDON

Emily. They settled on the smallest of packages—a quickie wedding without a lot of trimming and very little fanfare. Great for Emily, but a far cry from the gala wedding Marnie had hoped to pick up.

When at last Emily left, Marnie stood at her window and watched Emily putter out of the parking lot in a Geo Metro, then grabbed up her purse and keys and rushed out of her apartment, headed for Hancock Park and her mom's house.

She reached her childhood home in record time, but groaned when she pulled into the drive. The book club was meeting—she could see them all in the big picture window. That was the one thing she really didn't need today. She grabbed her purse, determined just to slip in, grab the letter, and slip out.

Mom, however, had other ideas. She was standing in the foyer waiting for Marnie when she quietly opened the door.

"Marnie!" she cried, and flung her arms around her, squeezing tightly for a moment, but then suddenly rearing back and frowning. "You're losing weight. I knew that would happen," she exclaimed. "You're not eating, are you?"

"Mom, I'm eating. I'm not losing weight. I weigh exactly the same as I did when I lived here."

"Oh, really? And when was the last time you weighed?"

"I don't know," Marnie said as she tried to dislodge herself from her mom's grip.

"Carol? Is that our Marnie?" Mrs. Campbell's familiar voice rang out, followed by Mrs. Farrino's gin-soaked smoker's hack. "Bring her in here. We haven't seen her in ages."

"Mom, no," Marnie hissed, but Mom grabbed Marnie's hand and pulled her into the dining room, ignoring Marnie's attempts to tug her hand back.

338

"Hi, Marnie!" the ladies called out, and Mrs. Campbell waved.

"Hello, Mrs. Farrino. Mrs. Campbell. Mrs. Randolph. Mrs. Donaldson."

"So come in, come in," Mrs. Campbell said, patting an empty chair. "Come do a Jell-O shot with us."

"A *Jell-O* shot?" Marnie echoed in disbelief, and looked at her mother.

"Why not?" Mom asked with a shrug. "You think we're too old for Jell-O? Now come in, Marnie, and sit down. We've missed you around here," she said, pulling Marnie into a seat at the table. She sat beside her, very close, as if she expected Marnie to bolt. Which Marnie intended to do the first moment she could.

"How's that new apartment?" Mrs. Randolph asked.

"It's great. I really like it a lot," Marnie said. In truth, it was a dump, but was the only thing she could afford and still pay off her debt.

"Carol says it's not in a real good part of Van Nuys," Mrs. Campbell said, wincing sympathetically.

"Ah, well...I couldn't afford the good part."

"Forget that—what happened to the wedding of Vincent Vittorio and Olivia Dagwood?" Mrs. Farrino demanded. "I thought there was going to be a big wedding somewhere but then I heard on *Access Hollywood* that they're just friends. Is that true, Marnie? They're just friends?"

Marnie had a sudden image of them all sitting around this table for weeks, speculating. "I have no idea, Mrs. Farrino," Marnie said. "I guess they're just friends."

"Horseshit," Mrs. Farrino said, and took another drag off her smoke. "Carol, pass me the Fritos, hon."

"Well, I guess they must be," Mom said as she passed the Fritos to Mrs. Farrino. "I saw in a magazine in the grocery store that Vincent is dating Olivia's assistant."

Marnie blinked. "*Lucy?*"

"Something like that," Mom said. She picked up a little glass that looked like it was full of congealed cough syrup. "Jell-O shot?"

"No thanks," Marnie said. "So okay," she added brightly, coming to her feet. "It's great to see you all again, but I really have to be—"

"Not so fast, Marnie," Mrs. Farrino said, and clamped a hand down on her arm, the cigarette ash hovering precariously over her hand. "Sit, sit!"

Marnie sat.

"What I want to know is if you are still seeing that handsome man. You know, the Texas one?"

Yes, she knew, the Texas one. The lonesome cowboy who made love like a man who had been stranded on a mountaintop his whole life. The man who could make her melt inside with just a look. The man who might have, maybe, actually written her a letter, but unfortunately, she didn't know for sure because she couldn't get out of the freakin' dining room to check it out.

"We, ah…we weren't really seeing each other," Marnie tried, and earned a bunch of snorting laughter from around the table for it. "Really!" she vainly insisted.

"Oh, Marnie," Mom said, laughing.

"And besides, he's out of the country right now," Marnie added smartly.

"Oh, that's a pity." Mrs. Campbell sighed. "I was hoping we'd see him again. He's so cute. I just want to eat him right up."

"I want to eat him right up, too," Mrs. Farrino said, and Mrs. Donaldson guffawed.

Marnie felt the back of her neck get hot and glanced at her mom. But Mom just laughed and playfully punched her on the shoulder. "Honestly, Marnie. Where is your sense of humor? They're just teasing you."

"Speak for yourself, Carol," Mrs. Campbell said, and the four of them howled again.

"Mom," Marnie said, pinning her mother with a look. "I really have to go."

"Then go on," Mrs. Farrino said with a flick of her wrist. "We're just having a little fun. No need to get your panties all in a wad."

They were not in a *wad.* "It's just that I have an appointment this afternoon, and I really have to go," she said, standing up. She waved weakly at the lot of them and said, "Bye."

"Bye!" the women called out.

"Marnie, honey, we're having soy enchiladas tonight. Go tell your dad you're here."

"Okay, Mom."

"Don't be late," Mom trilled.

"Okay!" she trilled right back, and as she exited, stage left, she heard them all laugh again when Mrs. Farrino remarked that Marnie had seemed a little too uptight even when she was a kid.

Marnie stalked to the kitchen, picked up the mail, and flipped through it, finally finding the one addressed to her. She glanced at the return address and her heart soared. *Thrillseekers Anonymous.*

She quickly tore it open, but her face fell when she withdrew an invoice with a yellow Post-it note stuck to it.

The note was from Michael, explaining that the invoice had arrived only last week, and he could find no record of it having been paid, and could she please shed some light on it? She glanced at the invoice—it was for John and Jim, the professional guests.

It was not a letter from Eli. In fact, Eli's name didn't appear anywhere on the damn thing.

Okay. All right. She'd pined, she'd hoped, and she'd had faith. Now she was just pissed. She folded the letter and stuffed it back into the envelope and shoved it into her purse. She marched out of the kitchen and into the hallway, headed for the door. As she passed the dining room, her mother saw her. "Marnie, where are you going? Don't forget the enchiladas!" she cried.

"Sorry, Mom, I've got something I've got to do," she called over her shoulder and went out, got behind the wheel of her car, and pointed it in the direction of the Thrillseekers offices.

The TA offices weren't really offices, but Jack's house off Mulholland Drive. Marnie had discovered this just before the wedding of the century that never happened, when she'd had to get a check for a vendor. He had a guest house on his property, set behind the main house and deep in some acacia trees, that served as their offices.

She lucked out—Jack and Michael were both there, going over a movie script. They looked a little surprised when she walked up to the glass door and banged on it— she could see them sitting just inside. Jack instantly got up and let her in.

"Hey, Marnie. This is a surprise," he said.

"Right." She took the invoice from her purse and shoved it at Jack. "Michael wanted to know about this invoice. I paid these guys at the lodge. This is for your records."

"Ah," Michael said, nodding as Jack took the invoice. He stood up, too, put his hands to his hips, glanced at Jack, and asked, "You drove all the way over here just to tell me that?"

"I was in the neighborhood," she said with a shrug. "I, ah, I told Eli you'd be getting an invoice for your records," she lied, and looked at the floor. "I guess he forgot to tell you?"

"Ah. I've only talked to Eli a couple times since he and Cooper left for Brazil," Michael said.

Aha, so there *was* a means of communication. Marnie bit her lip, absently fingering the edge of a lampshade. "Soooo...he's still in Brazil?" she asked, trying very hard to act innocently about it. "I thought that would have been over by now."

"It is," Michael said. "Right now he's in New Zealand."

Marnie's head snapped up at that. New Zealand? *New Zealand?* "New Zealand?" she exclaimed, forgetting her act. "He never said anything about New Zealand."

Michael exchanged another look with Jack. Jack put his hand on her shoulder. "He, ah...well, he had to go there in place of Cooper when Cooper's mom had emergency surgery. It was a last-minute deal."

"Oh," Marnie said, nodding. "Last-minute."

"Yeah. Last-minute."

She should have thanked them and left. She should have just let it go. But she didn't—she started talking to fill the awkward silence like she always did. "But he might have called and mentioned New Zealand, right? I mean, it's not like I'm entitled to an itinerary or anything, but, you know, we just survived the wedding disaster of the century, and it wouldn't have killed him to see if I was doing all right, would it?"

"No," Jack said firmly. "No, it would not have."

"*Thank* you," she said. "I'm not asking for anything but common courtesy here. Just some indication that he's human, and that he considers the feelings of people with whom he has worked closely. It's not often I get stuck in the mountains—like never—and my career didn't quite pan out like I'd hoped after that fiasco, but does anyone care about that? Nooo," she said.

"Ah…we care. We really do," Jack said, looking extremely uncomfortable. It was guy code, she realized—they were not going to dish Eli with her. Hell, they were probably all love 'em and leave 'em kind of guys.

Marnie suddenly felt very dejected and let her hands drop listlessly against her sides. "Okay," she said with a half-hearted shrug, "if you guys ever do another wedding, you know who to call, right?"

"Right," Jack said, patting her on the shoulder.

"I guess I'll just go now," she said, and turned around. Jack got the door for her. Michael walked up behind her as if he meant to tackle her if she tried to stay. "I moved to an apartment," she blurted, as if that meant anything to anyone in this room.

"That's great," Michael said. "You want us to tell Eli you came by?"

Marnie snorted. "Why?" she asked bitterly. "Don't bother. Anyway, I just wanted to tell you about that invoice," she said, and stepped out the door. "Okay. Thanks again." She reluctantly lifted a heavy hand to wave to them.

Jack and Michael glanced at each other, then at Marnie. "Bye," they said.

Marnie walked away, her heart heavy, her feet even heavier, and she thought, for the first time—okay, the second time—that she really hated Eli McCain. *New Zealand.* That bastard!

Michael frowned as he quietly shut the door behind Marnie's retreating back. "Did McCain say anything to you about having something going with the wedding coordinator?" he asked Jack.

Jack looked surprised. "No. Did they?"

"Are you blind?" Michael snorted. "What do you think? You saw her."

"Right," Jack said, looking confused. "That was pretty weird. But you don't *really* think there was anything going on, do you?"

"Why not?" Michael returned. "She's a damn fine-looking woman."

"Yes, she is," Jack readily agreed. "But this is Eli we are talking about. You know, the I'll-never-be-with-a-woman-again Eli."

That made Michael laugh. "You want my opinion? I think Eli will be the first one of us to be taken down by a woman."

"Nah," Jack said.

"Bet."

"How much?"

"A thou. And no interfering," Michael said, sticking his hand out.

"No interfering," Jack said, taking Michael's hand, "except to tell him she stopped by. He can take it from there."

"Deal," Michael said, shaking. "And I am going to enjoy spending your money, bro."

"But you won't be spending my money," Jack said. "I'll be spending yours."

"You're really pretty dumb when it comes to this stuff, you know it?" Michael said, grabbing two beers out of the fridge.

"Oh, and what are you, Casanova?" Jack snorted, taking the beer Michael offered him.

"I'm damn sure more successful than any of you ass-holes," Michael said, and the two men continued to argue about who was the real ladies' man over a couple of beers.

CHAPTER TWENTY-EIGHT

September 3 If I could have one night over, it would be the night of the storm. Do you remember it? I've thought of it a lot and sometimes the image is so vivid that I can feel your hair on my face or your breath on my neck. Not a day goes by that I don't think of you, Marnie. Not a moment exists without you in it somehow. I think of you when I see the sun glinting off the highest peaks, I smell you in the salt of the sea, and I hear your voice when we've bedded down at night and there is no sound but the crackle of the fire. You are everywhere, Coppertop, yet you are so far from me that I know I must be dreaming...

Did she think of him? Did she recall that night in the same way as he did, or was he building castles in his mind? Had he fallen over the edge again, had he tripped and broken his heart wide open? Would she be waiting for him?

Waiting. Why in God's name should she be waiting for him? He'd come to New Zealand on a whim, in a moment of cowardice. Michael had said he'd do it when Cooper had to bail, but Eli had jumped in without thought, acting from that place in his gut where all his fears and insecurities continued to live. It was embarrassing—he'd written her a dozen letters or more—love letters, letters he didn't think himself capable of thinking, much less writing—and they were all stuffed in the cargo pocket of his pants, none of them mailed.

He couldn't quite put down that small niggling fear that kept creeping, uninvited, into his thoughts, the one that he was the only one to feel this way, that he'd built her smile and her admission of love in the throes of lovemaking to something more than was really there. If he was the only one to feel this bond, he rationalized, then acting on it would make him an even bigger fool than one who wrote passionate letters to a woman who was halfway around the world and stuffed them in his backpack.

But as he led a run down some of the best Class V rapids in the world, Eli came to the conclusion that he was a goddamn coward if he didn't face his fears, and those were fighting words. No matter how it might go down, he had to know if he'd manufactured it all, or if Marnie really was The One.

Now that he was in Auckland, finishing up with the gig and preparing to leave by week's end, he'd called Marnie twice—both times on the cell phone TA had given her, and both times he'd only gotten voice mail.

But a thought had awakened him at four a.m.: her gig with TA was up. She'd probably given the phone to the guys. What an idiot he was. He glanced at his watch—it was nine in the morning in LA. He picked up the phone and dialed her house.

"Hel-*lo*-oo," Mrs. Banks sang into the phone when she picked it up.

"Hello, Mrs. Banks, it's Eli McCain. How are you?"

"Eli!" she exclaimed. "Have you come back from your trip? Where did you go again, Spain?"

"Ah, Brazil," he said. "I was, ah…hoping to catch Marnie."

"Good luck with that. Personally, since she moved out, I can't get her on the phone to save my life. Either she sees it is her mother calling and won't pick up the phone, or she is very busy with her life." Mrs. Banks sniffed. "I prefer to think she's very busy."

"She moved?" Eli asked dumbly. The thought had never occurred to him. He had gone on with his dreams of her, assuming she was exactly where he'd left her. Home. With Mr. and Mrs. Banks. In that room with clothes and magazines all over the floor.

"Van Nuys," Mrs. Banks said with disdain in her voice. "And not a very nice part of Van Nuys. I wanted her to stay here until she'd done a couple more weddings and could afford a better place, but what do I know? She had to go, and got out of here like the place was on fire."

"Oh," Eli said, his mind trying to absorb what Marnie's mother was telling him. She'd gone. Getting out like there was a fire.

"She's so strong willed, you know, and she always has been, even when she was a baby. If that little squirt wanted something, by God, she'd cry and rant until she got it. Until she could walk, of course, and then she just went and got what she wanted and couldn't care less if she got in trouble for it. So she decided she could get more business where there was a younger crowd and packed up all her things and moved to Van Nuys. Wouldn't even let us help her move. That's just pure stubborn for you."

"Do you have a number where I could reach her?"

"Oh, I have a number, but I doubt it will do you any good, Eli. She's *impossible* to reach. Three weddings, I think she said the last time we talked. That's a lot of weddings for one person to pay attention to, if you ask me. I told her I thought she should hire an assistant, maybe an apprentice like she used to be, but she told me she couldn't afford it, and of course, she probably can't, not with the weddings she's picked up, but if she tried to do more like the-one-that-didn't-happen-you-know-who-I-mean, she could afford an apprentice and a nicer place. But then she—"

"Mrs. Banks?" Eli gently interrupted.

"Huh? What?" she said, a little irritated that he had disrupted her train of thought.

"Do you have a number where I might leave a message?"

"Oh! Of course. Do you have a pencil?"

"Yes," he said, and wrote down the number Mrs. Banks gave him. "Thanks," he said when she'd finished. "I'll give her a ring."

"Oh, Eli. When you come back to LA you must—Oh, hi, Linda!" she said suddenly to someone else. "Come on in. I'm talking to Eli...*Eli.* Oh for God's sake, Linda. *Eli!* Marnie's hot friend."

Eli put his hand to his forehead and rubbed.

"Can you believe her?" Mrs. Banks muttered into the phone. "She's asked Marnie about you at least a dozen times, then tries to act like she doesn't know who you are."

"Thanks for the number, Mrs. Banks. I'll give it a try. Give my regards to Mr. Banks, will you?"

"Of course I will, sugar! You come by as soon as you can, all right?"

"All right," he said, and clicked off, rubbed his temples for a moment. Nice lady, but *man*.

He glanced at the number Mrs. Banks had given him and dialed. It took forever to connect, and when it did, his heart hammered with each ring of the phone, anticipating her bubbly voice.

He got the answering machine. *"Hi, this is Marnie Banks of Sophisticate Soirée, your complete wedding design and coordination services. I am with a client right now, so please leave your name and number and the proposed date of your event, and I will return your call promptly."*

"Ah...hey, Marnie," he said when he heard the beep, and felt his tongue grow thick in his head and grimaced at his ineptitude. "Ah...I'm in New Zealand, but I'm coming back to LA in a couple days and I was hoping maybe we could get together." He paused there, uncertain what else to say. "If you're up for it, why don't you give me a call on my cell. Okay. I guess I'll talk to you later," he said, and hung up.

"I guess I'll talk to you later?" he repeated aloud, shaking his head. "Jesus, McCain, how lame can you be?" he muttered, and turned off the light and tried to get some sleep.

He was not very successful, however, with the myriad of thoughts roaming his mind, and the next day was even worse. He expected his cell to ring, thought the call would come any minute. And it did ring, plenty of times—people in New Zealand. The guys back home. Even Isabella called, asking when he'd come to Escondido again so he could see her new puppy.

But never Marnie.

He slept badly another night and woke around four, unable to sleep. He called her again. He got her answering machine again. It would be about nine o'clock yesterday morning in LA, and he felt a sickening feeling in the pit of his stomach that he'd dicked around with his feelings way too long and had lost his opportunity. "Hey coppertop," he said quietly into the phone. "I'll be back in LA at the end of the week and I was hoping I'd get a chance to talk to you. Would you give me a call?" He paused, then added softly, "I'd love to hear from you."

Not able to think of anything else that didn't sound pathetic or stupid, he clicked off.

He did not hear from Marnie before he left New Zealand.

When Marnie heard his voice on her answering machine, it stunned her. She hadn't forgotten the rich resonance of it, but she had forgotten the way it trickled down her spine and lit her up. She sank onto a bar stool next to her phone and hit the play button again. And again. And twice more before she realized how pathetic she was, clinging to a stupid voice mail, and deleted it.

Eli'd had his chance. She wasn't going to fall into his arms again, no sir, because every time she did, she fell hard and then he went running just as hard in the opposite direction. So she'd had the most incredible experience with a man she'd ever had in her life, and she'd have given anything for it to continue, but obviously, Eli did not feel the same about her. If he did, he would have called or written her. Something. Anything.

He probably needed a ride from the airport. Loser.

When she received the second message, she laughed derisively. Oh sure, he wanted to talk to her—he was probably hard up after being in some remote New Zealand place with nothing around but a lot of goats. He should have introduced himself to a goat while he had the opportunity.

Marnie made herself forget him and went on with the plans for Emily Buckholtz's wedding. It wasn't easy to forget him, either—she had to keep doing it, over and over again. She had to keep busy, to stay on the phone or otherwise engaged, lest she slip back into the old pattern of thinking about him, waiting for the next sound of his voice, hoping against all odds that he would love her as she loved him. But that was a stupid, futile hope and she wouldn't risk feeling it again because it hurt too badly.

So she kept busy.

So good was she in her defense that she was caught off guard when she burst through the door of her apartment a couple of nights later to catch the phone before it stopped ringing and heard his voice, live and in person, on the other end.

"Marnie," he said.

Her name on his lips flowed over her like silk, and she said nothing, just dropped her planning book and purse with a thud to the floor at her feet. "Hey," she croaked at last.

"I've been trying to get hold of you," he said with a bit of a chuckle. "You're a hard woman to reach."

No, she wouldn't be so easily drawn in. "Am I?" she asked coolly, having regained her composure. "I hadn't noticed." She gripped the edge of her Formica bar, gripped it so hard that there was no danger she'd pass out with surprise or a sudden raging desire to see him.

"Yeah, well…you are," he said. "I guess I have it coming, huh?"

She said nothing. Let him do the talking for once.

"I, ah…I ended up in New Zealand," he said.

"So I heard."

"Right," he said quietly. "I was gone a little longer than I had intended."

The man was an absolute master at understating the obvious. "Huh," she said, gripping the Formica bar even harder.

"Look, coppertop," he said in a way that made her knees weak, "I should have called you earlier, but…but life got away from me, and I, ah…well, I—"

"Is there something you wanted, Eli?" she asked politely, as the burn of indignation began to creep up her neck. Should have called earlier? *Should* have? Of course he should have, the moron, but even worse, he should have *wanted* to call her!

"I'd like to see you, Marnie," he said. "I just landed in LA—I haven't even left the airport, but I was hoping I could see you and explain—"

"You know, I'm really booked up for the next few days. I've got a wedding next week, and there's so much that has to be done before then. I think this couple is actually going to go through with it, and since I couldn't just order up everything they need like the last time, I've had to do a lot more legwork, so I really don't think I have time for chitchat," she said peevishly, unwilling to hear yet another explanation of why he had failed to hold up his end of this relationship. Such that it was. Not a relationship, exactly. But *something*.

"I see," he said, disappointment in his voice. "I didn't really have chitchat in mind. But hey, if you're busy, you're busy." It seemed like a blast of cold air had suddenly hit the line, and she could just see the cowboy rearing his horse back, holding tight to his saddle.

"That's right," Marnie said smugly. "No time for chitchat or whatever else it is you might want to do. If you have a question about that disaster of a wedding, please, ask away. But if not, I've really moved on and need to get to some other stuff just now."

That was met with stony silence on the other end of the line. "No," he said at last. "No, I don't have any questions."

Marnie's heart sank a little. "Great," she said cheerfully. "Welcome back to the States, then. I'll...see you. Whatever," she said, and clicked off.

She dropped the phone and glared at it. She was supposed to feel victorious. Vindicated. Avenged for his poor treatment of her. But she didn't feel any of that. She felt mean. And a little heartless. And maybe...just a little foolish. He had sounded sweet and possibly even a little regretful at first.

"Bullshit," she said aloud, thoroughly disgusted with herself. "He probably wanted a roll in the hay, and then he'll freak out again, and guess who will be left holding the bag? No thanks," she said firmly. And besides, she didn't have time to dwell on it. Tonight she was going to shop for table decorations, and she really didn't need him clouding her mind.

And it was *so* not him clouding her mind when she couldn't find her keys. Or when she left her purse in her apartment. And it damn sure wasn't him that made her toss and turn all goddamn night, hell no. It was just a bad case of insomnia. A newly developed, she'd-never-had-in-her-life case of insomnia.

It took a week of solid work in LA before the sting of Eli's foolish hopes for love had worn off, and he was beginning to feel like his old self again. In fact, he was feeling so much like himself that he made a trip to Escondido to see Isabella, then sat in on a couple of meetings they had with Dream-Works for *Graham's Crossing*. Afterward, he spent some time with Cooper working up some stunt plans.

Yep, Eli McCain was back to normal—he'd retreated back into that comfortable place he knew, where nothing touched him and he touched no one. He just thanked God he hadn't made more of a fool of himself with Marnie, and that mercifully, he'd been stopped in his big plans to declare undying devotion to a woman again.

Oh yeah, he was feeling much better.

At least he was until one afternoon about a week after he'd been home. He was at the TA office, sitting on the cowhide recliner they all coveted, his boots up and crossed, tossing a baseball into the air and talking movies when Jack mentioned Marnie.

Eli missed the baseball and it crashed to the pine floors, bouncing up and knocking a coffee cup off the end table. Coffee went splashing all over the chair. "Shit!" Eli snapped and instantly jumped up, headed for the little kitchen for a rag.

"Damn," Jack said with a sideways grin. "That got quite a response."

"What did?" Eli asked irritably as he tried to sponge up the coffee stains.

"Marnie did. I guess she wasn't the only one who had a thing, huh?"

Eli stopped what he was doing and glanced over his shoulder at Jack. "What?"

"She's not the only one who had a *thing*," he articulated clearly.

Eli slowly straightened. "What do you mean, a *thing*?"

Jack laughed. "Look, Marnie stopped by while you were gone and she seemed plenty upset that you'd gone to New Zealand without calling her. Actually," he said, looking thoughtfully at Eli, "she seemed plenty upset that you'd gone to *Brazil* without calling her. I'm gonna walk out on a limb here and say that I think the girl was expecting a call."

Eli blinked, uncertain what to make of that. "I, ah…" Hell, he didn't know what to make of it, and absently scratched his five o'clock shadow.

Jack snorted at Eli's obvious confusion. "Dude. What's the matter with you? You used to be quite the ladies' man, right? Do I have to tell you that you should have *called* her if you like her? She was royally pissed."

"She was?" Eli asked, wincing lightly.

"Totally," Jack said with an adamant nod. "And I guess I have to tell you that if you do want her, and you didn't call when you were supposed to, that now you're going to have to grovel, aren't I?"

"Grovel," Eli repeated dumbly, his mind already racing ahead to just how low he'd have to go in and grovel, and being, astonishingly, perfectly willing to do it. Frankly, he thought he'd do just about anything to see her smile again and wanted to kiss Jack for giving him an excuse.

"*Grovel*," Jack said, a little louder. "Shit, don't tell me one bad relationship and everything you ever knew about women suddenly flies out that birdcage of a head you've got. Grovel, as in, slither in and beg for mercy. But most important," Jack said with a grin, "don't take no for an answer. Pull out the big guns if you have to. Flowers, dinner...you know the score."

Eli glanced up at Jack and smiled for the first time since coming back to LA "I haven't forgotten *that* part," he said with a wink, and tossed the rag at Jack. "Clean that up for me, will you? I've got some groveling to do." And he strode out of the TA offices on his way to grovel like he'd never groveled before.

CHAPTER TWENTY-NINE

Since Marnie wouldn't pick up the goddamn phone, Eli had to bite the bullet and pay a call to the Banks house in Hancock Park. He went early Saturday morning with the hope of avoiding the book club, but he had apparently miscalculated, judging by the look of things—there were five women, five steaming mugs, and a single book on the table.

They ambushed him at the door.

The dark-haired one—Mrs. Farrino, he remembered—tugged on her T-shirt to pull it down just a smidge farther to expose more of her overexposed cleavage.

Mrs. Banks was holding the door open for him. "Come in, come in, stranger!" she cried as Bingo came bounding out, his tongue flapping, to jump up and greet Eli with great enthusiasm, leaving dusty pawprints on his trousers. "Oh my, don't you look nice and tanned and..." Mrs. Banks let her gaze sweep the length of him as he tried to get Bingo off. "*Hubba hubba,*" she said with a wink.

"Hello, Mrs. Banks. And thanks. I think."

"Oh my, it's so good to see you, Eli," she said, beaming, and grabbed hold of his hand, yanking him inside. "Look what I've got!" she trilled to her pals.

"*Ooh,*" they all trilled back in unison as Bingo trotted off to have a sniff of the shrubbery. "If it isn't that cute young thang Marnie likes to play with," said one with a coy little wink.

"Marnie, hell," Mrs. Farrino said, eyeing him unabashedly. "She moved out. He's fair game. Eli, you look like you've been in the sun. Skinny dipping?"

"Oh, Linda! Don't scare him off!" Mrs. Banks scoffed. "Come in, Eli, and tell us all about your trip to Spain," she said, bustling him deeper into the dining room.

"Brazil," he kindly corrected her.

"Ooh, did you go to Mardi Gras?" the dyed blonde asked. "I always wanted to go to Mardi Gras. Did you go with anyone famous?"

"Ah…no," he said, nodding politely. "I think Mardi Gras happens earlier in the year. And I was not with anyone famous."

"Oh," she said, looking slightly disappointed, then shrugged and picked up her coffee cup.

"Coffee, Eli?" Mrs. Banks asked.

"No thanks," he said, quickly putting up a hand, which did not stop Mrs. Farrino from pouring a cup and holding up a package of artificial sweetener to her bosom. "Sugar?" she asked with a throaty growl.

"Thanks, but I'm in a rush," he said. "I just stopped by to see if you could tell me how to get hold of Marnie."

"Oh, that girl," Mrs. Banks said with a roll of her eyes. "I can give you her address, but you won't find her there. She's never home. I swear, she is a little social butterfly, just flitting from place to place," Mrs. Banks said, wiggling her fingers to indicate Marnie's flit.

"Really?" the blond one asked, perking up. "Is she see-ing anyone cute or famous?"

"Who knows if he is cute or famous?" Mrs. Farrino scoffed. "She sure won't bring him around here—I told you she's afraid of us."

"She's not afraid of us, Linda," Mrs. Banks scoffed. "You may scare that poor UPS man half to death, but Marnie is not afraid of you."

"Are you kidding? Older women are all the rage right now. If I were her age, I'd be scared to death to bring my boyfriend around someone like me," Mrs. Farrino said, stab-bing her very long nail to the table for emphasis.

"Shut up, Linda," another one said.

"Mrs. Banks?" Eli quickly and politely interrupted. "Could I have the address?"

"Oh, Eli, yes, yes, yes," Mrs. Banks said, and with a glare for Mrs. Farrino, she motioned for Eli to follow her into the kitchen as Mrs. Farrino explained to the others that she'd just seen an *Oprah* show about the allure older women held for younger men.

Mrs. Banks opened an address book and ran her finger down one page. "Aha. Here it is," she said, and took a Post-it note. "Now if you catch her, you tell that girl her mother would like to see her before she's carted off to the morgue."

"I'll tell her."

Mrs. Banks held up the paper. "Here you are," she said sunnily. "But don't be surprised if you don't find her. I know she has a wedding today, so she'll probably be out."

"Do you know where the wedding is, by chance?"

"Oh Lord, no." She laughed. "She doesn't want me to show up to see her work." Her smile suddenly faded into a sad frown. "I'd love to see her at work." She pouted for a moment, but she brightened instantly and handed the Post-it to Eli. "Good luck, Eli. And please don't be a stranger."

"I won't, Mrs. Banks," he said, pocketing Marnie's address. "I really appreciate it." He turned around and started out of the kitchen toward the front door.

"Oh sugar, you're not going, are you?" Mrs. Farrino called out to him.

"Yes, he's going, Linda. He did not come here to see you, he came to see Marnie, so I guess you'll have to wait for the next young man to prove your theory."

"Jealous!" Mrs. Farrino shouted at Mrs. Banks as she and Eli walked by.

"Do you see what I put up with?" Mrs. Banks asked cheerfully and opened the door for him. She patted his arm. "I really hope you two work it out," she said. "You're a good man, Eli. Marnie would be lucky to have you."

He cocked a brow at Mrs. Banks; she cocked one back. "You think I don't know what's going on between the two of you? She's a good girl," she said, and smiled fully. "*You'd* be damn lucky to have *her.*"

Eli smiled at Mrs. Banks. "I know," he said, and walked out the door, then turned halfway around. "Thanks," he said.

She waved her fingers at him, and he could hear the ladies inside calling her to come back and quit flirting with Marnie's boyfriend. Still wiggling her fingers, she shut the door.

Eli walked out to his truck, but before he could reach the driver door, Mr. Banks appeared, wiping his hands on an old red rag.

"Hey, there, Eli," he said, extending his right hand. "I was wondering when you'd come back around."

"Finally made it," Eli said, shaking his hand. "I'm trying to track your daughter down."

"Oh, that's easy," he said. "She'll be at the Fernando Wedding Chapel in Hollywood today. I took something to her earlier." He grinned and glanced at the house. "Just don't tell her mother," he said with a wink. "We wouldn't want her showing up to see Marnie at work."

"No, we wouldn't," Eli agreed. "Thanks for the tip, Mr. Banks."

"No problem. Now there's something you ought to know. Marnie can be a little like her mother sometimes, and by that I mean obstinate. I find if I just give her mother a little time to cool off, she usually comes around." He winked at Eli, and turned around, walked back toward the garage.

"Damn," Eli muttered to himself as he got in his truck. "Am I that obvious?"

He drove to her apartment in Van Nuys and had to agree with Mrs. Banks's assessment of it. It was a dump in a run-down part of town, and not where he'd like to see Marnie living. He'd actually like to see Marnie living in a very tasteful bungalow in Laurel Canyon. With him.

Mrs. Banks was also right that she was not at home. Nor was she at the Fernando Wedding Chapel, although some dude was there wrapping flowers around a column.

"She ain't here," he said when Eli asked. "She said she'd be back in a couple hours."

"What time is the ceremony?" Eli asked out of curiosity.

"Three."

Eli glanced at his watch. A couple of hours and a wedding would commence. He sighed and walked out to his truck. It looked like he was going to a wedding.

When he returned a couple of hours later, he was wearing a custom-made dark, pinstriped suit. He didn't want to be accused of not fitting in. He'd meant to arrive a little early so he could catch Marnie before everything got too hectic, but there'd been traffic on the 405, and now he was only a half hour away from someone's march down the aisle. It did occur to him that this possibly was not the best time to find Marnie, but he'd gotten dressed up and come all this way, and hell, all he wanted to do was ask her to please talk to him.

After the wedding, of course.

He walked into the back of the chapel, told the usher he was just going to peek inside before being seated, and slipped into the back.

He caught a breath in his throat. Eli had thought about her, dreamed about her, but he was not prepared for his body's visceral reaction to seeing her. Marnie was at the altar, setting a big floral display. She was wearing a simple, elegant green dress that skimmed her body and from which her legs, long and shapely, seemed to reach down for miles. Her hair, that bouncy mane, was pinned to the back of her head, and sparkling green earrings dangled from her ears.

He was content to just watch her, to feel the warmth of familiar affection as she moved around the massive thing, arranging the flowers just so, the frown of concentration on her brow.

Then she glanced at her watch, and even from the back of the small chapel, Eli could see her eyes widen with surprise, and she was suddenly marching toward the entrance, her arms swinging, her stride determined. And as she marched, her eye was drawn to Eli. She flashed a hint of a smile and looked away, then let out a tiny shriek and threw her hand up to her heart as she came to an abrupt halt.

"*Eli!*"

"Hello, Marnie."

Her mouth agape, she took him in, from the tips of his polished shoes to the top of his head. Her maple eyes softened, then quickly turned hard as she lowered her hand from her heart. "What are you doing here?" she demanded through clenched teeth.

"I had to see you."

"Now is not a good time," she said, and started for the lobby. But Eli was too quick for her and stepped into her path before she could beat her retreat.

Her brows dipped into a V and her hands went to her very curvy hips. "Eli, I have to do a wedding. You've seen me. Now please go...wherever it is you like to run off to."

"Ouch," he said with a soft smile and impetuously touched her cheek, stroking it with his knuckles.

Marnie's frown faded, but her eyes filled with sorrow, and she bit her lower lip.

"I need to talk to you, Marnie."

"Do you have to do this now? I am trying to work here, Eli. I am trying to move on with my life," she said, and he noticed that her eyes were filling with tears. "And you know what else? I don't want to hear what you have to say because whatever it is will just make me love you all over again, and then you'll run off and I'll be miserable, and I'd just rather we cut directly to phase three, which is you have your life

and I have mine, and even if we had fabulous sex and a fabulous time together, we don't have to keep making the same
mistake, and you can go on being a commitment-phobe and
a part-time pig and I can go on being a wedding planner
and we'll both be happy, so will you just go away now?" she
whispered frantically, and as she paused to draw a much-
needed breath, she dragged a finger under her lower lids to
wipe away the tears welling in her eyes.

"We don't have to do this now," Eli said. "But I'm not
going away. I need to talk to you."

She lifted her chin and folded her arms across her chest.
"You need to talk to someone else. Not me, Eli. I'm through
with us. Not that there ever really was an us, hello, but just in
case you are under the impression there was, there wasn't.
So if you don't mind, I have a bride to get ready and a wedding to handle, and I really, honestly, don't need this right
now." And with that, she started to walk away.

"I love you, coppertop," Eli said, surprised by how calmly
and easily the words came now.

She stopped dead in her tracks. Her shoulders lifted as
with a sigh, then sagged. She glanced at him over her shoulder and glared at him. "*Don't,*" she bit out, and with a shake
of her head, she walked out.

Eli shrugged, stuffed his hands into his pockets, and
walked out into the lobby. He was uncharacteristically
undeterred. He was willing to give her the space she needed
to come around to the truth, which was, he now had no
doubt, that she loved him.

He didn't know exactly how he knew it, but he did, and
as he walked past Marnie, he smiled and winked and chuckled quietly to himself when she dropped her head back

in dramatic fashion, then shook her head furiously as she stormed off in the opposite direction.

Thanks to Eli's unexpected appearance, looking totally-to-die-for, Marnie's wedding was ruined. Completely and totally ruined. She hardly saw Emily's walk down the aisle because she was scanning the small group of guests, looking for him. At the reception, she didn't notice that the bridal cake was damaged on one side, forgot to put out the disposable cameras, and very nearly forgot to give the bartender the bridal champagne flutes before the first toast. She was a total wreck, her head full of Eli, her arms full of wedding gifts and favors, and her eyes all but blind to the reception around her.

How dare he come back like this! How dare he just pop up at her wedding after nearly two months and act like nothing had happened! Oh no, he was not getting off so easy this time. She was through with him. Through. There was nothing he could say to convince her otherwise.

By the time the wedding was over, and the happy couple had been sent on their way, and Marnie had gathered up all the stuff the caterer wouldn't dispose of and packed it into her car, she was exhausted from the tension of waiting for him to jump out from behind a plant or a speaker, and furious with him for thinking she'd be waiting patiently for him to come round again. Bastard!

Marnie fumed all the way home about men and their humongous egos.

At her complex, she gathered up a bag with all the cameras, and the wedding cake top, and the two bottles of cheap champagne that had not been consumed, plus a couple of gifts and the guest album. Her arms full, she struggled up the steps to her second-floor apartment.

She noticed, as she was walking down the narrow landing, that there was paper stuck to her door. A *lot* of paper. Someone had covered her entire door with white paper—there were dozens of pieces stuck up there. She reached her door and stopped, her arms full, and squinted at the one directly before her.

September 2 My clients from New York passed around pictures of their wives and girlfriends while we sat around the campfire tonight, and I wished I had a picture of you so I could look at your smile whenever I want. I think how sad it is, judging by the pictures they passed around, that these guys will never know a smile like yours. It's the brightest thing in the universe. It makes your whole face light up. I may not have a picture, but I will hold the memory of it in my heart always.

"What the hell?" Marnie whispered, and leaned forward to look at another one.

August 23 I think I must be the biggest fool in the world, because there you were before me, and I didn't have the balls to reach out and grab you. I should never have left you in that tent, I should have grabbed you up and held you close while I had the chance. I think I will go flat out crazy wondering if I let my one true shot at happiness slip through my fingers...

August 15 There is a bird in the jungle that has a laugh that reminds me of you. The sound it makes is sweet and lyrical and I find it ironically amusing that the bird seems to laugh at us all day long as we trek through the jungle.

Marnie quickly put down all that she was holding and ripped the pages off her door, one by one, her mouth agape as she read them. *I love you*, one said. *I have missed you so much. I adore you, how could I not have told you so?*

And the one dated today, September 18:

I have made a huge mistake, Marnie, but I hope you will find a way to forgive me. You're right, I am a recovering commitment-phobe, and maybe a little bit of a pig. But I love you and I don't want to lose you because I don't think I can survive without you. Do you think you can give me one more chance? Do you think you could see your way to allowing me to love you and show you that I do? I love you. I love you. I love you.

"Oh God, oh yes," she muttered, and gripped the letters, held them tightly to her chest, staring blindly at her door. "Please be here, please be here, please be here," she chanted and turned around.

He was here.

Still dressed in that killer suit, he was leaning against the railing, a huge bouquet of flowers in one hand, his other hand stuffed deep into his pocket. He looked, she thought, charmingly uncertain with his head slightly bowed and one thick strand of golden-brown hair dipping over his eye.

Still clutching the letters, Marnie tried to move, but her feet wouldn't work. Eli pushed away from the railing, the flowers falling to his side.

Marnie pointed to the letters she held, stepped over her things, and started walking toward him. His expression was one of trepidation and hope as she came to stand before him. He cleared his throat. "Hey, coppertop."

"I don't know if I should kiss you or kick you," she said softly.

"You should probably kick me, but I'd prefer the kiss."

"You should have called me."

"I should have."

"Do you mean it?" she asked. "Do you mean what you wrote?"

He nodded solemnly. "Every goddamn word."

The corner of her mouth tipped up. "Do you promise you won't run away?"

He smiled then, that sexy, lopsided smile that turned her to jelly. "Marnie, I don't intend to let you out of my sight ever again."

She had a sudden image of Eli the cowboy, standing on a big prairie spread with her in his arms, and she wanted to be exactly there, in his arms. Without a thought to logistics, she launched herself at him.

She hit him with such force that she knocked the breath from him, but Eli caught her and buried his face in her hair as he held her tightly to him. "Oh God," he said, breathing her in, stroking her hair. "Oh God. I love you, coppertop. I can be a little dense, so it took me long enough to admit it and even longer not to fear it, but I am here now, stripped bare. I'll never let you go."

"Eli, damn you, I love you, too, and I never stopped loving you. I don't care if you're dense, I love you, too," she cried, and pressed her face into his neck.

He made a sound of relief and suddenly pushed her back a little, handed her the flowers, then swept her up in his arms and carried her to the threshold of her apartment.

He had to let her down to find her key, and they had to step around all her stuff, then drag it in so none of her shady neighbors would run off with the goods, but in Marnie's mind, it was as romantic as the cowboy who picked up the woman he loved and carried her into the hacienda, where he would make love to her all night long.

And would do so again the next day, and the next day, and the day after that.

CHAPTER THIRTY

When TA got the call to do the Nepal mountain climb with two Saudi princes, they gathered at their offices so they could decide who would lead in their usual fashion—rock, paper, scissors.

Jack, Cooper, and Michael waited a half hour for Eli, and when he didn't show, Cooper got on the phone, catching Eli on the second ring. "Dude!" he exclaimed when Eli answered. "Where the hell are you? We're setting up the Nepal thing."

"Oh, that," Eli said with an uncharacteristic amount of cheer in his voice. "You guys go ahead without me. I can do Nepal another time."

"What?" Cooper asked, unable to process the fact that Eli didn't want to do Nepal.

Jack looked at Michael, and Michael suddenly grabbed the phone from Cooper's hand and put it on speakerphone. "Where are you, Eli?" he demanded.

Eli chuckled, and the guys heard another chuckle in the background. A decidedly female chuckle. "I'm headed out of town," he said.

"Where?" Jack asked.

"No place you need to know. I'll be back in a few days."

"But...but what about Nepal?" Cooper asked again, as he was the only one of the guys to have missed Eli's falling head over heels in love with Marnie Banks.

"What about it? Have a great time," Eli said. "Look, I gotta go. And by the way...don't bother calling. When I hang up, I'm tossing the phone out the window."

Michael laughed and looked at Jack. "Toss it. We'll see you when you get back." He clicked off the phone and stuck out his hand, palm up. "You owe me a grand, Jacko. I was right—the man is in love."

"In *love?*" Cooper let out a loud guffaw. "What in the hell have you been smoking, Raney? That's Eli you're talking about."

"Exactly," Michael said with a grin. "And just as I predicted, he was the first of the mighty to fall."

Jack groaned and reached for his wallet. "I'll have to write you a check," he groused.

"You're both nuts," Cooper said, and plopped down in the cowhide chair.

"You couldn't see a hand if it was right in front of your face, Coop," Jack said.

"What are you talking about?" Cooper asked. "I think I know McCain just a little bit better than you two clowns, and there is no way that man is in love with anyone, and besides, who the hell would it be? The only women he's had any contact with are Olivia Dagwood and Marnie Banks..."

His voice trailed off and his eyes widened slightly as the truth sank in. "Nah," he said after a moment.

"Yeah," said Jack.

"No way," Cooper insisted, shaking his head, and the three of them began to argue about Eli McCain's capacity for falling in love. And then their capacity. And the three Thrillseekers left behind made another little wager about who might be the next of the mighty to fall.

ABOUT THE AUTHOR

In the Still Photography

Julia London is the *New York Times*, *USA Today*, and *Publishers Weekly* bestselling author of more than twenty romantic fiction novels. She is the author of the popular Desperate Debutantes, Scandalous, and The Secrets of Hadley Green historical romance series. She is also the author of several contemporary women's fiction novels with strong romantic elements, including the upcoming Homecoming Ranch trilogy, *Summer of Two Wishes*, *One Season of Sunshine*, and *Light at Winter's End*.

Julia is the recipient of the RT Bookclub Award for Best Historical Romance and a four-time finalist for the prestigious RITA Award for excellence in romantic fiction. She lives in Austin, Texas.

Made in the USA
Charleston, SC
19 April 2013